CAPTIVATING INNOCENCE

"What on earth are they doing!" Bethany mumbled into his nightshirt.

Adam tightened his hold, and his words sounded as if they were filtered through clenched teeth. "They're doing what husbands and wives do."

What kind of answer was that? But her curiosity was aroused.

"Does it hurt, do you suppose? Both of them are moaning so."

He chuckled. "No, it doesn't hurt. Far from it. It's intensely pleasurable."

Bethany placed her hand on Adam's firm cheek. "Say no more now, you can answer my many questions on the morrow when you're less annoyed by this nearness forced upon us." His jaw tensed beneath her fingers. She rubbed it gently, hoping to quiet it. There was a vague hint of bristles where his beard had been, and her fingertips tingled.

"Damn it, Bethany. You're torturing me beyond reason."

Other *Leisure Books* by Thomasina Ring:

TIME-SPUN RAPTURE

DREAM CATCHER

THOMASINA RING

LEISURE BOOKS **NEW YORK CITY**

A LEISURE BOOK®

June 1992

Published by

Dorchester Publishing Co., Inc.
276 Fifth Avenue
New York, NY 10001

The name "Leisure Books" and the stylized "L" with design are
trademarks of Dorchester Publishing Co., Inc.

Printed in the United States of America.

To *meine Augäepfel,*
my daughter, Jean Elizabeth, and my son, Mark Wilhelm—
the two loves of my life, whose lively spirits, loving natures,
and beautiful hearts make me know that wonderful dreams
are real and always come true.

Prologue

July 1754,
Williamsburg, Virginia

Adam rolled off Sweet Molly and patted her hefty thigh. "You're growing fleshy, my wench," he said with a chuckle.

"The truth ye speak, lad." She pushed a stray lock of tawny hair away from his ear and tweaked the lobe. "That gives more of Molly to pleasure a hardy young stallion, wouldn't ye say?"

Adam responded with a tired nod. As always, the romp with the woman had provided the searing moment of release he'd sought but that was all. He felt empty now, and he'd as soon take his leave at once and ride back to Wendover while the sun was still high. But manners prevailed, even in this small steamy room above the stables of Green's Tavern.

He nuzzled between the mounds of her large breasts, so recently the enticing targets of his inflamed attention, but now only flaccid reminders of the brevity of passion.

Molly gurgled a throaty laugh. "And tis it another shilling's worth ye'd be wantin', me tireless lad? Sweet Molly's prepared to spread wide for thee till your purse be empty or till I need climb down to serve the supper folk, whiche'er haps first."

Adam squeezed a handful of fleshy rump, kissed the dark star-shaped mole above her upper lip, and moved away—a part of their ritual, as was his jaunty answer. "Prepared you may be, my brazen wench, and shillings I have in quantity greater than your time, but one turn with such comeliness is enough for even this young stallion." He reached for his breeches, relieved to be off the lumpy flock mattress and free of her sweltering presence.

He would be back another day, and he knew she was as certain of that as he. The relentless fire in his groin—more often and powerfully it flared now that he'd reached his seventeenth year—would demand his return to her squalid cot within a fortnight. Only Sweet Molly knew how to extinguish that bedeviling blaze with her experience and the reward of a meager shilling.

How different she was from the prim damsels on the river plantations around Wendover. Those proper young ladies wafted the aroma of flowers and had skin as silky as their fancy London dresses, but they knew naught but how to tempt and tease while keeping their legs pressed firmly together till the bonds of a suitable marriage loosed them.

The bonds might loose a pair of spindly legs, but they sure as hell tied up the man, Adam fretted as he slipped on his shirt. He hadn't met one lass he'd bind himself to for life, though he knew from the flutter of their fans and the greedy lights in their wide eyes that a number of them, and their doting parents, as well, considered Adam Lawrence Barwick, the heir to Wendover, a suitable marriage prospect indeed.

Bloody hell, he'd be damned if he'd consider wedding and bedding any of the frivolous lot for years yet. Many more visits with Sweet Molly lay ahead for him.

"And so, Sir Long Blade, will we have a wee nip of that special brandy from your father's cellar 'fore ye leave?" Molly puffed her way off the cot, tugging on a soiled robe.

The pilfered brandy was another part of their ritual. "An extra reward for your sweet softness," Adam had called it that first time with her two years before when she'd initiated him to the pleasures of the flesh. He knew Molly had come to expect the nip as much as the shilling and, because she'd told him, his youthful verve and mighty weapon were a healthy contrast to those ol' coots who came here regularly for her services.

Remembering that compliment, he smiled with pride as he pulled the stopper from the dusty brown bottle and filled the waiting cups, giving her an extra dollop.

"To your sweet softness," he said, raising his cup.

"And to thy lack of it, me strong one," she responded with her familiar refrain, downing the brandy with one thirsty swallow. Her eyes glowed as he poured the contents of his unsipped cup into hers.

That, too, was ritual. Adam hated brandy, but he enjoyed watching the accommodating wench savor the costly wine his father served on only the most special occasions. He shrugged. Being with Molly

11

was a special occasion, even if it did occur with a tiresome frequency these days. The old man should understand. William Barwick had once been young himself and must remember the tyranny of passion.

Yet Adam knew his father would never approve of his afternoons with Sweet Molly, nor would he allow the "waste of fine brandy on tavern baggage." He could almost hear the gruff but highly proper voice declaring his strong displeasure should he ever learn the truth.

But his father didn't know and need never know, Adam assured himself. Only his stepbrother, James, knew where he was, and that ne'er-do-well was busying himself well enough in the next room with the black-haired slattern, Lucy. James and he had sworn an oath to keep their Williamsburg dalliances secret from the family at Wendover.

He cocked his head in amusement, watching Molly extend her talented tongue to catch the last sweet drop of brandy in the bottom of the cup. The star over her lip twinkled as she smiled her approval. The tongue and star came close to working their infernal magic yet again, causing a warning stir against his breeches. Perhaps there *was* time enough for. . . .

Molly's sudden cry and the crash of her fallen cup splintered his thoughts. Her face, contorted in pain, turned a vicious red. She grasped her throat, gagging loudly.

"Ye . . . ye've . . . *p'isoned* . . ." she croaked, straining for a scream, as her wild gaze fixed on him, questioning him, accusing him.

"Molly!"

Stunned and confused, he grabbed for the woman, desperately hoping to assure her that his father's brandy could hold no poison, that she would recover in a moment. But she shook violently and flailed against

12

him, gurgling a horrible noise. As she slid through his grasping arms and crumpled to the floor, her body convulsed wildly like that of a beheaded chicken.

Frantic, he reached for a water pitcher, filled a stained bowl, and tossed in a cloth. Fighting her spasms, he held the wet linen to her forehead. He lay across her, trying to quiet her, but she thrashed beneath him, defying his greater strength with her frenzied writhings. Her knee jabbed sharply into his stomach, her grasping nails tore down his cheeks, her clenched fist rammed his eye, his nose. He ignored the pain, aware only that she appeared to be in the throes of death.

His own blood dripped on her twisted face; a bubble of foam rose in the corner of her mouth. *Poisoned? Dear God, I must make her vomit.*

With a surge of strength, he curved her over his arm and thrust his finger down her throat. She gagged, but only a drop of warm liquid came forth. *"More,"* he urged, plunging deeper with his finger while he pressed his fist hard into her resistant stomach. "More, damn it!"

"Is this mayhem or pleasure you're wreaking in here, my little brother?" James Langhorne Wallace bounded with a swagger into the room. Lucy was close at his heels.

"I think she's dying. Help us, for God's sake," Adam pleaded, impaled by genuine terror for the first time in his life. Molly's thrashings had ceased and she lay limp in his arms.

James shut the door before walking toward Adam and the stricken woman.

"Dying, you say! What could she be dying from?"

He bent over Molly, who was quiet now—too quiet—took her from Adam, and carried her to the cot. Lucy sobbed loudly. Adam remained kneeling on the floor, his face bruised and bleeding, his brain whirling in confusion and despair.

"She's dead, that's God's truth," James said, covering the still body with a faded quilt. "What did you do to her, Adam?"

"I did naught," he answered, his voice as lifeless as Molly. "The brandy, James. She said the brandy was poisoned . . ."

"And why in heaven's name would you poison the brandy?"

"I *didn't*. For the love of God, you don't believe I would . . ."

His stepbrother's dark expression warned him. Adam stood. "I did not poison her," he said firmly.

"But you brought her the brandy."

"I brought her the brandy from Father's cellar."

"And you drank from it, too?"

Adam stood straighter, forcing strength he was no longer sure of back into his legs.

"No, I drank none."

Lucy started squealing. "Ye've killed 'er! Ye killed Sweet Molly!"

James rushed over to the hysterical woman and clamped his hand across her mouth. "Quiet, wench!" he ordered. "You'll have the whole damnable town up here. I need time to find a way out of this tangle."

Lucy squirmed in his grasp, her protests muffled by the large hand. James stared at his young stepbrother.

"You must flee, Adam. Go now, before it's too late."

"Flee? Why should I flee? I've done naught."

"And who would believe you?"

Adam's chest grew cold. *Who indeed?* The brandy would be identified by the Barwick crest. Horace Green, the tavern owner, knew he'd been with Molly. Lucy would surely bear witness against him. Who would listen to Adam? Who would believe the rough-hewn words, though true words, of a profligate youth? No one.

If he remained to defend himself and prevailed, even against all odds, with certainty this sordid episode would besmirch the Barwick name and he would suffer his father's eternal ire.

His father . . . *dear God* . . . his beloved but stern father would never forgive him. The room closed in on him, tilted crazily. He closed his eyes and took a deep breath.

"I see not how my flight could improve these circumstances," he said at last, surprised that his voice was strong and steady despite the emotions warring within him. "I must stay to defend myself in spite of the way this must look—"

"Nonsense!" his stepbrother interrupted with a frown. "That's foolhardy courage that would lead only to the gallows. Let me handle this matter." He looked thoughtful. "My plan is simple, Adam. I'll destroy the bottle and cross a few palms with silver. Green and Lucy will be well paid and quiet, I vow, and no one need ever know you were here this day."

James looked confident, but Lucy, still straining against his hand, was far from peaceful. Adam didn't trust her.

He considered his stepbrother's plan and regarded it as distasteful. Destroying evidence, crass bribery . . . How could such a pile of wrongs right anything?

Nor did he like the idea of running away. "A man must face his actions," he protested.

"What actions, Adam? Bedding a wench? You're willing to hang for consorting with a common wench?" James looked distraught. "I know not what's happened here," he continued. "Maybe Molly had a

15

weak heart and couldn't withstand your passion. I know only that she's dead. You say you didn't poison her, and as your brother I must believe you. But look at the evidence present in this room through the eyes of others. Be gone now. Let me do this thing for you."

Adam wavered. James's concern was evident; perhaps he spoke with wisdom.

"Provided I should accept your plan, I still see no need to leave you alone with such a task nor does it please me to have you shoulder my burden. Though I admit I don't like your scheme, I'll assist you in—"

"You will not!" James said, fire leaping from his eyes. "Tis far better if I do what's necessary by myself. You have no skill in such delicate matters."

Adam knew he was right. He'd always been too direct in his manner and had shunned devious paths. He'd never even been tempted to learn the art of persuasion—gentle or otherwise. James, who he'd often thought had the dark soul of a politician, was a master at it.

He sighed. "I will do as you say, though I have grave misgivings."

His stepbrother looked relieved. "Make haste, then, and ride west. Go visit with your uncle in Albemarle for a spell till this unfortunate incident blows over. I'll contact you when it's safe to return to us."

"And what will you say to Father?"

James snorted a laugh. "That you have tired of the Tidewater, that you're seeking manly adventures on the frontier for a few months and desire to reacquaint yourself with your mother's brother and his family."

"He will not understand my leaving without telling him farewell."

"Faugh! William Barwick thinks his son is blessed with the halo of an angel. He, too, ventured west when but a lad. Trust my way with him, little brother. He'll

16

be proud of you when I decorate my tale with your desires to prove yourself a man in his eyes." An edge of impatience crept into James's voice. "Now be gone so that I may begin to erase all evidence of your presence. You must be far from Williamsburg before this woman's body is discovered."

The hopelessness of his situation struck Adam like a sharp sword. He must trust James, it was his only hope. He left the room. As he descended the narrow steps to the stables, the musty shadows deepened his gloom.

James Wallace and Lucy watched through the tiny panes of the window until Adam rode away.

"And now a toast, my fine wenches!" he crowed, lifting the Barwick brandy bottle high. "I congratulate you both on performances worthy of the London theater."

"Was my death truly convincing?" Sweet Molly asked with a giggle, bouncing her purse of silver pieces on the tousled cot.

"Truly. The celebrated Mrs. Oldfield of Drury Lane could have done no better."

"And what of me?" Lucy questioned with a pout.

James kissed her soundly on the cheek. "You were perfect, my raven-haired love, though you were not required to bite my hand with such fervor. Twill be a fortnight before it heals."

"My deep apology, m'lord," Lucy said with a coy smile and a deep curtsy. He laughed and tossed her another piece of silver.

Molly tightened her robe and sighed. "I'll miss that lad, I will, he's a fine lusty one," she said. "But ye vow he'll be safe in Albemarle and return someday?"

"Someday," he assured her with smoothness. "Though you, my pet, must not be here to greet him. That well-earned silver should afford you means to stage a glorious resurrection in a new place."

A far better fate than the one waiting for your "fine one," he thought with pleasure. *My carefully wrought trap will assure that Adam Barwick will never return, save in a pine box.*

"Here, then, sweet whores," he said happily, "let's finish off this fine brandy and celebrate your bright days ahead with silver enough now to mend your tattered lives." *And to mine as the future heir of Wendover,* he added to himself with deep satisfaction. He took a hearty swig from the bottle before pouring a generous portion in the one remaining cup for the women.

Chapter One

April 1760,
Battletown, Virginia

"I dunno, Pa. He's right mean-looking." George Stewart leaned against Benjamin Berry's bar and warily eyed the sullen stranger seated alone across the room. "Think I'll wait till he downs a mite more of that rum."

"He's had 'nuff already to cross the eyes of an ox. What'sa matter, Bully Boy, ye growin' woman's breasts alla' sudden?" Bull Stewart laughed and thumped his son's barrel-like chest. "Shucks, Boy, even your good-for-nothin' sister, Bethany Rose, could pro'bly whop 'im. Better get on with your challenge 'fore it's too late."

"Your pa's right," piped in Johnny Davis, tossing a

couple of coins on the bar. "These say ye can wallop the tar outta 'im."

"He might not wanna fight." George didn't like the looks of the man. Big and solid as a mountain rock, he was, and near as immovable.

"Howya gonna know 'less ye ask 'im?" Johnny asked.

"He some pal of Morgan's? Rode up with 'im, didn't he?" George didn't cotton to picking a fight with any friend of Dan Morgan's. Morgan was the hands-down champion of Battletown these days.

"Nah, Bully Boy," his pa said with a sneer. "They prob'ly met up on the trail from Winchester. Anyways, Morgan's back yonder rolling 'round with Fat Moll. He ain't got no hankering for fightin' nobody today."

George finished off his tankard of ale and wiped his mouth with the back of his hand. Guess he'd have to go on and get it over with. There'd be no living with his pa or any of the others if he didn't. "Well then," he said, hitching up his breeches, "I'll just saunter over and make his 'quaintance."

On the other side of the bar, Benjamin Berry looked up with interest. "Gonna give us some entertainment this afternoon, Bully Boy?"

"Damn right, Berry. Better start takin' them bets."

George swaggered to the stranger's table. "Gotta name, fella?" he asked.

The big man didn't respond.

"Be ye dumb or deaf, or both? We friendly folk 'round here like to know a man's name. Wanna tell us?"

"I see no need."

The stranger's dark eyes studied George's face like he might've been lookin' at a bug, or somethin' lower even, George thought, welcoming the anger he felt simmering in his gut. *Makes it a helluva sight more*

*fun to knock the daylights outta a fella who riles ye up
a mite.*

Adam Barwick sized up the man hovering over him.
More stink than strength, he judged, and the eyes of a
pig and a bloated middle to match. A fight with him
would hardly be a contest, but the music of coins
ringing back on the bar tempted him. Morgan had
told him a fighting man could make a month's wages
or more with a good brawl here in Battletown. He
could use the money.

Hoping to sweeten the pot, he shrugged his shoulders with indifference and returned his attention to
his rum.

"Well, now, seems ye're not th' friendly sort. Could
be we don't want your kind here."

The stocky mountain man looked more anxious
than wise, and Adam saw the ease of baiting the
fool. "Could be," he said, edging his words with ice.
"What are you planning to do about it?"

The pig-eyed man spat on the table. "I 'spect I'll
beat the blazes outta you, that's what."

Adam's mouth twisted in a sardonic smile. "Want
to try it while I'm sitting or would you prefer I stand
up?" He heard more coins falling back on the bar. He
liked the sound.

"Get up, ye bastard!"

"I'd like to finish my rum first, if you don't mind." He
lifted his cup, relishing the flush of anger sharpening
the dull face of his opponent. The buzz of the tavern
had diminished considerably. Maybe he could raise
the stakes.

He shouted over to the tavern owner. "Mister Berry,
I believe this man here is suggesting we have a little
fight. What are your house rules in such a matter?"

"Odds depend on the bets," Berry responded, looking at the two uneven stacks of coins in front of him. "Right now I'd say it's about three to one, Stewart over ye, stranger."

"Your name Stewart?" he asked the man across from him.

"Damn right."

"You that good? Three to one?" Adam raised an inquisitive brow.

George Stewart bent over the table and stuck his face within inches of Adam's. "Damn right," he challenged through his gapped teeth.

The man's foul breath alone was enough to make Adam recoil, but he didn't move a muscle. Without taking his eyes off George, he shouted back to Berry. "What does the winner get?"

"Half the purse and free drinks on the house for the rest of the day."

"Sounds fair enough," he said, reaching under his coat.

George grabbed his arm and Adam lifted his other arm in a gesture of peace.

"Have patience, Stewart. I mean only to fatten the purse before we begin."

George grunted, but released his hold. He stayed hunched in a ready position, his squinted eyes on guard.

Adam pulled out a small pouch and tossed it on the bar, making sure it landed on the smaller pile of coins. He waited while the delighted Berry dumped out and counted this newest bet.

"Twenty shillings and a Spanish piece," the tavern owner announced loudly. "Ye've evened the odds."

Looking back at George, Adam smiled. "Still raring to fight?"

"Damn right."

"Would you prefer the contest be in here or outside,

Mister Berry?" Adam asked, keeping a cagey eye on Stewart.

"Outside is our custom, stranger."

"Then best we go on out, Stewart." Adam put both his hands on the table and leisurely unfolded himself from the stool. The shadowy light coming through the tavern's small windows added to the formidable effect he'd hoped for as his full height and brawn were revealed to the betting men in the room.

Coins plopped on the bar with a merry ring.

"After you, Stewart," he said with a polite bow and a sweep of his hand toward the door.

"No holds barred," Benjamin Berry yelled as he led his excited customers outside. They formed a rowdy circle around the two who had already tossed their buckskin coats aside, rolled up their sleeves, and were ready for action.

The match was far from graceful. Bully Boy Stewart was a master of Battletown methods with his elbows, knees, and teeth, but Adam had a punch that kept sending him down to the dust in ungainly sprawls. Again and again he waited patiently with a devilish grin while the man righted himself and came back at him, leading with his bull-like head and thick, groping arms. And each time, Adam let the man gouge, snarl, and bite just long enough to give the crowd some pleasure for their money before knocking Bully Boy down again.

Adam had gauged his opponent well. He was definitely more stink than strength. The man's stink was by far the bigger bother to Adam, and his need for a breath of fresh air spurred him to end the uneven match with a solid right uppercut to the jaw that lifted Bully Boy high into the air like a dusty feather. The thud as he hit the ground was unquestionably more solid.

The crowd cheered. Battletown had a new contender for its championship. Except for a bleeding ear, a few scratches, and a torn sleeve, Adam looked about the same as he had before the whole thing had started.

Bull Stewart and Johnny Davis were glum as they tried to revive Bully Boy. The others slapped Adam on his shoulders and herded him back into the tavern for congratulatory drinks.

Adjusting his eyes to the dim light inside, Adam saw Dan Morgan coming from the back room, a fat giggling woman in tow.

"Ye've got competition worthy of thee now, Morgan," one of the men shouted. "This stranger's done whopped the tar outta Bully Boy Stewart."

A raucous chorus of voices roared through the tavern. "Yeah, Fightin' Dan, show 'im a real fight!" "We're bettin' on ye this time, Morgan. Come on, give 'im hell!"

Daniel Morgan tossed a conspiratorial wink at Adam and raised his hands in surrender. "No fight left in me this day, gentlemen," he said with a big grin. "Fat Moll here's made a weak man of me, I fear." Bawdy laughter echoed around the room as he reached for a bottle of rum and took a hearty swallow.

"And there's yet another grave matter to consider, gentlemen," he continued. "Barwick over there and me's already had at it, last winter it was, back at Fort Loudoun. Four of the damndest hours I ever spent." He tipped the bottle in a salute to Adam. "It was a draw. Think I'd like to leave it at that."

Adam acknowledged the salute with a cocked eyebrow and silent appreciation. He'd never fought Dan Morgan in his life, never intended to, if he had anything to say about it. He admired the wagoner and had fought by his side in numerous skirmishes against the damnable French and Indians during the past few years. Adam hoped battles were behind him now that his conscription was ended and he could finally head home. But should he ever find himself in any kind of war, he wanted Morgan as an ally, not an opponent.

"Here's your winnings, Mister Barwick is it?" Berry thrust the now far plumper pouch toward him.

He accepted it with a smile and shook the pudgy man's hand. "Adam Barwick, sir. Pleased to make your acquaintance."

"One of them Tidewater Barwicks?" Berry asked.

"Once and future," he responded with pleasure. He'd been gone for six long years of unspeakable miseries and hardships, but he was free at last to return to Wendover where he belonged. In less than a week's time at a planter's pace, he'd be at his father's hearthside, and then, perhaps, he could pick up the pieces of his shattered life and begin to forget.

"Cease the formalities, Berry," Morgan ordered as he grabbed Adam around the shoulder, dragging the wench along with him. "Bring this man the rum he's due."

Nobody argued with Daniel Morgan, least of all Benjamin Berry, who'd profited mightily every time the man entered his tavern. He nodded quick assent, watched the two blond, bearded giants walk to the corner table, and hastened back to the bar for an armload of bottles and cups to quench their thirst. It had been a damn good day.

Adam barely noticed the frumpy woman with Morgan. Though she sat with them, she stayed quiet and in the background. The flow of rum, the frequent interruptions of congratulations, and the man-to-man camaraderie between him and Morgan fed his sense of well-being and his heady anticipation of better days ahead.

Only when the wench attempted to leave the table despite Morgan's protests did he pay her any heed. "C'mon, Fat Moll, stay close to your Danny, love. I may have need of you yet again . . ."

Moll? Adam tensed, eyed the woman. A thin shaft of sunlight fell on her doughy face. A star mole twinkled on the tip of her lip, a mole just like . . . in the exact spot where. . . .

"No!" he exclaimed, jumping to his feet.

Morgan looked up in surprise; the wench whimpered and tried to back away. Morgan pulled her toward him and held her in his grasp. "What in the hell's wrong, Barwick?" he asked.

Adam sat, not taking his astonished eyes off the woman. "Is it you, Sweet Molly?" he asked in a whisper.

She drew closer to Morgan and appeared to shrivel.

Morgan laughed softly. "Aye, she's a sweet one to be sure, but we fondly call her—"

"You're not dead?" Adam interrupted, still not believing he was seeing right.

Molly shook her head. A heavy silence fell over the table.

Morgan looked inquisitively at his friend, who had grown uncommonly pale as if he'd confronted a ghost, then down at Molly, whose round face had folded around a decisively guilty smile. Something was deeply amiss. "Seems you two might have a bit of talking to do. Shall I leave you alone?"

"No, Morgan, stay," Adam said quietly, his fiery eyes focused only on Molly. "I'd like a witness to this woman's revelations."

"Revelations? Weighty stuff, this sounds." Morgan hoped to lighten the atmosphere with his scoffing tone, but the hard set of Adam's mouth and the firm beat against his temples convinced him this was no time for a light touch. His brave friend had been struck a damaging blow of some sort and Adam's next words left no doubt.

"Weighty stuff indeed," he said, his voice like steel, his large fists tightened into cannon balls.

Morgan frowned. "Then let's get to the bottom of this. Speak your 'revelations,' woman."

Molly only shook her head.

"Then I have many questions," Adam said between clenched teeth. "And I expect honest answers."

Molly nodded, but hung on to Morgan.

"You were not poisoned that day in Williamsburg?" he asked.

"No, I only pretended," she responded in a thin voice.

"Pretended? For God's sake, why?"

"For silver, o' course," she said with a shrug.

"Whose silver?" Adam held his breath.

Molly squirmed. "T'other man's. Your brother, was he? Wasn't James his name?"

James? James had done this? Why, in the name of God?

"Speak the truth, woman! You say that James Wallace paid you silver to pretend you were poisoned?"

Molly raised her right hand. "God's truth. Aye, he did that."

"He paid Lucy, too?"

"Aye."

Adam exhaled an oath. The whole sordid scene had been staged? That damnable afternoon that had set him on his odyssey of suffering had been naught but

27

a contemptible trick? He'd trusted James, had heeded his advice. *What possible benefit could it be to James to have me gone?*

A stab of ice penetrated his heart. *Wendover!* Surely, by God, his father hadn't. . . .

He braced himself. He must hear all this woman knew.

"When did you leave Williamsburg, Molly?" he asked, his calm voice contrasting with the cold coil of apprehension in his chest.

"Less than a year after ye left us."

He said a silent prayer before his next question. "And what do you know of my father? Is he well?"

"He died, no more'n four months after ye had gone."

Adam flinched. Her words were like a hard, cruel blow into his ribs. He bit his lip, swallowed around the lump in his throat. William Barwick was dead. His father had been dead for nearly six years and he'd not known, had had no way of knowing.

Morgan reached over to pat him on the shoulder. "It's a large dose of bad news you're hearing today, my friend," he said.

Adam nodded and took a long, deep breath before looking up at Molly again. "What did my father know of me?" he asked at last.

"He thought ye dead, as did we all. There was word from the frontier that ye were captured by Indians, so they said. Your pa was sorely grieved, I heard tell."

His mind clouded with remembered thoughts. "I *was* captured by renegade Indians not ten miles from Williamsburg," he said softly, as if he were talking to himself. "It was a happening as peculiar as it was unexpected. It was as if . . . as if they were waiting for me." The realization struck him hard. *Dear God, that too was James's doing! The whole tangle of my life these past six years was that bastard's doing.* A hot, blistering anger flooded him.

"And what of Wendover?" he asked Molly.

"There was a new will, so I heard. That man got it."

"James Wallace is sire of Wendover?"

"Aye, that's 'im."

Adam slapped his hands on the table in an explosion of rage and jumped to his feet. "That bloody bastard—that *damnable* bloody bastard. God rot him in hell!"

Morgan's eyes were troubled. "Seems you might have yet more battles ahead after all, Barwick."

"Only one, Morgan, and a brief one," he said with fierce venom. "It will take but a swift thrust of the sword into one black heart . . ."

Morgan shook his head. "And be hanged for it, my friend. What good be that?"

"My peace" was all Adam said.

"Be reasonable, Barwick. It benefits you to move slowly in this matter. By rights, the land is yours. You need only present yourself to the courts—"

Adam cut him off. "The man must die—all else be damned." As his words echoed through the now-silent room, he quickly reached down for his long rifle and departed without farewell.

Adam was like a man swept up by the avenging Furies, Morgan thought with deep sadness. He'd seen that driven look before on men hard set on revenge. God almighty, he'd felt it himself. But he'd learned the hard way that strength sowed together with patience and reasoning reaped the better harvest. He knew Adam Barwick to be an intelligent fighter, a worthy, brave comrade-in-arms whose mettle had been tested time and again under fire.

"Above all, strategy is the key," Adam had told him once. Morgan prayed now that the long trip to the Tidewater would force his friend to remember his own wise words.

Molly looked shaken, ashamed. "Can't ye stop 'im, Danny?" she asked.

Morgan heaved a sigh. "Only God can stop him now." *And perhaps a bit of time for sober thought,* he added to himself with fervent hope. He reached for the bottle.

Not five minutes later, Adam bounded through the door again, his already-seething rage boiling with a new fury.

"The stinking lowlifes stole my horse!" he shouted, riveting the attention of every man in the tavern. Nobody moved, except Johnny Davis, who slithered unnoticed back into the shadows.

Morgan stood and walked over to Adam. "Who in God's name would steal your horse, Barwick?"

"The bloody Stewarts, that's who," he roared. "Who here can tell me where the bastards live?" The silence in the room was palpable.

"Surely ye must be mistaken," Berry said, placing his towel on the bar. "Those Stewarts be dumb and mean, but they wouldn't—"

"The bastards took my horse," Adam interrupted, his nostrils flaring. "The stable lad coughed out the truth to save his own scrawny neck. Now either one of you men here is going to tell me where I might find the scum, or by God every eggshell head in this room will be cracked."

Mumbling low disclaimers of any knowledge of the Stewarts' whereabouts, all of the men appeared to move back a step. All except Daniel Morgan, who stood tall by Adam's side. "Speak up, you cowards!" he bellowed. "The Stewarts are often in Battletown. Where's their home?"

"The Hollow," said a weak voice in the corner. All heads turned toward Johnny Davis, who hunkered further into the shadows.

"Where?" prodded Adam.

"The Hollow," Johnny repeated, cowering. "They live in Wildcat Hollow, 'bout five miles down a ways, I think."

"Give me the directions, you son of a polecat."

Johnny shook his head and cringed into the corner. "Never been there meself, Mister." He looked around in panic. "Some of ye other fellas know, dontcha?" he pleaded.

"We've none of us been there, Barwick," Berry said, coming to Johnny's rescue. "It's a wild area back in the hills, 'cross the river and then south a ways, I think. Nobody else I know of lives down there but the Stewarts."

"Nobody else'd wanna live in the godforsaken place," said one of the men with a scornful laugh. The tension relaxed in the room, but it remained hot and taut in Adam's face.

Dan Morgan watched his strong friend clench his fists, his eyes burning like twin dark coals. He knew that Barwick now had two missions of revenge and harbored no doubts he'd pursue them both with hard, relentless passion. God in heaven, Adam had good reason to be so driven but Dan felt concern for his friend, though he knew he'd prevail. Hell, the Stewarts and James Wallace deserved to die. In the latter case, however, he prayed that Adam would heed his advice and move slowly rather than in incautious anger. Perhaps this nettling detour would cool him down and bring needed reasoning into his further actions.

Adam turned away from the gaping crowd. "I'll be on my way to the Hollow then," he said to Morgan.

"Do you plan to walk, my friend?"

He shrugged. "My rage is sufficient to give wings to my boots."

"I have no doubt," said Morgan with a chuckle.

"But unless those wings can hoist you over the oaks and pines, a horse will carry you far faster. You may borrow my mare, Patsy. She's a mite old, but she's well shod for the rough country."

Adam looked thoughtful. "Patsy would be a help, but borrowing's out of the question, for heaven only knows when I'll see you again. Could I buy her?" He offered his coin-filled purse.

Morgan waved him off. "She's worth less than a third of that fat pouch."

Adam poured out more than half the coins and held them out. "Take these or I'll walk."

With a resigned sigh, the wagoner accepted the money. "Patsy's yours," he said, clasping his friend's shoulder. He looked deeply into Adam's fiery eyes. "Godspeed, Barwick, but after you've retrieved your horse and settled with the Stewarts, think long and hard about taking a more judicious approach in that greater wrong that's been done to you."

Adam nodded, a wisp of a smile curling his lips. "I thank you for the mare, Morgan, but your advice, I fear, travels not nearly so well. Nor would I pay you a shilling for it."

Morgan reached for his hand. "You're right, my brave comrade, no man's advice is worth a shilling. Above all, strategy is the key."

Adam's eyes flashed. "Strategy be damned," he said under his breath and left the tavern.

Benjamin Berry walked over to Morgan. "Blasted no-good Stewarts doin' a fool thing like that," he said, shaking his head. "The man will kill them for sure."

"Aye, and they deserve no better," Daniel Morgan responded. With a weary sigh, he turned away. He hoped mightily the Stewarts were all that Adam Barwick killed.

Chapter Two

April 1760,
Wildcat Hollow, Virginia

Bethany Rose Stewart pulled the bowstring taut and squeezed one eye shut. Holding her breath, she sighted down the long shaft of the hand-hewn arrow. *Steady*, she told herself. *Now*.

With a zing and a thud, the arrow landed precisely in the center of a knot on the oak's trunk.

Without a pause, she reached quickly over her shoulder for another arrow, rearmed the bow, and pulled back the string in one swift movement. *Thwang!* The second arrow nestled hard beside the first.

"Damnation, I'm still not fast enough, Constant,"

she complained. "The crow yonder called thrice between my hits."

Frowning, she ran over to the tree and yanked out the arrows. After inspecting the tips, she returned to the boulder and crouched behind it again.

She took a deep breath, pushed a wild sprig of copper-red hair away from her determined face, and waited for the crow to resume its cawing. Timing its steady beat, keeping her eyes focused on the oak's knot, she repeated her exercise. *Zingthump!* One. *Thwangthump!* Two.

Again the second arrow lined up beside the first, but this time Bethany smiled brightly.

"I did it, Constant!" she squealed. "I hit them true in less than three caws." She wrapped her arms in glee around the skinny dog and hugged him close. The mongrel signaled his approval with a wet lick of his freckled tongue on her cheek.

The two rolled playfully on the hard soil, oblivious to the stinging stones and grainy dirt. "I did it! I did it!" she sang over and over and Constant barked in happy harmony.

Flushed with enthusiasm, Bethany retrieved the arrows and propped them against the oak. She hung the bow and arrow bag on a low branch, moved from under the speckled shadows of the spring-tender green leaves, and leisurely sprawled on her back. How glorious it was to have a free afternoon. Pa and George had gone to Battletown for the day and wouldn't return before nightfall. She'd finished her chores with dispatch by midday, and long, warm sunlit hours of blissful solitude lay ahead for her. *Time*, she thought with delight. Fingering the small leather pouch around her neck, she smiled. *Time to dream.*

Content, she idly watched puffs of white clouds float across the blue sky.

"There's an owl," she said. The dog, who lay next to her faded brown skirt, lifted his ears when she spoke but soon returned to his own reverie.

"No, its middle's growing now," she said with a giggle. "It's a pig, Constant. A great fat pig with a curly tail, and the sun's turning it pink."

Her toe reached over to nudge a soft spot behind the dog's ear. "Think on it, my Constant, a fat pink pig. Tis a wondrous omen, promising full trenchers on the table with heaps of scraps and bones left for you." The dog yawned, then placed his warm muzzle across her bare foot.

Bethany continued watching the lazy motion of the pig-cloud, waiting with dreamy patience for its next transformation. It spread, stretching wide its head and tail, growing four long legs, a small set of silver-tipped wings. A horse—a *flying* horse!

Her eyes sparkled. "It's the sign for the prince," she said with a catch of expectancy in her voice. Her heart fluttered like the wings of a hummingbird nearing an open blossom. He was coming at last just as her dream catcher had promised!

She watched with wonder as the winged horse sped across the sky. *He'll come for thee on a swift, white steed, your beautiful prince with rich, dark hair like a beaver's fur and with eyes as blue as the summer's sky,* her treasured amulet had whispered to her again and again in its wind-like song. *He'll carry thee with gentle peace to lands beyond the blue-clad heights. The heavens themselves will tell thee when it's to be.*

"The heavens themselves will . . ." she repeated softly, the words as sweet as honey on her tongue. "The heavens themselves . . ." A gasp of joy leapt from her throat. Trembling with excitement, she sat up and circled her arms around the dog. "It's to be, Constant! It's to be!" she cried into his mottled neck. "The prince is on his way to us, perhaps even now. The heavens have given us the sign." Constant seemed to nod in complacent agreement as he snuggled up against her.

Bethany ruffled the short hair of the dog's dull coat, stirring up a puff of dust. She wrinkled her nose. "And just look at us, will you? We've more dirt on us than a pair of oxen in a drought." She looked with dismay at her filthy bodice and skirt. She had little other clothing. How could she welcome her prince garbed thus? She felt a twinge of panic.

Looking up at the sun, she saw it was still high and bright. Good, there was warmth and time enough for drying the thin, worn homespun if she hurried.

"Wake up, Constant," she ordered. "We have work to do and the stream yon is beckoning. We need get washed and ready." As she started to unlace her bodice, the dog's ears raised and a low growl of warning rumbled from his throat. Bethany froze, instantly alert. Someone was coming.

Crawling to the tree, she grabbed her two arrows, reached up quickly for the bow, and pressed hard against the trunk. Constant stood erect next to her, his insistent barks shredding the peace of the Hollow. Her attempts to hush him were futile. Resigned that whoever or whatever was coming would be forewarned, she armed the bow, waited, her nerves as taut as the bow's string.

The dog quieted at last, but remained by her side, stiff as a sentinel poised for battle, his long nose pointing toward the steep brush-covered hill in front of them. Bethany's acute senses followed the subtle movements of the bushes and picked up the tenuous sound of slowly moving horses' hooves on the stones.

Three horses were coming. *Three*. Her brow furrowed. She had only two arrows. She could do naught but be on guard and wait.

When she saw the men come into the clearing, her tense fear was replaced with surprise. Pa and George? Why in heaven's name had they returned so early from Battletown? She felt a chill of disappointment; her blessed hours of solitude were at an end.

Lowering the bow and straightening her shoulders, she sighed and watched her pa and brother approach. And how did they come upon the extra horse? she wondered. A fine chestnut it was.

They stopped in front of her. She gnawed at her lower lip as she checked their moods. Worse than usual, she noted with despair. George looked as if he'd been battling a pair of black bears, his swollen eyes and bruised face a sure sign he'd taken on something that had whopped him to a fare-thee-well. Her pa was as sour and bitter as the pokeweed he chewed and her heart sank. The remainder of her day boded ill, she feared.

"Wastin' time again, are ye?" Bull Stewart grunted.

"No, Pa." She raised her bow tentatively. "I've been but practicing with—"

"Hog's swill!" he blurted impatiently. "Time with the bow be wasted time for a worthless woman. What 'bout your chores?"

"They're mostly done," she said, keeping her voice soft. "I need only to—"

Bull raised his whip. "Need only to what, lazy wench? What have ye left undone?" he roared.

Constant bared his teeth and growled. Bethany placed a quieting hand on the dog's neck, fearful his protective stance would anger her pa even more. She moved forward cautiously to shield the animal.

"I intended but to launder my clothing," she said,

eyeing the whip warily and bracing herself for its lash.

His scoffing laughter struck her instead. "Damn fool woman, ye'll be th' death of me yet with your infernal washin'. Makes holes in the clothes, it does. Wears 'em out 'fore their time and 'taint needed. Ye're as all-fired addled 'bout cleanin' up as your ma was, maybe a sight worse." Though his face remained puckered with disapproval, he lowered the whip and she breathed easier.

"Get on with your foolishness then, but keep your hands off mine and Bully Boy's garments. We don't cotton to the stink of new-washed stuff." He narrowed his eyes. "I s'pose ye haven't started our supper yet?"

"Aye, I have," she responded. "Tis in the kettle, near ready, a wild turkey I killed this morn." She hoped that would quiet his displeasure with her a mite. He relished turkey.

But his eyes remained hard. The pokeweed wiggled ominously as he worked his mouth around it. "We left ye chores aplenty back at the cabin, Bethany Rose, and I 'spect to see them dispatched well, ye hear me?"

She nodded. She'd done all he'd ordered and more and prayed he'd find no fault with any of it.

"C'mon, Bully Boy, let's cease this useless palaverin' with your fool sister and head on t'home," Bull grumbled, turning his horse. "I'm hankerin' for a bib of corn whiskey 'bout now."

George, who hadn't spoken a word, looked mighty sullen and disagreeable to Bethany. He grunted and turned to follow his pa.

Noting again how bruised and battered he was, she ventured her help. "I could prepare a poultice for your swollen face."

Her brother shrugged.

"Nah, woman," Bull said, shooing her away with

his hand. "Bully Boy here's got no need for your fancy ministerin'. He's the new champion of Battletown, I'll have ye know. Done won himself a new horse."

Bethany's brows shot up in surprise. George *won?* She hated to think what the defeated man looked like.

As the men headed for the cabin, she was relieved they were leaving her alone for a spell. She hoped the whiskey would improve their tempers, but she had her doubts. Most times it just made them meaner.

She grasped the pouch that hung around her neck. The warmth of the magical metal inside radiated through the leather, giving her comfort. "I wish . . . I wish I need never go home again," she whispered. *No! Tis not a proper wish,* her mind screamed. She frowned and shook her head. "Heed me not, my dream catcher," she pleaded. "My words sprung from my selfish heart, and I meant them not. Protect my pa and brother and our home as well."

She held her breath, closed her eyes, and held the pouch tightly, willing her evil wish to be expelled. The amulet pulsed a light response through the leather and she relaxed with a sigh.

From its perch high in a nearby sycamore, a mockingbird trilled, warbled, and chirped its medley of borrowed songs. Constant rubbed against her skirt. Aroused from her musings, she realized that time was slipping away and squinted up at the sun. "It travels too swiftly, Constant," she moaned. "Now my clothing will never dry."

For a moment she wondered why she'd deemed it so important to wash them. *The prince!* As the memory of the winged horse she'd seen nudged into her consciousness, only a faint glimmer of her earlier excitement flickered in her breast. Pa and George ofttimes dampened magic, she realized with a pang, but she was determined they'd never make her lose faith in the dream catcher's special promise. Her prince *would* come for her, though now that the spell of her wonderful afternoon had been broken, she figured he'd be delayed a mite.

"Tis not likely he'll come this day, anyway," she confided to the dog with a mix of sadness and resignation. "And Pa's right that scrubbing makes holes in the clothes." She looked down at her soiled skirt. "My petticoat peeks well enough through the holes that be there already," she added with a wry chuckle.

Constant began scratching at his ear, reminding her that at least part of her initial plan did need tending to. It had been days since they'd bathed.

She ran to the oak and dug out the hunk of soap she kept in the bottom of her arrow bag. "C'mon, boy," she yelled. "Neither of us gets holes from washing!"

With the dog running after her and yapping at her bare heels, she pulled off her clothes and tossed them aside. The two plunged happily into the cold stream.

On his way in pursuit of the horse thieves, Adam cursed the sorry mare. Her pace was slower than a weighted-down sloop on a windless day, and he felt damnably sure he could be making far better time on his own feet.

Though he admitted he was grateful he had the grizzled animal. The steep, heavily forested terrain with its treacherous limestone outcroppings would have sorely challenged his travel-worn boots. Patsy's shoes were far sturdier, and her legs, too, steadier than his this afternoon. Those numerous cups of rum back in Battletown were taking their toll, and a dull ache hammered at his temples. He realized he hadn't eaten a bite since the stale hoecake he'd shared with Morgan at dawn.

"God rot it all," he grumbled. His world this day

had turned as bitter as the taste in his mouth.

Two unforgivable wrongs had been foisted upon him. One, the long-ago workings of a devious Satan, cut deeply into his soul and cried out for fierce retribution; the other, a callow act by cowardly dolts, was naught but a temporary annoyance resulting in this frustrating detour.

He muttered an oath, damning the Stewarts and the delay they'd caused him. Now he must find the bastards and retrieve his horse before he could head eastward to wreak revenge on the dastardly James Wallace.

A bloody pox on them, his mind growled as he shifted his weight on the laggard mare.

Adam noted that the Stewarts also were being forced to travel slowly through the torturous hills. His keen, trail-wise eyes had found it easy to track them thus far. Flattened brush, an occasional hoofprint, and still-warm droppings from the horses were clear markers for him that the mountain men had passed not long before.

Reaching a high flat ridge, he pulled on the reins to stop Patsy and dismounted, thinking it perhaps wise to pause a spell.

Morgan's parting words—his own words cleverly thrown back to him—rang still in his ears. *Strategy is the key*.

He'd rest the mare, uncloud his thoughts, and devise his plan to be rid of this nettling problem with the Stewarts as swiftly as possible. As for his strategy in dealing with James, that would have to wait until he'd settled this first matter.

Far below him, a small stream meandered from the base of an opposite mountain and coiled its way lazily around dark boulders and through a curved patchwork of tangled greens, browns, and yellows.

He believed it likely he'd found Wildcat Hollow, and a whiff of grayish smoke rising behind a nest of trees bordering the stream indicated he'd located the site of the Stewarts' cabin. "Nobody else I know of lives down there but the Stewarts," Benjamin Berry had told him.

Very well, he thought. *Let the scum crawl into their filthy lair, and I'll catch them there off guard.*

But he must quell his impatience. He would wait till the sun was low on the horizon, till the two men were sated with food and drink. . . .

Adam had learned well the ways of his Indian captors. Surprise, he knew, was ever more than half the battle. The lesser half required sure hands with tomahawk and blade, and he was skilled with both. Should they put up any kind of battle, he was confident he'd prevail.

He drew in deep breaths of fresh mountain air to help him relax. He needed some time to garner his strength and shed the effects of the rum. This rocky ledge high above his prey would be a suitable stopping place; perhaps after he'd eased his hunger he would nap awhile. The sun told him he had about two hours before he should make his move.

The gray speckled mare he'd bought from Morgan had no pack of supplies, so he would have to forage for food. But the woods abounded with wild blackberries, ripe for the picking, and their sweet juice would be sufficient to restore his energy. A few handfuls of berries and a brief sleep would prepare him well for his task ahead, he told himself with a warming surge of satisfaction as he began gathering his supper.

It was, he noted, the first satisfying moment he'd had since knocking Bully Boy Stewart to the ground for the final time back in Battletown.

* * *

The eerie squall of a vulture circling above awakened Adam a short while later. Feeling refreshed, he greeted the intruder with a near smile. "Be patient, my black-winged hunter of death," he muttered as he sprang to his feet. "I'll leave carrion behind for you soon enough." As if in reply, the bird dipped a wing and glided over the ridge and out of sight.

He checked the sun. Far too high for his attack, he judged, but low enough for him to begin his journey down to the Hollow. The smoke still puffed behind the trees, signaling his target.

"Come, Patsy, let's be on our way," he said, pulling the mare's reins. He chose to lead the animal down the mountain, more sure now of his own legs.

Moving carefully, he steered the mare away from stones so that her shod hooves wouldn't make a clatter and wended a circuitous path around thickets and bushes to avoid any telltale movement of branches or leaves.

As he neared the bottom, he pulled up short, puzzled. He'd heard laughter rising from the Hollow's stream, the unbridled laughter of a youth at play. *A youth?* Adam frowned. He hadn't taken the Stewarts for family men. Had he come upon the wrong Hollow?

He pulled aside the leafy branches of a wild gooseberry and squinted toward the sparkling ribbon of water beyond the boulder-strewn meadow. A volley of splashes disrupted one spot of the otherwise quiet stream. Soap bubbles bounced around a frolicking pair—a well-lathered dog and a slender youth whose arms whirled like a windmill in a lusty breeze as he tried to rinse the animal.

The pleasant scene was punctuated by the lad's good-natured laughter echoing through the hills. For a brief moment, Adam's spirits lifted like the rainbow-splattered bubbles that drifted over the happy pair, but the black cloud of his mission in Wildcat Hollow quickly lowered about him.

Surely, he'd happened upon a neighboring Hollow. No one connected with the Stewarts could be so lighthearted. He would have to ask the youth for proper directions, but common sense dictated he shouldn't surprise the two while they bathed. He'd stay hidden till they were out of the water and the boy was dressed. Then, with plenty of noise, he'd warn them before he approached and assure them of his friendly intentions.

Adam stroked Patsy's neck, whispered that she should stay still, and sat beside the mare. Through an opening in the budding gooseberry, he watched the pair splash about in the water. He wished he could join them; it had been more than a week since he'd had a proper bath. Idly, he noted a scattering of dark clothing on the shore and a bow and two arrows nearby. His lips curved in a nostalgic smile as he remembered the long-ago joys of his own carefree youth. He, too, had once known such simple pleasures.

He sighed and his mood darkened. *Once, but never again*, he reminded himself. With growing impatience, he saw the sun was balanced atop the opposite mountain and readying itself to slip behind. Soon the shadows would deepen, making his journey to the Stewart's Hollow more troublesome. Indeed, he might have to wait till morning if he should find from the lad that the Stewarts' place was yet distant.

Weary at the thought of further delay, he decided to question the boy at once. As he started to rise, the youth and dog, with a whoop and a bark, ran toward the shore.

Adam stopped, midway between crouch and standing, momentarily incapable of further movement. The lad was not a lad.

His hand gripped the bush. *Dear God, has Venus herself ascended from the stream?* His eyes widened then narrowed in an effort to comprehend the vision before him. She was sculpture in motion—a silken image carved from ivory clay, still gleaming with moisture as if newly molded by a master artist and just this moment brought to life.

He beheld her, suspended as if in a dream. A thin wisp of air escaped through his parted lips, carrying with it the tattered shreds of coherent thought.

She was truly a wonder, bathed in the pink translucent glow of the lowering sun. His eyes filled with the sight of her—her ripe breasts like rounded alabaster tipped with soft rosebuds; the tapering of her slender waist; the gentle curves of her hips; the dimpled navel above her firm stomach; the small mound of copper marking like an arrowhead the tender place between her long, perfectly carved legs.

He was spellbound, powerless but to stare at her as she turned away from him and glided with the ethereal steps of an angel across the shoreline. Her wet, dark red hair streamed like a silky curtain down her back, nearly screening the sweet twin pillows of her lovely buttocks.

She began to dress. The heavenly nymph disappeared beneath the folds of earthly clothing.

She was, Adam realized with a soft nudge of regret, neither vision nor dream.

A mind-clearing slap of insight followed rapidly, striking him hard. For these past fleeting moments, his reactions had been passing strange; he had not been himself. He shook his head. He'd not been himself at all. Mist-filled fantasies had never before been part of his nature.

· He wondered at his peculiar conduct, attributing it at last to the surprise she'd given him and the long span of time since he'd had a woman. Only now, after its intensity had diminished, was he aware of the powerful throbbing in his groin.

He'd allowed worldly lust to perplex his brain.

His brows pulled together as he chastised himself. *Visions, dreams, nymphs! They're naught but the stuff of folly*. He took comfort in the knowledge that his hard, colorless world of reality had ever scoffed at such nonsense. And rightly so, for muddled thoughts, like women, could weaken a man, make him vulnerable.

A spark of anger at his own foolishness ignited a more sensible view of the scene before him. The woman, he saw now with eyes free of enchantment, was but a simple mountain girl in shabby dress. Her bare feet moved in ordinary fashion across the bleak rock-filled meadow like any earthbound creature. The black dog by her side was a mangy cur, the ridges of his ribs visible even from this distance.

The world indeed was hard and colorless, as was the life of those who inhabited this ugly Hollow by whatever name it was called.

He remembered his purpose for being in this dreary place, and time enough had been wasted. Lad or girl, it mattered not. He must inquire where he might find the Stewarts.

With a loud clearing of his throat, Adam pulled on Patsy's reins and continued his descent, making certain this time that his arrival would be well announced.

Bethany tensed, even as Constant began his warning growl. She grabbed up her bow and arrows and scurried behind a boulder, eyeing the hillside with alert caution. The thicket of gooseberries rustled ominously, signaling the approach of . . . what? Who? She heard someone whistling and the sound of nearing hooves. Constant ran forward, barking loudly.

With her heart clambering in her chest, she pulled back on the bow's string and waited.

A tall man leading an ugly, spavined mare broke into the clearing. A cold clutch of fear stiffened her spine. The stranger was fierce-looking! Menacing. Constant cowered in his giant shadow and, with tail lowered, skittered with a whimper back to her side.

She cursed the dog under her breath. He'd drawn the frightening man's attention to the boulder where she crouched.

"Halloo!" he shouted between cupped hands in her direction.

She jumped reflexively, then tightened her grip on the weapon.

"Is there someone there who can tell me where I am?"

She responded by releasing the arrow. With deadly precision, it sped toward the stranger, lifted the wide brim of his hat, and carried it backwards with a resounding *swish* into the bushes.

Stunned silence followed. The man stood still, his arms held stiffly away from his sides. Only his wild sun-streaked hair moved. It was near the color of his buckskins and now, unfettered by the hat, it waved restlessly about his head, disconcerting her further, adding to her terror.

She rearmed the bow quickly, warily watching his hands for any sign of movement toward hidden weapons. Something warned her she must stay on the offensive with this bearded giant. With but one arrow left, she had to convince him to leave. Immediately.

She aimed carefully at his large chest. A knob of fear clogged her throat, but she prayed she could make her voice convey the firmness of her will. She took a steadying breath.

"This next one goes straight through your heart, Mister, unless you make haste and get away from here!"

Chapter Three

Adam believed her. She'd sure as hell proved her accuracy with that bow by removing his hat with her first shot. Hoping to assure the woman she was safe, he held his hands away from his own weapons and eyed her warily. Dare he try to reason with her?

She was guarded by the boulder and kept her aim steady, but he calculated the bowstring was yet a hairbreadth from being fully drawn. He trusted his own quick reactions.

"I bring you no harm, ma'am," he ventured. "I'm looking for Wildcat Hollow, the Stewarts . . . They stole my horse and I mean to . . ."

The string tightened. He lifted his hands in surrender and nodded his resignation. "You win, woman, I'll leave you now."

She stood with bow drawn, as sturdy as the rock in front of her. "I don't believe your lying words about the horse, Mister. Now *get*."

She was a Stewart all right. Maybe a mite brighter than the men, but surely as mean. *Damnable wild mountain woman*. She'd bested him, he knew, frustrated at his own carelessness. He'd allowed a slip of a girl to outwit him. He decided he'd better comply with her command—partially, at least. He would hide up the mountain, wait till dark, then attack the cabin. If they resisted, he reckoned he now had three Stewarts he might have to kill in order to retrieve his horse.

He turned slowly, keeping a sharp eye on the bow. He'd be damned if he'd take her arrow in his back.

"Get!" she shouted.

With a shrug that he prayed she'd construe as reluctant cooperation, he pulled Patsy along and walked back through the gooseberries.

Bethany watched him disappear. The bushes rustled in his wake, and the clatter of the mare's hooves slowly diminished as the pair climbed the mountain. Only when she was convinced the stranger was truly on his way did she relax her guard. Taking in a ragged breath, she lowered her bow.

Constant rubbed against her skirt, and her hand trembled as she patted his neck.

"Damnation," she whispered. A troubled frown creased her brow. "I was scared to a fare-thee-well, Constant, and could ne'er have let the arrow fly." She shook her head. At least he had believed she might, and the danger was past—for the moment.

Who was he? Strangers seldom came upon the Hollow. He must have followed Pa and George. A lone wanderer, perhaps, bent on stealing the chestnut horse George had won fair and square in Battletown. Well, she'd taught the bastard horse thief a lesson about meddling with the Stewarts.

"Let's be going to home," she said to the dog with a worried sigh. Casting a final hard look at the darkening mountain, she thought she discerned the stranger's movements high up, near the top. A vulture floated over the stony ridge above like a grim host welcoming the man's approach.

Bethany shivered and headed back toward the cabin. She wanted to tell her pa and George about the horse thief, alerting them to the danger he might yet hold for them. But she saw it was too late when she arrived home. Both men were deep in drunken slumber, sprawled on their backs across their pallets in the cabin's front room. Though still clothed and booted, their belts were loosened and their unlaced shirts had gaped open. Their slack jaws and mouths flapped rhythmically under the pressure of their noisy snores.

Bethany wrinkled her nose. A familiar enough sight this was, but tonight she might have need of them. Dismayed, she knew they'd be useless till morn and meaner than hornets then.

She gathered up the greasy trenchers of turkey scraps and the bottles they'd left on the floor and walked back into the cabin's other room, a smaller cubicle that served as a kitchen and her own sleeping quarters.

The hearth's fire was near dead under the kettle, but the air was hot, heavy with pungent smoke. The lopsided chimney had never drawn properly. Her eyes stinging, she pulled aside the stained oiled paper from the window, welcoming the cooling brush of light wind across her heated cheeks.

No time for resting, she reminded herself, lighting a pine knot. Its flame sputtered, throwing shadowy fingers that clawed against the log walls and grasped upward toward the beams beneath the weather board roof. Straw skittered over the dirt floor as her bare feet hurried across. She had chores to finish, despite her weariness. The recent tension in the meadow had truly exhausted her and she rubbed her lower back.

The meager remains of the wild turkey still bubbled in the kettle, and its strong aroma assaulted her nose. She grimaced. Her stomach was way too tight for food this eve.

She banked the fire, relieved that wood enough for the morning fire was stacked by the hearth. After letting Constant finish off the scraps in the men's trenchers, she placed them into a bucket. She'd wash all in the morning, she decided, too tired tonight to fetch water from the creek that ran behind the cabin.

When she snuffed the pine knot, the sudden, inky darkness made her shiver, despite the heavy warmth of the room. A stir of warning prickled her nape. Instinctively, she reached for her amulet and held it tightly. *Soothe my nerves, dear dream catcher*, she pleaded silently.

The amulet pulsed through the leather, comforting her.

After shedding her clothing and slipping into a thinly worn nightdress, she went back to the window. The sky was moonless and without stars. As her eyes grew accustomed to the darkness, she saw the mountain, looming black against the pewter clouds. Was the man still up there, or was he even now stealthily approaching with devious plans to steal the horse while they slept?

She couldn't allow it! She noted George's hard-won chestnut tethered to the tall pine outside her window. It was her duty to protect her family and their possessions, but a chilling twinge made her chin tremble. She felt woefully alone.

Shaking her head stubbornly, she straightened her shoulders and tightened her lips. *Nay! I'll not give in to such weakness.* She pulled over a low stool and sat, picked up her bow, and placed it firmly across her lap. She had only one arrow left, but she'd stay awake on guard through the night, here, by the window.

If the bearded giant should be fool enough to return, she pledged she'd put an arrow into his heart without hesitation.

The prince came to her. He was beautiful, strong, his long dark hair shimmering in the moonlight, his bright blue eyes twinkling with captured stars. Mounted on his fine white steed, he held his hand down, reaching for her. "I am here," he said.

His irresistible touch was gentle as he pulled her toward him. She floated upward and joined him high upon the horse. His hard body pressed against her, pervasive, sweet. His muscled arms encircled her, possessed her. She was with him at last, content, protected. The steed sped them through the night, toward the hazy blue mountains that held captive the sleeping sun— the very sun, restless now in its dark prison, that the mountains would release in a red blaze of glory in the morn.

She smiled, the warm wind a caress upon her face, the light steady beat of the mount against her thighs a perpetual pulse, growing stronger. She was the prince's woman, a swelling blossom, moist, wanting, aching for. . . .

The horse reared, whinnied. Flashes of light struck her closed eyelids and a deep rumble vibrated against her ears.

Bethany awoke with a jolt. The dream's gauzy veil was mercilessly torn away from her eyes as she saw spears of lightning lashing the darkness and heard the roars of angry thunder reverberating in the hills and in the surrounding forest. She stiffened to attention as her eyes focused more clearly. The stranger was outside! He was untying the chestnut's tether, speaking low words to the agitated animal. A powerful wind whipped his long hair into flames of burning bronze.

He was the devil himself. She wanted to recoil, to hide beneath the window, but she found herself standing, her bow armed and ready.

"You've been warned, Satan!" she screamed, releasing the string.

The man ducked, and the arrow flew over his shoulder, plunging with a quiver of futility into the pine behind him.

Terror gripped her. He crouched, then moved relentlessly toward her. A tomahawk bulged from his raised hand. Impaled by fear, she held up the stool.

A sharp crack split the night. A spike of fiery light blinded her, and a blast of sound staggered her. The stool fell from her hands.

She reached for the windowsill, striving for support, but it was too late. Her fingers fluttered across the splintery wood as she crumpled to her knees in the swirling darkness. Her last thread of conscious thought wove a bleak thin tapestry of discovery . . . *Dying . . . There was naught else. . . .*

Adam threw down his tomahawk and leapt through the window. He must save the woman! The lightning-severed pine had slammed into the cabin, and the loud crackle of flames above mingled their threats with the deep grumbles of thunder.

"Where are you?" he shouted into the darkness thick with the odor of sulphur. No response. What in God's name was he doing? Moments ago she'd tried to kill him. Was she even yet aiming one of her blasted arrows at him?

That mattered not! He couldn't leave her to die in this infernal place.

"The cabin's burning, woman! We'll settle our disagreements later, but for now we must get outside."

A dog barked and Adam pressed against the wall. When his boot touched a soft bundle on the floor, he looked down, and the bundle moved, groaned. Flickers of lightning illuminated the woman lying curled at his feet; she was quiet, as though in a deep sleep. The dog ran to his side, whimpered, and began to lick her pale cheek.

The acrid smell of burning wood spurred him to action. Shooing away the dog, he swiftly gathered the woman into his arms and climbed out the window. The dog followed them.

Adam lay her carefully on the ground. In the expanding orange glow, he saw that she breathed, her small breasts rising in a rhythmic pattern against the nubby fabric of her tattered nightshift. No longer was she the harridan who had threatened him, but once again the nymph who had enchanted him. He shook away the vision and stooped to tend to her, to find what injury had stunned her so—to awaken her if he could.

She moaned as he cradled her head. With quick, deft fingers, he felt for lumps beneath the tangled riot of copper curls. He found none, no reason there to cause her lack of consciousness. At least, thank God, no falling beam had struck her.

Her neck was cool, the tiny pulse beneath his thumb reassuringly strong and even. He pulled up her sleeves and examined her arms. Save for a pair of bruises beneath one shoulder, they were unharmed and flawless like creamy silk. He pushed away the image, forcing himself to concentrate on the bruises. Old ones, they were, not fresh. He frowned. Had those bastards struck her?

Gently, he turned her over. He thought he heard a sigh as his fingers moved down her spine. He ignored the poignant sound and carefully, through the twisted cloth of her nightdress, touched each small knob of her back, prodding, checking for damage. Only when he reached the final one, the one deep in the warm cleft of her buttocks, did she react.

He pulled back as she scrambled to her knees. She flung herself around and faced him, her dazed eyes large, catlike.

"Who are you?" she asked in a whisper.

He started to answer, feeling a surge of pity blend with the dead ashes of his anger, but she gave him no time to explain. The fire in her eyes singed him as she stared at him, and then she took in the scene around her. Shocked comprehension flashed across her face, and she sprang to her feet.

Before he could stop her, she was running like a deer toward the cabin.

"Pa! George!" she screamed, disappearing into the thick smoke.

Chapter Four

She must find them! The cabin's roof was aflame, the burning pine smashed across it—across the very area where they slept. Fighting the billowing smoke, Bethany raced into the front room.

She had entered hell itself. Tongues of fire licked the jagged pieces of weatherboard dangling above her, fallen beams were crisscrossed on the floor, their splinters sparking, smoldering, ready to burst into full flame. The heat seared her face, stung her eyes. She winced and slapped her arm over her nose and mouth.

Pa's boots. He was trapped under a beam! And George. . . there beside him.

In a frenzy, she reached for the beam to release them, but found it too hot to touch. Wrapping her hands with the skirt of her nightdress, she struggled to raise the heavy log. The smoke bit at her eyes, filling them with tears. She strained, grunted, but couldn't budge the wood.

"Pa! George!" she cried in desperation.

Something swift and strong shoved her aside. She staggered and fell to one knee on the heated dirt. And then she saw a pair of huge hands lift the beam, tossing it back into the smoke as though it weighed no more than a leaf.

It was the stranger who had done it. Her brain whirled in a confusion of fear and gratitude but there was no time for either. Jumping up, she ran to her family.

Pa and George were free now, but sleeping still, their snores silenced by the bedlam of noise around her.

She must move them outside! Pulling at her pa's boots, she tried to drag him toward the door.

"I'll do it. Get out of here!" the man shouted to her, pushing her away again. Already he had George flung over one of his massive shoulders. Before she could blink, he had her pa over the other. *"Go!"* he ordered.

She stumbled into the yard. He followed her and placed the men on the ground. Red hot cinders spewed into the night sky; the growing flames behind her cast a harsh orange light—the eerie brightness of an autumn's noon.

A muffled roar shook the seething air. She fell to her knees, sickened by the sound. The cabin's roof had caved in. Spasms of nausea wracked her, and dry, violent heaves tore against her seared throat. Her home was gone.

She looked up at the stranger. He hovered over her like a mountain, the sweat on his broad brow luminous in the fire's angry glow. His dark brown eyes studied her; they looked sorely troubled.

"Thank you for saving them," she said softly, the words scratching over her parched tongue.

He turned away, coughed. "They're dead, woman."

She gasped. "Dead?" Trembling, she reached for her pa's hand. It was cold and rigid. George's hand, too. Their faces were contorted; their chests bloody and broken, crushed. . . .

"No!" she screamed, leaping to her feet. "No! No! No!" She beat her fists against the man's unyielding back and pummeled him again and again.

Facing her, he grasped her wrists with one hand and placed a restraining hold with the other on the top of her head. "Calm yourself," he said, his eyes almost gentle.

But she wasn't assuaged. She struggled against him. "Let me go!" she squealed, kicking out at him.

He stared at her. "Where will you go, woman? Do you wish to follow your men? Believe me, it's far hotter than even this hellhole where they've gone."

She spat in his face. "Then kill me, too, you murdering horse thief! You've taken all I had . . . all I ever had." She loathed the sobs that made her angry words a gurgle but he had heard them. His heavy brows drew together, his eyes grew large and glinted—with surprise?

She cared not what the glint was. This man had wrought this horror.

"I did not kill your family," he said quietly. "It was the lightning, the tree . . ."

"Ha! And you're the Satan who brought the storm."

He took his hand from her head and placed it on her shoulder. "I shall not harm you, woman." He released her with a sigh. "May you find peace where you will," he said, and walked away.

Bethany sagged. A heavy rain began to fall; the heavens themselves seemed to be weeping with uncontrolled sadness, as desolate as she. She raised her face and let the stinging drops wash away her tears. Though she wanted to hang on to her heated anger, it dissolved under the flow as well. She felt limp, as though her bones, like everything around her, had turned to water.

"Do not leave me," she whimpered.

Adam turned. She was like a tiny doll made of sodden cloth. Her once-wild hair clung in dark red strands against her pale, rain-splattered face. Her large, unblinking eyes riveted him. They were liquid with despair, as green as the sea after a roiling storm. A wave of compassion swept over him.

"I'm here," he said, moving toward her.

She stiffened at his touch. He dropped his hand and his eyes searched her face. The rain was a heavy veil between them, blurring his vision. He knew not how to comfort her.

"Follow me then," he said at last. "We need to find shelter." He drew back and started for the woods, glancing over his shoulder to see if she would obey.

She stood fixed to the spot where he'd left her, unmoving. He slowed his steps and felt a stab of frustration.

"Come, woman!" he bellowed.

She jumped as if he'd struck her. Then, as she moved to follow him, he couldn't help but note her courage. Though she looked befuddled and lost, she held her chin high and walked with firm steps behind him.

He found a dense cluster of pines nearby with widespread, drooping branches that overlapped to form a protective canopy. A thick, springy carpet woven from the dried needles and spiny cones of years long past covered the ground beneath his boots. Ghostly wisps of mist coiled in the damp green darkness, but the air was redolent with the spicy scent of pine. Spikes of rain slid off the tightly clasped branches above and were deflected into a watery curtain that separated the circle of quiet from the chaos that lay beyond.

With a sigh of exhaustion, he sat and waited for her to join him. He longed for his pipe. The woman stooped and entered the copse. He could barely see her but sensed her tentative movements, heard her jagged breaths and a soft squish as she sat in the needles. She had placed herself far away from him, he noticed, as far as she could manage and still be within the shelter. He suspected she'd huddled into a knot.

Neither spoke. Adam welcomed the silence, he needed time to think. After this night's terrible happenings, what must he do next? Find a suitable home for the woman, of course, but where? Battletown? It was naught but a rowdy crossroads, no place for. . . .

"Why did you come to wreak this terrible destruction upon my home?" she asked. Her voice through the darkness was tenuous, the thread of accusation strangely thin after her earlier outburst.

"I came for my horse," he replied.

"You came for my brother's horse."

He started to protest, but held his tongue. The woman was damnably hardheaded. But, wait, did she say her *brother?* He felt a feathery pull of satisfaction. He'd assumed the disgusting Bully Boy had been her husband. He scowled at himself. And what possible blasted concern was it of his *what* the man was to her? She was a Stewart and mean-tempered like the lot of them.

Reasoning with her would be next to impossible,

but he felt honor bound to help her.

"Do you have kin, woman?" It was, he figured, a beginning. Likely the hills swarmed with Stewarts.

Her response quavered over a sob. "None now. There have been but the three of us since Mama was . . . was taken by the Shawnees."

Adam frowned. She was truly alone—a bloody damned orphan.

"Surely, there are folk you know nearby?" He stared across the darkness.

"I know no one," came the tiny reply.

"Bloody hell, woman. Where the devil can I take you?" His harsh tones annoyed him as much as the exasperating circumstances. He cursed himself, realizing he'd become sorely mean-tempered himself.

"Take me? What in heaven's name do you mean?" Her question rang loud and clear from the other end of the copse. At least she'd recovered her voice.

"What in hell do you think I mean?" he heard himself growl. "We must find you a place to live."

She was silent. He restrained his urge to go to her and shake a response from her.

She spoke at last, her voice distant, dreamlike. "My home is here, and I shall stay, for I must be here when he comes for me. I have the promise."

"The promise?" Good Lord, the night's events had deranged her.

"The promise of my dream cat. . ." Her slow, soft words drifted away into the mist. He heard her even, gentle breaths and knew she'd fallen asleep in mid-sentence.

Dream cat? He shook his head. His problems had multiplied beyond reason. He had a madwoman on his hands.

As he pondered what new tests he'd confront on the morrow, his eyelids grew heavy. He, too, should sleep.

But the night air had chilled, and the pitiful woman was so sparsely clothed. He removed his buckskin coat. Following the smooth sounds of her breathing, he crawled in the darkness until he found her. After draping his coat over her huddled form, he returned to the far end of the copse and fell deeply asleep.

Bethany awoke at dawn, her hand clamped around her amulet. The haze of sleep lifted slowly. Reluctant to let it float away, she snuggled into her pallet and pulled her cozy quilt closer around her. Bristly needles chafed her cheek and her eyes flew open.

Where am I? No pallet was beneath her and she was surrounded by tree trunks. The air was coarse against her nostrils, a pungent pine scent trapped beneath the biting smell of singed wood. A torrent of stark memories flooded her mind, and she jumped up with a strangled gasp. The coat that had covered her fell heavily to the ground. She stared at it, terrified. *Where is he?*

She saw him then, spraddled across from her, asleep, his rifle beneath his hand. Should she grab it? She took a step toward him, but a clutch of fear stopped her. She didn't dare! The man was ruthless.

And yet he'd stayed with her through the night of terror, had provided her warmth with his buckskins. He confused her with his stray moments of kindness or had she only imagined them? Her brows knitted. No man possessed tenderness. She touched her amulet. No man save her dream prince.

She looked down at the stranger. This horse thief was worlds away from any maiden's dream prince. He was rough and foul-tempered, with the dark, searing eyes of the devil and unruly hair the color of parched grass. Even in sleep he frightened her, his ungodly strength awaiting only a flicker of consciousness to be unleashed. His booted legs were like mighty oaks, his sinewy arms, so peaceful now, could strangle a bear. His hands could toss away a burning log as though it weighed no more than a. . . .

The awful memory cut through her like a spear of sharp ice. Her family was dead.

She ran from the copse. The desolate scene before her jolted her to a halt, and her throat constricted. Pa and George lay broken and still. Beyond them was their home—her home—a rubble of smoking, sodden ashes. The crooked chimney, its stones blackened, stood alone like a solemn mourner bent with despair.

Churner, the milk cow, grazed in the stubbly field beyond as if this dawn were no different from all others. *But it is, Churner,* she wanted to cry. *Dear God, it is.*

Her own world, Bethany knew with deep sadness, would never be the same.

Constant sat by the dead men. He lifted his ears when he saw his mistress, rose slowly, then walked toward her with his head bowed.

"You understand, boy," she said quietly, kneeling to hug the dog. "We need to be strong," she mumbled into his neck. Tears sprang to her eyes, but she forced them back. She had much to do this day. She looked around, fighting the mad compulsion to flee into the woods and find solace in forgetfulness. But she knew that would solve nothing, for she'd never forget. She fingered the amulet. At least she still had her dreams.

The old shed remained standing. Tools would be there, rusted most of them but useful, and it held some meal and dried meat. The forest abounded with game and timber.

Feeling heartened, she ran to the shed, pulled open

its creaking door, and peered inside. Why, she had a wealth of tools and supplies left! Somehow, she would rebuild; she was certain she could.

Welcoming her renewed confidence, she was eager to get to work, and one task cried to be done before all others. She lifted a pick. Her first duty was to lay her pa and brother to rest.

Drawing from her deep wellspring of courage and hope, Bethany Rose Stewart began digging at the muddy, stony soil.

What was that infernal pounding? Adam stirred and reached for his rifle. He stood in an instant, fully alert. His coat was at his feet in a neglected heap. The crazed woman had left, was out there in the yard—doing what, in God's name?

He peered through the trees. She was striking at the ground with an oversized pick, her face taut with determination. He groaned. She was digging graves, he guessed, and going about it all wrong, though her intensity and the dents she'd made in the soil provided evidence that she would accomplish her task eventually. In about a week, he judged.

Hell's blazes, he could do naught but dig the graves for her, though he felt strongly that the Stewart men deserved to be left for the vultures. Bloody bastards. They'd been cowardly, drunken horse thieves who'd probably beat the woman and she, through some distorted devotion, deemed it necessary to give them a proper burial.

Cursing the fates that had steered him to Wildcat Hollow, he walked over and pulled the pick from her hands.

"Fetch me a shovel if you have one, woman," he commanded. "I'll dig the graves."

"You'll . . . *you'll* . . ." she sputtered, stepping back. "Give me back my pick."

He squinted at her, purposely made his face hard. "Fetch me a shovel," he repeated, and slammed the pick into the ground.

She flinched, then stood stock-still and stared wide-eyed at him. *Don't be defiant*, his mind begged her. Her large dark-lashed eyes glistened up at him. They were filled with pain and questions, a disturbing look of pure innocence that pressed against his heart and pushed it strangely askew.

Adam turned his head. He felt vulnerable under her bright green gaze, bared of his dogged assurance and stripped of the confidence and competence that were his mainstays. He didn't want her to see the unseemly frailty that had come over him.

He took a deep breath. "With a shovel I can make quick work of your family's graves," he said, keeping his eyes on the ground in front of him. "If you'll tell me where I may find one, I'll fetch it myself."

"No need, I'll get it for you," she said.

He stood, watching her run to the dilapidated shed. In a few moments, she returned with a rusty shovel and handed it to him. Without meeting her eyes, he fiercely stabbed the dull tool into the wet dirt and began digging the holes.

Bloody hell, what am I to do with this woman?

Strange that he should help me, Bethany thought. He was unpredictable—blustery and stubborn one moment, quiet and reasonable the next. At least with her pa and George she'd known what to expect. With this man, she wasn't sure.

Oh, well, he would be departing today. He seemed eager to be on his way, so his peculiar temperament was of little concern to her. She hoped he'd leave something behind for her. She'd need the tools and the milk cow. The chestnut horse, she saw, had returned and stood over by the trees next to his spavined mare. He'd take them both, she guessed.

She kept busy while he dug the graves. She milked the cow, using an old wooden bucket from the shed, then speared a rabbit with a pointed stick, skinning it with the man's knife that he let her borrow.

That was kind of him, she thought. She could tell he didn't relish giving the knife to her, and yet he did, despite his grumbles. After building a fire with straw and twigs, she skewered the rabbit and roasted it well before calling him for breakfast.

He thanked her—*thanked her!*—after he ate and had insisted she eat with him, too. A strange man, he was.

The graves were nearly finished. She searched for sturdy sticks and found four that would make suitable crosses. She used strands of frazzled rope from the shed to tie them. And then, with a sinking feeling, she watched the man lift the broken bodies of her family and lower them carefully into the holes. It was over. They were at rest at last.

She walked to the man's side and stared down at Pa and George. Tears stung her eyes. When he bent to lift a shovelful of dirt to throw upon them, she reached out to stop him.

"Do you know proper words?" she asked.

"Proper words for what?"

"For burying . . . for sending them to heaven."

Something very like a scoff escaped his lips, but his face reddened as he swallowed it. She looked at him questioningly, and he looked away.

"Please?" she said, low.

"Our Father, which art in heaven," he began tentatively. "Though I walk through the valley of the shadows of death, I shall fear no evil . . ." He paused, cleared his throat. "What were their names?"

"George."

"Both of them?"

"Aye, my brother was George, Junior, I suppose."

He looked uncomfortable and closed his eyes as if he were dredging a distant memory. He spoke at last, his voice strong and uncommonly sweet, "Unto God's gracious mercy we commit you, George Stewart and George Stewart, Junior. The Lord bless you and keep you. The Lord make His face to shine upon you, and may . . . may He forgive you for your earthly sins. The Lord give you peace above and your woman, here, peace below. Amen."

Bethany sobbed as he began to fill the graves, then ran back for the crosses and a small bunch of wildflowers she'd gathered.

When he nodded that he'd finished, she knelt beside the mounds. "Farewell," she said in a broken whisper and stuck the wooden crosses into the fresh dirt and placed a sprinkling of yellow and blue flowers on each of the graves.

She stayed beside them for a long time, her head bowed, the beautiful words of the stranger echoing still in her ears.

The sun did peculiar things to her hair, Adam thought as he watched her. Colors other than red danced through the curls—gold, silken bronze, and burnt umber. Her hands were small, the nails broken but the fingers that splayed across the damp dirt were finely shaped, almost delicate. He wondered about the leather pouch that hung between her breasts. It contained healing herbs, he suspected. Likely she'd have a way with herbs, most mountain women did.

She puzzled him. How could a creature who looked so near like an angel spring from the ugly seed of a man like George Stewart? And how could she be bowed with sorrow over the loss of those drunken scum who'd abused her?

He knew so little about her, understood her even less. Yet something about her tugged at his heart, and he didn't understand that, either. Pity, he figured, was at work and a sense of responsibility.

When she rose and faced him, he wasn't prepared. His fingers tingled, wanted to reach out to her, to touch her.

"You may go now," she said with a finality that lashed him.

Her oval eyes were like jade in candlelight, he thought incongrously. They captivated him. Her long black lashes swept over them, covering them, as she looked down. He held his breath.

"I thank you for digging the graves," she continued, "and for the words you spoke."

"I'm not leaving you," he blurted out. She unsettled him, but for God's sake, did she truly think he would abandon her?

Her eyes snapped up, and a trace of fear skipped across them. "What do you mean?"

He measured his words carefully. "I mean that you cannot stay alone in this wild place. You'll go with me, over the mountains"—he nodded toward the blue ridges behind him—"and we'll find a settlement there where you can live protected."

Her reaction surprised him.

"No!" she screamed, striking out at him. "Only the prince can take me over the blue mountains!"

The prince? She made no sense. Once again he found himself holding her wrists captive and waiting with strained patience until her struggles quieted.

She wearied at last, and her incoherent protests ceased. Not until he was sure she wouldn't dash madly into the woods did he release his hold. She rubbed her wrists and impaled him again with her gemstone eyes that burned now with frustration—and defeat.

He'd won, but he felt no flush of victory.

Then she did a strange thing. She reached for the pouch around her neck and clasped it in her hand. She closed her eyes and her lips moved silently as though in prayer.

Her action troubled him. Suddenly, a bright light suffused her tear-stained face, and she opened her eyes and smiled up at him radiantly. His heart skipped a beat.

"Aye, I'll go with you," she said with surprising firmness. "The dream catcher says I must, for the prince awaits me beyond the blue mountains."

She spoke as if she'd regained her senses, but he made no sense of her words.

The dream catcher? Adam felt a shudder of unease. The woman was clearly unbalanced and, he knew without a doubt, she would be a heavy burden of responsibility.

He dreaded the days ahead.

Chapter Five

Bethany couldn't stop jabbering. Her jaws had become unhinged, and all morning long, as she helped the man find items about the place that had survived the fire, she talked incessantly.

She figured her tightly coiled nerves had sprung loose and were unraveling in an uncontrollable string of words.

The man paid her no heed and busied himself pulling out supplies from the shed.

" . . . and I've sorely missed Mama since she was taken on that black day more than ten years ago," she continued in her unbroken stream of chatter. "She was beautiful and kind and taught me all I know except the bow, which I taught myself because I vowed ne'er again to be helpless when danger came . . . Oh, and here's a hemp sack that'll hold the tools."

He nodded, stuffed the sack full, and dragged it toward the chestnut horse. Looking contemplative, he left the sack on the ground and opened the large leather pack that hung across the still-saddled horse's back. Without even a moment's search, he pulled out a long-stemmed clay pipe and a small pouch of tobacco.

Bethany crinkled her brow. How could he know the pack's contents?

Her brain lagged far behind her tongue, however, and the questioning thought was buried beneath her continuing babble. "We need to find a way to take Churning along with us and Henry if he's still around and Constant, of course, though he can walk himself . . ."

The man's dark look of alarm stopped her. "Churning? Henry? Constant? Who the devil are—"

She interrupted him with a smile. "Churning's the milk cow yon, Henry's the ox, and this is Constant," she said, bending to pat the sleeping dog.

He didn't respond. Leaning over, he stuck a straw in the embers of the cook fire and lit his pipe. He puffed on it, his bearded face clouded in thought.

"I'll look for Henry while you rest a mite," she said. "He's likely back in the trees, since I've never known him to run anywhere far, not run at all, really, his being as slow of foot as of wit as oxen tend to be. But his back's strong and could carry the sack of supplies you've gathered with ease."

Her voice was going faster than her legs, but once back in the woods she quieted at last. The silence surprised her and was, she had to admit, a welcome relief. Her own ears felt tattered; the man's must be ringing like a bell!

What in heaven's name was wrong with her? She shrugged and squinted into the leafy shadows looking for Henry, whose hide, alas, was nearly the same color

72

as the tree trunks. She doubted if the man had heard even one of the numberless words she'd spoken this morn, he seemed so deeply occupied with his own thoughts. Spotting the ox in a cluster of sycamores by the creek, she ran forward to coax it back where it belonged.

As she prodded the sluggish animal toward the clearing, she found herself wondering what kind of thoughts a wandering horse thief might have.

By God, her endless talk would drive to drink even those upright Moravian settlers who trek down the Valley, Adam thought, scowling as he drew on his pipe. She was mighty high-strung, skittish as a cat beset by fleas. She had cause enough, he supposed, losing so much all at once as she had, and hadn't she said she'd never left the Hollow? It was likely she'd feel some apprehension about the journey ahead.

Well, bloody hell, so did he. He had sufficient worries without having to tend to a nervous orphan and her pitiful assortment of underfed animals.

Surely, he'd find a cabin within a day or two where he could leave her and her motley possessions. They'd accumulated a heavy load for their journey across the mountains, damnably heavy, and it would slow their pace. And now she wanted to bring along a cow and ox.

With such a cumbersome caravan, he figured they'd be able to travel no more than two miles a day at best, less than a quarter of the distance he could cover if he traveled alone. Damn! He was itching to reach the Tidewater to wreak his vengeance on that bastard James. Was heaven itself bent on slowing his revenge?

The woman emerged from the trees, pushing the lumbering ox ahead of her. Her face was shining with

73

triumph, and, he noted without surprise, her mouth was going full speed.

" . . . found him, as you see, behind the sycamores. I fear Pa's and George's horses have gone for good, they were a restless pair and ever ran off when they had a chance, but we have enough with your mare and my chestnut, don't you agree?"

Hold a minute, he thought with exasperation. He raised one brow. "*Your* chestnut?"

"Aye. 'Twas my brother's, won fair and square in Battletown so Pa said. Now, I reckon it's mine." She looked damnably sure of herself.

Adam glowered at her. "Am I hearing right, woman? You're intending to ride the chestnut?"

She hesitated, then fixed her big emerald eyes on him. "Tis my horse," she said with firm conviction.

"We shall see," he mumbled, and moved away quickly. Bloody stubborn woman.

At least he'd quieted her. She remained peacefully silent as he packed the bundle of supplies atop the ox, stayed silent as he roped the cow and ox and tied one to the makeshift yoke he'd attached to the chestnut's harness, one to the mare's. A raucous chorus of birdsong rang in his ears, but the woman, thank God, was quiet.

He wanted to depart by noon. Squinting up at the sun, he saw he was on schedule. Good, the preparations were done. He was ready.

"It's time we mount," he said.

She didn't answer.

"I said . . ." He looked over his shoulder, but she wasn't to be seen. *Blighted devil, where's she gone now?*

He saw her at last by the graves. Saying her final farewells, he reckoned, trying to stem his impatience. He'd give her another minute before calling her.

Dream Catcher

Counting the seconds as he watched her, he realized with a low groan that she was woefully ill-clothed for this journey. Her thin nightdress was torn and singed, and she had no shoes. He muttered an oath and tried to remember what, if anything, was in his pack that would serve as clothing for her.

Bethany looked up. The man seemed to be waiting for her; he must be ready to start over the mountain. "I'm coming!" she shouted, and ran toward him.

He looked impatient.

"Is it time we leave?" she inquired.

"Aye, though I believe you need sturdier clothing before we begin."

She looked down at her frayed nightdress and felt her cheeks flame with a rush of heat. He was right, of course, it was not suitable wear. "But I have no other garments," she said softly, feeling helpless.

"I have a shirt in my pack," he said, heading for the chestnut horse. "Though it's likely to engulf you, it will be far better protection than what you have."

He pulled a bundle of gray cloth from the pack. It was indeed a shirt, she saw, a shirt large enough to fit even him. Strange that he knew it would be there. Could it be the horse was truly his? She remembered he'd earlier shown signs of being familiar with the pack's contents. Had he been telling the truth from the beginning? Were Pa and George the horse thieves?

Her mind struggled to sort out her disturbing thoughts. As he thrust the shirt into her hands, she wanted to blurt out an apology, but she held her tongue. "Thank you" was all she said, keeping her eyes lowered.

Damnation, it is his horse. He spoke truthfully, and I came near to killing him, she thought as she pulled the coarse linen shirt over her head. It smelled of soap. As it dropped around her, she felt lost in the

75

folds of fabric. It fell shorter than the nightdress, but the shoulders drooped halfway down her arms and the sleeves covered her hands.

"'Tis big," she said matter-of-factly, and rolled up the sleeves.

He made a funny sound, something between a sneeze and a snort. Surprised, she stared up at him. The mirth on his face was undisguised, though he attempted to control it. His face had grown red, his dark eyes danced, and she heard the sneeze-snort again.

His humor was catching and she thought how peculiar she must look in the oversized shirt. "'Tis b–big," she repeated, feeling a bubble of laughter rise in her throat.

"Aye," he agreed with a vigorous nod. His mouth tightened in a valiant effort to restrain his amusement, but his eyes glistened.

Bethany couldn't hold back a tentative giggle, then felt it explode into a full-blown laugh. The big man's deeper laughter joined hers, and the sound was irresistible. Her shoulders shook and tears ran down her cheeks. She had no control over the moment, didn't even attempt to control it. All her tension, fear, sorrow, and strain of the past hours slipped free.

"Oh my," she said at last, wiping her nose with the back of her hand and pushing away the tears from her cheeks. Relief washed through her like a warm balm. She was rejuvenated, sure of her own strength again. She straightened her gray-draped shoulders, ready for the journey ahead.

The man had recovered his formidable bearing; he looked sober and slightly disconcerted. She studied his broad face, tanned from the sun, rugged but handsome nevertheless, she thought, wondering at the same time why such a thought would come to her. True, he was far different in appearance from Pa and George, and those two had been so similar, like peas in a pod. But he was far different, too, from the picture she held in her mind of her beloved dream prince. She'd seen few men and never realized they could display such variety of form. There'd been Pa and George, a couple of old trappers who had passed by once—and then there was her prince. Now, she saw, there was this man, too. Strange how. . . .

"Why do you stare at me so?" he asked, his voice low.

She jumped and turned away with a flush of embarrassment warming her cheeks. "I was . . . I was but considering how . . ." She shook her head. "Tis naught," she heard herself say. "Shall we leave now?"

"Aye." He walked to the chestnut and prepared to mount, then paused and looked back at her. "It *is* my horse, you know." It sounded oddly, as if he were requesting her permission.

She nodded.

"You may ride the mare. Do you need assistance up to the saddle?" he asked.

She stepped back, gripped with a new fear. "I know not how to ride."

"Bloody hell, woman! Before you were demanding to ride the chestnut, and now you're telling me—"

"I never learned," she said simply. He looked angry as the devil again. She retreated another step, watching him warily.

"God rot it all! Now I must re-tie the damnable animals," he grumbled.

She was sorry to cause him such trouble but didn't dare risk raising his ire further by speaking. Even an apology might unleash his wrath. Pa and George were so often that way.

He made quick enough work of the task, though she noted his movements were somewhat exaggerated and well accompanied by grunts of exasperation. She could do naught but stay out of his way and pray his temper would improve.

"Come," he said when he finished.

She complied with haste. His huge hands grabbed her waist and before she knew what was happening he'd hoisted her atop the chestnut and plopped her soundly on the front of the saddle. She sat sideways, terrified at being seated so high above the ground with the big animal restless beneath her. She was even more terrified of the man who jumped astride behind her.

Damnation! she thought, eyeing the blue mountains ahead as their caravan slowly began moving forward. Her waist and bottom still vibrated from his rough handling. This journey on horseback boded to be a far cry from the one in her dreams.

Chapter Six

He didn't bring them to a halt until near sundown.
Bethany would have cheered had she dared. She was
sorely tired and plagued by unfamiliar aches. The
ceaseless, rolling gait of the horse had been partly
to blame, but she sensed her unrelenting tension was
the major culprit.

During the long hours of the ride, she'd sat rigid,
trying with all her might to avoid bumping against the
man so close behind her. Above all, she didn't want
to raise his hackles again. But despite her efforts,
too often she'd find her elbow jabbing into one of his
hard ribs or her hip slipping back against his firm leg.
Each time she'd wiggle forward quickly and murmur
an apology.

The man hadn't appeared to notice any of it. He'd
remained mostly silent, his serious eyes concentrat-

ing on the torturous path through tangled brush and around thick walls of trees or jagged outcroppings of gray rock. When he did speak, he mostly grumbled—to the animals that trailed behind.

Possibly he'd forgotten she was seated there in front of him. *A good thing*, she thought. She'd been wishing she could disappear.

"We'll stop here for the night," he said at last, pulling back the reins, his first words to her since they'd started out.

"Aye, it's a suitable place." A safe response, she figured.

He dismounted and reached up to help her down. As pleased as she was that he'd stopped, she realized she'd been dreading this moment and hoped her stiff body wouldn't snap in two between his burly hands. But he was far gentler bringing her down than he'd been earlier getting her up. She slid off the horse with surprising ease and only a twinge of complaint from her tight muscles.

As he untied the mare, ox, and cow, she surveyed the spot he'd chosen for their night's rest. A narrow stone-filled brook rippled nearby, promising water for them. Though dotted with rocks and boulders, the steep ground was clear enough to accommodate all of them and thick with wild grass to feed the animals.

A tremble of excitement coursed through her. She was in the blue mountains! Passing strange it was, though, how nothing was blue as she'd expected. Myriad hues of green abounded and clumps of grays and browns and even an occasional wisp of yellow, lavender, or white peeked from the buds of bushes. But not a trace of blue was to be seen, save the sky above, and that was streaked with gold and pink from the lowering sun.

"Why did they appear so blue back in the Hollow?"

she heard herself asking, too filled with curiosity to abide by her pledge to keep quiet until he spoke first.

"Why did *what* appear so blue?"

His dark expression was as testy as his words. Oh dear, she was irritating him again. She swallowed the lump of fear that clogged her throat.

"The mountains?" she ventured timidly, moving back.

He shrugged with disinterest, wiped his dusty hands on his breeches, and turned to unload the supplies. A heavy sigh of relief pushed against her lips but she held it back, letting it puff out her cheeks instead.

"The mist causes it, I guess. I've never given it much thought."

"Oh." Her acknowledgement sounded fluttery to her, riding as it did on her sigh.

Feeling useless, she watched him sift through the sack and pull out an assortment of items. She wasn't accustomed to standing by while others worked but was reluctant to step forward to assist. He'd surely chastise her for being in the way.

When he tossed an ax on the ground, however, she saw a way she could help.

"I'll gather the wood for our fire," she said happily, reaching down for the tool.

"You will *not!*" he exploded. She stopped in mid-reach. "Cutting wood is men's work," he added with force.

"It is?" Her whispery voice reflected her astonishment.

"Damn right it is."

"Oh." She pulled herself upright. *Men's work?* What did he consider to be a woman's work? She hesitated to ask him, thinking it far wiser to figure that out for herself.

81

Her face brightened. Of course! She could hunt for their supper. That should please him, and she'd be out of his way.

Wishing she had her bow, she settled instead for a long sharp stick she found nearby. She lifted it, liking the way it fit in her hand. She'd speared many a turkey and squirrel, had even got a fox once. Smiling, she headed for the trees.

"Where do you think you're going, woman?"

His bellow stopped her. Surely, he didn't object to having supper.

"To spear food for us?" She'd intended to sound confident, but he had her speaking tentatively again.

"Bloody hell, I'll take care of that. You'd be fool enough to venture into the woods with unshod feet?"

She looked down at her feet, dumbfounded. "I never wear shoes after the first spring moon," she said. "My feet are accustomed to—"

"You will *not* go after food," he blustered his command, pinning her with his eyes to the spot where she stood.

He was glowering. She didn't move, fearful that even a blink of her eyes would ignite him further. *Dear God, can I do nothing to please him?* She wondered.

He lifted the ax and moved toward her. She would have cringed, but cold terror held her firmly erect. When he stopped, he stood so close to her she could smell the smoky scent of his buckskins. The tip of her nose almost touched his huge chest. As if a strong skein of fiber were pulling them, her eyes were drawn upward and met his. Suddenly, she couldn't breathe.

The light in his dark gaze wasn't anger. She didn't know what it was, but it did peculiar things to her, made her backbone tingle, her insides quiver.

"A man gathers wood, a man hunts," he said, his

voice low, patient . . . kind? His words rolled through her ears as his soft breath spread like honey across her upturned face.

She dropped the spear and tried to nod her assent. His deep brown eyes burned into her, setting off a trail of sparks that ran a convoluted course to her fingertips before reversing and sweeping like wildfire clear to her toes.

"Do you understand, woman?"

"Aye." *No*. She understood naught.

"Good." He turned away and walked toward the forest.

Stunned, Bethany watched him. What had happened to her? It was something other than fear she'd just experienced. Fear had long been her companion, but it had never made her knees so wobbly, never made her head fill with cobwebs.

Before he disappeared behind the trees, she found her voice.

"What does a woman do?" she asked weakly.

He looked back, and she detected a hint of a smile on his stern face.

"For now, *sit*," he ordered.

She sat.

Adam cradled a load of wood in one arm and dragged along the deer he'd shot. Frustration, though, was his chief burden. Soon he'd be facing the woman again, and her presence sorely muddled his brain. She was damnably impulsive, her behavior a constant riddle to him. Had she learned to do nothing properly down in that Hollow? In many ways she was as unruly as a child.

He paused, then shook his head. Dear God, if only she *were* a child, that would make his responsibilities toward her far simpler, and he'd be spared those blasted physical yearnings that swept over him from time to time when she was near.

The journey this day had been torture. Her soft body against his thigh had lit flames that had taken strength beyond reason to quench. The woman was a tender wildflower with maddening powers that drew him toward her while his senses warned him to stay distant.

He studied the ground beneath his boots and kicked a small stone against a tree. He must watch himself in her presence, battle his weaknesses.

She feared him, he thought. Good, that was as it should be.

Nodding, he started on his way again. Surely on the morrow they'd come upon a settlement. In the brief time left, he'd remain on guard. He would stay distant, he determined, stay in control.

She was seated where he'd left her, perched on a boulder, the mangy black cur asleep at her feet. Once again, she was holding the leather pouch that hung about her neck, and her eyes were closed.

What was it she'd called the dratted thing? Her dream catcher? *Dream catcher*. Damnable nonsense! Naught but a foolish superstition.

He built the fire and began stripping the deer. Out of the corner of his eye, he saw the woman approach. He steeled himself and tried to concentrate on his task.

"It's a fine one," she said softly.

Adam tightened his jaw, said nothing. She came no nearer, but he felt the disturbing pressure of being watched. He came close to cutting his hand.

The deer had more meat than they could eat before it spoiled, but he'd chosen it for the skin. They needed the hide and, if time allowed, he would make the woman a pair of moccasins. Maybe her wits were too dull to know the dangers of unshod feet in the mountain wilderness, but he'd be damned if he'd let her continue in such a manner.

Dusk had nearly fallen before he finished stripping, gutting, and cleaning the animal. After cutting the choicest morsels from the carcass, he carried them to the woman.

"Can you cook, by chance?" he asked, holding out to her the still-bloody pieces of meat and purposely maintaining a severe expression.

Her face shone as if he'd offered her a handful of priceless diamonds.

"Aye," she said with enthusiasm, then looked up at him, a cloud of caution darkening her eyes. "May I?" she asked, her voice timid again.

He nodded. "Women cook."

She took the meat from him with a radiant smile that warmed him like an August sun.

As she ran back to the fire to start preparing their supper, Adam stood for a moment, ordering his senses to muster their forces and step back into line. Everything around him was bathed with a copper glow—the sky above, the stones beneath his feet, the wild grass yon, and the grazing animals. Even the fire burned copper. It was as though the setting sun had brushed the whole world with the same vibrant color of that woman's hair.

He closed his eyes. Bloody hell. Only with great effort was he able to pull himself together. But even as he built another fire to dry the skins and stretched them on poles, the copper light persisted in bedeviling him.

Bethany felt content after supper. He would allow her to do some things for she had cooked for them, and he hadn't complained about the herbs she'd added or the trenchers she'd carved from the thick branch of an oak. After they'd eaten, she'd gone to the brook to wash their few utensils without even a trace of a grumble from him.

He had wondrous supplies in his pack. Coffee beans she'd found, a tin cup, even a small pot. She'd boiled some coffee for him, the way she'd done for Pa and George many times. Unlike them, though, the man had insisted she drink a portion from his cup. It had tasted hearty and strong.

Using a bit of the cornmeal they'd taken from the shed, she'd made hoecake and had topped it with berries she'd picked.

Now the man sat quietly across the fire, puffing on his pipe. She realized her weariness had fled and she smiled into the darkness and reached for her amulet.

"Why do you do that?" he asked, startling her.

"Do what?"

"Touch the pouch that way."

Pa and George had never noticed, it had ever been her secret. She wiggled back in the dirt, reluctant to tell him.

"It's naught but a habit," she lied.

"You called it your 'dream catcher.' "

She had? Bethany froze. When had she said such a thing? Dear heaven. . . .

"It's naught," she repeated, holding it tightly in her hand.

He pursued his question no further, and she relaxed again, watching the orange flames dance into the air.

"Do you have a name?" His question interrupted her reverie.

"Aye, Bethany it is. Bethany Rose."

There was a long pause.

"Bethany? That's an interesting name. It was the

place of Lazarus, you know."

"Lazarus?"

"In the Bible."

"The Bible?"

"Do you not know the Bible, wo . . . Bethany?"

"Nay. What is it?"

"A book."

"Book?" She was befuddled. He kept using words she'd never heard.

The light of his pipe glowed. She couldn't see his face but hoped she wasn't displeasing him with her many questions.

"My name is Adam," he said at last.

"Adam," she repeated slowly, the strength of the word striking her as her tongue hit the roof of her mouth and the final sound vibrated through her lips. "Pa" and "George" had required but air to speak. "Adam," like the man sitting before her, was far more solid.

He rose and walked back to the other fire, where the skins were drying. He added more wood and stood there awhile, rearranging the poles and adjusting the skins. The low flames outlined his massive frame with gold, softening his formidable size while, at the same time, extending his power beyond him into the encircling night.

She could feel it reaching back, wrapping around her like a protective cloak.

"They won't dry sufficiently by dawn," he said in quiet tones, but the long silence that had preceded caused his words to ring uncommonly loud.

Her mind raced. What on earth was he talking about? "Dry? What won't dry?"

"The skins." He came back to the ebbing cook fire.

He'd gone about the task competently, but she knew he was right.

"No," she said with a nod of agreement. "They'll require another night's fire at the least." Then a wonderful idea struck her. "We could hasten the drying by using the morrow's sun during our journey."

He grunted an objection. "I see no way to carry it stretched out as it need be."

She didn't contradict him, but a possible solution had popped into her mind. It would take but a simple contrivance, and she'd assemble it herself, while he slept.

Meanwhile, the pile of uncooked meat he'd discarded nagged at her. They shouldn't leave it behind to spoil.

"We have salt, I believe," she said after another period of silence.

"Salt? For the hides?" he scoffed.

"Nay, for the meat. I know how to prepare it so that it keeps well. 'Twould be a shame to let it be food for the vultures when we might need it ourselves."

"There's game aplenty in these mountains," he said.

"Waste is the devil's handmaiden, my mama taught me." She paused, wondering if she was being too bold. He made no comment and she sensed no added tension in his manner. She continued hesitantly, "'Tis but easy work for me . . . if . . . if I may, that is?"

"Do what you will, Bethany," he said with resignation, or was it weariness? At least it wasn't a mule-headed denial. "I'll fetch the salt for you," he added.

"Thank you, Adam, but that can wait till the morn." She jumped to her feet. "The meat must be readied first, and . . . and if I may but borrow your knife again?"

Glory be. He handed it to her without a word, without, even, a sigh of complaint.

Her spirits soared as she washed off the hunks of meat, slivered them as best she could, and wrapped the thin pieces around sticks. A woman was allowed to do more than cook and wash, thank the heavens.

After bracing the wrapped sticks on poles high beside the skins, she poked the fire beneath and added extra wood. She checked the heat, holding her palms level with her handiwork. 'Twas perfect, she decided, pleased with her accomplishment.

When she returned to the cook fire, she saw that Adam was asleep, curled on his side, his rifle wrapped in his arms.

No longer fierce, she realized, looking down at him. His awesome strength was harnessed now, but present still in the pulse at his temple that beat beneath the stray lock of hair that was the color of warm sand, present still in the veins of his powerful hands and the broad curves of muscle on his arms.

She wondered why he had removed his coat in the night's chill, noticing then that he'd laid it on the opposite side of the fire, where she'd sat before. A bundle of cloth formed a small pillow above it. She smiled in gratitude at his thoughtfulness.

"No longer fierce indeed," she murmured. Her heart began an odd sort of rhythm. It felt . . . it felt as if a bird had flown into her chest, was raising its head, and preparing to burst forth in a full-throated song.

Not since her mama had gone had anyone prepared a bed for her. She wasn't accustomed to. . . .

Bethany chewed at her lip and frowned. She could depend no longer on those things she was "accustomed to." Her world had changed beyond measure, and she knew with apprehension that she was woefully unprepared for whatever may lay ahead for her.

Were all folk outside the Hollow as strange and unpredictable as this man Adam? Would she ever be able to learn what was expected of her? What was *not* expected of her?

She clutched her amulet. Maybe Adam would teach her. She had quantities of things to learn before she could meet her prince. *Please tell Adam to help me know the proper ways before he leaves me.*

The dream catcher pulsed twice against her hand. She smiled.

Now then, before she slept she would build the platform for the skins to dry on tomorrow. She must do it very quietly, though, for she didn't want to awaken Adam.

Chapter Seven

Damned clever. Adam lifted his brow at the ingenious device she'd strung together with poles and ropes during the night. He could see it would work well, would attach behind one of the animals and be dragged along, holding the skins taut toward the sun. He might have thought to make it himself, if he'd had his normal store of wits about him.

He had risen early, when the sky was yet holding on to its drab predawn blanket. The cooler air heralding the sun's coming had awakened him, and he'd lowered his sleeves and pulled his collar higher. Now, tenuous traces of pink wove through the heavy gray above, and the surrounding forest began to stir with birdcalls.

The woman still slept, her small form snuggled beneath his buckskins, a straggle of copper hair peeking over the top. She was a tiny bundle of warmth in the morning's chill.

Without allowing himself to consider why he'd suddenly found his own covering to be excessive, he rolled up his sleeves, pushed down his collar, and distracted himself by punching the almost-dead cook fire into sparks that ignited the fresh wood he'd added.

"Is it morning, already?"

He jumped slightly at the sleep-swollen question, then glanced over his shoulder. She was up, stifling a yawn, his coat wrapped tight about her. Her hair was an unruly mass of blazing curls, brighter than the flames at his feet.

"Aye, tis morning." He felt the corners of his mouth curve whimsically upward before he could order them back down where they belonged. He turned away and poked with unneeded intensity at the fire.

"Thank you for the coat's warmth."

He knew she was holding it out to him but wouldn't let himself look at her.

"Keep it till the sun's higher, I don't need it." An understatement, he realized at once. Beads of perspiration had sprouted on him in devilish places, undoubtedly caused by his closeness to the fire. He backed away a bit, taking care to steer clear of her.

But she wasn't there. She was wandering merrily off to the woods as if he hadn't warned her about. . . .

"Stay here!" he commanded.

She stopped, looked back at him, her face flustered.

"But I . . ." Her cheeks reddened. "I must . . . behind the trees, already I've had to, when you knew not . . . My feet weren't harmed, and truly, Adam, you must allow me to . . ."

His chest constricted and his own face grew hot. Of course. He'd been callous not to consider her needs.

"Go, then," he said, trying for an unconcerned shrug as he busied himself again with the fire.

He admired it, I believe. Bethany was proud of the skin-drying platform she'd built. He'd made no comment but had readily transferred the skins and tied the device behind the ox. While their breakfast had cooked, she'd salted down the deer meat and encased the preserved pieces in a scrap of the hide.

Once again they were on their way. He'd promised her they would stop earlier than yesterday, saying something about needing added time for a "special task." She wasn't entirely clear what he meant, but a shortened journey this day appealed to her.

Though her bottom still ached from yesterday's ride, her spirits had improved considerably. She wasn't sure why, figuring it was a mixture of happenings. True, she feared him less, though she vowed she'd be heedful not to anger him. He even spoke a few words to her while they rode—brief words, once about the fine weather, once a grumble about the "dastardly slow pace."

Aye, it was a mixture of small events, but they added up, providing her with strengthened hope that last night's plea to the amulet would be answered soon, that he'd start teaching her some of the many things she needed to know.

They came upon a cabin a little past noon. As he pulled to a halt, Bethany felt the tension that throbbed through his arms, saw his hands tighten on the reins.

"Shhh," he cautioned.

She held her breath, sensing danger. Were there folk in the cabin? Would they be unfriendly? Or—and a sliver of gloom pricked her, its dark tip surprisingly sharper than danger itself—what if they were friendly? Would he then leave her here with them? Leave her this very day before she knew the proper ways? She grasped the dream catcher and closed her eyes. Her newest plea seemed the perfect solution. *Let it be empty.*

He dismounted, pulled her down hastily, and placed himself in front of her.

"Ho!" he shouted. "Is there someone in there?"

She noted his hands were poised near his tomahawk and knife, tensed, ready to move in an instant. Hidden behind him, close enough to smell the reassuring animal scent of his coiled power, she felt totally secure.

When no response came from the cabin, her spirits lifted. She attempted to peek around him, but his elbow nudged her head back.

"Stay quiet," he ordered, his voice low.

Suddenly, Constant began barking, scaring her so that she reflexively hid her face into the back of Adam's shirt before kicking out at the dog, trying to silence him. Sharp pain radiated up her leg as Constant clamped his teeth into her foot.

"Ow!"

Quicker than lightning, Adam whopped his hand down against the dog's neck, knocking him away from her. Constant yapped and cowered in the dirt, then crawled up beside her, his black eyes watery with apologies.

Adam raised his arm, and the blade of his knife glinted in the sunlight. "No!" Bethany screamed, pushing hard against his hand with both of hers. "Don't kill him!"

The look he threw at her was naked with fury. "The cur bit you, he must die."

She shook her head wildly as tears filled her eyes. "The bite's naught. He was but reacting to the fright. *Please don't . . .*" she sobbed.

He lowered his arm. Constant whimpered, and Bethany knelt to embrace the dog, burying her wet face in his scrawny neck. "It's all right," she murmured over and over. "It's all right now."

Adam's deep voice came to her muffled, filtered through her overwrought emotions.

"It's a blessing this bloody place is empty, or the commotion raised by your bloody dog might have got us shot." He was on his knee beside her, his arm across her back. "Here, let me see that foot."

Still trembling, she held Constant close and sat, meekly sticking out her foot for his inspection. Looking with concern between the dog's ears, she saw the small marks of his teeth above her toes. Truly naught, she repeated to herself, relieved, but a speck of blood, only a wee bit of puffiness—a mere trifle and surely not worthy of the man's violent reaction, nor, indeed, such careful attention.

Her foot disappeared as he gathered it up in his large hands; it grew warm inside his firm clasp. With a surprisingly gentle finger, he dabbed away the blood, smearing them into a reddish-brown stain across the top of her dusty foot. She felt only a little pain as his hard thumb pressed the tiny tracks of swelling.

"See, I told you tis naught," she said, attempting to pull away. He wouldn't let go. Damnation, she could minister to such a meager wound in a trice. She needed but water and a sprinkling of the proper weed. "If you'll release me, I can—"

"You *cannot*." His hold around her ankle was like a vise, and he moved her foot closer to him with a yank that was far from gentle. "Bloody hell, woman, we must get this washed off at once."

"That's what I . . ." *intended to do* was stifled against his shoulder when he swept her up into his arms so swiftly she nearly choked on the words. As he carried

95

her to a narrow creek behind the vacant cabin, she squirmed her protests as best she could, frustrated by his unnecessary pampering. And yet, a bothersome voice inside her was chirping a different tune. She was experiencing something very close to pleasure, wrapped in his arms and pressed against his hard chest, the beat of his strong heart caressing her ears. A feathery wisp of recognition floated across her mind. Only in her dreams had she felt so. . . .

The wisp vanished without a trace as he put her down, rather rudely, she considered. When he plunged her foot into the cold water, she winced. Definitely rude.

He bathed the wound well and wouldn't let her help, shooing away her hands and reprimanding her every time she tried to offer any assistance. *Bloody stubborn he is*, she fussed to herself, liking the satisfying punch of emphasis added by the new word she'd learned from him.

"There. Let the sun dry it, that will hasten the healing," he said gruffly, apparently finished.

With a scowl etching a deep line between his thick, tawny brows, he stormed up the creek's bank toward the cabin. Bethany stood, letting the soothing water lap against her ankles. It soaked the frayed hem of her nightdress hanging below the bulky gray shirt, but she didn't care. She wished the creek were deeper, for she longed to give herself and every stitch of her dreadfully soiled clothing a vigorous soaking.

She was reluctant to follow him, sensing a need to stand there in the creek alone for a spell, free from his overpowering presence. He unnerved her with his peculiar manner—fire one moment, ice the next. He shifted from blistering anger to warming concern to chilled disinterest faster than the wind shifts on a temperamental autumn day.

He made her so . . . She screwed up her face in an attempt to describe his effect on her. So off balance.

She was as limp as old dimity, more weary than a whipped workhorse after a long day in the fields. The conflicting emotions she'd experienced during the past hour, heaped on top of the woes, turmoil, and unrelenting challenges of the previous days, had drained her.

With a sigh, she left the creek and plopped down on the soggy bank. Constant crept over and laid his soft muzzle across her lap.

"I forgive you," she whispered, scrunching her fingers into his neck. The dog licked her hand and settled himself against her.

Bethany looked up at the bright blue sky, but there were no clouds to watch, nothing to show her what might lay ahead. Feeling woefully unprepared for the future, she reached for her dream catcher. *Help me find the strength I must have.*

As she opened her eyes, a refreshing breeze wafted across her face like a promising whisper. She nodded, then stood and patted away the dirt from the back of the borrowed shirt. The time had come to join Adam up at the cabin—the *empty* cabin, she remembered with satisfaction. He might be needing her help with the chores.

And maybe . . . maybe this eve he'd begin teaching her some of the things she needed to learn.

"They didn't leave behind much, did they?"

Adam whirled around. She stood in the doorless opening, the sunlight dancing in her fiery hair. Before he could speak, he had to swallow the aborted breath that had lodged in his throat.

"Not much. Looks as though they abandoned the place before last winter." After a quick glance at her foot to assure himself the injury was as slight as she claimed, he concentrated on the floor and counted a few uneven planks.

"It's a sorry spot they picked to build a cabin," he continued. "The ground is pocked with limestone, unsuitable for farming, and the grass and creek are inadequate for any quantity of livestock. Only a fool-headed dreamer would settle here."

"They had mighty dreams, I sense." As she walked into the room, he moved back toward the wall. "The floor is wooden, I've never seen . . ." She paused, testing the planks with her bare toes. "'Tis far finer than dirt."

Her awestruck face shone as she looked around. "It's so *large*, and is that truly another room back yon?"

"Aye, and as empty as this one." He'd considered the cabin a hovel. Her big green eyes seemed to be seeing a marvel. He frowned and checked the desolate place again, wondering if he had missed something. No, it was still dirty and ugly.

"And what's this inside the window?" Her finger tapped one of the small distorted panes.

"Glass. Most every home has glass now, haven't you seen—" He stopped himself. She'd seen precious little in that squalid Hollow, he realized with a tug of pity. She was like a traveler from a primitive era, cast on the shores of an alien world she knew nothing about and they'd only come as far as the bloody mountains, for God's sake. So many wonders lay ahead for her. Why, the sight of Wendover will . . . He trapped the thought, held it squirming beneath the clamp of his remembered pledge to be rid of her as soon as possible. He had no intention of taking her as far as Wendover. They'd find a settlement way before then.

"Glass? *Glass*." She seemed as fascinated with the texture of the syllable on her tongue as with the miracle beneath her fingertips. "How wondrous! Look, Adam, you can see the sunshine through it."

"Heavily filtered through the cobwebs," he commented, feeling compelled to add a dab of reality to the magic she insisted on weaving around the humble dwelling.

"Cobwebs, faugh, we can be rid of those with ease."

She startled him by reaching down and ripping off a piece from the bottom of her nightdress. With a few enthusiastic wipes, she whisked away the webs.

"See? They're gone," she exclaimed, beaming as brightly as the rays through the window.

Adam decided to change the subject. "I found two pallets rolled in the corner," he said. "Vermin-infested, I suspect, but I gave them a good shake and put them out to sun. We may be able to sleep softer tonight."

"Any blankets, perchance?"

"No, but I checked the fireplace and it draws well enough, so we may be warmer, too." A vagrant thought wandered through his brain. *Nestled close together we could be even warmer.* He kicked it away with dispatch, but not before a whisper of heat glided across his nape.

He grumbled and headed for the door. He had to get busy. Many chores awaited him and much needed to be done to justify stopping early today. Already valuable time had been wasted.

"And what's this?"

Her lightly spoken question stopped him. She was standing in the corner, holding up a shaggy straw broom. Damn. He'd have to explain.

"It's a broom, for sweeping the floor. See, like this." He took it from her and demonstrated, making a path through the accumulated debris. A few tiny rat bones clicked across the wood.

"That's truly marvelous," she said with a small intake of breath, but she made no move to reclaim the broom.

He shoved the handle toward her. "Women sweep," he said. She nodded happily and took it from him.

Very good, now she would be well occupied inside. As for himself, he had work to do—outside, thank God.

Everything in the room was crackling. The pine knots he'd brought from the woods crackled as they surrounded them with light; the flaming logs in the hearth crackled; even the deer hide in Adam's hands crackled beneath his knife.

Bethany's jangled nerves joined in, popping and crackling, as she sat on the cabin's floor, her knees drawn up to her chin, watching him work. She had nothing else to do, and she was miserable being so useless, being such a bother. Besides, she didn't want the blasted things.

He was making her a pair of moccasins, he'd said, explaining they were the kind of shoes Indians wore. She'd never cared for shoes and hated the winters when she'd had to limp around in George's castoff boots, their toes, sides, and heels stuffed with cloth so that she wouldn't step out of them.

Shoes were uncomfortable, restricting, and she wasn't pleased she'd have to wear them. *Indian* shoes at that. She wanted no part of anything Indian. The heathens had taken her mother from her.

"I need to get a measure of your foot." His unexpected words snipped into her string of silent complaints.

With considerable effort, she managed to suppress the groan that would signal to him she was less than delighted with this "special task" of his. She stretched out her legs.

He folded a piece of deer skin around one foot and with studied concentration made several light marks in the hide with the tip of the blade. The material was soft against her flesh, wonderfully pliable. For a few moments, the room's crackles were subdued. She watched his large fingers move nimbly from her toe to her heel, their light pulse of warmth through the hide setting off peculiar tingles that scurried willy-nilly up her legs.

Her small gasp surprised her. Surprised him, too, she saw, for he looked up, puzzled.

"Am I pressing too hard on the wound?"

"No, it's all right." The wound was all right, true, but that odd tingling she'd felt . . . What in heaven's name was that? She bit her lip to keep from asking. Anyway, the strange sensation had passed, and he was occupied again with his measurements.

When he finished, he sat back and began cutting the hide.

"What's that yellow dusting on the bite?" he asked.

Does he note everything? "A sprinkling of a weed's flower, I know not what it's called. Mama taught me about its healing powers."

"Is that what's in the pouch you call a dream catcher, healing weeds?"

Her heart quickened and she clasped the amulet. "No." Damnation, why hadn't she simply said aye? It would've been a lie, but no one save the prince should ever know her secret; her mama had warned her.

She continued talking, hoping to distract him from his troublesome curiosity. "I found the flower by the creek. It's wee and furry like a baby daisy."

He looked over at her. The pine knots' white flames flickered recklessly in his dark brown eyes. She could see a question about her dream catcher forming, and her mind rushed to find a way to stop them from reaching his lips.

"Did you like the sugar I made?"

It worked. He bent back to his task, but she saw a faint smile curl his mouth.

"It was fortunate the folk had left the plug and its bucket in the maple tree that way," she went on, breathing easier. "The rising sap had been caught well, and the bucket was nigh full for us. I used but a mite of it. I relish the sweetness of the syrup and the sugar it makes after a firm boiling."

He was silent for a while as he laced strips of deer skin through the strangely shaped pieces of hide. They were formed for feet, she could tell. Shoes. *Bloody* shoes. She shifted her still-sore bottom on the hard floor and let a sulky cloud drop around her.

"Of little necessity, however," he said.

Shoes? Glory be, maybe he'd come to his senses.

"Oh, sugar tastes well enough, I suppose," he added, as he punched another hole in the deer hide and threaded the long strip through it. "But it's hardly the stuff of survival, like corn and meat."

And like shoes, he apparently believed.

Bethany leaned back on her hands. Something more than shoes had darkened her mood. What was it? She searched for the answer through the thicket of possibilities in her cluttered thoughts and found a particular thorny one that snagged her at every turn. Uneasiness. She was constantly uneasy in this man's presence.

Why? Yet another question, she discovered, unwilling to plunge into that new thicket she'd reached. It was even more tangled than the first.

She straightened up and shook off her sulkiness. It fit her no better than Adam's shirt. She had many things to be happy about. She was warm and well fed, and tonight there would be a roof over their heads.

"I like this cabin," she said, feeling brighter. "One could live well here, I believe."

His grunt sounded negative, but she wasn't deterred.

"Had there been folk here willing to accept me, would you have left me?"

His hand paused, but his next jab into the hide was a fierce one. "I suppose I would have."

His words stung. Strange they would affect her so. Surely, she hadn't expected him to want her around any longer than necessary. She was an awful bother. She stared at the deerskin between his fingers and flinched as he shoved the strip through. She felt the rough scrape between her ribs as if he were lacing a hole he'd punched into the middle of her chest.

Unbeckoned, a fat tear spilled from her eye and rolled down her cheek. She wiped it away hurriedly. She was being such a ninny!

"I'm a true burden to you, Adam. I'm sorry." She heard her words pop out, as unexpected as that silly tear. She chewed at her lip, waiting in the heavy silence for his response.

"No need to be sorry," he said, examining the moccasin on all sides before putting it down. It looked finished.

Without further comment, he began lacing the second shoe. She couldn't ignore the twinge of disappointment. Had she hoped he'd deny she was a burden?

The crackles grew louder, increasing her edginess. She went to the fire and poked it hard enough to set off a hefty spray of sparks. After adding a log, she watched the flames grab hold of the wood and begin to devour it.

Damnation, another evening was speeding by, and Adam had shown no signs of complying with her plea to the dream catcher. She wished he'd talk more. This world outside of the Hollow was filled with mysteries and she craved to learn about at least a few of them before she had to face other places, other . . . strangers.

Her heart tightened. She circled her fingers around the amulet to reassure herself that all would be well eventually. If only she could think of a way to get him to talk to her. . . .

A glimmer of an idea sparkled. Maybe he was a man of few words, but he did respond to her questions. It would be a beginning, she thought with a smile. After wiping the soot from her hands, she returned to her spot on the floor opposite him.

"May I ask you some questions, Adam?"

"About what?"

About everything. No, that wouldn't do. She thought hastily, praying she'd find a good starting place and reminding herself to phrase it as a question.

"Where are you heading? After you're rid of me, that is." She tacked on the last part to be on the safe side.

He looked troubled and threaded two holes before he responded. She tensed. Maybe she'd begun all wrong.

"The Tidewater," he said at last.

"The Tidewater? What's that?" Questions, she found, were easy to form when she was so woefully ignorant.

"It's flatland, south and east of here, down by the James River. I grew up there."

He'd provided a lot of information to digest and she was delighted. She worked on it awhile. Land could be flat? She'd imagined the whole world held mountains. "South" and "east" she knew. The sun and the blue mountains rose in the east; the birds flew south in the late autumn. "River" she'd also heard. That was a great body of water. The Shenandoah it was called. A "James," too? There must be two rivers.

"The Tidewater." He grew up there. Her next question came quickly. "Why did you leave the Tidewater?"

He clenched the hide and she drew back. Maybe she shouldn't have asked that question.

"I was deceived."

He looked angrier than the devil, but she sensed his anger was directed elsewhere, somewhere as distant as his clouded gaze. She was too curious not to continue. "Deceived? Someone lied to you?"

"Far worse than lies. The man will die for his trickery."

Bethany noted the venom in his words, though she didn't understand. "Are you returning only to kill him?"

"Aye, that I am." He glowered at the shoe. "But I'm returning, too, to my home."

Home. It had a wonderful sound. She wished she had one to return to. She fought back a wave of self-pity, feeling greater concern for the man opposite her.

"Which is more important to you? The killing or the home?"

A long silence followed. Adam's hands tightened on the moccasin. She waited, holding her breath.

"They're of equal importance to me, as tied together as these skins." He looked at her then, his stern expression setting off a drumbeat of warning in her breast. "Cease the questions for now, Bethany. Your moccasins are finished. Here, see how they feel." He tossed them to her.

Thomasina Ring

She stared at them, disconcerted. Her head was filled with additional questions, but she'd have to pose them another time. His answers tonight hadn't solved any mysteries, anyway. Indeed, they'd opened new ones that she sensed were far more important than her lack of knowledge about worldly matters.

She felt an urgency to explore the anger that seethed in Adam, a desire to help him quiet it before it destroyed him. He, too, needed help—more, perhaps, than she did.

But for now, she would try to avoid irritating him further. Despite her misgivings about the shoes, she picked them up and slipped them over her feet.

They topped her ankles but didn't bind, and they fit her like a second skin. She wiggled her toes, taking pleasure in the tickle of nubby fur. As she stood and walked around, the moccasins' warm embrace added a spring to her steps. Why, they were far better than bare feet!

"They're wondrous," she exclaimed. "Where did you learn—" She stopped herself, interjecting a ringing "thank you" instead.

He seemed pleased with her approval, and his broad smile reached clear to his eyes. Her heart skipped a beat. She wanted to give him a big hug but she figured he'd object.

Meanwhile, she was gratified to see his eyes cleared of anger. Their dancing light slipped around her as warm and comfortable as her new shoes.

"Thank you," she repeated. Her own smile, she suspected, was as wide as the great Shenandoah.

Chapter Eight

Adam whacked the branch across his knee, taking perverse pleasure in the resounding *crack* as the wood splintered apart. He flung the jagged pieces to the ground. Blazing hell, but it was a relief to get outside.

The night air was cool, exactly what he needed. Three more seconds in that sweltering room and he'd have incinerated on the spot. The glowing hearth was bad enough; the woman's radiant smiles had made the place an inferno.

Her mangy dog sat over in the trees' shadows like a scrawny lump, watching him with guarded eyes. Adam wanted to whop his bony head—damnable undisciplined cur. He slammed another branch instead and relished the sharp sting against the heels of his hands. The kindling was required for the morning's fire; making it, he was discovering, satisfied a more pressing need.

He was agitated . . . *wham*! . . . stuck here in these mountains with a . . . *crack*! . . . maddening woman who'd reduced him to a muzzy-headed . . . *slam*! . . . addlebrained fool.

Flipping the sweat from his forehead, he paused and clamped his teeth. Only one mile they'd covered today—one mile—and there were hundreds to travel to Wendover. If he continued at this pace, James Wallace would die of old age before he could run his sword through the bastard's black heart.

He *must* be rid of that worrisome woman and her blasted caravan of animals soon. Bloody hell, he had revenge to wreak, justice to tend to and here he was, trapped, wasting precious time with trifles like sugar and moccasins.

His jaws relaxed and his tongue played across his lips. He hadn't tasted sugar in years. It had become but a web of sweetness nestled in the far corners of his memory. Only a memory, until tonight, when she'd put a sprinkling on the hoecake and added a tiny clump to his coffee. Her eyes had sparkled like sunlit emeralds when she'd licked the brown grains from her fingertips. He remembered well the one tempting speck that clung to the corner of her mouth, the urge he'd had to nibble. . . .

Wham! The kindling stack grew higher beside his boots.

Later, he straddled a log and smoked his pipe, his calmed mind as clear as the night's sky. It had grown late, the sliver of the new moon leaning westward, the low, two-note call of a lone quail beating the same steady cadence as Adam's heart.

For the first time in days he had no distractions, no disorderly jumbles in his brain and now, in these blessed hours of quiet, he vowed he would lay his plans for revenge against his stepbrother, James. Not once since Sweet Molly's revelations in Battletown had he truly thought the situation through with a clear head.

Though at present he was saddled with unwanted responsibilities, he assured himself he wouldn't remain that way long, only a few days more, at the most. Then he would move with haste but he had to have his strategy in place—a workable, firm strategy.

Strategy is the key. He nodded. He would hearken to his own tested advice. What was the wisest path he could take to regain Wendover? Dan Morgan had possibly spoken the truth. It would be foolhardy to storm the place and kill James. True, the blackguard would have his due, and Adam ached to see him writhing beneath his sword. But at its end, such a path could lead him even farther away from his birthright.

Adam tapped the bowl of the clay pipe against the log, and a clot of dead ashes fell to the dirt. He ground them with the heel of his boot. It might well be that he should choose to pursue the legal route instead; slower, true, but perhaps in the long run more effective. The knowledge that he was alive and that his father's will could be legally overturned would cause James grievous torment. He could then watch James dangle without mercy on the twisted ropes of his own heinous deceit. He'd see him struggle to no avail and suffer the tortures of hell as the noose tightened, bringing him disgrace, dishonor, and finally, by God, the loss of Wendover. For a man like James, that would be death itself—a slow, painful death.

Adam smiled into the darkness. Morgan had tried to

tell him, but he'd been too hotheaded to listen. Choosing the legal path indeed would inflict far greater injuries to James Wallace than would a swift blade.

He ran his fingers through his beard and frowned. He didn't know the ways of the courts, and he would need the assistance of a trusted advisor, but who?

The low hoot of an owl echoed his question. Like summer lightning, the answer flickered. There might be such a man. Uncle Hallston Lawrence, his long-dead mother's brother. Adam hadn't seen him since he was a lad, but remembered he was a magistrate, a gracious man who was learned in affairs of the law.

Where was it that his uncle lived? He had been headed there on that dark day of treachery. Brierwood, the home was named. In Albemarle, wasn't it? Near the blue mountains, he remembered, close to their eastern slopes. It would be less distant from here than to the Tidewater, a mere few days journey, once he was free from. . . .

Bethany. His heart quickened and a subtle quiver ran down his spine. She was so easily enchanted, so filled with childlike wonder with the simplest of objects—a broom, a pair of moccasins. So quickly she found pleasure in matters worthy of little note, and her delight had touched him with its golden glow more than once. For suspended moments she'd made him forget the hard cruelties of this world, had made him believe that. . . .

Adam furrowed his brow. The world allowed no space for golden glows. Nor did he, if he wanted to keep his wits about him.

He slapped his open palms against the log between his legs. His decision was made.

Aye, once he was free from Bethany Rose Stewart he'd head straight for Albemarle County and the home of his Uncle Hallston.

*   *   *

The prince had grown taller. She gasped when she saw him changed that way, but was comforted when he reached for her and pulled her up to him, wrapped her within his strength and whispered his familiar refrain, "I am here." The white steed raced them through the night and through the shaded mountains that opened to them. His breath caressed her ears as the warm wind caressed her face. The light pulsing against her thighs began its tender magic, setting off gentle rays of soft throbs that spread through her in waves like sweet, thick syrup. She moaned into his chest.

"Will it be soon?" she asked.

"Aye, soon." His words stroked through her hair. The darkness was touched with a pink glow, grew brighter with streams of lavender and gold and there, ahead, she saw the flowering meadow beckon to them, inviting them to enter. The vivid colors sparkled in the sunlight, fondled her eyes with their beauty. She pressed close against him, and the steed quickened his pace. The pulse grew stronger, its power prodding an ache of longing for a deeper fullness that only the prince could provide.

They were almost there. She clung to him.

"I am ready . . ."

Bethany opened her eyes. The newborn sun was a ball of red through the glass window. She blinked, but the spell of the dream covered her like a gossamer veil. It had been different from the other dreams. It had carried her with added swiftness far nearer to the promises that before had remained hidden behind the blue mist. She'd seen the meadow with the colors that dazzled, had felt the swelling anticipation of a glorious fulfillment beyond any she'd ever imagined.

The anticipation lingers even yet, her fog-wrapped brain whispered, *and it's settled in a mighty peculiar spot, too*. She shifted her legs restlessly on the pallet, unsure of this new sensation, but unwilling to let it go. Not yet, not until. . . .

"Breakfast is ready, if you can bestir yourself."

Oh no. Does he always rise before the sun? She was truly awake now.

Good grief, cooking breakfast was one of the few chores he'd allowed her, and she'd been a worthless slugabed. She wanted to moan. Would she forever be more bother than help to him?

Bethany struggled to rise quickly, but her night-dress was twisted above her knees and she was tangled up in the gray shirt. "I should've cooked the breakfast. Oof! It's not right that you must—mmph!—do everything while I do nothing but sleep." Her feet touched the floor at last.

His back was turned, thank heavens.

"There was little enough to tend to," he said, piling their trenchers high with a hodgepodge of victuals, most of them remains from last night's supper. "We need to get under way early this morn. I hope to put more distance behind us today."

And more between us, she thought uncomfortably, noticing his manner was frostier than usual.

She pulled on her new moccasins. "Aye, I'll scurry out and milk Churning."

"That's done already."

"Then I'll tie the animals."

"Tis done."

"Pack the tools?" Her voice was getting weaker. Surely, he'd left something for her to do.

He shook his head. "Just eat, please."

She had little appetite, but she ate.

By noon they'd reached a wide, inviting stream. Bethany prayed he'd stop, if only for a short while.

She longed to bathe and give the nightdress a scrubbing, but he seemed bent on haste this day, so she didn't dare suggest they pause.

They didn't, and it was late afternoon before he pulled them to a halt. She was delighted, for they'd come upon another stream, wider and even more inviting than the first.

"This will do," he said.

"Indeed." *Indeed*.

"We've covered three miles, I reckon."

"I reckon so." She had no idea what "miles" were, but she was determined to be as agreeable as the dickens.

"I'll prepare the site," he said, handing her down from the horse. "You're to do naught till the fire's ready for cooking."

"Naught?"

"Absolutely naught."

"But I . . ."

His beard twitched. "But you what?"

"Would like to . . ." His hands still lightly held her waist, and those peculiar tingles were radiating through her again. " . . . to wash some things?"

"Wash what things?" He pulled away his hands and rubbed them against his breeches. The tingles lingered around her middle.

"My nightdress . . ." His warm brown eyes made her think of sugared coffee. "The shirt you're wearing if you'd like . . ." Why was her voice so whispery? "And myself, of course."

The pause lasted a halting heartbeat. She was unable to move her upturned face; her gaze had locked to his permanently, it seemed.

"Aye, of course," he said with a deep huskiness, then turned from her. "Do so while the sun is yet warm, and I'd be grateful for a clean shirt."

He stripped off his shirt and handed it to her before walking away. Bared now, his shoulders and smooth back looked even larger and more heavily threaded with muscles than she'd considered possible. Her fingers prickled.

Bethany stood transfixed. She couldn't have moved if she tried. Her bones had turned to syrup. She took in a deep breath and dug her hands into his wadded shirt; its smoky-woodsy scent wafted about her like a comforting cloud. Oh my, she thought, her brain reeling. That wasn't uneasiness she'd just felt—or was it? It appeared to be its kin, but something quite different, too. She wished she had a name for it.

The bath was glorious. Bethany floated about happily in the stream, letting the cold mountain water bathe away soot, grime, and exhaustion. Adam had given her a hunk of soap from his pack, and she already had washed the nightdress and his shirt, spreading them across laurel bushes to dry in the sun. His other shirt, the one she'd worn since leaving the Hollow, would have to get its soaking another day, for she'd be needing dry covering after her bath.

She had found a hidden cove that provided privacy, a commodity she'd too seldom had when she'd lived with Pa and George. She hadn't liked it on the occasions they'd stood on the bank and watched her bathe, chastising her all the while about being "addled about washin' " and ridiculing her "useless woman's body unfit for anythin' worth doin'."

Feeling ashamed, she would try to hide under the water, and they'd leave her alone finally, snorting their crude laughter as they returned to the cabin. She would soap herself all over again.

The memories weren't pleasant ones, and she pulled them from her mind with a tug of sadness. Poor Pa and George. They'd loved her, but they couldn't stop themselves from tormenting her; it was just their way with the world, that was all. She wondered if they continued to act the same up in heaven. How were the angels reacting to their taunts?

They'd smile, she guessed, and go on ignoring them and strumming their harps until Pa and George softened and became enchanted and then they would smile, too.

She hoped that for them. Not being an angel, she'd never succeeded in making them smile.

"May you find peace above and your woman, here, peace below," Adam had said over the graves. Aye, she thought with a sigh, they were beautiful words.

Feeling more peaceful than she had in days, she finished her bath and started toward the stream's bank. Adam's soap smelled like bayberry, and it sudsed far better than any she'd made. She'd have to ask him about it.

Bethany didn't see the men approach until Constant growled. Alerted, she grabbed for Adam's huge shirt. She pulled it over her head and was struggling with the laces when they walked from the trees.

"Well, jes' look whut we found, Sammy."

Panic gripped her. She stared at them in terror, clutching the shirt's gaping top closed. There were two—the grizzled trapper who'd spoken and a half-naked Indian. *Indian!* And she had no bow! She wanted to run, to scream, but stark fear held her pinned and voiceless.

The stocky trapper moved toward her, a deadly light squinting from his yellowed eyes. His face was spidery with grimy wrinkles.

"Tis our lucky day, boy. We found ourselves not only an ox and milk cow but somethin' e'en better—a flame-haired lassie." His serpent eyes raked her from head to toe. Spittle foamed in the dark corners of his twisted mouth. "I got a powerful hankerin', I tell ye. Let me at her first, then ye can have the leavings." Leering, he came toward her, groping at his breeches, pulling out his man's thing. It was threatening, like a limp, pale snake with a squirmy head.

She recoiled. *Adam! Help me!* But the scream hung frozen in her throat as the man's ham-hock hands tore her hands away from her shirt and with a fierce thrust, shoved her backwards. She landed sprawled before him in the dirt. She scrambled to her knees, but he pushed her back, hard. Her head hit a rock, the air rushed from her lungs, and then he was all over her, his weight like a heavy stone holding her down. His clammy hands pushed the shirt up to her neck and clawed at her flesh. His bony knee pushed between her legs.

She was dazed from the blow to her head, drained of breath, and drowning in venomous stench. *Fight it, fight it!* her mind screeched. She became frenzied, thrashed out at him, fought him like a crazed catamount with teeth and nails, with arms flailing and legs kicking. But nothing stopped him. He was everywhere, his grunts filled her ears, his fetid breath smothered her face, his rough hands clamped her breasts, squeezed and mashed them. Flaring pain burned red against her eyes and icy terror blinded her with sharp, glaring white.

Dear God, no!

She heard a muffled bark, a sharp thump, a grinding groan of agony then a splatter of wetness hit her face. The man above her jerked once and was suddenly still.

She stiffened as his stony body pressed down hard, heavier. And then he was gone from her. A big brown boot had kicked him away.

Adam! Relief shredded through her fear. She was free, the cool air brushing across her skin quieting the fevered stings. But she lay stunned, unable to move, unable to comprehend. Something terrible had almost happened to her; she didn't know what exactly, only that it was something vile and hideous—worse than the torturing pain she'd suffered.

And Adam had stopped it; Adam had saved her.

She looked up at him through swimming tears. He was a wavy blur, but the glow of deep concern in his dark eyes penetrated into her soul. She tried to smile her gratitude but found her swollen lips incapable of movement.

He knelt beside her and pulled the shirt down, covering her nakedness. "It's over, you're all right," she heard. His soft words, his gentle touch stroked the taut string that had held her rigid, and it sprang loose. A great sob exploded from her throat; she began to weep like a babe.

"Here, now, it's over," he crooned, drawing her into his arms and holding her close. "It's over, Bethany."

She trembled within his embrace, wracked by the violent sobs that lashed through her like storm-tossed waves. She couldn't control them. Over and over they struck her, billowed out of her. It was as though a lifetime of pent-up miseries had gathered into one massive force and were driving her to let them spurt out in rising swells. *Mama's gone. The heathens took her 'n I wish they'd taken ye.*" "*Good-for-nothin' lazy wench.*" "*Useless woman's body, unfit for anythin' worth doin'.*" "*I got a powerful hankerin'* . . . *Ye can have the leavings.*"

They rushed, overrunning one another. She pressed her face against Adam's strong bare chest and let them all gush out in heaving spasms that rocked her ribs, tore at her throat.

"Shhh. It's over now. You're all right."

She desperately wanted to believe him, but her insides kept convulsing and her shoulders wouldn't stop shaking. His arms pulled her closer, his hand cradled her head.

"Are . . . are you sure? All right? Am . . . am I?" she blubbered into the silky hairs of his chest.

"Aye, you're all right. It's over now." His deep voice was soothing, his refrain reassuring. *It's over now. It's over.*

She began to quiet. It was over. She was all right. The tears flowed, but the sobs ceased wrenching her. Unwilling to leave this cocoon of safety, she stayed where she was, wrapped in his arms, inhaling his strength.

Adam was making her all right. No one but her mama had ever comforted her like this, no one except . . . her prince.

But Adam wasn't the prince. Bethany grew quieter. Her face was tight against his chest, the steady rhythm of his heart pulsed against her ears; her lips were salty with a mix of her tears and his sweat.

A small voice told her to pull away, while a stronger voice told her to cling to him.

She clung.

He moved first. "Better now?" he asked, his breath a whisper through her hair.

"Mmmm." She attempted to nod, but she was locked so tight to him that only her lips could flutter her muffled assent. "Much metter mow."

He released his grip, gently squeezed her shoulders, and backed away slightly, still holding her arms to steady her. Though she was reluctant to leave his secure warmth, she straightened her back and raised her head.

"Thank you," she was able to murmur. The shirt had

gaped open, exposing her breasts. She pulled it closed and worked shakily with the laces. Something warned her not to look up into his eyes, but she couldn't stop herself. Her fingers paused. His face was tense, his jaws beneath the tawny beard clenched, but his dark-lashed eyes gentled her with their questioning concern.

"We must tend to your bruises." His penetrating gaze stayed fixed on hers, held her as close as his arms had done.

"I'll fetch herbs," she said softly, unable to look away.

"You're not to leave my sight, Bethany."

I don't want to, ever, she thought, then realized with a pang that she was being foolish. He meant only as long as he was her protector and even during that brief period his order was impractical.

She unhooked her gaze from his and looked down, finished her lacing. "I understand" was all she said. But she didn't. She didn't understand what he did to her to make her feel so dependent on him, so . . . so liquid and warm inside.

As she stood, she saw the trapper, rolled in a stiff curl beside her in the dirt, a tomahawk embedded in his skull.

She gasped, covered her mouth with her hand.

"You killed him?"

Adam unfolded himself from the ground and brushed off his breeches. "Aye, and none too soon, I'd say. His mother should've smothered the bastard in his cradle."

"Adam! That's cruel to say—"

He interrupted her with his angry outburst. "*Cruel*? He was about to rape you, Bethany, and would have killed you in the process without a fare-thee-well. I know his kind. I have seen too many innocent, broken bodies left behind by the likes of him." His harsh tones held a bitterness that distressed Bethany. He yanked the tomahawk from the man's shattered skull and wiped it fiercely in the dirt.

She shuddered. "What is 'rape'?" she asked.

He stared at her. "You don't . . ." He looked away, was silent for a moment. When he spoke again, his voice was subdued, patient. "Rape is forcing one's self upon a woman against her will."

"Oh." The horrible man had surely done that but Adam had said he'd been "about to rape her." Was there something more? She felt sick.

Adam changed the subject. "Your dog saved you, you know."

"Constant?"

He nodded. "He ran for me, barking like crazy, and led me back here."

"Bless him." She looked around for the dog, but didn't see him. "Where is he?"

"Ran off in the turmoil, I guess. He'll be back, the cur sticks to you like glue."

Bethany felt a shiver of unease; something was terribly wrong. Constant wouldn't have left her side without good reason. Perhaps he'd found another danger, someone else to. . . .

The memory jolted her. "Adam! The Indian . . . There was an Indian with this awful man."

"An Indian? I saw no one . . ." He tensed, and his alerted senses cut through the charged air like sharpened arrows. "Listen," he said, low.

She heard it—a distant barking.

"Come!" Adam shouted, grabbing her hand. "Stay near me!"

Chapter Nine

Constant had the Indian at bay. He'd knocked him down and had him well restrained with his front paws on his shoulders. The dog's sharp teeth were bared, aimed at the savage's neck.

"Good boy," Adam said as he approached, Bethany in tow.

With pride, she could see Constant was in full control. How he'd done it, she wasn't sure. Indians were swift warriors, not easily overtaken. She'd seen them in action only once, and the memory gave her icy shivers, but Pa and George had told her many stories about the red men's devious, clever ways.

Adam took charge. He picked up the Indian's bow and arrows and tossed them back into the bushes, then he checked him thoroughly for additional weapons. There weren't many hiding places, Bethany noted. The heathen wore only a breech clout on his greased body. He was rigid with fright and his rounded black eyes were like those of a cornered deer.

She felt a surge of pity.

"Stand," Adam ordered.

The Indian slowly rose to his feet. Bethany gasped her surprise. He was but a boy, no older than three and ten summers was her guess.

"Adam, he's but a—"

"Hush. I'll handle this."

She bit her lip.

"Do you have a name?"

The youth nodded. "The wh–white man, Jake, c–called me Sammy," his soft voice quavered.

He had on a pair of moccasins much like hers, Bethany saw with a warming sense of fellowship.

"Your white man is dead." Adam spat his words, and there was not a hint of compassion in them.

A chill ran down her spine. *Treat him with mercy*, she pleaded, and reached for her amulet.

"What were your stinking plans—yours and your vile friend's?" Adam growled.

"He sp–spotted a cow and ox. Pl–planned to take them, b–but he saw the wo–woman yon and . . ." He bowed his head. "Jake was not my fr–friend," he said to the ground. "He was e–evil. He o–owned m–me."

"Owned you?" Adam asked.

Owned him? Bethany didn't understand.

The boy only nodded and stared at his moccasins.

Adam walked away. He looked exasperated as he ran his fingers through his light hair. For long moments he stared at the bushes as though they would tell him what to do. She held on to her dream catcher.

Finally, he went back to the Indian. "I must tie you, Sammy, till I know more about you. If I find you're lying, you're as dead as the bastard Jake." The words were harsh, but his tone had softened considerably.

Heartened, Bethany squeezed the amulet.

They left the boy tied to the tree and went back to the cove to retrieve her moccasins and the clothes she'd washed. Adam was quiet during the short walk. He looked sorely troubled again; she suspected Sammy had something to do with it.

"What did the lad mean when he said the trapper owned him?" she asked, perplexed.

Adam's voice was as deep and heavy as his mood. "People buy other people sometimes. It's called slavery."

She studied that information and found it disturbing. "That's an ugly thing, I vow. People can be *bought?* Like blankets and rifles?"

A shadow darkened his face. "It happens every day, Bethany. I keep telling you, the world is an ugly place."

Not all of it, she wanted to cry out. The budding bushes showed promises of breathtaking beauty to come, the call of the meadowlark was beautiful, the heavens were oft so beautiful they brought tears of joy to her eyes. And people, too, could be beautiful. Adam was, she thought, looking at him. His long hair gleamed gold in the sunlight, the bronzed flesh of his massive back and shoulders stretched taut and smooth over his wonderful strength.

And his eyes—*his eyes*—with those heavy lashes blacker even than the deep brown orbs they fringed. The memory of the way she'd found herself drawn to those shining depths triggered a tiny pulse of anticipation down low in her insides, and that triggered yet another memory—her powerful dream that morn.

Peculiar. She knotted her brows and quickened her steps. She had fallen far behind, and he'd stopped

123

to wait for her. He wore the pained expression of patience stretched to the limit. He'd made his demand clear: She was to remain in his sight at all times. After today's terrifying events, she was more than willing to comply.

The trapper's body lay where they'd left him. Seeing it, she cringed. The bugs already had found him. Armies of ants and flies were crawling and hovering.

Bethany's stomach flipped and she covered her mouth.

"Dear God, we must bury him."

"No, damn it."

"Please?" She felt as if her soul itself was peering from her eyes, pleading for him to understand.

"After what he did to you, you'd have me—"

"Please," she repeated. That pitiful bug-ridden mound held no resemblance to the man who'd hurt and threatened her and he had been a fellow being, even though a disgusting one. They couldn't leave him unburied. They couldn't! She'd never be able to find peace knowing they'd left him without the covering protection of the earth.

"Please, Adam?"

There was a weighted silence. "We'll have to go back for the shovel," he said at last with resignation bordering on downright displeasure.

"Tis not far." *Thank you*, she felt like shouting. *Thank you, Adam.*

He picked up her moccasins and handed them to her. "Put them on, woman. Maybe you can walk faster in them."

She smiled and slipped them over her feet. "Aye, I can run if it would please you."

The burial was swifter than the earlier one. Adam dug the hole with fierce energy. She had insisted on "words" again, but he grunted out only a few. He knew that the combined liturgies of the Pope of Rome and the Archbishop of Canterbury wouldn't carry Jake whatever-his-name off to heaven.

He watched her place a tiny cross and a wild daisy on the fresh dirt, and once more he was amazed by her seemingly limitless capacity to forgive the unforgivable. It went beyond innocence, transcended anything he'd ever encountered.

Was that what the parsons and other weaklings referred to as unconditional love? If so, he'd never experienced it and was damn sure he wanted no part of it. Life demanded unclouded eyes and a hardened heart.

With a blinding flash of insight, he knew he'd be remiss if he didn't warn Bethany about the pitfalls of innocent trust and misplaced compassion. She needed to arm herself better for the real world and shed her foolish belief that all could be well—indeed, that *anything* could be well.

"Thank you," she said simply after they'd finished. "We've done all we could."

Adam moaned, picked up the shovel, and plucked the sun-dried shirt and nightdress off the laurels.

"Let's be on our way," he said. "We need to put poultices on your bruises, there's supper yet to prepare, and we still have Sammy to dispense with."

"Sammy? What do you mean 'dispense with'?"

Her big questioning eyes ripped into him. Hell, he didn't know himself what he meant. How could he explain his own dilemma about the boy's presence? He was damnably confused.

He prodded her forward. "Give me time to consider the matter," he said, unwilling to commit himself one way or the other. "We can't let our guard down, just because he's a boy."

She didn't look convinced.

"Go on," he urged.

She obeyed. He followed her, trying not to look at her. He didn't succeed. Her mussed red hair bounced around her shoulders and trailed like silken ribbons down her back; the curves of her bare calves were clearly visible between the shirt and the moccasins. Her round, little bottom pushed against the coarse linen of his old shirt and undulated as she took her purposeful strides.

She'll drive me berserk, part of him complained. *She's by far the loveliest woman I've ever seen*, a larger part taunted, tormenting him with its unsettling honesty.

"We must feed the boy," Bethany said when their supper was ready.

"I thought you hated Indians." Adam sounded gruff, but she detected a teasing lilt.

She contemplated his statement, then shook her head. "No, I think not. How could I hate them? I've known no Indians."

"The Shawnees are Indians. They took your mother, you said."

The stab of that memory was still sharp, but she had found comfort long ago in her faith that things had gone well for her mama. "True, but I've always felt in my heart that they've treated her kindly," she said, keeping her voice light. "Mama was a beautiful, loving woman, and I know that no one could ever harm her. I like to think they made her a queen."

Pain flickered in Adam's eyes as he looked down at her. She held her breath, afraid of what he might say. "I was held captive by Shawnees for a spell, Bethany. Do you know what they do to white women?"

She felt the blood drain from her face, then reached for a trencher and filled it with deer stew. "You see only evil in the world, Adam. I prefer to believe my mama has found happiness."

He was quiet. When she handed him the trencher, her hand trembled. "Give it to the lad, please," she said.

"He's a Shawnee, Bethany."

Was he testing her? She lifted her chin. "Tonight he's a hungry boy."

He held the trencher and studied her face. She could almost hear the tension snapping in the air between them. She wished he'd say nothing further, but she could see the challenging words forming on his lips.

"This world is filled with evil, Bethany Rose Stewart, and it's folly to see it otherwise," he said at last. "Your pretty pictures are the stuff of dreams with no substance. Dreams are destructive."

He seemed so sure of himself, but he was dead wrong. She straightened her shoulders. It was time he heard the truth.

"No, Adam, it's hatred that brings destruction, not dreams. Dreams are like love. They sustain and nourish." She looked deep into his shadowed eyes, fighting his powerful will, defying him to contradict her. "You'll never convince me otherwise. Never."

"Folly," he repeated with a shake of his head and took the food to the boy.

Adam untied Sammy so the lad could eat and left him unfettered after supper. It had grown dark, and the three sat around the cook fire. Sammy cowered in the shadows, but Adam demanded he stay within the glow where he could keep his eyes on him. He made Bethany sit even closer in the circle and kept himself and Constant between her and the Indian.

She had reapplied the herb poultices to a couple of her more swollen bruises, one on her left breast, the other on her stomach. She held the cold wet packs beneath the shirt and was thankful her other bruises and abrasions required no further attention. She was thankful, too, that Adam kept the fire going strong, for the night air had grown chill.

When she wiggled forward to be nearer to the warm flames, Adam adjusted his position likewise, maintaining his line of guard.

He's overprotective, she thought. Poor frightened Sammy posed no threat to her.

Adam began questioning the boy, and she listened with attention.

"How long were you with the trapper?"

"Four summers, five winters" came the reply.

So long a time? Tears pressed against Bethany's eyelids. She batted them away.

"What did he make you do?"

"Scout, mostly. Kill game, cook."

At least the poor soul had stopped stammering, Bethany thought.

"Did he abuse you?"

"M–many times."

She detected his stifled sob, and her heart constricted.

"Who sold you?"

"He took me. I had str–strayed into the forest."

"You're Shawnee?"

"Aye."

"From west of the Valley?"

"It was called by us the 'Valley of the Daughter of the Stars.' The great river ran through it."

"The Shenandoah," Adam said softly, as if to himself. He poked at the fire with a stick.

"Did your people attack the white settlers?"

Sammy shook his head. "Nay, Father, my family group were friends with the white men. They taught me your tongue."

Adam stared into the fire, then turned to Bethany. "He speaks the truth, I believe."

"Aye." She held back the sigh of relief, but she suspected her eyes were dancing with it.

"I will tie him tonight, to be certain, but I'll reconsider loosing him in the morn. It's likely he'll have to accompany us."

"Must you tie him?" The thought distressed her.

"Aye." He stood. "We must sleep. I dare not trust him this soon. The Shawnees are known for their trickery."

"But it appears truly unneeded. He's harmless."

"You're too quick with your trust, Bethany. I'm tying him." He tossed the stick into the fire and walked toward the boy.

She tightened her lips, flinched when he ordered Sammy to rise and go to a nearby oak. How would he be able to sleep lashed to a tree? *You're wrong,* she wanted to scream out to Adam. *You're being unjust.*

But she remained silent except for a fretful murmur of strong disapproval, which she doubted he could hear.

"Can you ride, Sammy?"

Adam's question to the boy floated back to her across the fire. The sounds of rope being wrapped around the tree tightened her chest.

"Aye, Father. I have a pony, back in the forest."

"Did the dead bastard have a mount?"

"Aye."

"We'll find them in the morn. You shall join us on our journey till we find a suitable home for you." His voice sounded woefully tired.

Thomasina Ring

A wave of sympathy for Adam washed over her. He now was burdened with two who were without homes. He had *two* to bother him now. Despite his untrusting nature, though, he was being considerate enough not to leave either Sammy or her alone in the wilderness. She supposed she should be comforted that he hadn't seen fit to tie her to trees every night.

She heard Adam's voice drift back to her. His next words softened her anxieties for Sammy. "I'm lashing only your wrists, and the rope's long enough so that you may lie down to sleep. Don't try to break loose, now. The dog will be watching you, and I sleep light."

"Aye, Father, I stay quiet." A rustle indicated the boy had lain on the dried brown leaves beneath the oak. "And thank you, Father. Have a good night."

When Adam returned to the fire, he was without his buckskin coat. Though he looked as stern as ever, she couldn't help but smile.

"That was kind of you," she said.

"Kind?" He didn't seem too delighted with the compliment.

"Aye, you were truly kind to allow him to lie to sleep and to give him warmth with your coat. He has such little covering, and it's cool this eve."

"You have little enough yourself," he grumbled. "Hardly a dram of fat and gristle on your bones and but the two pieces of thin clothing to cover that. We'll have to sleep near the fire this night for warmth."

She reached under the shirt and removed the poultices. They'd worked their magic, the swelling was nearly gone.

"Where's my clean nightdress?" she asked.

"Yon. I'll fetch it. Stay where you are."

He was gone from the fire's circle but a moment, then was back, handing her the nightdress. She felt a twinge of uneasiness. His eternal watchfulness was becoming difficult. She needed to dress, hadn't relieved herself in hours. Was he going to hover over her while she did *everything?*

She didn't know how to approach the subject of privacy. Perhaps it didn't truly matter, but a peevish voice inside her protested. She stood and fluffed out the nightdress.

"I'll put it on, I guess."

Adam didn't look interested in going anywhere. Her toes jiggled nervously inside the moccasins.

"I should change now, I suppose."

He didn't move. Damnation. Oh well, he was giving her no choice. She began unlacing her shirt.

He twirled around and faced the fire. Relaxing with a smile, she swiftly removed the shirt and pulled the nightdress over her head. It smelled clean, like his bayberry soap. Despite the temptation to pause for a moment and enjoy the luxury of fresh clothing against her skin, she hastily donned the soiled gray shirt for added covering.

"'Tis done," she said when she'd tightened the laces.

"I'll accompany you to the trees if you have need to . . ."

"I think I do," she said weakly. "But, Adam, I . . ."

"Come then."

She followed with reluctance.

He stood a decent distance away from her, but insisted that Constant guard her behind the bushes.

Bethany made a sour face in the darkness. Adam was becoming somewhat of a bother himself.

They had brought along the pallets from the cabin. Bethany squirmed fitfully on one; Adam lay quiet, apparently in deep slumber, on the other. An arm's distance separated the two.

Thomasina Ring

She couldn't sleep. Disturbing memories stormed through her groggy brain. She saw the leering trapper coming toward her, felt his clawing hands tear at her, smelled his abominable stench. She flopped over on her side and curled up her legs. He was still there, crouching, sneering. She groaned, beat the pallet with her fist, and knotted herself into a protective ball.

The mountain night resounded with mournful noises—drones of insects, the frightened whispers of leaves, the distant wail of a wolf, a whippoorwill's insistent cry like a woman in distress.

She clamped her hands over her ears and stared out into the darkness. The fire had grown low and she was cold. Would morning never come? She jerked around to her other side, squeezed her eyes shut, and coiled as tightly as she could.

Sleep stayed as distant as the thin crescent moon that hung in the midnight sky above.

She sat up, scowling. Shivering, she wrapped her arms across her chest, scrunched her shoulders, and kneaded her fingers through the sleeves of the shirt and her nightdress.

Beside her, Adam slept like a babe. *You'd think he lay under a wrapping of goose down, he looks so warm.* Maybe if she moved closer. . . .

Struggling to be quiet, she maneuvered her pallet nearer to his, only a hand's distance away this time, and already she felt warmer.

He radiated more heat than the fire. Settling down once again, she believed for sure she'd be able to sleep.

She fell asleep, but the terrible memories stampeded back upon her. Inky blackness opened to blotches of grimy wrinkles and bubbling foams of rank spittle. Yellow eyes squinted, leered. Slimy serpents—hundreds of them!—slithered toward her. Groping hands, scaly and big as tree trunks, grabbed at her. A deafening scream split the air.

"No! Dear God, no!" She thrashed and flailed, and then, suddenly, she was being pulled forward. Warm arms encircled her and she was enveloped with the scent of bayberry.

"I'm here," she heard. "Shhh, 'twas but a nightmare. You're safe. Go back to sleep."

Her pounding heart slowed to a soft rhythm. She smiled into the warmth, snuggled close to his strong chest.

"You're here," she breathed into the wonderful bayberry. She clasped her arms around him, nestled into his strength, and slept in deep peace at last, perfectly content.

For Adam, fully awake now, a long night loomed ahead. He didn't need this—this bundle of heated softness wrapped against him. He buried his face in her hair, a silky cloud of sweet-scented roses. *Cease these bedeviling thoughts,* he commanded himself. Her breasts nudged through his shirt and lit twin circles of fire on his chest. *Don't notice. Think of other things. Think of Wendover . . . of Albemarle . . . of the Indians. . . .*

Damn. Now they had Sammy with them—a bloody Indian boy to add to the already cumbersome caravan. Would this journey never end? As he frowned into the night, his hand slowly rubbed her back, and he drew her closer.

She nodded in her slumber and tightened her hold. *Dear God, does she know what's she's doing to me?*

No. She was so innocent she could have been born yesterday. But the full-blown ripeness pressing into him was a fierce reminder that, innocent as a babe or

133

not, she was an intensely desirable woman. He was ripening pretty thoroughly himself, he realized with growing discomfort. His aching groin was aflame, his shaft rising like a phoenix swollen with renewed life against his breeches. He stirred restlessly, ordered it to back down.

She sighed and wiggled closer, ensuring all too well that his order would go unheeded. Blighted devil, but he was in agony and there was naught he could do but remain where he was. The woman required the comfort of his presence, that was evident. Reasonable, too, considering the fright she'd had this day. But he was suffering the bloody torments of hell.

He knew it would take the strength of Hercules to resist her, to resist his own needs, but he was determined to do so. *Think of other things. Forget she's here. Ignore the way her sweet breath is whispering on my neck. Forget the alluring curves of her petal-soft body. . . .*

Defying his will, his rebellious hand slid down her back, cupped her buttocks through the thin nightdress. The shirt had worked its way up around her middle. Her rounded flesh burned into his palm. He groaned, stiffened. *Good Jesus, stop me.* He pulled away his hand, let it settle on the wadded clump of fabric at her waist. *Safer there,* he thought, *away from her flesh, away from her heat . . . away, please God, from my unholy desire to take advantage of this beautiful creature's trusting nature.*

A sliver of sanity stilled him. Adam Barwick had been a Titan in the frontier battles he'd been forced to fight, was a man without mercy when faced with evil but never had he been a beast. Never.

"You're safe," he murmured, cradling her head in his hand. "Safe as a babe in her nurse's arms."

But, dear Bethany, you must beware of being so trusting, his mind pleaded. *This world of ours too often smites those who dare to trust unwisely.*

It was a long while before he could fall asleep.

His hair had grown less dark and he was yet taller than before, but she knew he was her prince. "I am here," he said as always, and all else became the same— the floating upward to join him on his white horse, his arms even stronger around her, the gentle wind across her face. The throbbing pulse of the swift steed once again began its wondrous magic.

"Aye," she said. The multihued meadow beckoned to them. They were almost there. The beating pressure sent swollen waves through her, overlapping waves, like thick, heated honey. She clung, and a driving force impelled her to open wide to him.

"Aye," she breathed into his lips, "I am ready . . ."

"I am ready." Her voice, a sweet zephyr across his face, stroked Adam awake.

Dear God, she was there in his arms, so close their heartbeats had fused into one. Her leg was over his, her warm center throbbing with softness against his breeches . . . against, dear heaven, his swiftly swelling shaft.

She was ready, she had said. Ready? Well so, by God, was he!

Be gentle with her, he warned himself as he fumbled with his buttons between their tightly clasped bodies. The sweet heat between her legs warmed his fingers, drew them toward the moist spot of loveliness she was offering him. His breathing was shallow, and his hardened shaft pushed free from its unbuttoned prison. She was there opened to him, waiting for him, the small folds of her maidenhood

135

like a delicate blossom tipped with drops of nectar. His hand covered the blossom and he felt it quiver in response to his touch. Her desire pulsed near as strong as his and filled his veins with liquid fire.

She wanted him; he was mad with the wanting of her. Gentling her, he moved his hand slowly, savored the way she pressed herself upward against his palm, inviting more of him—all of him. *You shall have me, my sweet,* his heated brain promised, *but we must go slow for you. You must be made even readier before I . . . Be tender,* he commanded his fingers as they began their careful exploration of the dewy satin petals that unfolded beneath his touch till he found her tiny swollen button of passion. *Tender . . .* he reminded his thumb as it flicked back and forth across the little pulse that grew stronger, more rapid, began to rise to meet him.

Her moan was like a harp's string against his ear as her body arched toward him. His blood ran thick, hot with his flaming need for her. *Slow,* he repeated to his fingers, slickened now with her desire.

Her breath caressed his mouth. "Soon, my sweet," he whispered. As the tip of his tongue touched her honeyed lips, they parted for his kiss. He paused one thumping heartbeat and looked down at her upturned face. The first light of dawn was brushing them with its tenuous glow, and he ached to see the magical luster of desire in her gemstone eyes.

But they were closed to him. The dense lashes a sweep of shadows across her pale cheeks. Her face was at rest, its gentle peace defying the storm of passion raging within him, the convulsing storm beneath his fingers.

Dear God, she was asleep. She didn't know . . . she didn't know what she was . . . what he was. . . .

Adam groaned, low. Hastily, he removed his hand. Trying not to awaken her, he unraveled himself from her and bounded to his feet.

Bloody hell! He'd almost. . . .

He buttoned his breeches quickly and flung two hefty logs on the fire.

Chapter Ten

Damnation, Adam was truly in a foul temper. She'd never seen him so tense, so prompt with growls. All morning he'd issued clipped orders to her and the boy as he moved about with undue haste preparing for their day's journey.

Bethany was more than a little fidgety herself. She'd awakened that way, in fact; it had something to do with her dream, but she couldn't figure out what. She only knew there'd been a special promise of fulfillment, much stronger than ever before and then it had vanished in a whiff, leaving her tight as a drawn bowstring and strangely unsatisfied.

She fingered her amulet. *Why is the dream so different now?* She heard no answer, but Adam's impatient roars would have drowned out sounds far louder than her dream catcher's soft voice. He was commanding her to follow them as they hunted for Sammy's pony and the dead man's horse.

She bristled. Good grief, she needed a moment alone to consider the changes in the familiar vision, the strange changes she sensed happening within her body.

"Must I come?" she complained. "Constant can stay with me, and I should clean up the breakfast things."

"Come, woman. Cease your stubbornness."

"And who's the stubborn one?" she mumbled under her breath as she reluctantly moved forward.

The dream must be growing stronger because she was nearing the prince, she consoled herself before she joined them. Her heart leaped an extra beat; that was it, she was sure. She smiled inwardly. Adam's constant glower encouraged no open smiles.

They found the two mounts—Sammy's dun-colored pony and the trapper's dusty black stallion. The pony was obedient and gentle and appeared happy to see the boy; the restive bucking horse was as mean-spirited as its former owner. Bethany was terrified of it. Adam kept it under control with sharp words and vigorous handling, but she backed away with genuine fear from its angry snorts and raised hooves.

Both animals had packs on their backs stuffed with useful goods, much of it, according to Adam's grumbling assumption, "ill-gotten, I vow." They had blanket rolls, too. Blankets! The trapper's horse carried a long string of blood-matted beaver furs across its withers.

Adam's temper grew increasingly sour as the morning progressed. She wondered if she might somehow be the cause for his snappish mood. She'd likely been a terrible nuisance awaking him with her nightmare fright and then sleeping against him throughout the night. She had needed his strength, but perhaps she'd truly bothered his rest. That had never been her intent.

"I'm sorry if I disturbed your sleep, Adam," she ventured when they were ready to depart.

He responded with a low grunt as he placed her up on the front of the chestnut with far less gentleness than she'd become accustomed to.

Oh my, she fretted, this day boded not well—not well at all.

"Is the old Indian trace atop the ridges nearby, Sammy?" Adam asked when they'd been under way for an hour or so. His few words thus far had been addressed only to the boy, who rode back behind the animals. She seemed to have disappeared entirely from his mind.

"Aye, Father. Beyond the next crest, about five furlongs farther."

"Why does he call you 'Father'?" she inquired, unwilling to sit like a stump the whole day. She longed to know what a "trace" was, too.

"They consider it a term of respect."

"Oh." She looked back at him. His eyes were focused well over her head, his face a hard-set mask of disgruntlement. She'd have to find out about traces another time.

Adam held the chestnut's reins with his left hand. With his right, he kept a firm grip on the reins of the dead trapper's unruly black stallion. Bethany, sitting sideways as usual, was glad the ill-tempered steed was behind her, out of her line of vision, but she couldn't forget its presence. She heard its frequent snorts and could tell by Adam's ongoing jerks of restraint and harsh words that it was a mighty handful.

Adam's left arm, a protective barrier across her middle, was steady as a rock. His sleeve was rolled up, and for a long while she occupied herself by counting the sunlit golden hairs on the large expanse of his bronzed arm. She'd only learned her numbers through nine and ten, so she had to begin back with one numerous times, and then she'd lose her place.

It was a bit like counting stars in the heavens, she thought, wondering why she found the exercise fascinating rather than boring.

Eventually, the passage through the trees widened enough for Sammy to move forward to ride beside them. She ceased her endless counting and began watching the young Indian with interest. His sleek body held the softness of youth, but he sat stiffly erect in his saddle, and she could denote signs of latent strength that would develop someday into cords of muscle and sinew, not perhaps the equal of the arm that now lay across her, but something near. His long hair was stick-straight and blacker than a crow's wing.

She felt a warming kinship with the youth, sensing that perhaps he might become her friend. A slight jolt of the chestnut jostled her hip backward against Adam's rock-hard thigh, and she detected his tight constriction before she could jiggle away. She frowned concentrating on Sammy again. She was sorely in need of a friend.

Adam had let the Indian retrieve his bow, and it hung now from the boy's saddle. A bag of sharp arrows was across his shiny copper shoulders.

Bethany envied him. She missed her own bow and had longed to fashion a new one for herself, but there had been so little time on the journey. Besides, she figured Adam would never allow her to have one. Pa had called her practice with the bow "wasted time for a worthless woman." Adam, she suspected, would be of like mind.

Thomasina Ring

"Your bow is a sturdy one," she said to Sammy.

The boy smiled with pride. "I made it from a strong hickory."

"Do you shoot well?" It felt good to have someone who would talk to her and his smile warmed the frosty air around her considerably.

"Aye, I never miss."

"Are you swift, too?"

He nodded, and his face broke into a wider smile. "As swift as the hawk's flight."

"I shot two within three caws of a crow once," she said, remembering the joy she'd felt that afternoon which seemed so long ago.

Sammy looked at her, his mouth agape. "Did you shoot them true?"

She nodded. "Aye, true," she said with a small surge of satisfaction.

Adam's stern voice punched away the surge. "Are you sure the trace is ahead?"

She obviously was still invisible to him; he was speaking only to Sammy. A sullen fog threatened to cloak her, but she did some punching of her own to keep it away. She saw no need to let him control her moods along with everything else.

Adam and Sammy talked on about furlongs and traces, which were incomprehensible to her, so she shut her ears and directed her mind elsewhere. The buds were less open here, only a tinge of fair colors peeked from the tips of green, but their glorious promise of full blossoming was apparent to eyes willing to see it.

The clouds puffed ever-changing shapes, and she watched them for signs. There was another fat pig promising food aplenty; a great log house with a jeweled roof promising shelter; a downy pallet promising soft rest. Good signs, all of them, and they calmed her. The air was fresher. They'd come higher, were nearing the crest of the blue mountains that weren't blue, after all.

Her brow crinkled. So little was as she had dreamed. The amulet pulsed against her chest. *But it will be*, it crooned. *It will be.*

When they reached the Indian trace, she saw it was a weathered path, nearly as rugged and rolling as where they'd been, but cleared enough for easier passage. Adam headed them south, toward the bright yellow sun that hung high before them. Sitting as she was, facing east, Bethany felt the warming rays against her right cheek. Sammy had brought his horse up on Adam's other side and rode behind the restless black horse, helping Adam in small ways to quiet the animal.

Giant outcroppings of rock and tall pines bordered the path and loomed before her. Occasionally there would be an opening, and she could see groupings of lower mountains, lush in their dark greenness, and now and then she spotted great stretches of land beyond—flatland, by the looks of it, that spread to the distant horizon like a huge patchwork quilt tinted with a breathtaking variety of more tender greens. A blue mist lay suspended over the quilt's end.

Was that the Tidewater? She glanced back at Adam to ask him, but his gaze was as distant as the far blue mist and intensely deeper. She held her tongue.

But she couldn't control her eyes. The sun bathed Adam's face with a luminous glow. A thin web of lines radiated across his bronzed temples before disappearing beneath the golden halo of his wavy hair.

Her fingers tingled with an urge to trace through the lines, to smooth them with her touch and then to wander back through the thickness of that rich, tawny hair. She was suddenly warm and wiggled on the saddle.

"Do you need to stop?" he asked. He didn't sound too pleased.

She shook her head and stared ahead at a gray wall of limestone. "Nay, I'm fine, thank you."

But was she? What in heaven's name was happening to her?

They stopped for a short rest around noon. Bethany rubbed her saddle-worn bottom and welcomed the opportunity to stretch the kinks out of her limbs.

Adam tied the stormy black stallion to a tree away from the other animals. He allowed Bethany to go behind the bushes escorted only by Constant, but his giant shadow hovered nearby.

He offered his canteen of refreshing, cold water to both her and Sammy before drinking from it himself and then he passed it around again. She was heartened to note the ride had worked away some of his grumpiness. His eyes had softened, and though he said little, his growls had lifted to a more normal huskiness. Even his tensed mouth had loosened some, and once, when a splash of water from the canteen dribbled onto her chin, it curved upward in a near smile. The fullness of his bottom lip intrigued her. It looked moist and pillowy.

Under the spell of his vastly improved temper, Bethany's own tension relaxed. The already-bright day turned exceedingly brighter.

"How far would we be from Rockfish Gap?" Adam asked the boy.

She sat happily on a rock, no longer bothered that he talked more to Sammy than to her. That near smile and softer expression made her know she wasn't invisible to him. Why that pleased her so much, she couldn't say, and she was far too placid at the moment to search for a reason.

"A great distance yet, Father. At our pace, the moon will grow full and wane to darkness and wax near to half-size before we reach it."

"Three weeks?" he said with a groan.

Sammy nodded. "We move very slow."

Adam frowned, but reached down to rub Constant's neck. He poured a big dollop of water in the cup of his huge hand for the dog, who lapped it up with loud slurps, wagging his tail all the while.

Bethany smiled. He'd grown fond of her dog.

"Then we should start riding again soon," Adam said. "I'll check the ties on the animals yon, you two remain here and continue your rest. And stay close to one another. Sammy, watch over the lady. You too, Constant."

Her smiling eyes followed him as he walked toward the long train of animals that trailed behind the chestnut. Patsy, the mare, was first in line, then Churning, the milk cow, and, at the end, the sluggish ox, Henry.

The mean stallion, away from the rest and tied to a gnarled black walnut, strained at his ropes. Would the animal never tire? Her confidence that Adam could control him soothed her.

Sammy's soft voice broke into her rambling thoughts. "Did you truly shoot two within three caws?"

Bethany jumped, then looked at the boy and chuckled. "Aye, that I did."

"Could you show me how?"

She stood. "I've had no practice in days, but I'd love to try."

"Here, take my bow and arrows. I'll be the crow, you aim"—his raven-dark eyes surveyed the area—

"aim at that dead pine branch yon."

The bow was longer and sleeker than hers had been, and she relished the feel of it. With enthusiasm, she hung the bag of arrows across her back.

"May I have one practice shot?" she asked.

"Aye."

After placing the nock of the well-crafted arrow in the bowstring, she closed one eye and pulled her arm back, aiming carefully. The string was taut between her fingers, and the smooth wood and prickly feather of the arrow nestled with familiar comfort against them. She held her breath. *Now.* The arrow flew true and stuck fast into the target branch. A frightened flock of sparrows lifted from the pine, filling the air with their beating wings and startled cries. Constant let out a bark of joy.

Bethany and Sammy laughed. "That was surely true," the boy complimented her. "Now that you've practiced, show me your speed."

"Aye," she said, her heart quickening with the excitement of the challenge. "I'll rearm first, then you set the pace with your cawing and, mind you, make it neither faster nor slower than the black crow's."

Sammy began, so near to the sound of a crow that she looked at him in amazement, then grew tense, concentrating on the rhythm.

"Caw . . . caw . . . caw . . ."

The arrow flew with a resounding thump into the branch. Her hand shot back for the next arrow.

"Caw . . . caw . . ."

Wild turmoil broke out behind her—a ferocious whinny, an angry shout. She twirled around. The black horse had broken free, reared on its hind legs, its strong front legs thrashing high and poised to crash down on . . . *Adam*! Adam was trapped, on the ground beneath. . . .

She had no time to think. The armed bow was already pulled taut and she aimed at the black beast's neck and let the arrow fly.

Sammy gasped, the horse bellowed, dark blood spewed, Adam scrambled away from the crushing hooves. Bethany stood rigid, not breathing. For a frozen moment, everything was as still as death. Her heart thumped a maddened, rapid drumbeat that threatened to choke her.

She dropped the bow and ran toward Adam.

He was on his feet, his face and clothing covered with the stallion's spurting blood. The animal lay behind him on its side, quivering, its black eyes bulging and streaked with red.

"Get back!" he ordered her.

She stopped, watched stunned as he pulled the long rifle from his back, loaded it with powder and aimed at the dying beast's head. The blast of the rifle shocked the charged air and echoed against the rocks and surrounding mountains.

Her hand fluttered to her beating chest. "Dear God, are you all right, Adam?"

He wiped his face with his sleeve. "Aye. How did Sammy shoot so quick . . ."

"The lady shot, Father, not I."

Adam stared at her. The horse's gore dripped from his thick eyebrows, from his once-tawny beard and hair. "The lady?" He blinked away the blood and once again wiped his sleeve across his face. The smoking rifle dangled from his other arm.

"I owe you my life," he said at last. "Thank you, Bethany."

He turned around. Tears flooded her eyes.

"And I owe you mine," she whispered as he went to comfort the disturbed train of animals. She didn't know if he had heard her.

147

Chapter Eleven

Bethany snuggled beneath the blanket Sammy had given her and held her new bow close to her chest. Though sleep had come easier recently, it was keeping a pesky distance tonight. Too many fascinating thoughts scurried about her brain.

Nothing had been the same these past few days. She smiled, recounting the wondrous changes in her life since that frightening afternoon when she'd shot the crazed horse.

Adam's new attitude toward her had colored her world with the radiant hues of a rainbow. No longer did he restrict her to his addled idea of "woman's work," and the two of them, along with Sammy, had become a true team.

She indeed appreciated Adam's open approval. It made her see she *did* have courage, *did* have a good mind, and *could* do some things well.

And she had two companions now—two real friends. Before, she'd never had an opportunity to have even one.

Aye, there'd been many exciting changes. Her bow was only the latest. She drew it closer, savoring the curved strength of the smooth wood. Sammy had made it for her at Adam's suggestion.

"She should have her own," he'd said to the boy several nights ago. "We'll stop earlier tomorrow so you can begin fashioning one for her."

They'd stopped earlier each day after that and even paused for rest more often during the shortened journeys. Adam's impatient haste had seemingly vanished and so, too, had his hard-as-granite temperament.

He'd started teaching her things! He was teaching Sammy, too. When he'd learned that neither knew their numbers beyond nine and ten—*nineteen,* she reminded herself—he'd taught them through a hundred, then up to a thousand.

She still lost track, though, when she would idly try to count the hairs on his arm as they rode. Once she had attempted to hold her place with the tip of her finger—with the lightest touch—and he had jerked away his arm as though her finger had been a red-hot fire tong.

She'd been more guarded about such careless actions since then. Adam didn't cotton to being touched and she didn't find it too all-fired comfortable, either. Even their inevitable brushes against each other on the mount had begun unleashing those bothersome tingles.

Frowning, she squirmed under the blanket. Good heavens, those tingles were a continuing puzzlement. What on earth could be causing them?

She directed her thoughts down a different path.

He was teaching them letters, too. He'd draw them in the dirt with a pointed stick during their long afternoons. Both she and Sammy knew the whole alphabet now, and this day he'd shown them how to put a few together to make words. "Dog," they'd learned. "Cow" and "Ox." Next came "Sammy" and "Bethany" and "Adam."

"Adam" she'd liked best of all. It looked as strong as it sounded. She had scratched it in the dirt numerous times—twenty-two, she'd counted when he had questioned why she'd written such a great long row of his name.

"See, I'm practicing my numbers at the same time," she'd quickly told him. Her face grew warm, just as it had this afternoon. She didn't know herself why she'd done it.

She and Sammy would be able to read and write, he'd told them. She loved learning all she could and words were especially wonderful to know, though she couldn't figure out why people would ever need to read and write. Scratching words in the dirt took such time and effort while speaking the things were far simpler and quicker.

Nevertheless, she looked forward to tomorrow's lessons. There were so many words to learn to spell, and she wanted to know them all. If Adam believed it important they be able to read and write, that was reason enough for her.

In fact, *anything* Adam believed important sounded reasonable these days. Oh dear, *he'd* become truly important to her—too important, perhaps, for he would be leaving her behind without a fare-thee-well when they found folk willing to take her. Sammy, too, maybe, though he'd never discussed the matter with either of them.

Several times she'd noted puffs of smoke in the

nearby hills and she'd find herself praying he wouldn't turn toward them.

He hadn't, but someday they were bound to run across a closer settlement—and what then? Her dream catcher's message had been clear of late. She was to find her prince *beyond* the mountains; should she be left within them, she'd have to find a way to go on by herself, if need be.

Damnation, she'd had so little time to talk with Adam about the things she believed he needed help with—that pent-up anger with the man in the Tide-water who had deceived him, for example.

She feared for Adam. Revenge, as she'd told him this eve as they'd relaxed by the cook fire, could only destroy the spirit.

He'd mumbled an objection, showing a hint of his former stubbornness, and his private anger glowed as hot in his eyes as before.

"Being too forgiving is far more dangerous, Bethany," he'd said. "Bowing and bending to evil can only create additional evil."

She prayed he'd see otherwise before he left her and that she could be assured somehow that he would steer himself from his destructive goal.

She wrapped her hand around her dream catcher. *Please help Adam find peace without having to kill the man who tricked him.*

The tiny pulses through the leather were a soothing lullaby, quieting her fevered thoughts. Adam was indeed a highly special man. She hoped he'd be pleased tomorrow when she and Sammy sprang their little surprise.

At last, with a soft smile on her lips, she fell asleep.

"Step up on the rock here, set your left foot in the stirrup, hold to the mane with your left hand, the saddle's pommel with your right. Then reach up with your right leg and push yourself up and . . . mmph, there you go . . . across him. See how easy it is? Want to try it without my help?" Adam could sense Bethany's apprehension at being astride the chestnut, but it was time she learn to ride a true horse.

She'd already conquered the pony. Sammy had taught her without his knowledge, and they'd astounded him this morning at the start of their journey. There she was atop the little animal ready to ride beside him, her big green eyes sparkling her triumph.

"I can ride," she'd said proudly. His amazement must have done fierce things to his expression, for she flushed and her hands tightened on the reins. "If you don't mind, that is?" Her voice dropped along with her thickly lashed eyelids.

"No, of course I don't mind, but are you sure? How the devil did you . . ."

The emerald eyes dazzled up at him. "Sammy taught me. I was quick to learn, and I'm damnably good, he says."

He expected she was. She'd been quick and damnably good with everything he'd taught her. But he couldn't stop the twist of regret from quirking his mouth. Sammy had taught her; he should have thought to do so himself.

"Ladies don't say damnably," he'd chastised mildly.

"Then I'm bloody good."

He had made a face. "Nor do they say bloody."

Her lips puckered into a rosebud pout. "Then I don't think I want to be a lady. What is one, anyway?"

He'd laughed. "A lady is a gentle woman, Bethany. It's true you'd find it a strain."

One thin copper eyebrow arched. "I assume the world has found no need to form a word for a gentle man, since I'm sure there are none."

"They're called simply 'gentlemen,' and there may be one or two out there. My father was one."

The light sprinkling of freckles on the tip of her pert nose had wiggled as she lifted it with a haughty sniff. "Tis a quality that doesn't run in families, I vow."

Sammy, sitting atop Patsy, had come up to them then, interrupting their genial sparring, and they'd started the day's journey.

Adam couldn't help but smile. Lord, but she'd altered since they'd set out on their journey. She'd been an untamed hellion at first, then like a frightened mouse, confounding him all the while with her disarming beauty and incredible innocence. He cringed still at the discomforting memory of how near he'd come to violating that innocence.

As he watched her bravely adapt to the chestnut's greater girth, he told her to hold on to the pommel while he led the horse at a slow pace. "Get the feel of it beneath you," he said.

Her teeth worked at her bottom lip, but her enchanting eyes looked down at him with a heart-stopping quantity of trust. "I'm ready," she said.

He started walking the animal, looking straight ahead.

"Why, it's far less bumpy than the pony," she said at last, as they headed back toward their campsite.

"At a walk, perhaps. At a faster gait, you'd think otherwise, and I'll need to teach you how to accommodate to the quicker rhythms with your legs and—uh—posterior."

"Posterior?"

"Bottom."

"Oh."

He glanced at her. She had a bemused expression he couldn't decipher.

"I believe I should know that. Could you teach me now?"

Blighted devil, what had he got himself into? His fingers reached to loosen his collar only to find he'd removed his shirt hours ago for her regular washing routine.

How in hell should he begin? "Well," he started, his mind still searching, "what you do is push down on the stirrups and tighten your calves, knees, and thighs, ready to . . ."

"Thighs?"

He wanted to groan. "The inner part of your legs, here," he pointed to his own, hoping she wouldn't notice the bulge that was forming in his breeches. Too often of late he was afflicted with nettlesome arousals over the merest of trifles, it seemed.

"See, your feet are there firm in the stirrups. I've adjusted them for you. Keep your heels down, toes up. You rise when the horse is down; you lower when his back rises. By using the strength in your—uh—inner legs you keep your—uh—bottom from being battered."

She looked puzzled. "Could you show me?"

"I could demonstrate, I suppose." Good idea. The exercise would be a needed diversion. "Here, I'll help you practice your dismount, then I'll take a turn and you can watch."

He bent to help her slip her left foot out of the stirrup, but before he could give her proper instructions as he'd intended, she'd swung her right leg across the front of the horse.

"No, no, bring that leg over the back, and back down," he warned her, but she'd already started sliding off with unstoppable momentum. He freed her foot from the stirrup in the nick of time and had to grab for her with both hands to brace her fall.

Her nightdress and shirt rose as she slid down, and he found his hands holding first a pair of silky hips, then a narrow waist, and finally the warmed hollows under her arms.

He had halted her descent, but her toes dangled above the ground.

"Are you all right?" he asked, knowing at once *he* wasn't. The entire front of her bared lush body pressed against him, the curves of the sides of her tempting breasts nuzzling against his thumbs, their soft tips pushing into the skin of his chest. Every nerve in his body sparked alive and began a headstrong dash in one direction, forward.

He held her suspended for a long breathless moment as he struggled to spur himself into sensible action. He knew he could do naught but ease her down to her feet, and he did, at last, but the final two inches of descent, as she slid over his aching bulge was both agony and intense pleasure.

"Good heavens," she spluttered, "I didn't do that at all well, did I?" Her clothing was clumped around her neck like a disheveled ruff. Her lively eyes gleamed with humor at her awkward position and showed not a trace of embarrassment.

"Ummm" was all he could say. How could she be oblivious to the torment she was causing him? Two contradictory urges bedeviled him—to pull away quickly; to stay exactly where he was till he died. Which could be damn soon, he realized with crunching discomfort.

He pulled away.

With a flurry, she straightened her clothes. "What a mess I am," she complained. "Now you will go on with your lessons, won't you?"

"Lessons?" His brain had stopped working.

"The horse . . . the inner leg and posterior thing you were going to show me."

"Oh." Hell, he was beginning to sound like her.

He wasn't sure it was safe for him to mount, considering his condition, but he jumped up on the horse, anyway, praying he wouldn't damage himself for life.

Bethany attempted to concentrate on his movements as he trotted before her on the chestnut, but she was distracted. For one thing, his breeches were all lumped out in the front in a peculiar fashion. She feared she might have given him a bad bruise when she'd fallen against him. Then, too, those blasted tingles had attacked her again and lingered yet. Perhaps she should make herself a purging potion of feverwort before this annoying condition worsened.

"Did you see how I rose and fell against the horse's rhythm?"

She jumped, he'd stopped right in front of her.

"What?" she asked, flustered.

"My movements, did you note them?"

Thank heavens, his bruise had lost its swelling. "I'm sorry, Adam, you were going too fast, I believe. I couldn't note, truly."

"Bloody hell, woman, I have to bring the horse to a trot to show you properly. Pay attention."

Again, he'd grown short-tempered with her.

"I was just concerned about your bruise, I guess," she said in the way of an apology. She saw no need to mention the tingles.

"My bruise?"

"There." She pointed. "It seems to have healed on its own well enough, but should it flare up again, I'll make a poultice for it."

His bottom lip curled and the corners of his mouth twitched as if he might be trapping a runaway laugh.

What, she wondered, could be humorous about a simple expression of concern?

"Show me again, I promise to be more attentive," she said.

He did, and she was.

It looked easy enough, and she itched to try it. He gave instructions all the while, "As the horse's right leg and shoulder move forward, lift up from the knees, partially stand with more weight in the stirrups, heels down. When his left leg and shoulder start forward, go down. With practice, the rhythms become natural and require no real thought."

He brought the horse back to her and dismounted. "Ready to try? No trotting today, mind you, just test the motions while the horse stands still." She was pleased he'd become the old Adam again—the *new* Adam, she corrected herself.

She was fired with determination to master today's lesson. Mount, perform a simple set of movements, and then dismount properly, without his help if she could manage. She loved basking in his glow of approval when she conquered a new task with ease.

"Stand back a ways, I want to mount without your assistance." He stayed within grasping range, but that bothered her not at all. Her confidence wasn't nearly as strong as her determination—not yet, anyway.

His earlier instructions marched in an orderly row through her head. *Stand on rock, left foot in stirrup, hold with left hand on mane, right on pommel, right leg over . . . push up.* "Ooof."

She'd done it! She beamed down at him, and his nod of approval stamped a handsome seal over her success.

"Good work," he added needlessly, but she loved hearing it.

She reached for the reins and relished the feel of the

sturdy leather in her hands. Adam moved in closer, cautioning her that she was to keep the horse still.

Because she was perched up on the mount, her eyes were level with his. Such a pleasant face he had. She experienced a sudden wild craving to rub her cheek into his beard. Could it possibly be as soft as it looked? Instead, she squeezed her knees into the horse's sides.

The chestnut moved forward, but Adam quickly grabbed the reins and turned the animal's head to stop him.

"Ho there, Nutmeg. I said to keep him *still*, Bethany."

"Is that his name, Nutmeg? I didn't know he had one." She was sorry she'd upset Adam, but it wasn't her fault the horse had decided to start going.

"His name is Nutmeg, and you're to sit quiet up there or I'll pull you off this instant."

"Don't shout, please."

"I'm not shouting!" he shouted.

"You're scaring Nutmeg, Adam." No, he was scaring her; the horse was receiving tender pats on his neck and warm assurances.

She received nothing but a scowl. Adam's tone had moderated when he spoke again, but his words were less than warming. "I should never have started this fool lesson. Women aren't supposed to ride astride, anyway."

"They aren't? Why on earth not?"

"It's not considered proper."

She looked down and saw her knees were showing, but they'd done that off and on all day when she'd been astride the pony and Adam hadn't uttered any complaint. She adjusted her clothing to hide her knees best as she could.

"How do women ride, then?"

"Sidesaddle."

She screwed up her face. "That's highly impractical, I vow. I much prefer to ride as men do." She hoped he'd agree to continue his lesson, but he took his own good time coming to a decision. She waited, striving for patience.

As he contemplated, he ran his finger slowly back and forth across his full bottom lip. She watched the steady movement with fascination until she realized her tongue was following along, running back and forth over the inside of her own bottom lip. *Damnation, there go those tingles again*. She almost forgot what she was waiting for.

"I guess you're right," he said with a tired sigh, jolting her mind back into focus. "Astride is far more efficient, and under our circumstances, propriety is hardly necessary."

Well, that was settled, thank heavens. She smiled her victory. "Let's see if I have it straight."

She went through the routine several times on the quietly standing horse. "His right moves, my heels down, I tighten calves, knees and whatchamacallits to lift up bottom. His left moves, I sit."

"Once more, keep your back good and straight. That's it, and relax your upper body more." He prodded her ribs gently. "Good, keep loose like that, and you'll feel the horse's motions."

Loose? She was downright limp. She squirmed on the saddle, frustrated. How could she understand the instructions when the horse sat still as a stone? "I'll never get it right till you let me bring him to a trot so I can truly feel the motions," she complained.

"Tomorrow, maybe. You've learned enough today."

He was right, she supposed. She was finding it difficult to concentrate. She must be getting tired.

He insisted on helping her dismount, but at least

she came down the right way this time. When his hands circled her waist, the tingling returned.

Worrisome, she fretted. She decided to look for feverwort right away.

The feverwort purge was a mistake. Bethany groaned with agony most of the night and feared she was losing her entire insides.

"Did you eat something we didn't?" Adam asked with concern after she'd returned from the bushes for what must have been her tenth trip. His solicitude should have been a comfort, but nothing was a comfort. She wanted to die.

"Don't bother me," she said with a moan and yanked the blanket over her head. Another severe cramp knotted her gut and she pulled her knees up and started rocking to fight the pain.

He pulled the blanket away from her face and pressed his big warm hand against her forehead. "You've no fever. Haven't you any idea what could be causing your throes?"

"Go away, let me die." She meant it.

"No, damn it, come here."

Damnation, but he was bullheaded. He lay down behind her, unpinned her knees from her chest, and drew her back against him. She tried to re-curl her legs, but the flat of his hand was pressing on her stomach.

"There now, does that help?"

"Nothing helps," she groaned.

"Shhh. It will, try to relax."

Relax? Not bloody likely with her stomach stuffed with knotted clumps of rigid rope. She winced as another spasm hit, tightening the rope. His warm palm pressed and the hard lump melted beneath his touch.

Again it happened—pain, tightened lump, warm press, gone. Again, and yet again. Bethany was too weak to resist his ministering. And so, too, apparently, was her malady. Gradually, the spasms became less frequent, less fierce, and then, at last, they disappeared. Her stomach unknotted beneath his hand, became smooth and quiet.

She stretched out her legs and leaned back against him.

"'Tis gone, I believe."

"Are you sure?"

As she nodded, she felt his chin on the top of her head. Her matted hair was entangled in his silky beard. A stray tingle wiggled across her scalp, and she frowned.

"Damnation," she said with a moan of frustration. "The blasted things continue yet, and I nearly killed myself trying to purge them."

With renewed anxiety, Adam pressed his palm against her stomach. "Continuing yet?" he inquired. Dear God, what was attacking her? But he felt no recurring knots, her stomach was flat and smooth.

Hold a minute, did she say purge? *Purge?* He raised up on his elbow and looked down at her. Long strands of copper hair clung to her moist face. She was on her side. Her eyes were closed, but the lids flickered.

"You took a purge? What, for God's sake and why on earth did you do such a thing?"

She rolled over on her back. The nearby fire cast an orange glow on her widened eyes.

"I took a potion of feverwort, Adam. It often cleanses peculiar ailments."

Fresh concern for her stiffened him. "You've had an ailment? Why haven't you told me?"

She sat up, pushed her hair behind her ears, and sighed. She stared into the fire. "It seemed small, not worthy of note, but it's become increasingly annoying."

He was determined to find out what had afflicted her. After all, he was responsible for her well-being.

"How does it manifest?" He'd seen no signs of ailing. She'd been as spry as a colt since he'd met her.

She shrugged. "It's hard to explain. A mite like unbeckoned shivers running hither and yon, only deep inside. Once when I was a young girl I ate some wild berries and I got all itchy, and Mama gave me a feverwort potion and the itching ceased right away, so I—"

"Are you plagued now by the shivers?" he interrupted, his concern making him impatient. Lord, she'd talk the ears off an elephant.

She was still a moment. "No, not a one, but they come and—"

"You must tell me if you ever feel them again. Do you promise?" Hell, he didn't know what he would do about it, but he should know if she was suffering and if they ever found a settlement, perhaps there would be a physician.

"Do you promise?" he repeated.

She nodded. The flames bathed her porcelain-pale face with its flickering light, the shadows of her dark lashes framed her oval eyes. Without warning, she turned those eyes toward him, and her searching gaze locked into his. His heart turned a lopsided somersault.

"It's nothing, I'm sure," she said. Her whisper was barely audible.

Why couldn't he pull away? "I hope not, but you must tell me if the shivers return." His own voice sounded distant to him, as if spoken through gauze—green gauze, soft, incredibly beguiling green gauze that wrapped around him, pulling him toward. . . .

She blinked, releasing him. Shaken, he drew back.

"I felt one," she said.

"Felt what?" Wisps of green yet clouded his brain. Her brows pulled together. "One of them, a shiver, just then, when you . . ."

"Did it hurt?" Concern had cleared his head. Dear God, don't let her be truly ill.

"No, just peculiar. It was deep, down low, and not a shiver, really, for it wasn't cold. More of a tingle it was and definitely warm. I can't imagine what causes it."

Comprehension hit him with an unsettling wallop. Adam stood quickly. He didn't know whether to laugh or cry. Doing neither, he poked at the fire.

"It sounds like a minor ague, Bethany," he said at last, carefully avoiding her eyes. "I wouldn't worry about it if I were you and, please, dear woman, don't take another purge for it."

"Believe me, I won't. The purge was far worse than the blasted tingles." She rose and with a grimace dashed back into the bushes.

Adam shook his head and looked with consternation into the fire. "Blasted tingles?" he murmured with a faint smile before puffing a huge sigh. *Aye, a feverwort purge is not the remedy for those, dear Bethany.*

He threw the stick into the flames and grew deeply sober.

Nor, he knew, must he ever allow himself to believe that he should be the remedy.

He ran his fingers through his hair. Dear God, they *must* find a settlement soon as this situation was fast becoming impossible.

Chapter Twelve

Sammy spotted the cabin first. He'd ridden ahead on Patsy to scout while Bethany and Adam lumbered along with the animal train.

"There are folk up yon," he announced with excitement after returning at something surprisingly close to a gallop.

Adam pulled the chestnut to a halt. "What kind of folk?"

Sammy shook his head. "Don't know, saw the cabin only. There's smoke from the chimney."

Bethany, who'd stopped the pony alongside Adam, felt her heart sink.

"How far?" Adam asked the boy.

"Round the bend. The cabin's just down off the trace a ways."

Adam looked thoughtful. "We'll approach with care.

You two ride behind me. As we near, dismount and stay hidden behind the trees. Sammy, cover me with your bow."

"I'll cover, too," Bethany said, a mite irked he hadn't included her.

He hesitated before nodding his assent. "Get back now, both of you, and watch for my signal to dismount." As he started forward slowly, he tossed a final command over his shoulder. "Sammy, take care of her if something goes wrong."

Sammy sat taller on the mare, proud as a turkey cock. Bethany peppered Adam's back with a nasty look. She was a far better shot than Sammy, and Adam knew it and knew, too, that she'd be the one who would be doing the caretaking should something go wrong.

Should something go wrong. Her palms grew moist against the leather reins. Why would Adam even think of such a thing? Why, he could defeat a horde of armed men with one hand tied behind his back, and with her and Sammy protecting him, he'd prevail against any number of unfriendly folk.

She gripped the reins tightly. But suppose they welcomed him? Had it happened at last? Had they come upon folk who might be willing to take her off his hands? Apprehension clutched her. They were in the mountains still. She wasn't ready to have Adam leave her behind, not nearly ready.

He stopped ahead, dismounted, and tied the chestnut. With his finger pressed against his lips, he signaled to them, then began walking down the the hill.

After tying their animals and grabbing their bows, she and Sammy ran to follow him. Constant tagged along at Bethany's heels.

"Keep low," Sammy whispered.

Her throat was too tight with tension to remind the boy that she'd started ducking before he'd thought of it.

Crouching behind a tree, she watched Adam approach the cabin. She armed her bow, finding herself hoping someone vicious like Jake the trapper would come storming out. The three of them could dispense with that kind of threat with ease.

But she knew at once with heartrending certainty that wasn't going to happen. The cabin was set in a tidy clearing. A neat string of laundered garments hung between two trees—a woman's dress and clothing for a lad alongside a man's shirt and breeches. Savory cooking aromas drifted on the smoke from the chimney.

Though she stayed alert, her senses told her Adam wouldn't be needing her help. They'd found a settlement. Good folk, probably. She was likely seeing her future home, and she wanted to cry.

"Ho there," she heard Adam shout as he stood outside the door. "We're friendly wayfarers, would you welcome us?"

He, too, must have noticed the signs of tranquil habitation. His arms were relaxed by his sides.

A man came to the door, and Bethany tensed, drawing back the bowstring. He was tall and slender with tawny hair near the color of Adam's. When she saw the stranger's smile was as broad as the door and heard his hearty greeting, she lowered the bow with a fretful moan.

Good heavens, with the warm handshakes and slaps on shoulders, one would think they'd known each other since childhood.

Adam pointed up to the trace and back to the trees where she and Sammy still hid, and she heard bits of what he was saying, "Be beholden . . . train of animals . . . young Indian . . . wearisome journey . . . woman . . ."

That she'd come last didn't improve her mood.

"Come on out, Sammy and Bethany," Adam called. "David here tells me we're welcome and have shelter for the night."

Sammy seemed as reluctant as she was to move forward. He looked at her with eyes as round as a bird's nest. She motioned that they should comply and led him out from the trees.

But when she saw the woman, she stopped in her tracks. Sammy, following so close that he bumped into her, stopped, too.

Bethany couldn't believe her eyes. Though dressed in calico and apron, the woman apparently was Indian. Her skin glowed copper like Sammy's, her hair, black as pitch, laid in two long braids over her slender shoulders.

She was beautiful, and her smile was open and full of tenderness, but Bethany was hesitant to go closer.

"Come on, you two. Mister Owens and his wife want to greet you."

Though Adam's soft command spurred her feet ahead in tentative steps, her mind wanted to rush back behind the trees. Sammy matched his pace with hers, staying directly behind her.

Was Adam going to leave her with an Indian woman?

The introductions were brief. Bethany stood straight and clasped her hands in front of her, wishing she had something sturdier to hang on to. Her knees shook beneath the nightdress, but the stonelike clot of apprehension lodged in her chest held her upright and rigid.

Their names were David and Mina Owens, and they had a son named Jonathan. Bethany didn't see him right away; he hid behind his mama, much the way Sammy attempted to hide behind her.

"Come, my dear, we'll find clothing for you and the boy," the Indian woman was saying, reaching out for her hand.

Her touch, voice, and smile would soften stone itself, Bethany realized, but she still couldn't move. She looked to Adam for directions.

He nodded, and his dark eyes sent her a message of reassurance, melting her resistance. "Go with her, Bethany. She will care for you and Sammy."

She reached back for Sammy's hand, noting it was as damp as hers and trembling slightly. The woman's hand was warm and persuasive as she led them toward the cabin.

Jonathan and Sammy stared at each other. The boys were near the same size.

Bethany looked back at Adam. "You will stay, too?" she asked in a quavery whisper.

"Aye, for tonight we all will stay," he said.

But tomorrow? What's to happen on the morrow? she wanted to scream out to him. She clamped those questions down in her tight throat. Pulling Sammy along with her, she meekly followed the woman into the cabin.

Adam had no idea why he'd done it, but he'd told the Owenses that Bethany was his wife. He'd been protecting her, he guessed, but from what? Appearances? Good grief, a man and woman traveling together in the frontier without the benefit of matrimony would hardly be accused of scandalous behavior and certainly a couple like David and Mina, who likely had never stood before a parson, wouldn't consider it so.

And yet he'd said it, and now he was held to the fiction. Hell, he'd been longing daily for more than a month to be rid of the woman, and the first minute he found folk who might well take her in, he'd blurted out that she was his wife.

Not bloody likely they'd be willing to shelter a married woman whose husband wanted to leave her behind.

Unless, that is, the wife should insist she wanted to be left. He felt a surge of hope. That would do it. He'd talk with Bethany, tell her what foolishness he'd spoken. He felt certain she'd prefer to stay here with the pleasant couple. She would surely cooperate.

Heartened, he ran up to the trace to lead the animals down to the Owenses' property for water and feed.

By late afternoon, he was aware he'd made a serious mistake. Bethany was not being cooperative, not cooperative at all.

He'd been talking with David Owens when she popped out of the cabin, her face flushed and puzzled.

"I must speak with you, Adam. Alone." Not schooled in social graces, she didn't give David a glance, let alone an apology.

Adam excused himself, and David gave him an I-understand-how-it-is-with-the-little-woman shrug.

"You could have warned me you were going to tell them I'm your wife, for heaven's sake," she chastised him, keeping her voice low. "I was truly at a loss for words when Mina kept calling you my husband and I knew not what I was supposed to—"

"*You?* At a loss for words?" he interrupted with a chuckle. He'd intended to give her a sober, reflective explanation, but her appearance had unhinged his resolve. She'd bathed and was clothed in a neat, well-fitting dress of a soft brown material printed with tiny green flowers. Her copper-red hair coiled about her face in damp curls and was tied back with a perky green bow that matched her eyes.

He'd thought her beautiful before. Now she was distractingly ravishing. And crisp and snappy as a fresh-picked bean.

"Don't laugh at me, Adam *Barwick*. That is your name, I gather, since you introduced yourself as such to the Owenses, and now that I'm *Mrs*. Barwick, I'm glad to know at last you have a name other than just Adam."

"You never asked my name," he retorted. Lord, she was lovely—a spitfire, true, but without a doubt a gorgeous one. He knew he needed to take control of the conversation, but for the moment he could do naught but feast his eyes on her.

"And what does it mean that I'm your wife? I don't understand why you said . . ."

"I erred, and fully intended to speak with you to explain—"

"*Erred?*" she interrupted, her hands on her hips, her voice rising to a stormy pitch. "Aye, please *do* explain to me, *Mister* Barwick!"

He glanced back at David, who sat on a bench next to the cabin's door, smoking a pipe, looking damnably amused. Quickly cupping his hand on her elbow, Adam guided Bethany out of the man's earshot.

"Keep your voice down, woman. I'll explain over there by the tree."

Though her pretty face puckered, she didn't resist his directions.

"Now calm yourself and listen to me," he said when they reached the leafy shadows of the maple. She huffed, but otherwise stayed quiet.

"I said what I did without thinking, Bethany, and I'm truly sorry." He paused, trying to choose his words carefully, avoiding her eyes as much as possible.

"It's just that my upbringing was such that I considered it necessary that I protect you from . . ." Her lips were wiggling at him. " . . . from any thoughts of impropriety, so I . . ." Her forehead wrinkled. "I said what I said, but I . . ." Her captivating eyes were wide and expectant. " . . . but I believe if you wish to stay behind we can arrange it." His voice had diminished to a timbre he barely recognized.

"If I wish to stay, we can arrange it?"

Good. She'd got the message. "Exactly. You need only tell them your desires to be free of me, and they'll understand."

"I'm not sure that I understand."

She wasn't making it easy.

"Just tell them you don't wish to be married to me any longer."

"But I don't know if I wish that or not, we've been married such a short time, you see."

It was hard to classify the glint in her eyes, but with growing discomfort he suspected it could well be defined as sly.

"Bethany, we're *not* married, you know that."

"If we were married, would they keep me?"

"Not unless you insist they do so."

"Then it's my decision to stay or leave with you?"

He nodded. "I think that's correct, and I'm sure you'd prefer to . . ."

She twirled around before he could finish, and the green bow taunted him with a wicked little flounce. "You should come on into the cabin now, *Mister* Barwick," she tossed back over her shoulder. "Mina's got a tub of hot water ready for you, and I believe she expects your wife to assist you in your bath."

Adam rolled his eyes skyward and counted to ten . . . very slowly.

*   *   *

Bethany was delighted. Adam wouldn't be leaving her behind, after all. She liked the Owenses, believed even that she could have enjoyed living with them. They were kind folk, and their cabin was spacious and clean with wooden floors and glass in the windows.

But her dream catcher wanted her to go beyond the mountains to find her prince. She was convinced now that all of the life-changing events of the past weeks had been the amulet's doings. It was leading her to the prince of her dreams.

And the wisdom of the dream catcher was clearly visible. It had sent Adam to guide, to instruct, and to protect her along the way. The *whole* way, thank heaven.

She felt like giggling. For the day, she would have to pretend to be Adam's wife. He had "erred," he said. Little did he know that his error was the dream catcher's doing, its way of ensuring he not leave her until he could hand her over to her beloved prince.

Adam was glowering when he walked into the cabin's sleeping room. She smiled brightly in return and tested the tub's water with her finger.

"'Tis far warmer than a creek in July and a true joy, you'll find," she said.

He grunted. "I'll bathe without assistance, woman. You may go to the other room."

"Nonsense. And have Mina think I care not enough for my husband to wash his back?"

"Bethany." It had the sound of a firm command. She ignored it.

"Hurry off with your clothing, Adam. I'll wash them for you later, and Mina's brought a fine stack of fresh garments belonging to David for you to wear till yours dry." She lifted the stack for his approval.

"Bethany, leave at once."

172

She shook her head. "A contented wife assists her husband. I'm contented, Adam."

He threw her a look that had the force of a tomahawk. She refused to blink.

"Bloody hell, woman, you asked for it," he growled as he yanked off his shirt and boots and began unbuttoning his breeches.

She was determined to stand her ground. Mina had said that a wife washed her husband's back, and if she ran into the kitchen now, the woman would surely be suspicious.

Besides, she'd seen naked men—Pa and George, anyway. They'd been less than modest over the years.

Adam wasn't being very modest, either, she saw with alarm. He'd got angry enough to challenge her, and she knew she had to win. She steeled herself and stood beside the waiting tub without moving.

At least her body didn't move. But when he stalked toward the tub, naked as a jaybird, her insides began raising a ruckus. Fighting to hang on to her defiance, she refused to close her eyes, but she ordered them not to see. They did, of course.

He was nothing like Pa and George. Oh dear, he truly wasn't. He was hardened muscle and sinew from his broad shoulders and chest tapering all the way down his entire long length clear down to his toes. The uncomfortable tingles striking her, now of all times, only added to her confusion. Her blink was unavoidable. She figured she looked as stunned as she felt, for his blatant smile as he stepped into the water had victory written all over it.

Damnation, she wished he at least had the decency to sit under the water. But he stayed standing, facing her, with one wicked eyebrow raised.

"Soap me, wife," he ordered, his eyes sparking with devilish humor.

173

"What?"

"Soap me."

"All over?" She kept her gaze glued to his face.

"Indeed all over."

"But . . . but there's so *much* of you." He couldn't be serious, could he? She backed away, struggling to recover her sanity.

"Well?"

He wouldn't even let her think, for heaven's sake.

"Uh, wet. You need to be wet before soaping." She doubted she was making sense.

With obvious delight, he scooped up great handfuls of water and began pouring it over his head, shoulders, arms, chest, and, she guessed, all the rest of him. She turned her back to him before he finished his infernal splashing. But he'd splattered her in the process, and the volley of sprays on her face had cleared her befuddled mind—cleared it with a vengeance. She had to regain control of this situation or he'd win for sure. *You're not leaving me behind, Adam Barwick!*

She grabbed the hunk of soap and twirled to face him.

"Turn around," she ordered. "And *sit*."

Glory be, he obeyed. With a flurry of lather, she began her onslaught, and she wasn't gentle. She soaped his hair and face, making sure a substantial quantity of suds got into his eyes. Working on his ears next, she gave them a yank to get behind them good and dug into their insides a bit while she was at it. He spluttered and complained. She cuffed his head and told him to sit still.

Bethany was beginning to enjoy herself. The sponge was rough and she made it rougher as she attacked his neck, shoulders, and back till his sun-bronzed skin turned rosy pink. There was such a great expanse of him to cover, and she took her time scrubbing as hard as she could all the parts visible above the water. She hoped fervently he'd tire of the fierce treatment before she got to those parts beneath the water.

"That's enough," he said with a subdued growl, grabbing the soap from her hand. "I'll finish by myself, woman. Go launder my clothes."

She smiled sweetly and dried her hands.

"I'll see you at the supper table, Adam," she chirped as she bundled up his soiled clothing and left the room.

Chapter Thirteen

Adam had a dimple in his chin. Bethany was taken aback when he appeared at the supper table. He had shaved off his beard after she'd left him that afternoon.

She hadn't been able to keep her eyes off him, though she tried like the dickens to avoid staring. That dimple was most appealing, and his jaw was square and firm. She'd been curious what he'd hidden beneath that beard. Now, she realized, it did seem a shame to hide such a treasure of a face.

The evening had set in, and the Owenses and their guests were gathered in the cabin's large kitchen-sitting room.

Sammy and Jonathan had become good friends. The lads were transferring a complex pattern of strings between their hands—a cat's cradle, they called it—and their laughter from the corner was as bright as the hearth fire that warmed the room. Sammy was dressed in some of Jonathan's clothing, and the two raven-haired boys almost looked like brothers, though the Owens lad had far lighter skin and his sky-blue eyes were like his father's.

Adam and David sat by the fire, smoking their pipes and conversing. Bethany had never seen Adam so relaxed, nor had she seen him so talkative. Strange, she thought with a twinge of sadness, with others he seemed not at all tense and argumentative as he so often was with her.

His garments had not yet dried, so he still wore David's. Both the shirt and breeches fit snugly and provided a disconcerting emphasis to his hard rippling muscles. He'd tied his long hair back with a strip of leather, and the hearth flame's glow softened the angular lines of his strong jaw.

Oh dear, she was staring again. Mina, who sat sewing across from her, must have noticed.

"Your husband is indeed a handsome man," she said with a knowing smile. "You've not been married long, I vow."

Bethany's cheeks warmed and she straightened on the pine settle. "No, not long at all, but a full turn of the moon."

"A month."

Damnation, even an Indian woman knew more than she did.

"Aye, a month," Bethany repeated with a nod, placing the new word on top of the growing stack of new words in her head.

Why, this very room held a staggering number of objects she'd never seen, let alone known the word for before this evening—beeswax "candles," a "braided rug." They'd eaten off "pewter plates" with "forks" and

177

"spoons of metal" and had sipped "tea" from cups of "stoneware." She'd put a "brush" to her hair and had it tied now with a "ribbon." And one of the greatest wonders of all, the Owenses had a "looking glass!" She'd seen herself in it, too. A strange experience that was. Not at all like the wavy reflection she'd seen in the stream back in the Hollow.

She wasn't pretty. Not like Mina with her big black eyes and shiny braids. Her own eyes were truly uninteresting. A peculiar shade of green they were, and though she'd known her hair was red, she'd never noted how wild and untamed it was.

"And where will you and Adam be heading from here?" Mina asked, interrupting her thoughts.

"Oh . . . through Rockfish Gap." She remembered hearing Adam mention the place.

Mina nodded. "And then . . ."

She didn't want her to know she hadn't an inkling. "The Tidewater, I suspect."

From across the room, Adam contradicted her. "We're headed toward Albemarle. David was just giving me directions."

Albemarle? A mouthful of letters that was.

"You'll like Albemarle, I vow," Mina said to her. "It's rolling land, with soil the color of your hair."

Bethany touched her hair with a self-conscious gesture. "Red dirt?"

The Indian woman laughed. "Aye, bright red."

"Have you lived there?" Bethany longed to know more about her.

"For a short while only." She frowned and her needle paused. "As more settlers moved in, David and I thought it wise to move up here. We're more comfortable without neighbors who question how an Indian woman came to be married to a white man."

Bethany had been dying to ask that question herself, but remained silent.

After breaking the sewing thread with her small white teeth, Mina looked at David, who was deep in conversation with Adam. Her eyes glistened with a tenderness that gave Bethany a thrill of excitement. Mina loved her husband deeply. That was the way a woman looked when she'd found her prince.

"I was born Indian, to a Pamunkey queen, I was told," Mina continued in her musical voice. "But I grew up in the home of a white family in Henrico County, so I know little of Indian ways. My peaceful tribe was raided by a lawless band of white men when I was but a babe. The Cartwrights found me squalling amidst the carnage. All of the others had been slaughtered. They took me into their home and raised me as one of their own."

Bethany's eyes brimmmed with tears. Adam kept telling her the world was cruel and Mina's story lent credence to his dreary assumption. But goodness had prevailed. The Cartwrights had been there for Mina and now she had David and true happiness. All *could* turn out well, despite the presence of cruelty, just as she'd always believed. She fingered her amulet and vowed to help Adam see that, too.

"How did you meet David?" *Did he carry you away on a white steed?*

Mina smiled. "We met as children. The Owenses were neighbors to the Cartwrights. He and I knew from the age of four that our futures would be entwined. By the time we were six and ten—"

"Sixteen," Bethany corrected with pride.

"Aye," Mina agreed with a soft chuckle. "By *sixteen* our love was so great that no one on this earth could have separated us."

"Did anyone try?" Bethany was horrified. True love could be separated?

Mina nodded. "Many, my dear. We were of two bloods, and some believe strongly that the two should never merge." She glanced at Jonathan. "I see my beautiful son and know their belief is false. He embodies the strength of both our peoples."

Bethany knitted her brows. Blood was merged in marriage? How did that occur? And how did a child come about?

Adam and David rose from their chairs, and David began banking the fire while Adam stretched and yawned.

Mina smiled. "Our men seem ready to sleep, I suppose we all are tired." She put down her sewing.

"Aye, I truly am," Bethany admitted.

"Sammy and Jonathan will sleep on pallets in this room. The two have taken a liking to each other, have you noticed?"

Bethany said she had. Indeed, Sammy looked contented and playful, the way a mere lad by rights should be.

"I'll fetch you a nightdress, my dear. You and Adam may share our room. Jonathan's bed is a mite small, but for two so recently wed, I'm sure that will present no problem."

A bed? Bethany was excited. She'd never slept on a bed. Such a luxury would be marvelous. She was sorry she was having to share it with Adam, though, for he'd leave her so little space.

And she knew it would be difficult to keep from bumping into him during the night, but she was determined to try with all her might not to. He'd been ill-tempered as the devil after that one time she'd disturbed his sleep.

* * *

Bethany scrunched over to the edge of the flock mattress as far as she could go without falling to the floor, but it was no use. Adam was simply too large. He, too, was scrunching over on his side, but they continued colliding into each other.

The nightdress Mina had given her was sheer "muslin"—another new word!—and was airy and delicate. Adam was wearing one of David's too-short nightshirts.

Despite her efforts to avoid contact with him, her feet occasionally ran into his long bare legs, and her bottom kept meeting his.

"I'm trying not to touch you, Adam," she whispered.

"Good." He didn't sound at all pleasant.

"The bed is small, and you're . . ."

"Shhh. Stop talking and go to sleep."

She closed her eyes. He adjusted his position with a mumbled oath, and his leg skimmed across hers before he pulled it away as if he'd encountered a flaming poker. Her eyes popped open.

For certain he despised being touched. She wiggled away from him till her toes dangled over the mattress, struggling to make herself as small as possible.

Staring into the darkness, she figured she'd never get a wink of sleep this night. Adam wasn't sleeping, either, she could tell. Damnation, they'd both be crimped into knots by morning.

Suddenly, from across the room, she heard disturbing noises coming from the Owenses bed. She lifted her head in alarm. She'd thought they were sound asleep. In the darkness she couldn't see them, but from the awful sounds she feared they'd become ill.

Flipping over, she tapped Adam on the shoulder. "Something's terribly wrong with Mina and David.

They're thrashing and moaning," she breathed into his ear.

"Mmmm?" He raised his head slightly, then buried it back into the pillow without further comment.

"Adam, they're ill, we must help." She couldn't believe his lack of concern. She persisted. "Adam . . ."

His groan was audible. "They're all right, go to sleep."

He was impossible! Well, *she* wasn't going to lie quiet while two kind people might be dying in front of her. She started from the bed.

Adam pulled her back with a grip that would have stopped a bear. "Get back here," he hissed.

She had no choice. He held her captive. "We must see to them!" she spit out, but her complaint was a subdued splutter against his tightly clamped hand.

"Bloody hell, be quiet. Don't bother them *now*, for God's sake!" The urgency in his whispered command got her attention.

She stilled and twisted around. His hand released a mite, but he kept it close to her mouth. "Why not?" she questioned. "They sound in pain, they may need us."

"Shhh." He put his finger across her lips. "Believe me, Bethany, they don't need us now, and they're not in pain."

"But—"

"Shhh."

Damnation, he was unreasonable. He had her clasped against him in a miserably awkward position. How could he be so sure they weren't suffering?

The sounds from across the room grew more frenzied and Bethany was beside herself with anxiety for them.

"Adam, please free me, we really must help," she begged. Sometimes he responded to heartfelt requests. But not this time. He clutched her so close she wasn't sure she could breathe.

"They don't need our help, damn it."

She wanted to cry out in frustration. "What on earth are they doing?" she mumbled into his night-shirt.

He tightened his hold, and his words sounded as if they were filtered through clenched teeth. "They're doing what husbands and wives do."

What kind of answer was that? But her curiosity was aroused. What was it Mina had said? Good heavens. . . .

"Are they merging their blood? Is that what you mean?" Her questions were so heavily muffled by his chest she could barely hear them herself.

"What?" His restraint loosened enough for her to wiggle up so her face was next to his.

"Are they merging their blood?" she repeated.

His soft laugh ruffled across her lips. "That would be one possible way of describing it, I guess."

She thought awhile. Merging blood? Were they cutting each other, for heaven's sake? She shivered. "Does it hurt, do you suppose? Both of them are moaning so."

He chuckled lightly. "No, it doesn't hurt. Far from it. It's intensely pleasurable."

His assurance puzzled her. "How do you know, Adam? Have you done this thing?"

"Aye, of course, but . . ."

"You've had a wife?"

"No."

"But you said . . ." Now she was truly perplexed. "I don't understand."

His sigh was a long one. "It's difficult to explain, Bethany. A pair indeed should be married before they . . . But young men have a fierce drive for . . .

So they often do this . . . this thing before they wed, but . . ."

His hesitant speech confused her as much as his words. He obviously was extremely uncomfortable. She couldn't see his face in the darkness, though it was very near. And their bodies were not only touching, they were veritably melded together. Knowing his distaste for such, she figured that was adding a large measure to his discomfort. Surprisingly, she found having his hard strength against her quite comfortable indeed.

But she needed to make him feel better. She placed her hand on his firm cheek. "Say no more now, you can answer my many questions on the morrow when you're less annoyed by this nearness forced upon us." His jaw pumped its tense movements beneath her fingers. She rubbed it gently, hoping to quiet it. There was a vague hint of bristles where his beard had been, and her fingertips tingled. Her attempts to calm him came to naught. The pumping in his jaw increased greatly.

"Damn it, Bethany. You're torturing me beyond reason." He spoke with a huskiness unlike any she'd ever heard from him.

"I'm truly sorry," she breathed her earnest apology. Her lips were but a whisper away from his and brushed against them as she spoke. "If you'll let me go, I promise to be quiet, and I'll stay as distant as I can under the circum—"

His lips stopped her. He'd hushed her before with words, with his hand, or with his finger. But this time he was using his lips, and they . . . they felt soft as feathers, tasted sweeter than honey. It seemed perfectly natural to flick her tongue across them. He groaned, and the feathers became something quite different—a delightful persuasive pressure, decidedly the most pleasant sensation she'd ever experienced. Lips against lips. A true wonder, she decided, too enthralled to question why he'd chosen this different way to silence her. She returned the pressure, savoring the way his mouth responded with fevered movements urging her lips apart. They complied, willingly.

The tip of his tongue played across her teeth, then tested the roof of her mouth, as though he, too, sensed the presence of honey. Oh my, that felt good. He was sending waves of sweet pleasure that lapped through her far beyond his touches—a surge of waves she welcomed and encouraged. Vaguely familiar waves but with a fiery force that was somehow new, fresh . . . Words scattered away from her.

Her fingers laced through his hair drawing his head yet closer. Whatever was happening, she wanted it to continue forever.

His mouth was devouring hers; no, hers was devouring his. It mattered not. There was hunger, his and hers, and it would be sated, though she knew not how and wasn't concerned about how. Adam would know. Adam. . . .

"Adam?" She'd spoken. His lips had left hers, but they were so near his heated breath was like a whispered promise.

"Move back, Bethany." His hand was tense against her shoulder, opposing her instinctive desire to move forward.

"But why?" Her disobedient fingers wound through his hair, crept around his head to bring him to her again. She felt a shiver course through him, from his scalp beneath her fingertips down through his arm and hand that held her and, finally, like a corded ribbon through his long body pressed against her.

"Don't . . . please don't . . ." He'd grown rigid, but his deep voice quavered his plea—a plea that despite its softness was layered with warning.

She heard it, removed her hand, and pushed herself away. She was trembling.

"I'm sorry, Adam." She could think of nothing else to say. She sensed he was suffering, and that she had caused it.

"I'm to blame, Bethany. Forgive me." With a combined sigh and groan, he flopped over and turned his back to her.

She was confused. She should forgive him? For what? For giving her such intense pleasure or for taking it away? Nothing made sense any longer. She had relished the feel of his mouth on hers, the deep plunges of his heated tongue, felt still the pressure of his hand on her bottom, pulling her up against him.

He'd stirred wild responsive forces within her that ached for something more. And yet, she'd made him miserable. Tears stung her eyes. How could whatever had happened between them bring her such pleasure while bringing him nothing but misery?

Now *she* was miserable, filled with tremors she didn't understand and, at the same time, felt completely empty.

She scooted to her far edge of the bed and knotted up into a small ball.

Holding her amulet, she drifted at last into a restless sleep. The prince did not come to her that night.

Sammy stayed behind with the Owenses. The couple wanted him, and Adam knew the boy had found a loving home.

Bethany had wept when they'd told him farewell. She'd agreed with Adam that the lad would be better off with the family, but she'd hugged Sammy tightly, like a reluctant mother parting from her son.

It had been a wrenching scene, giving Adam a heavy lump in his throat.

Leaving her cow and ox behind had been her own idea. "To express our gratitude," she'd said to the Owenses. He had started to protest. They were, after all, her only property. But she'd been adamant and, deep down, he was relieved to be rid of the sluggish animals.

Mina had provided her with a small bundle of clothes, and she wore the same attractive flower-printed dress she'd had on yesterday. Her tattered nightdress she'd left behind "for dusting rags," and she'd returned his shirt, freshly laundered.

Sammy kept his pony, so there were only the two of them and the dog, Constant, of course. Bethany rode the mare; Adam was astride the chestnut. Both steeds were loaded with the few supplies they'd considered necessary for their continued journey, but their pace was far sprightlier without the slower animals.

Uncle Hallston's Brierwood in Albemarle was only a few days away, he figured.

How the blazes was he going to explain Bethany? What in hell was he going to do with the woman? Stay well away from her for one thing. Good Jesus, she was the most responsive woman he'd ever held in his arms, and she had no earthly idea what transpired between a man and woman—what could easily have transpired last night. He'd come damnably close to giving her a full demonstration of "blood merging," as she'd called it.

Daylight helped; their faster pace helped. His resolve was strong. He'd keep his distance from her.

"Why did you decide to head for Albemarle rather than the Tidewater?" she asked.

187

"A change of plans." He'd be damned if he'd tell her anything more.

She brightened. "Then you've given up your destructive idea about revenge?"

Hell, no. He weighed his response carefully. "I've determined a more efficient strategy. Now ask no more questions."

She was quiet for a while, but he could tell from her fidgeting that she wasn't going to remain that way.

He was right. "Revenge will gnaw away at your gentle, kind spirit, Adam."

"Who the hell said I had a gentle, kind spirit?"

"I did."

He grumbled. "You speak nonsense. Had I possessed such a weak spirit, I would have been long dead."

"I didn't say 'weak,' Adam. I said 'gentle and kind.'"

"It's one and the same."

She responded with a tilt of her head and a wry smile that said "I don't believe you." He glowered at her. She lifted her nose and brought the mare to a trot, moving ahead.

He watched the green ribbon bounce at the back of her head and noted she kept a good seat. She'd learned to ride well, had indeed learned many things well in the past weeks. Including, he thought with disgruntlement, numerous new ways to bedevil him. He clucked Nutmeg into a gallop and overtook her.

"Stay beside me, woman." He pulled alongside her and they slowed to a walk.

"You're mighty grumbly today," she said at last.

"Maybe it's a grumbly day." The clouds were thick and it looked like rain.

She sighed. "I'm not too pleasant, either, I guess. Leaving Sammy was difficult and I didn't sleep well."

He glanced at her, her cheeks were slightly flushed.

He hoped like mad she wasn't going to start bombarding him with questions about the facts of life. For damn sure, that was a subject he wished to steer away from entirely.

Thinking quickly, he opted to distract her by providing her some information about his Albemarle strategy. He might be needing her cooperation.

"Perhaps I should discuss with you my plans for after we arrive in Albemarle," he offered. Knowing her avid curiosity about everything, he figured she'd leap at the bait.

"Glory be, does this mean that Adam Barwick is willing to actually *talk* with me about something important?" The gleam of excitement in her emerald eyes overpowered the sarcasm she'd attempted.

"First of all, you must get it into your stubborn woman's head—and keep it there—that my purpose is to wreak revenge on that Tidewater bastard."

She wrinkled up her face with disapproval.

"Nothing will deter me from that goal," he added, throwing her a look of warning. "My goal is revenge. It has been since you've known me, and it will continue to be till the wrong done to me is righted. Do you have that basic fact in your mind?"

She nodded, but he'd never seen a more sour expression.

"Now the next thing you need to know is that only my strategy has changed. On our journey, I've had time to think things through with a clear head, and I've decided to launch my revised scheme from Albemarle." He paused, checking to see if she was listening. She was.

"There are folk there who might assist me." No need that he could see to mention they were relatives. "But I must be cautious. I've been absent many years, and I'm thought to be dead, so I've been told, so when

189

I arrive, I'll not reveal myself as Adam Barwick at first. I must know what has happened in my absence, how people view the Tidewater villain." This potential problem had occurred to him. Uncle Hallston could have been charmed by the devious James and it would be foolhardy to trust him till he found it safe to do so.

"Who will you be?" she asked.

"I'll think of a name. The important thing for you to understand is that whatever my name becomes you must call me by that name." He caught himself, adding, "Assuming, that is, you're still with me at that point." Blighted devil, surely she wouldn't be.

"I've been meaning to talk over that matter with you, Adam. You mustn't leave me before we're beyond the mountains."

"And why is that?"

She looked hesitant to speak. Truly out of character, he thought with a touch of amusement.

"I should have mentioned this earlier, and had I done so we could have avoided some of the—uh—discomfort we encountered yesterday, for you'd have understood why I couldn't stay behind with the Owenses." She fingered the leather pouch around her neck, seeming to search for the right words.

"'Tis just that I was told not to tell my secret," she continued, worry crinkling her smooth forehead. "But I believe you should know; otherwise, we might find ourselves arguing again should we find further settlement in the mountains."

She toyed with the pouch and grew quiet. He pulled at his earlobe, trying to quell his impatience. He didn't succeed too well.

"What is it I should know?" he prompted.

She took a deep breath, then smiled over at him

with a powerful radiance that came close to unseating him from the saddle.

"My dream catcher has ever foretold that a prince would carry me beyond the blue mountains. You're not the prince, of course, we both know that. And thus, I was reluctant at first to journey with you, as I'm sure you remember."

He did, but said nothing, hoping she'd eventually get to her point.

"Of late, the dream catcher has given me the clear message that my prince awaits me beyond the mountains and that you are taking me to him." Her eyes glistened with confidence. "So now you understand."

Understand? He understood that she was addled enough to believe some hocus-pocus talisman was guiding her destiny, but it was beyond comprehension that she'd consider he'd ever swallow such nonsense. He would try to bring her down to earth gently.

"A prince, you say? How will you know him?"

"I've seen him."

He quirked his brow in surprise. "And when would that have been?"

"Many times—in my dreams. He has hair as dark as a beaver's fur and eyes bluer than the summer heavens, and he rides a . . ."

"In your *dreams*? Bethany, for God's sake, dreams aren't reality. You're pursuing a make-believe phantom—a bloody fantasy!"

"My prince is real." Her face was as set and determined as her voice.

He shook his head. "You're doomed to disappointment, woman. Wipe those gossamer cobwebs from your brain. There's no prince waiting for you. Your dream catcher's naught but a silent stone."

"It's metal, and it sings."

"Stone, metal, it makes no difference. It's what it

is and naught else—and I'm sure it doesn't sing."

"It sings only to me."

Blazing hell, there was no sense trying to reason with such fuzzy-headed obstinacy. A scattering of raindrops began to fall. He scowled at the sky, pulled to a stop, and ordered her to do likewise. After dismounting, he dug into the pack for their deerskins, tossed one to her, and threw the other over himself.

"We'll continue despite the rain," he said. He was more eager than ever to get this damnable journey behind him. She'd drive a holy saint crazy.

But he couldn't help feeling concern for her. Lord, how he longed to convince her to let go of her foolish superstitions, but mere talk would never accomplish such a feat. The world itself would have to teach her. She'd be forced to shed her illusions, of course. Life always stripped away illusions. But in her case, he prayed it would do so without further pain. She'd had enough already.

When they were under way again, he spoke no more about the dream catcher. He'd take her beyond the mountains. At least he could do that for her. But there was no way he could assure her he'd be handing her over to a prince. As far as he knew, there wasn't one to be found in the whole colony of Virginia.

"Am I to continue to pretend to be your wife?"

Her question jogged him alert. "What are you asking?"

"Your wife? Am I to continue to pretend . . . when we reach the place in Albemarle where you'll pretend to be someone other than who you are?"

Hell, no! One day of that charade had come close to ruining him forever. Maybe it had; his groin had developed a permanent ache. He said instead, "That won't be necessary. I should be able to find a home for you before I reach my destination—beyond the mountains, I promise—but if I don't, I won't repeat that stupid mistake. I'll introduce you as my sister."

Good idea. He wished like the devil he'd thought of it yesterday. Sharing a bed with her again was definitely not in his plans.

"You weren't stupid. The dream catcher made you do it."

He groaned. "Stop that nonsense."

She shrugged under the deerskin. It covered her flaming hair and that alluring ribbon that tormented him.

Dear God, everything about her tormented him. A mere glance from her eyes set him ablaze; one small touch gave him a fevered arousal; the passion in her kisses last night had unleashed a desire so powerful that. . . .

He raised his face and welcomed the cold sheets of rain. Bethany had spoken right about one thing, at least. He wasn't her prince. They both knew that, she'd said.

Adam hoped that silly dream catcher might be right, too. It would be a godsend if she found her "prince" in Albemarle.

Lord knew, she was ripe for a husband—overwhelmingly ripe. He wished one for her. She deserved a man who would provide her happiness and fulfillment.

Lucky bastard. He tightened his grip on the reins and gave himself a firm reminder. His only duty was to leave her safe somewhere—and intact. Fully intact.

Meanwhile, he pledged to the desolate sky that he would keep his distance from her.

Chapter Fourteen

Late May 1760
Albemarle County, Virginia

Bethany gasped. "What *is* it?"

"It's a house. Stop staring, for God's sake, and come along. We'll go to the rear door and, remember, I'll do the talking."

She was too startled to talk, she could barely think. The building was huge. Could it possibly be a dwelling? If so, ten families must reside in it. Eight glass windows were on the front of the house. *Eight* and they were stacked, four below and four above. Only a true giant could peer out from those at the top. A shudder of fear ran up her spine. Were there such folk? She'd thought Adam must be the tallest man in the world, and even he could not reach that high.

The house was dark red and made with an odd kind of stone that was flat and even. Two big chimneys of the same stone were on either end, indicating two kitchens were inside. She reckoned ten families would require that many.

She'd seen a wooden shingle as they'd approached proclaiming the place was called "Brierwood." The name had not struck her as sinister. Then, too, Adam was with her, and he showed no apprehension. She followed him with only the tiniest of qualms.

Adam was bearded again. He'd said it would add to his disguise. She hadn't figured yet if he was more handsome with or without it. Both ways she'd found highly attractive.

As he led her toward the back of the large house, she pulled her eyes away from him. Oh my, what *were* all those things?

More buildings were behind the large structure, some built with the same peculiar red stone, some of weatherboard. Large areas of land were marked off with a series of logs put together in a pattern she'd never seen—open enclosures of some sort, with groupings of animals in each. Numerous animals. Horses together in one area, pigs in another, cows and sheep back on a far hill in yet another.

The animals were all normal-sized, she saw with relief. Adam halted the chestnut and dismounted.

"Stay close to me and listen well—and try not to say a word," he admonished.

She nodded, but since her ears were buzzing with a mix of anxiety and curiosity, she doubted she'd hear him above the roar. With certainty, she knew her tongue wouldn't be moving. She dismounted and joined him.

"Stairs," he explained without her asking. He'd started doing that often in the past weeks, anticipating her questions as if he could read her thoughts.

Stairs. A clever building device, far easier to ascend than a rickety ladder. She added the word to her ever-growing vocabulary and, after watching how Adam stepped up the three rising pieces of wood, she followed close behind.

He knocked on the door. She held her breath and stood rigid, clasping her hands at the front of her calico skirt.

The plump woman who opened the wide white door was not a giant, but Bethany was startled nevertheless, for the woman's skin was near as dark as burnt wood. Good heavens, did folk come colored in every shade of the rainbow?

Adam spoke first. Bethany tried to listen well, as he'd ordered. "Good day. May I speak with the gentleman of the house?"

"Mister Hallston Lawrence, he's back in the lib'ry, I'll fetch him."

"Library," Adam muttered in way of an explanation after the woman had left the door. "A room of books."

She nodded, though he'd told her very little. She still didn't know what "books" were. At the moment, she was far more concerned about Mister Lawrence. Might he be purple or green? And, since he was the gentleman of the house, he was certain to be one of the giants who could see out from those upper windows.

He wasn't. In fact, he was only a head taller than she, and his skin was near the shade of her own, only a mite more pink. But his hair was peculiar enough—stark white and as puffy as a haystack it was. He wore a white shirt with fancy ruffles down the front, black breeches, and shiny shoes with metal squares atop them. Though his face seemed kind, she relaxed only slightly.

"Good day, sir," Adam said with a stiff bend of his waist. "I'm George Stewart, this is my sister, Bethany, and we're seeking honest labor. Would you have need of extra hands?"

So he was to be George Stewart? Her dead father? Her head was so stuffed with confusion that one more oddity hardly mattered. At least he'd let her keep her own name.

The man shook his head but smiled. "I have more hands than I need, Mister Stewart, but you may try my neighbor to the south, at Ridgecrest. He was telling me only yesterday that he was woefully short of help. Castle's his name. Robert Castle."

Adam hesitated. "A near neighbor?"

"Aye, down that way but two miles or so." The man pointed ahead with a chubby finger. Frilly ruffles hung from the end of his sleeves, and they covered half his hand. "His land's down by the river. He's an honorable man and a dear friend. Doesn't own slaves by choice, so there's a good chance he'll hire you on." He gave Adam a quick appraisal and nodded his approval. "You appear to be a sturdy man, and if you're as honest as you're big, he'll be pleased to have you."

He'd only given Bethany a brief glance. She wondered if Robert Castle would be pleased to have her, too.

Adam thanked him and took her by the elbow.

"Godspeed and good fortune," Mister Lawrence said, and closed the door.

Adam was disappointed. He'd wanted to work for his uncle, for it would be far easier to become privy to the man's relationship with James Wallace if he could be truly close. At least Castle's place was nearby, and the men were friends.

Thomasina Ring

The situation wasn't ideal, but it was still far better than disclosing his true identity before he knew if Uncle Hallston could be trusted.

"Fence," he said to Bethany when he saw her looking with puzzlement at the posts and rails.

"And the house's peculiar stone?"

"Brick. It's not stone. Handmade it is, from clay set in molds and put into hot ovens called kilns."

She took it all in and seemed to be content with his simple description. But the wonders for her were many, so he wasn't surprised when she continued her questioning chatter. "When I saw the upper windows, I thought giants lived inside. What's their use way up high like that?"

He couldn't resist chuckling. Her naïveté and colorful imagination were a constant source of both amusement and amazement to him. "The house has two floors, or stories, they're sometimes called. You walk from one to the other by using stairs—a staircase."

He could tell she was forming pictures in her head and storing the information in prompt order. Lord, she was hungry for knowledge and exceedingly quick to learn and he relished feeding her fertile mind.

Though he'd tried, he hadn't found a suitable home for her before now. They'd stopped at two cabins since they'd left the mountains, but he had considered neither to be acceptable havens for her. One of the couples had been sullen and taciturn and would have worked her hard. With them, her life would have been even drearier than it had been in Wildcat Hollow. The second couple had disturbed him more. At least the man did. His beady eyes had examined Bethany as though she might have been a sugared, buttery puff paste, and his lips had virtually smacked as he looked her over.

Damned if he would leave her with scum like that. Then and there, he'd made the decision to skirt further habitation and take Bethany with him on to Brierwood—now, possibly, to Ridgecrest. She required his protection still, and he needed to be close at hand until he was assured she would be cared for properly.

At both cabins, he'd introduced her as his sister, and it had worked well. They'd been bedded separately.

In fact, he'd kept his pledge to avoid any additional physical contact with her, though he'd been sorely tested from time to time. God knew, her lush ripeness, so often only a short reach away, had been a continuing bedevilment, and she'd grown increasingly desirable to him with each passing day.

Now that they'd come at last upon a more populated area, he hoped fervently he'd find a willing wench soon. He was badly in need of a woman.

"It will seem strange to call you 'George,' Adam."

"You should start practicing it now."

"George, George, George." She frowned. "It doesn't sound like you."

"What does that mean?"

"George takes but air to speak. Adam, like you, embodies great strength."

He'd never given his name a second thought, and her words gave him a rise of pleasure. He glanced sideways at her. He'd learned to avoid full looks as much as possible. "Just call me George," he said with all the gruffness he could muster.

"What if Mister Castle doesn't want us, either?"

He shrugged. "I'll think of something."

Suddenly, Bethany pulled the mare to a stop. "My God," she gasped. She was as pale as a specter.

"What is it?" He jerked alert and saw at once what she'd spotted—a speeding rider on a distant hill, heading back toward Brierwood. The man was way too far to be a threat, and he was not on their path. Why in God's name had she reacted thus?

"He's the prince," she whispered.

Her cheeks were flushed now, her wide emerald eyes glossed with excitement. Adam felt a grinding pang of what? Envy? Balderdash.

"He's a man on a white horse, Bethany. Nothing more." He eyed the distant rider. He looked ordinary enough; indeed, he was only a man on a white horse.

But she sat transfixed, her face aglow with happiness. "I told you he'd be here," she said.

"Don't raise your hopes too high. The world is full of dark-haired men riding white horses, and we know nothing about this one." *Damn it, woman, listen to me*. But she paid him absolutely no heed. Her gaze was fastened on the rider, and it remained fastened till he disappeared over the hill.

"Was he going to the Lawrence house, do you suppose?" she asked at last.

Adam wanted to shake her soundly. She needed sense put into her head. He was annoyed, too, by that syrupy smile all over her face.

"How the hell would I know where the fool's going? Come on now, we have no time to waste on silly dreams." His harshness surprised him, but it didn't appear to bother her one tad.

Glowing and smiling with renewed assurance, she brought Patsy to a spry trot. "Aye, *George*," she said over her shoulder as she moved ahead of him, her voice oozing sweetness. "Let's be on our way."

He scowled at her and angrily nudged the chestnut into motion. Damn, but she was a bloody nuisance!

When they arrived at Ridgecrest, she slipped from euphoria to unabashed awe, making Adam more comfortable. He was accustomed to her ever-constant awe and figured he could handle it with a calmer spirit.

"The river down yon I believe is the James, the same that flows by the home of my birth, though that's many miles distant from here," he said. "The James is far wider and swifter in the Tidewater. It's newer here, nearer its source."

But she was staring at the house, her mouth agape. "Tis even bigger than the other."

Neither his uncle's Brierwood nor this Ridgecrest were half the size of Wendover, but he realized that to her eyes they were grand indeed. As they approached the house, he anticipated her questions. "This one's built of native stone—fieldstone—and it's been white-washed, which is why it's gleaming white rather than the natural gray of the stone. Those slatted wood pieces on either side of the windows are called shutters. They close to keep out cold winds or bright sun."

"Why are we going to the front?"

"This is the rear, the front faces the river. See, the outbuildings are back here."

"What are the outbuildings for?"

"Various things. A kitchen, smokehouse, a stable for horses, homes for servants, that small one yon is a privy."

"A privy?"

"They may call it a 'necessary' here as they do in the Tidewater. It's a—uh—place to go when . . . It takes the place of a chamber pot."

"A chamber pot?"

He groaned. "The creek, the bushes, whatever . . ."

"Oh," she said with comprehension lighting her eyes and a tinge of blush coloring her cheeks. "Necessary is indeed a good word for that."

A tall, slender man walked out from the stable. He had silver hair and an aristocratic demeanor, despite his simple white shirt and buckskin breeches. Shading his eyes, the man watched them approach and raised his arm in a friendly wave.

Adam returned the wave. "That's Mister Castle, I vow," he said to Bethany under his breath. "We'll dismount here and walk over to him. Let's hope he hires us."

"He will," she said brightly. "My dream catcher just told me this will be our home for a spell." She dismounted with confidence and busily straightened her skirt.

He threw her a shadowed glower. "Bethany, you know what I've told you about putting too much faith in that non—"

"Just wait and see, Adam . . . *George* . . . Mister Stewart."

Good thing she reminded him. With her infernal distractions, he'd almost forgotten his dastardly new name.

Robert Castle had clear blue eyes and the lean, angular face of a tenth-generation English nobleman. A pure breed, Adam could tell, possibly a true gentleman.

"Good day, sir," he began, then repeated his earlier speech, adding that Mister Hallston Lawrence of Brierwood had suggested he inquire at Ridgecrest.

Castle introduced himself and offered his hand. His handshake was firm. "Stewart, you say? From where have you traveled?"

Adam noted with discomfort that though the man spoke to him, his gaze appeared fixed on Bethany.

"From a hollow in the lower Shenandoah Valley. Our home burned, we lost our pa and all else," he answered.

A fleeting glimmer passed across the man's eyes before they turned to his own. Adam couldn't decipher its meaning, but he put himself on guard. He waited for Castle's response.

"And what of your mother?" he asked, looking deeply into Adam's eyes.

"Dead, I suppose. She was taken by—"

"No, sir. She isn't dead," Bethany interrupted, and brazenly stepped forward. "The Shawnees took her eleven summers ago, but I prefer to believe they've treated her well and made her a queen."

Robert Castle paled slightly, then smiled. "I prefer to believe that also, Miss Stewart."

Adam wanted to punch the man. He'd sure as hell better stop feasting his eyes on Bethany that way, or he'd beat the bloody tar out of him.

"Aye, indeed I do need additional help, as Hallston Lawrence told you, Mister Stewart," Castle said with a polite, easy manner. "A longtime, faithful hand wed one of my house servants last week, and the two with my blessings have gone to settle in the upper Valley. So, as you see, your arrival is welcome." He gave Bethany another quick glance before continuing.

"I'll introduce you to Angus, my foreman. He'll be pleased to have your assistance beginning in the morning. I'm sure you both need a good night's rest before undertaking any chores. You'll sleep in the men's house with Angus and my other men." He returned his gaze to Bethany and then, with a broad smile, faced Adam again and added, "Your sister will have a room in the main house."

Adam's hands clenched into fists by his sides. "Neither of us stay till you tell me more," he said, his jaws tight. "Wages, duties, that sort of thing, Mister Castle."

"Why, of course."

The aristocrat looked most amenable. Adam searched his eyes. He wanted to trust him, hoped like the devil his motives weren't what they seemed.

He'd be damned if he'd put her in the hands of a bloody lecher.

"You would assist Angus with a variety of tasks, from shoeing horses to tilling the fields. It's fair work, with proper wages. Twenty shillings a week I paid Stephen, who'd been with me more than five years. I'll start you at nineteen. If I'm as pleased with your work as I fully suspect I shall be, you'll be raised to twenty in one month."

"And what of my sister?"

"She'll work in the house, assisting Ida, the widow Mrs. Pumphrey, with serving, cleaning, and the care of my wife, who's somewhat sickly. Her wages would be five shillings per week."

The "sickly wife" bothered Adam. Castle looked to be in his forties; he'd likely still be desiring the pleasures of a woman. As much as he longed to be nearby his uncle to continue his own plans, he was not about to consider Castle's offer till he was assured of Bethany's safety. He decided to take his time, to feel out the situation—and the man—further.

"My sister will require patience and some basic instructions. She's had little experience with a modern home. She's eager for learning and quick to understand. I've attempted to teach her throughout our long journey. She knows her letters and numbers now, but there's much still for her to know."

Castle looked inquisitive. "Why did you wait till the journey to teach her letters and numbers? Did you not consider that a duty even in your hollow?"

Adam was taken aback, but recovered quickly. "I was away for many years, captive of Indians for a while, then sold to and enslaved by French fur traders in the far west on the upper Mississippi. Finally, when I escaped and was wending my way home, I was conscripted as a wagoner by the English soldiers. I served at several forts, including Duquesne, now called Pitt, and most recently at Loudoun. I'd just been released from my conscription and had reached the Hollow when we had the fire."

All he'd said was true. He'd learned long ago that directness, based on fact, served him well. The only fiction he needed to concoct for this man was that Bethany was his sister and that he was George Stewart.

He wished to hell, however, that she'd been more discreet and hadn't stared at him so wide-eyed throughout his discourse. He'd seen no earlier requirement to reveal his sordid history to her.

Castle didn't appear to notice Bethany's surprised reaction. "Angus served with General Braddock's forces in the disastrous defeat of '55, and he too was at Loudoun for a spell. You two will have much in common," he said.

Adam stiffened. "Before I agree to your offer, I must be assured my sister is safe in your house." The man looked intelligent and should understand Adam's meaning.

A tightening around Castle's eyes indicated he had. "Mrs. Pumphrey is a kind woman who will both guide and shelter her, Mister Stewart. Your sister will sleep in the same room as Ida."

That took care of the nights but what of the days? Adam decided on a further demand. "I must be allowed to see her daily, to talk with her to be ensured she's well."

"One of her duties will be to serve the men their meals. You will see and talk with her daily. I appreciate your brotherly concerns—uh—George. May I call you George?"

Adam nodded, but continued searching the man's

eyes. They were seemingly honest. God, he wanted to trust him. But dare he?

"Will she have a day of rest?" he asked.

"Aye, you both will have Sundays free. It's ever been my custom at Ridgecrest that no one works on the Sabbath."

So Castle was a God-fearing man? That boded well, if true. But it had been a long time since he'd been in the company of a God-fearing man, so he wasn't sure he'd truly recognize one.

"My sister and I must be allowed to spend our Sundays together as I want to continue instructing her with her letters and numbers." He truly did, he realized. But he figured, too, that Bethany might learn more in the house than he could in the fields about his uncle's attitude toward James. The Lawrences would be frequent visitors, he assumed. Spending Sundays with her could allow him to glean helpful knowledge from her.

He'd know quickly if Castle was to be trusted, and, with the information Bethany could supply about the Lawrences, he'd soon know too if Uncle Hallston could be trusted.

Castle nodded his agreement about the Sunday demand, but Adam noted an unsettling hesitancy.

"Ida and I both will assist you with her continuing instructions."

Adam was less than delighted with that proposition, but he kept his displeasure hidden behind a stolid expression and said nothing.

Castle lifted one silver eyebrow. "I'm curious as to how you learned your own letters and numbers, George. Your history as you tell it would appear to preclude much schooling."

Adam bit down on his lip. Deception indeed was a tangled web. "There was a traveling tutor when I was a lad. My pa hired him as a hand one summer, and he taught me in the evenings," he lied. "Some of the English soldiers in the forts provided me with books and additional learning." Hell, he hoped that satisfied him.

It appeared to. Castle pursued the subject no further.

"I'll fetch Ida, for I believe when you meet her you'll feel secure about your sister's safety in my home," he said, then after excusing himself, he headed toward the house.

"What do you think, Bethany?" Adam asked. He wasn't convinced he could trust the man.

"He's truly a pleasant gentleman, I vow."

Her glowing face reflected her blasted confidence that all would be well. Lord, she was so swept up by her blind trusting nature and that damnable singing dream catcher that she was incapable of reasonable thought. The decision to leave or to stay at Ridgecrest would have to be of his own choosing—only his. Bloody hell, he prayed he would make the right choice.

"Did you speak the truth about the Indians and the traders and the forts?" she asked softly while they waited for Castle's return.

"Aye."

"Your life has been a hard one, Adam."

"George," he reminded her.

Bethany acknowledged his correction with a nod, then she looked up into his dark brown eyes, trying to fathom the forces that battled yet in their depths.

Did she truly know him? For weeks he'd been her steady companion, her teacher, her guardian. Though he was as grumpy as a hungry bear with her at times, at others his gentle tenderness had wrapped about her like a furry cloak.

She ached to tell him that she'd grown accustomed to having him near and appreciated his arranging to continue his guard over her. She wanted him to know she wasn't ready to tell him farewell—not nearly ready, not till she could help him quell those mighty demons that beset him.

Even the prince could wait till that was done, she'd tell him.

But she found she couldn't speak at all. Adam was returning her studied gaze, and a warm shiver skimmed across the top of her back. So often his looks felt like soft touches.

And it was happening to her again. Something far stronger than gratitude or the need for his protection was binding her to him. Like a silken ribbon, it drew her toward him in ways she couldn't understand.

The ribbon tugged at her now, and she still didn't know what to do about it.

A long moment lapsed before she could speak, and even then she didn't know the source of her words. "Do you wish to stay here?"

He didn't respond, only continued looking into her eyes. The feathery shivers multiplied, ran down her shoulders, through her arms. Before she could stop it, her hand reached for his and circled his fingers, held them tightly. He made no move to withdraw from her grasp.

"Do you?" she repeated in a whisper, not entirely sure what she'd asked in the first place.

"I don't know what I wish," he said, low.

Then he did a peculiar thing. He moved his fingers around her hand and encircled it in his own grasp. Her fingers fluttered like a small bird before snuggling down with quiet contentment within the warm nest. Through the haze that clouded her mind, she realized he'd not only accepted her touch, he'd welcomed it, returned it. Not since that haunting night when his lips had silenced her had she felt so. . . .

He gave her hand a gentle squeeze before releasing it and stepped back.

As he pulled his eyes away from hers, she detected the deep rumble of a moan before he cleared his throat. "We shall stay only if I deem it safe for you, Bethany."

She was awash with tingles and took a deep breath, hoping they'd disperse. Her breath expelled in a great, quivery sigh.

He ran his fingers through his hair and glanced at her. A sidelong glance, not a full look, thank heaven. She concentrated on his silky beard. The sun dappled it with gold, and she remembered the intriguing dimple in his chin that was hidden beneath. She rubbed her fingertip across her thumb.

He continued, "If I accept Castle's offer, you must promise to tell me if you're ever mistreated or if you should—uh—become uncomfortable in any way."

She was uncomfortable now, but she couldn't tell him that. She was certain he meant something other than this now-familiar affliction that he himself seemed to bring upon her.

"I promise," she said, her voice as weak as she felt.

Castle was coming toward them with a short, round woman in his wake. Bethany pressed her hands into the sides of her skirt. Both she and Adam turned and faced the pair, waiting.

Ida Pumphrey's face was a wreath of crinkly smiles. Bethany saw at once that she was as kind as she was wide.

But Adam, of course, viewed her with suspicion.

"Bethany will require patience and guidance," he said after the introductions. "You must assure me you will honor my demands in that matter."

"I brought five children up to be diligent adults, Mister Stewart, through care and love and with naught else save the able assistance of a gentle husband. My grown children have scattered hither and yon, my beloved man is dead. I welcome your sister into both my care and my heart."

Bethany suspected Ida Pumphrey's heart was as big as her bosom. She hoped Adam could see that, too.

In the end, he seemed to, but not until he'd asked the woman additional questions that were less polite than probing.

Finally, after repeating to Mister Castle his earlier requirements of daily contact with her and their spending their Sundays together, he gave his acceptance.

He remained wary and on guard, however.

As she walked toward the house with Mrs. Pumphrey, she called back to him, "You'll care for Constant, won't you, George?" She knew he would. He'd grown fond of the dog, and Constant doted on him.

Adam reached down to pull the dog close and gave him a pat. "He'll be fine," he assured her, watching her closely.

She longed to smooth away the dark concern on his face. "I shall be fine, too," she said, keeping her voice light. "Please have faith in the good of these folk."

His scowl deepened, so she added, with a smile she hoped conveyed the rush of warmth she felt for him, "I'll miss you a great deal, Ad . . . George, but I look forward to our meetings."

She meant it. Oh my, she truly meant it.

Chapter Fifteen

"I need talk with you," she whispered into Adam's ear as she placed his supper plate before him. "When you've finished, I'll meet you out by the stable."

He nodded and glanced up at her. "No hurry," she added under her breath before speaking up for all to hear, "eat well, brother, the hog pudding this night is delicious."

Every man around the table was secretly eyeing her. Little wonder, Adam thought, stabbing into the hearty dish with his fork. Bethany looked far more delicious than the hog pudding, far more delicious even than the plum tarts on the corner cupboard. The white bodice she wore was most becoming, though he wished the front were higher. He didn't relish the others getting glimpses of her tempting bosom.

None of them dared stare outright at her in his

presence, nor would they risk a comment about her beauty, but he was acutely aware of the way the air sizzled whenever she was in the room.

Being her protective brother had turned into an ever-increasing responsibility.

He was curious why she'd asked to speak with him at such a late hour. As a rule, they held their brief conversations after the midday dinner before resuming their respective chores. It had been her routine to return to the main house before the men finished their supper, letting the kitchen women serve dessert.

But tonight she stayed, busying herself by assisting with the late-evening tasks. She was fidgety, and that disturbed him. So far, he'd been content that she was both happy and safe at Ridgecrest. Certainly, she'd adapted well during the past month, demonstrating her agility at conquering the myriad new things she'd had to learn. She'd grown exceedingly competent, never making a mistake more than once and there had been precious few of those, considering the challenges she'd faced.

Ida Pumphrey had done as she'd promised, and more. She'd guided her well, and he knew Bethany was truly fond of the woman. And Robert Castle had remained a gentleman throughout, though Adam still had doubts about the man. Castle was unduly attentive to and protective of Bethany, frequently seeming to treat her more like a ward than his servant.

Was Castle the cause for her need to talk with him tonight? He watched her place a cleaned spit on the wall rack. The bow of her apron jiggled against her narrow waist as she lifted her arms, and her full skirt swayed in a restless motion. She was full of nervous energy and he was impatient to discover why.

When she turned, he caught her eye and nodded his head toward the door. She acknowledged his signal by telling the cooks and the men a pleasant "good night" and leaving the kitchen.

Adam waited a couple of minutes before excusing himself. "The pudding is a mite heavy for my taste, and you fellows can battle over my dessert," he said. "I'm going outside for my pipe."

Martha, the plain-faced cook, fretted over his lack of appetite, but the men, fully intent on their suppers now that Bethany had departed, paid him no heed.

He found her standing in the shadows of the stable. Honeysuckle perfumed the pungent layer of animal smells, and the air was redolent with the mix—beauty mingled with brute strength.

Adam lit his pipe and studied her face before speaking. "Is there trouble, Bethany?"

She shook her head. "No, Mister Gloom and Worry, I'm fit as a fiddle and fine as wine." Her voice was cheerful, animated. "Tis that I've heard something of Wendover, and I know how long it's been since you first told me to keep my ears open for that, and so I'm eager to tell you."

His heart thumped an extra beat. "What have you heard?"

"They were here for dinner today, as you know, the Lawrences. All of them, even the two young ladies— Mistress Polly Lawrence and their houseguest, Mistress Evelyn Mason. Oh my, they dress like princesses. The Mistress Mason was wearing a pink frock that was frothy as a strawberry compote and—"

"Bethany."

She clamped down on her lip and quirked a smile. "I'll save all those fancies to entertain you with on Sunday," she said. "It's just that the visits by the Lawrences provide me with great fascination. Tis always a festive occasion, and I—"

"Wendover," he reminded her.

Her ruffly white cap bobbed atop its bed of tidy copper curls. "Mister Lawrence and Mister Castle were talking over their brandy, and I took the pot of coffee in to refill their cups. I heard Mister Lawrence say 'Wendover,' so I fussed around at the sideboard a mite, stacking the dishes and cutlery and such in order to listen, though I would seldom do that, of course."

She stopped and straightened her shoulders. The moonlight burnished her skin with silver, highlighting the alluring curves of her breasts. He fought the distraction and concentrated on the ruffles of her cap.

"And?" he prompted.

"And I heard him say"—she lowered her voice in a charming imitation of Hallston Lawrence's gravelly voice—"that dastardly Wallace is likely to lose Wendover unless he ceases his profligate ways and his wayward penchant for gambling.'"

Adam removed the pipe stem from his mouth. "Are you certain? He said 'dastardly'?"

The cap bobbed. "Aye, and all the rest is exact, too, though I've no inkling what 'profligate' and 'penchant' mean. I've had a bloody hard time keeping the full sentence firm in my mind till I could tell you."

He felt like hugging her. He'd been waiting to hear those words, with his patience stretched near to the point of breaking. His uncle disapproved of James! He now could approach Hallston Lawrence with his truth and enlist his able assistance.

"The message pleases you, I vow," she said, tilting her head and smiling broadly.

"Aye, it does indeed. Thank you."

"May I ask why?"

His finger gave her upturned nose a light tap. "No, you may not, little sister, and you must promise not to breathe a word of this to anyone."

Her smile faded and a brush of worry crossed her silvered face. "Is this Wallace of Wendover the man who deceived you?"

He turned away with a scowl. "Aye."

"And you're still driven to destroy him?"

He tightened his jaw. "My resolve is firm, Bethany, and I don't want to hear another of your tiresome lectures on the evils of revenge. Say no more."

But he knew he might as well have told the earth to stop twirling on its axis.

She walked around to face him. "I have no lecture tonight, but I would like to remind you . . ." She paused under the pressure of his warning look. "I must remind you that it sounds as if Mister Wallace is destroying himself well enough without your assistance, so you should now get on with your life and forget about him."

He attempted a threatening growl, but it came out as a weary moan. "Damn it, woman, you profess not to lecture and then you proceed to lecture." Exasperation laced through his tone as he continued, "Get this one truth etched into your stonelike head and keep it there. *I* will destroy James Wallace. It is *my* life and I'll run it as I choose, and *you* will never change my mind, even if you learn every damnable word in this bloody universe and speak all of them at once!" He'd built into quite a roar.

She worked at stifling something maddeningly close to a wry grin. "You say 'one truth,' and then you list at least three matters, Adam. Which of them shall I keep in my stony head—that you'll destroy this Wallace person, that you'll run your life as you choose, or that I'll never change your mind?" Her voice was sweet as sugar.

He deeply desired to wring her neck. He found himself chuckling instead and muttering, *"Touché."*

"Touché? What does that—"

"Forget it," he interrupted, raising his hand in surrender. "Go on to your bed, Bethany. I'll see you tomorrow."

"Don't you want to hear about the prince?"

He frowned. "What prince?"

"My prince."

She fingered her dream catcher. She'd begun to fashion pretty little containers for the foolish amulet, and tonight it was held in a puff of green cloth that was strung with a thin silk ribbon of the same color. Why did her every mention of this phantom of her fanciful imagination cause a churning bubble in the pit of his stomach?

With unease, he noted he had to feign his disinterest. "So, what of him?"

"His name is Marshall, I believe."

"Marshall?"

"Aye, you must promise to keep my secret, too. Marshall Lawrence, Mister Lawrence's son, he rides a white horse and his hair and eyes are those of my dreams, and he—"

"Hold a minute, woman. You're saying you think Marshall Lawrence is going to carry you over the blue mountains? *Marshall Lawrence?* The son of an aristo—"

"I'm already over the mountains, Adam. You brought me, remember?"

He ignored her remark, his brain racing at a furious pace. She had reason to believe his dandified cousin could be her promised prince? He'd seen Marshall Lawrence a few times and had been unimpressed. He was a true snob who looked down his nose at the servants in a demeaning way that had rankled Adam. And she truly was thinking that sniveling coxcomb could be her prince?

A stab of concern pierced him. Marshall Lawrence had been a frequent visitor to Ridgecrest of late. Had he. . . .

"Has this man touched you, Bethany?" By God, he'd kill him if he'd laid a finger on her!

She stepped back and looked up at him, puzzled. "No, Adam. But why are you so angry with me?"

"I'm not angry with you," he growled. "I just want to know why the hell you think Marshall Lawrence is your bloody prince."

Her lip quivered. "I told you . . . the white horse, the hair, the eyes . . . and the way he looks at me now and again, and truly, Adam, I don't understand why you're reacting so—"

"*Looks* at you? Bloody right he looks at you!" he heard himself shouting. "Any man with blood in his veins looks at you, Bethany, for God's sake. You're an unusually beautiful woman."

His outburst echoed through his ears, and then there was complete silence until a horse whinnied inside the stable.

Bethany stared up at him, and his heart twisted. Her widened eyes were brimming with tears, and a large one spilled out and began rolling down her cheek.

"Pl–please don't be angry, Adam," she sniffled. "I thought you'd be happy for me." Her lashes swept down, releasing a cascade of teardrops. She smeared them away with her fingers, but fresh ones streamed forth. Her wet cheeks glistened in the moonlight.

He couldn't bear to see her so distraught. She'd misunderstood, had mistaken his concern for anger. Chastising himself for upsetting her, he reached out to cradle her chin in his hands and lifted her face toward his.

"I have no anger with you, Bethany. You must

understand it's concern for your future that sometimes puts such harshness into my words." With his thumbs, he wiped away her tears, and his fingers combed back the wisps of curls that had fallen around her ears. "See, I'm far from angry," he added, hoping his calmer tones would assure her. Though his brain warned him to withdraw his hands, they remained where they were, seemingly glued to the moistness of her soft cheeks; his fingers wrapped through her silky hair and stayed there.

And though he was well aware of the potential danger a steady gaze held for both of them, he could do naught but look deeply into her eyes. *Beware*, his mind called out weakly even as he fell again under her spell.

"Why?" Her whispered question was a caress across his lips.

"Why what?" Only a tiny corner of his brain noted with alarm that he'd lowered his face quite near to hers. The rest had become helplessly caught up in a whirlwind of confusion.

"Why . . . oh, why everything?" She blinked, and her lashes, when they lifted, were like black lace studded with teardrop diamonds.

Her strangled sob broke the spell. He gathered her into his arms and held her head against his wildly beating chest. He buried his face into the top of her linen cap.

Freed from the hold of her magical eyes, he retrieved a few shreds of coherent thought and began to weave them into a semblance of sanity. Forcing himself to ignore her ripe body against him, he focused what little concentration he could muster on finding a way to answer whatever she was asking him. Damnably difficult, when he was so blasted unsure what that might be.

"Tell me what it is you want to know, and I'll do my best to explain—if I can, that is," he said at last. Her arms were locked around his waist. That was all right. She needed something to hold on to.

Her sigh was wavery, but she'd ceased sobbing, thank God. "So many things, Adam. I'll try hard to be brief."

She'd turned her head, but held the side of her face tight against his chest. He knew she was chewing on her lip, as she did so often when she was ordering her thoughts. He found himself smiling and drew her closer to assure her he was waiting with patience.

"For one, I guess I want to know why you become so mean-spirited every time I mention my prince."

Had he? Surely, that hadn't been the case. But he was far from in the mood to argue with her.

"If I seem mean-spirited, Bethany, it's because I don't want you hurt." His hand kneaded her shoulder while he spoke. "High expectations can too often be toppled, and they fall with a crash, breaking things—things like your heart, for example. I don't want that to happen to you."

Her arms tightened around him; she was quiet for a spell. His thumb gently rubbed the warmed hollow at her nape.

"Does that mean that you believe the prince is naught but a 'high expectation'?" she asked.

He closed his eyes, struggled to choose the right words. "Your prince may be real, I hope that for you, but I prefer to call whoever your future husband might be a solid flesh-and-blood man of this earth rather than some airy dream phantom prince. And you'll find him, I feel sure, but you'll only be able to recognize him once you've cleared your head of those fantasy cobwebs you've woven. Meanwhile you must . . ."

He'd lost his train of thought. She had squirmed closer, and her firm stomach was pressing against his aching arousal. Dear God, this was no way to conduct an important conversation.

But she was listening, he believed. Damn it, he had to continue. Where was he?

"Uh, meanwhile you must stop looking for things like dark hair and blue eyes and white horses, but you should wait for a suitable man who will love you and care for you in the way you deserve." He was speaking too rapidly, compelled by a deep urgency to bring this uncomfortable situation to a speedy end.

"Do you hear me?" he heard himself ask.

"Aye," she responded, and with profound relief he felt her pushing away.

"How will I know such a man?" she inquired.

He held her shoulders, determined not to falter now that she'd released her pressure against his groin. But he couldn't avoid her wide, emerald eyes.

"You must be cautious." His voice was like a croak; he cleared his throat. "Men can be animals, Bethany, and many will desire you. Keep them distant till your heart tells you otherwise."

Hell, he was botching this whole thing miserably. She didn't understand a thing he was saying. He wasn't certain what he was trying to say, either.

Her next question added to his discomfort. "Am I truly beautiful as you said?"

"Aye." Damn it, he was croaking again. He dropped his hands and moved away from her. "Remember that and remain cautious" was all he could think of to add.

She fidgeted with her hair and straightened her cap. Though she emitted an aura of uncertainty, he sensed he'd made some inroads with her. Lord knew, she was smart, and she'd heard him. Maybe, he prayed, she'd heed his words.

"I owe you my gratitude, and not for the first time," she said, eyeing him, he could tell, but he didn't face her. "I have many more questions for you, Adam. I know nothing of love between a man and a woman, let alone what they do to seal that love, and I trust you will guide me in such matters."

Bloody hell, what had he gotten himself into?

"I'm truly confused," she continued, "for though my dream catcher's songs assure me, your strong words strike me as truth also. I shall learn to listen to my heart as you advise. I'm not sure I yet know its voice."

He nodded his approval, but was disturbed by the peculiar turn his simple motives of comfort and protection had taken. *Listen to one's heart?* Had he truly given such advice? He didn't even know what the hell that meant.

Though she seemed as subdued and tentative as he felt, her voice had a lilting lift. "On Sunday, I trust you'll instruct me about this thing between a woman and a man that I understand not. I must know, Adam, before you leave me. Will you promise me that?"

"I promise," he said without enthusiasm.

"And I'll be cautious," she said, "though of what I'm not certain. Have a good night, my dear one. You're more than a brother to me, you know. You . . . you're my guiding star."

With that parting salute, she ran toward the house.

Adam stood silent for a long while, and then, with a low moan, headed to his own quarters.

When Bethany entered the small bedroom she shared with Ida Pumphrey, she saw the woman was still awake, sewing. Though she enjoyed her company, tonight she wished for solitude. She sorely needed to think through Adam's words.

Thomasina Ring

"You're mighty late coming in this eve," Ida said, not taking her eyes off her stitching. It wasn't a question, but Bethany knew the genial woman expected a response.

"I helped Martha and the others tidy up and then spoke for a while with my brother." She sat on the edge of her bed and removed her cap. Noting it was a mite mussed, she plumped it and set it beside her on the quilt. Her fingers lingered on the rounded top of the smooth linen cap. Adam's face had been there and an enveloping flush of warmth followed the thought.

"Your new dress is near ready. It's lawn, ye know. Mister Castle purchased the bolt of fabric last week. Ye should have the lightness of lawn for your summer frocks, he says, now that the days have grown so warm."

"He's too kind to me, and so are you, Ida. Your stitching is truly fine. My own is coarse and rough, and I long to learn your skill."

"You'll surpass my puny skills with the needle before ye know it, Bethany Rose, and in the meanwhile I relish making ye pretty clothing. Keeps my withered fingers agile, it does, and the good Lord knows ye needed a set of frocks." She smiled, fluffing the fabric out on her lap. Pale lavender it was, the color of the lilacs blooming in Ridgecrest's garden. A roll of purple ribbon atop the chest beside the woman indicated Bethany's new dress would be decorated unlike anything she'd ever owned. Far too fancy for a servant girl's daily wear but it would be perfect for her Sunday outings with Adam.

The realization he'd be one of the first to see her in it gave her an unexpected rise of pleasure.

"Tis indeed admirable the way your brother frets over your well-being," Ida said, making Bethany wonder if she could read her thoughts.

Her cheeks grew hot, but her response was quick. "I've been a heavy burden of responsibility to him these past months. At times he frets needlessly, but I've learned to expect that from him, so it doesn't truly bother me." Did it? Tonight he'd had her in tears but he'd comforted her out of them. Those soothing circles he'd drawn on the nape of her neck . . . She rubbed her upper arm, trying to dispel the warm shiver lodged there.

"Ye two are so different 'tis hard to believe you sprang from the same parents. You're like sunshine, he's thunder and lightning."

Bethany looked with caution at the woman. Was she suspicious? She wasn't eyeing her, and her pleasant face remained placid.

"Only our father was the same. His mama died young, then Pa married my mama." It had been thus with her and George, and the two of them truly had been unalike. She hated lying to Ida Pumphrey, but she prayed the explanation satisfied her. She'd promised Adam to keep his secret and she owed him her allegiance.

And she felt she should defend him, too. "You compare my brother to a storm, and he's often growly and fiery, true. But he's strong as a black bear and reliable as a pack animal, and ofttimes he's gentle as a colt." She stood and began to undress.

"Aye, he's all of those, though only the sister sees the colt, I vow," the woman said with a chuckle. "The bear and mule we've all seen."

Bethany smiled beneath her skirt as she swished it over her head. She'd seen the bear and mule many times herself.

"Don't get me wrong, child, all of us at Ridgecrest have come to admire George Stewart. Mister Castle and Angus both have told me he's the best hand this place has ever had."

Her heart swelling with pride for Adam, she removed her shift and slid the sheer linen night-dress over her head.

"He's admired," Ida continued, "but ye, my dear, are loved by everyone at Ridgecrest."

"Not by everyone," Bethany reminded her, trying to keep her voice light. "Mrs. Castle truly dislikes me, I fear."

"Faugh, that hardhearted termagant dislikes every-one. Pay her no heed," she said, squinting at the needle's small eye and pushing the thread through.

Bethany sat back on the bed with a sigh. "Tis the only spot of sadness for me at Ridgecrest. I long to please her, and yet all I do displeases her. I know I'm an 'ignorant mountain girl,' as she tells me daily, but I'm truly trying, though I may never achieve the perfection she requires. I still confuse the linens on occasion and at dinner today I placed the wrong forks for the dessert course."

Ida Pumphrey looked up from her sewing. "Your errors have been amazingly few, child. When I think of the distance ye've come in a brief month, why, I'm proud as a mother hen. Stop fretting, now, and turn down your covers. It's time we both get some sleep." She put aside the dress and, wheezing from the effort, heaved her wide body up from the chair.

"She calls me 'Bella Mae,'" Bethany said with disgruntlement, folding back the quilt and slipping between the soft linens on the feather mattress. It was like sleeping on a cloud, and she hadn't yet grown accustomed to its airy luxury.

Ida snorted a mild laugh. "She calls me 'Ada,' and I've worked here fifteen years. She does it on purpose, I've decided."

"Why, do you suppose?"

"Meanness. She's an unhappy woman who's shielded herself inside an armor that allows no closeness. Purposely using the wrong name for a person is a form of separation, and it shows a lack of caring. She cares for no one but herself." She snuffed the room's candles, and the moon's glow through the window washed the darkness with an eerie light.

Bethany stared up at the shadows of the cross beams on the low ceiling. "Surely, she cares for Mister Castle. He's her husband."

There was a heavy rustle from across the room as the woman climbed into her own bed. "God's truth, the poor man deserves to be loved, but fate wedded him to a woman with no heart."

"He should have listened to his own heart before marrying her," Bethany said with a frown of worry. Dear heaven, was it possible to hear one's heart wrong?

"He had no choice, child. The marriage was arranged by their families. A merging of dynasties, it was." She paused, and Bethany turned her head toward her, knitting her brows. "Little good it did," the woman added, then chuckled. "Nary a babe resulted for the noble bloodline. I'd be surprised if that chunk of ice ever allowed him close enough to start one."

Bethany's heart quickened. There it was again—merging bloodlines, babes. Dare she ask Ida her bedeviling question? A peculiar shyness gripped her. No, she mustn't be direct, but perhaps she could inquire about other troubling matters.

"How did you know you loved Mister Pumphrey?" she asked, holding her dream catcher tightly.

A sweet sigh drifted across the room. "Oh my, I suppose it was the way he made me feel when I was with him. It's hard to explain, child, but ye know. Ye just know when ye find your mate. You're drawn to him, want him to touch ye. Why, the first time Will kissed me, I knew he was the only man for me."

"Kissed you? What's that?"

The pause was like the ripple of a satin ribbon. "A lover's kiss places a man's lips upon a woman's," the gentle voice said. "It's a special prelude to even more intimate touches that set wonderful fires in your body. Ye have much to look forward to, child, and your heart will tell ye when you've found the man of your dreams."

The amulet pulsed as fast as her rapid heartbeat. *Lips upon lips?* Adam had *kissed* her that night and she'd truly been aflame. His every touch seemed to set blazes within her. Even his eyes upon her at times had been like burning torches that. . . .

"Have a good night, Bethany Rose. Sleep well." Ida's voice sounded like a contented smile.

Bethany was finding it hard to breathe, impossible to return the "good night."

Adam? Was her heart telling her Adam was her prince? *Adam?* Adam felt naught but a sense of responsibility for her. He was obsessed with his hatred for the man who'd deceived him and had no room in his heart for love. Like Mrs. Castle, he kept distant from people, shielded himself from them. And then, a contradictory thought struck her with stunning swiftness. There had been times . . . oh my, a number of radiantly beautiful times . . . when he had indeed opened that shield and brought her inside with him. She swallowed the gasp that leapt to her throat.

Her dream catcher throbbed against her palm. *What are you saying to me?* she asked it. Her ears buzzed with its confusing song. *You'll know your prince. Your heart tells you who he is. Your heart. . . .*

But her heart was whirling like a crazed tumbler and said nothing she could understand.

She pushed her face into the pillow. Dear heaven, what if it should speak Adam's name to her? What then?

My God, is it possible that Adam is my prince?

Her next plea to the pulsing amulet was a soulful prayer.

Open my ears to my heart's voice and have it speak with truth and wisdom.

Chapter Sixteen

"Aye, tis guid to raise me boots on a stool, lean back, and cradle a mug of rum. Saturday eves bring a touch o' heaven to a working man's life." Angus McInnes's rich, musical Highland brogue was trailed by a sigh of contentment.

Adam reached over to pour another gill into the burly Scot's cup, then refilled his own. "It's true sustenance to weary bones and tortured souls," he agreed.

Angus's pale blue eyes glinted beneath his heavy red eyebrows. "Tortured, are ye now, George Stewart? When ye've landed work in the fairest homestead in the Virginia colony?"

Adam shrugged off the questions with a half-hearted grin. "An overstatement on my part. Shall I say restless souls?"

Angus laughed. "Aye, a man's soul be e'er restless

on this mortal coil, and only rum or a bonnie lass can lay a temporary quiet on its fevered brow. We're sadly without the one this midsummer eve, but the guid God's blessed us with twa flagons of the other."

The two were alone in the men's quarters, both of them having chosen not to join the others on their merry jaunt to a crossroads tavern up at Cabellsville. "Ye fellers don't know what you're missin', I wager. Plump wenches be there who know how to soothe away a hard man's woes," Mike had cajoled as they'd saddled their horses.

But Adam hadn't been tempted, though he wondered why the hell not. God knew, he sorely needed the release a woman's company could provide, but Mike's mention of "plump wenches" had been like a bucket full of icy water dumped over his head, reminding him too well of Sweet Molly and the mighty woes that had befallen him as a result of her so-called soothing.

Besides, a nagging sense of apprehension had gripped him this evening. About what, he wasn't sure, but it had to do with Bethany. He needed to be here. She might require his protection.

The two cups of rum had muffled the apprehension. Indeed, they had made him scoff inwardly at allowing himself to fall prey to a premonition with no substance. He should have joined the men. He needed the solace of a woman far more than that offered by rum.

" . . . but with oxlike stubbornness the fool Braddock insisted we build the plank road and march in our blazing red coats in regimental file through the wilderness and 'twas teeming with the wily Indians armed to the teeth by the devious French. Ready they were to pepper us guid, too. Colonel Washington tried to tell the bloody English general, but . . ."

Angus was recounting his favorite war tale; Adam knew it by heart by now, but pretended to listen with interest.

"You should speak with more respect for our glorious English army," he chastised him mildly, as he always did. Hell, he'd been appalled himself by the fools thinking they could stage classic battlefield maneuvers in a war against Indians. But, after all, he was English and he enjoyed needling the good-natured Scot.

"For meself, I'm a Virginian and proud of it. The English be damned," Angus exploded.

Adam chuckled. "You sound like my friend, Dan Morgan. He often told me he was a Virginian first, a bloody good shot second, a lover of women third, and that the English part came down at the bottom of a mighty long list of more important priorities, including rum and good food."

Angus looked up with interest. "Ye ken Fightin' Dan? A braw one, he is. Was with me at Fort Chiswell and I saw him get five hundred lashes across his back for knocking the brine out of an upstart officer." He shook his head. "Bravest man I e'er saw. Didn't blink an eye through the thrashing, stood stalwart as the cat-o'-nine made bloody ribbons of his skin, and he counted the lashes. *Counted* them. 'He gave me only four hundred ninety-nine,' he told me once. 'Just guess I owe old King George one.' "

Adam knew that story well, too, and he'd seen the scarred proof on Morgan's back. He wanted to change the subject. The conversation was darkening his mood, reminding him with fierceness of his own battle-ridden past.

"I hear Colonel Washington's left the militia. I served under him at the Duquesne victory. What's he doing now?" he asked Angus.

"Got himself wedded last year to a rich widow lady, he did. Lives over in Mount Vernon by the Potomac and, so I hear, divides his time between developing one of the best damn self-sufficient plantations in the colony and representing Frederick County in that do-nothing House of Burgesses down in Williamsburg."

At least they'd got off the subject of war. Adam took a hearty swig from his cup. The rum was taking hold and he welcomed the numbing fog creeping around his brain.

"Do you plan to spend the rest of your days here at Ridgecrest, Angus?"

The amiable Scot shook his head. "Nae, lad. I have a dream, I do, and saving my shillings, too, to make it come real."

Bloody hell, did this hardened, tough, levelheaded man before him say he had a *dream?* Adam swallowed another big gulp of rum.

"Going to find meself a bonnie wee lass to wed, I am, and when the time's ripe, I'm taking her with me out to that fertile Valley and buy us a tract of land. From the first day I saw that Valley, George, I knew that's where I belong."

"Why the Valley, for God's sake? There's fertile land aplenty here in Albemarle, and the Tidewater's bountiful."

He shook his head of thick red hair. "The Tidewater's bought up by a handful of dandified planters, and they've pretty much taken over Albemarle, too. Look at Lawrence and Castle, though Castle is a man apart, I allow you that."

Adam had to agree. Castle and his slave-free plantation was run far different from places like Wendover and Brierwood. Run as successfully, but truly different.

"All of it is too *English* for my taste, lad," Angus continued. "The Valley, now, that's a place where a man can breathe free, can live free of the English yoke. There are *individuals* there, Scotsmen, Irishmen, Dutchmen. Independent folk, George, like our friend, Fightin' Dan. They're the future, not those inward-looking land barons down in the Tidewater who grow dynasties rather than corn."

Adam looked hard at his companion. The Scot didn't know he was lambasting Adam's own heritage. The Tidewater was filled with his kin and he damned well planned to be part of it again, to form his own dynasty. It was his right—his birthright, by God.

But he held no anger toward Angus. The man talked of independent folk and that had a pleasant ring to it.

Angus stood and brought another bottle over to the table. Adam let him refill his cup, though he knew he'd have a roaring headache in the morning. Sunday. Bloody hell, Bethany expected him to tell her the facts of life tomorrow. He emptied the cup with two swallows and poured himself another big portion.

"So you're taking your bonnie wee lass to the Valley. Are you working on finding her?" Adam's speech was slightly slurred and came punctuated with a hiccup.

Angus smiled. "Maybe that depends on ye, Stewart."

"Me?"

He nodded. "I'd like your permission to call on your sister now and again, get to know the bonnie lass a little to see if—"

"*No.*" Adam was stunned by the strength of his response. His brain was suddenly as clear as crystal. Or was it? He was acting abominably, truly stupid. Angus was a fine man, as big and strong as he himself and far kinder. He would be a perfect mate for

Bethany, and it was, after all, her decision to make, not his.

"Sorry, Angus," he said, looking over at the disconcerted Scot. "I've grown so protective of Bethany that I forget at times she's grown up now, with a mind of her own. I'll ask her tomorrow if she'd like you to visit her."

He felt rotten. A stray thought warned him he was going to feel more rotten if Bethany agreed to the proposal.

Nonsense, he reprimanded himself, pulling up to his feet.

"I've had enough rum for one night. Think I'll go outside for a breath of fresh air. Want to join me?" He hoped not, he wanted to be alone.

Angus stood and offered his hand. "Nae, I'll just stay here with the bottle a bit longer. Thank ye, Stewart." His handshake was warm and firm. His hand matched Adam's in size.

"I'll be in later. Have a good night, my friend."

For a while, Adam leaned against the weatherboard of the men's quarters, smoking his pipe and letting the cool mountain-kissed air disperse the remnants of the rum's fog.

His thoughts, however, remained in disarray. The conversation with Angus had bothered him, but was that only because of the way it had shifted hither and yon, traveling from cruel realities like war and thrashings to such things as the man's wispy dreams of a happy future with a "bonnie lass" among independent folk?

No, Angus's words about Bethany were nagging at him, too.

Her head was so filled with fanciful clouds that she could well find enchantment in Angus's dream. He wanted happiness for her, didn't he? If anyone could transform a dream into reality, the burly, no-nonsense Scot might be that man.

So why the hell did the thought of Bethany with Angus make his stomach churn? That was the rum's doings, he decided, pushing himself away from the building. He'd walk it off. Taking long strides, he began pacing the grounds of Ridgecrest.

As he passed the tall boxwoods that bordered the garden, he stopped, jerked to a halt by peculiar sounds coming from beyond the hedge. He yanked the pipe from his suddenly clamped teeth.

What the hell. . . .

Bethany had her nose stuck in the fragrant center of a pink rose when Marshall Lawrence came up behind her.

"Ah, there's a far fairer blossom amongst the others this eve, I see." The voice was smooth, deep—startling.

She jumped, pricking her finger on a thorn and whirled around.

"My sincere apologies for intruding upon your reverie, *bella mia*, I was but taking a stroll," he said with a polite bow of his head. His rich, dark hair picked up the glow of moonbeams.

Though fascinated, she pulled back. "My name is Bethany, Mister Lawrence, though Mrs. Castle calls me 'Bella Mae,'" she said impulsively. She didn't sound like herself. Her words were as fluttery as a butterfly's wings. The eyes looking down at her were the blue of a summer's sky.

His ripple of soft laughter floated across her ears. "I know your name, my lovely—Bethany Rose Stewart. *Bella mia* is Spanish for 'my beauty,' and that's the way I think of you."

It was? She wanted to be thrilled. Instead, a warning, like a cold, steel rod, stiffened her back.

She couldn't speak, could only stare at him with stunned eyes. He was the image of her prince, but something was wrong.

"I've given you a start, haven't I? You will forgive me, I trust?"

Smooth . . . honied. She trembled.

"Come, my dear, sit with me on the bench yon where we can have a talk to put you at ease." He cupped her elbow.

She tensed and pulled it away from him. "No, sir. I must go inside now." There'd been no warmth in his hand and she was truly uneasy.

"Nonsense. I've been waiting to find you alone."

He moved toward her with unexpected swiftness, impaling her with terror as his hands clamped her shoulders and pulled her relentlessly forward. His arms imprisoned her and then, with a suddenness that defied her frightened protests, his lips fell hard upon hers.

He's kissing me! It was loathsome.

She struggled, but he was strong. As his tongue invaded her resistant mouth, his hand ran down her rigid back, reached her buttocks, and pulled her tight against him. A wave of nausea struck her.

"Relax, my sweet, you want this as much as I do," he coaxed before moving his lips in a moist trail down her neck.

An ugly vision flashed across her mind. A slimy snail was crawling, leaving its tracks on her skin.

"*No,*" she pleaded, pushing at his shoulders, madly squirming to get away from his grasp. A violent memory lashed at her. *The trapper!* He was like the trapper!

"Unloose her!"

The rough voice tore through her fevered brain,

then soothed it like an angel's song. Adam. The disgusting Marshall Lawrence had dropped his arms, was moving back. He'd been pushed back, pushed away from her by a ferocious shove. For a frozen moment, she wondered if he had a tomahawk in his skull. But he was standing, his face contorted in anger, glaring at Adam.

"Your sister invited me this eve, Stewart," he said.

Bethany was numb. She shook her head in denial, but Adam wasn't looking at her. He glowered at the man.

"You're not to touch my sister, even if she sends you a thousand invitations, Lawrence. Do you understand me?"

She'd never seen him so angry.

The dark-haired man brushed the shoulder of his frock coat and fussed with the lacy ruffles that stuck out from his sleeves. "If you were a gentleman, sirrah, I would challenge you to a duel," he said with a sneer.

"And you'd also die," Adam said through clenched teeth.

He stepped between her and Marshall Lawrence and stood solid as a mountain boulder, facing the man. She stared at his back, reveling in his strength and grateful for his protection, but trembling still.

He blocked her view of the man she'd once considered her long-sought prince. She shuddered and held on to her dream catcher. Though warm in her cold hand, it was silent.

"Leave now," she heard Adam say to him. There was a muttered oath, then a haughty "harumph," followed by the sound of steady, purposeful footsteps as the man left the garden.

Adam stood with his back to her, his hands gripped tightly by his sides. She was afraid to speak.

When he turned to face her at last, she lowered her eyes and pressed her nails into her palms.

"Did he speak the truth, Bethany? Did you invite him here?"

She tried to shake her head, but it wouldn't move. She clamped her lips together. They were sore from the man's brutal kisses.

His sigh was a whiff of sadness. "He's not your prince, you know."

Her throat clogged with the tears she wouldn't let climb to her eyes. "I know, Adam," she said so softly she could barely hear it herself.

"I'll walk you to the door," he said, placing his hand lightly at the middle of her back and guiding her forward. Her steps were halting, then grew more sure under his gentle support as they walked side by side across the mossy stones.

The secure warmth of his firm hand against her back was like a soothing balm. She wanted to keep it there forever.

But they arrived at the house's wide front door, which was standing open, and he removed his hand to step aside and let her enter.

She paused and dared to gaze up at him. His eyes, dark and troubled, pierced through her heart and into her soul.

At that moment, she knew.

Adam Barwick was her prince.

With a sharp intake of breath, she heard her heart shouting his name so loud that she believed the heavens themselves could hear it.

"Adam?" She wanted to shout it, too, but managed only a whimper.

"Shhh." His finger was across her lips. Like a lover's kiss, her heart sang. "George," he reminded her in a whisper.

"What?" He wasn't making sense, but she didn't care. *It's Adam! It's Adam!* was all she could truly hear.

"George, is that you out there with Bethany?" Robert Castle had walked into the large hall. "Is everything all right?"

Oh, aye, everything is perfect. Her smile, she suspected, stretched from ear to ear.

"Aye, Mister Castle, I found my sister sitting alone in the garden and thought I should bring her to the door. It's grown chill, and she's without a wrap."

Bethany felt like exclaiming she was far from chilled. She was on fire, in fact. But she continued to stand there and smile, looking up at the distinguished silver-haired man, then back to the tawny-haired, bearded giant who, she decided then and there, was the most handsome prince of a man in the whole wide world.

"You must come in out of the chill, Bethany," Mister Castle said, putting an arm around her heated shoulders to draw her inside.

Adam, behind her, seemed to stiffen. "Run on up to your room, Bethany," he said, sounding gruff.

Then he addressed himself with grave formality to Robert Castle. "May I have a few moments of your time, sir? The black stallion appears to be favoring a rear leg, and I think you should have a look at it."

Bethany stood at the door and watched the two men walk toward the stable.

She was sorry about the horse, though far too elated with her own magical discovery to dredge up true concern. But she did find it puzzling that Adam had requested Mister Castle's assistance. He could make the stallion well all by himself. He had a wondrous touch with ailing animals.

Oh my, Adam's touch was *indeed* wondrous. *Every-*

thing about the man was wondrous. With his name ringing in her ears, she ran happily up the wooden staircase to prepare for bed.

She wanted to scream out her news. She wanted to dance a jig. And, glory be, tomorrow was Sunday. Tomorrow she would spend the livelong day with her prince!

Chapter Seventeen

By the time Adam came for her, Bethany was bubbling with suppressed excitement. Equal measures of anticipation and anxiety worked like yeast on her jumbled emotions. Throughout the morning she'd tried with every sobering thought she could conjure to punch down her rising expectations but to no avail.

Adam didn't love her. But surely he would discover he did. He was driven by revenge. He'd forget all that nonsense once his heart filled with love. How should she tell him he was her prince? She'd find both the ideal time and way.

Her heart, pure and simple, had become a warming oven, and her love for Adam was swelling like runaway dough.

His first words to her were perfect, "I am here."

Indeed he *was* there, glorious atop his chestnut,

holding the reins of the spotted horse Mister Castle had offered her for the Sunday outings. Beautifully glorious in the open-neck white shirt that rippled lightly over his muscled arms and back and in his buff breeches that molded tight around the strong curves of his sinewy thighs and legs.

A heated flush warmed her cheeks. Seeing Adam with her eyes cleared of fantasy cobwebs was a dizzying experience. Oh my, he was truly real—and truly wonderful.

She almost tripped over her leather slippers as she ran down the front steps to join him. After handing up to him the basket of food she'd prepared for them, she mounted her horse, choosing to ride sidesaddle like the demure ladies she'd seen. She didn't want to muss her new lavender dress.

Adam nodded his approval of her ladylike perch. She hoped he'd noticed the dress, too, but he didn't comment.

Constant stood wagging his tail behind the horses, and Bethany giggled at the faithful animal's happiness. He loved accompanying them on their weekly outings. Life at Ridgecrest had agreed with Constant. He'd grown a bit of meat over his bones, and his black coat had developed a healthy sheen.

As they rode alongside the quiet James, heading up river to their favorite picnic spot, Bethany, as usual, chatted gaily about one thing and another, trifling things, but Adam never complained. She was never sure he listened, though at times he'd surprise her by speaking up. He'd been attentive after all.

Today her tongue was particularly animated. She couldn't help it.

"Even the dusting is a joy, for the Castle's furniture glows beneath my rubbing. Yesterday I spent a half-hour on the comb-back spindles of the winsome settle, and . . ."

"Windsor," he supplied with a smile. "It's called a Windsor settle."

"Windsor," she repeated. His *smile* was winsome. She forgot what she was talking about.

He took advantage of her pause. "Are you finding time to read daily?" he asked, as he did every Sunday.

Adam kept his eyes on the path ahead and seemed oblivious to her frequent glances in his direction. She thanked the heavens for that, because the time and place weren't yet ripe to tell him she loved him, and she suspected it was written all over her face.

"Aye, I'm reading at least an hour a day. Mister Castle allows me to visit his library when my morning chores are done, and often he's there to guide my selection of books, even has me read aloud to him and helps me when I stumble. Yesterday he introduced me to the poetry of John Donne, and though I had difficulty with numerous words, the beauty of it filled my . . ."

"Donne?" He didn't sound pleased. "His religious works or the other?"

Oh dear. Her cheeks were warming again and she fidgeted with the reins. "Uh, both, I believe." Angels were mentioned. She hoped that qualified as "religious."

He looked stern but, thank goodness, changed the course of the conversation—or so she thought.

"I see you're wearing yet another new frock," he said with a frown. The frown bothered her. She'd hoped for his approval and had thought the lavender beribboned dress quite becoming on her.

"It's lawn. Ida made it from a bolt Mister Castle provided."

"Damn it, Bethany, that man is far too attentive," he said with a grumble. "You must be careful around him."

A wedge of discomfort shoved into her euphoria. He was issuing her that warning again. *Men can be animals, Bethany, and many will desire you. Be cautious.* He'd been right about the beastly Marshall Lawrence—but Mister Castle? Surely not. The man had ever been a lamb of a gentleman with her, always kind, more like a caring father than a. . . .

"You're wrong about him, Adam," she blurted out. "Wrong, wrong, wrong." She had to believe that.

"You remain too trusting, woman. By God, experience alone should have taught you by now that blind trust is foolhardy. Why, that coxcomb Lawrence you invited to—"

"I *didn't* invite him," she interjected, a sliver of anger further diminishing her good spirits. Damnation, did he truly think she was to blame for that ugliness? And, besides, she trusted Adam. Was he telling her that was foolhardy?

They rode in silence for a few minutes.

When he spoke at last, his weighted tone squeezed all traces of airiness from her mood. "I must leave Ridgecrest soon, Bethany. God knows, I should have left days ago. It's only my determination to be sure you're safe that's kept me here so long. Primarily now, my suspicions of Castle hold me prisoner—that and your bloody innocence."

"You're leaving?" Those were the only words she'd heard. The rest had scattered like a weak sprinkling of hailstones across the frozen surface of her mind.

"As soon as possible."

Oh no! He *couldn't* leave her. Not now. Not, please God, *ever*. Adam was her prince. She must tell him. Once he knew, he'd surely stay. But a numbness had gripped her jaws, and she said nothing.

When they reached their picnic spot, her spirits were flat as hoecake, and as twice as heavy. She wanted to flee behind the trees and cry till her eyes hurt.

But Adam was the animated one now, fussing with the linens in the basket, setting out the food, and talking constantly. Not at all like himself. He was trying to cheer her, she figured, but it wasn't working. Only one thing would cheer her, and lighthearted banter about his appetite for cold collar of veal was hardly going to do it.

"I'm not hungry," she said with more petulance than she intended. She punctuated her remark by kicking a pebble into the glasslike stillness of the narrow river and causing a remarkable disturbance in its placid surface.

She'd like to jump in herself and *really* mess up the blasted river.

"Want to tell me what's wrong?" he asked, startling her.

He was standing behind her. She'd thought he was back there with the basket and his beloved veal. Disconcerted, she crossed her arms and kneaded her elbows.

"No." Yes, she did but she couldn't. He wasn't ready to hear her truth.

He moved up beside her, and the two of them watched the water become like a mirror again. She sadly wished the turbulence of a disturbed heart could smooth out with equal swiftness.

"Something I said?"

She nodded.

"My comments about Castle? My accusing you of inviting Lawrence?"

She shook her head twice. He'd slanted his eyes

toward her. She felt them but kept her own gaze on the river.

He ran his fingers through his hair, a true sign he was exasperated. Well, good, so was she.

"What then, for God's sake? How can I defend my words if I don't know what the hell I said to upset you so?"

A flutter of hope skipped across her chest. He cared that she was upset? Maybe, then. . . .

"You said you were leaving." It had popped out of her like the silly cloth jester in that jack-in-the-box toy Mister Castle kept in his library. She wished she could stuff it back and close the lid. But it was too late and she steeled herself for Adam's response.

"Bethany, you've always known I'd be leaving. But didn't you hear me say I wouldn't go till I knew you were safe?"

"I'm not safe yet," she said quickly.

"Damn it, don't you think I know that?"

He kicked a sizeable pebble with the toe of his boot and churned up the water to a fare-thee-well. She felt worlds better. He wouldn't leave her till he thought she was safe. All she had to do was convince him she'd never be safe without him.

As she was figuring how she might accomplish such a feat, he surprised her by reaching for her hand, removing it from her elbow, and pulling her toward the grassy hillock where he'd set their basket.

"We can eat later, I think we should talk a spell. I promised you that, remember?"

He looked uncomfortable as the dickens. But his hand felt so good wrapped around hers that she had trouble remembering what he'd promised to talk about.

Oh. The man and woman thing. Now *she* was

uneasy. If she knew all that, would he then think she was safe?

She already had an inkling what this thing entailed. Her body had been trying to tell her every time she'd been near Adam. It was a simple matter of loving someone, and the complicated other thing followed quite naturally, she was sure. She was, in fact, looking forward to the whole beautiful experience.

Now that she knew he was her prince, her impish next thought surprised her not at all. She would much prefer Adam show her rather than try to tell her, but he'd sat quite a distance away from her, and his furrowed brow indicated he was preparing a long lecture.

She'd play dumb, she decided. Until he discovered that he loved her and could never leave her, she'd just pretend not to understand a word he said.

While she waited for him to begin, she removed her fancy slippers and let the soft grass soothe her bare feet.

"You'll remember, Bethany, that I warned you that men can be animals, and you witnessed that last night," he began.

Adam had never acted like an animal with her, she thought with an inward smile, save, of course, those times he'd demonstrated mulish stubbornness.

"Marshall Lawrence is a snob of an aristocrat who thought it would be a lark to dally with a lovely servant girl and it's precisely because he *is* an aristocrat that he would never entertain the thought of wedding you. But you can be damnably sure he would have—uh—taken your gift of maidenhood without compunctions of conscience—"

"Maidenhood?" she interrupted. Playing dumb was fairly easy.

His fingers ran through his hair again. Beautiful hair, it was, streaked gold by the sun, its loose waves rumpled by the summer breeze. Instinctively, she wiggled an inch toward him.

"Your maidenhood can be given but once, thus a woman must be watchful that she save that gift for the man she weds," he said.

Her eyebrows squiggled. "Only once?" She had hoped this thing would be done numerous times. Whatever, since she fully intended to wed Adam, she was eager for this gift-giving occasion. Her bottom slid sideways another inch.

"Aye, you give it but once," he said with a nod. "It's the most precious gift a woman gives to a man. Thus, you must protect it till your heart tells you you've found your true mate."

Well, her heart had done that, all right—resoundingly.

He yanked up a long stem of grass and worked his lips around it for a spell. His lips intrigued her—the way the bottom one was a tad fuller than the top, for example. She remembered well how they'd felt against hers and shifted another inch or two.

Realizing he was waiting for a question, she pondered but couldn't think of one that made any sense. Which was as it should be, she supposed, since she wanted to play dumb.

"Where's my maidenhood?" was the first thing that entered her mind.

Oh my, now he truly looked uncomfortable. He tossed aside the grass stem and, leaning back and bracing himself with his elbow, turned toward her. He didn't appear to notice she'd closed the gap between them considerably.

"Damn it, Bethany, ask Ida that question and all others about like matters. It's impossible for me to explain it to you."

Back went his fingers, combing through his golden

waves. Her own fingers tingled. That's where they wanted to be.

"But you promised, Adam." A smaller wiggle followed.

He shook his head and sat up. He pulled his booted legs toward him and encircled them with his strong arms. She maneuvered at least five inches while he was distracted.

"It's highly unsuitable," he said.

"Why?" She was close enough to see the pulse of tension at his bronzed temple and longed to ease it—when the time was ripe.

"Because it is" was his grumbled response.

"Then I'll never understand, I guess, since I'm far too shy with Ida to ask such questions." She attempted a proper pout. "And thus I can't be safe, and you'll never be able to leave me."

"But I must . . ." He stopped in mid-sentence when he turned his face toward her, his startled expression a clear signal he hadn't expected to see her so very near him.

The time had come.

"Kiss me, Adam," she whispered.

"What?"

The pulse at his temple had become a drumbeat, and her fingers covered it.

"Kiss me," she repeated, rising on her knees to position her lips a mere breath away from his.

His no was a tickle of a touch.

Her fingertips soothed the throbbing pulse beneath them, then wandered back through his hair, fondling his ear along the way.

"Please." Her lips brushed his—a stronger tickle this time.

His head shook his refusal beneath her fingers. She didn't retreat.

"No, Beth . . ."

Perfect. His *B* had made full contact, and she rose to greet it.

His kiss was precisely as she remembered it, soft and warm—far better, now that she knew what it was and why it was doing what it was doing to her.

He stiffened to pull away, she pushed in closer.

"Mmmm," she muttered, testing with her tongue for the honey she knew she'd find on his lips. It was there, waiting for her.

She searched for more, and, with one deep groan, he became increasingly accommodating, opening to her exactly as she wished. Ah, he tasted wonderful. He *felt* wonderful. She anticipated his arms wrapping about her. They came. She welcomed his sigh of surrender as he pulled her over him and lay beneath her.

Their mouths worked in unison, receiving, responding in a magical rhythm. Her tongue teased his, his returned the favor, explored her lips, her teeth, and then, at last, began the deep thrusts she'd awaited and had hungered for. The waves of fire he unleashed were stronger than she remembered. Delightfully stronger. She traced her fingers around the shells of his ears before finding their warm centers and instinctively offering answering thrusts.

A shiver ran down his long, hard body. He liked that. She smiled into his mouth, repeating the pattern, tracing and thrusting. His moan mingled with hers, setting new fires, finding new paths to set ablaze, new places swelling with desire.

Her skirt and petticoats had crept above her knees. They should be higher, but he would take care of that. He'd know where to touch her, where the flames had started to build, where her want for him was strongest.

No surprise, then, when his hands glided with tantalizing assurance up her legs, pushing the wispy fabric ahead of his fingers as they traveled their heated journey across skin so sensitive it sprang to life beneath his touch. By the time his hands settled on her bare bottom, she simmered with liquid fire.

The sensations were far more real than her dreams, far more intense. But her dreams had prepared her. Her steamed brain assured her there was more ahead, a great deal more, and she wanted all of it. Adam had spoken of a gift she had to offer, but he was giving her a gift, too. And her entire body and its rampaging heart were telling her she wanted it. Oh my, she wanted *him*.

An inner voice suggested she unlace her bodice for him, and she did, though her fingers were reluctant to leave his ear, and she had to wiggle a bit, for he held her atop him so close.

The wiggling triggered new shivers in him, pleasured him. She obliged him by moving her hips beneath his wonderful hands, spreading her knees over him.

As she touched down upon the throbbing bulge in his breeches, she knew at once she'd reached home. Her gift had reached his. All thought departed at that moment and her body's fiery sensations took full control. When he rolled her gently to her back and his hand slid up to cover the swelling spot that ached for him, it was the most natural thing in the world. His fingers strumming there, both natural and wondrous; her dress falling away from her shoulders, exactly the way it should. His lips circling the tips of her breasts, pulling them into his mouth, suckling them, a pure, natural delight fueling added fires that rushed down to greet his pulsing fingers.

She arched to him and the pressure increased. Adam would give her the release she craved and, at the same time, she'd give him release. Only she must free him. That her fingers moved to his buttons was perfectly natural.

Adam had lost surprise and resistance long ago, but a few shreds of consciousness floated yet through his turbulent mind. There was no stopping for them—for her, at least. He couldn't allow himself to enter her, but he'd bring her the rest of the way.

She was almost there, like heated satin beneath his fingers, slick with her want, reaching for him, vibrant, seething. His own scorching want wasn't important, hers was vital. His defenses had melted under the flames of her surprising, innocent seduction, and he'd gone this far. He would satisfy her, he owed her that. But he would betray her no further. He owed her that, too.

Dear God, she'd released his turgid shaft! It had thrust free, lay quivering with desire across her silken stomach. *Stay there, go no nearer,* he ordered it, even as he felt her rise toward him, her convulsions growing beneath his hand.

He lifted over her, watched her ecstasy-bathed face as she approached the brink she sought, heard her gasp as she came nearer . . . nearer.

"That's it," he coaxed. "Let it go, my love."

She did, with powerful spasms that reverberated through his arm and coursed clear through him. His own release came suddenly, without warning. Guided by a frenzy of rapture, her hand had circled his shaft, held it tight against her writhing stomach. His explosion was swift, mighty, and he felt his seed spew free in pulsating bursts.

He fell limp across her, reached up to wrap his fingers through her disheveled damp curls, and buried his face into her neck.

"Oh my," she whimpered softly.

He nuzzled his beard into the hollow of her shoulder and nibbled a trail of light kisses up her cheek, till he reached her ear.

"Oh my," he echoed.

She tightened her arms around his back but otherwise lay still.

Gradually, his heartbeat slowed from a racing gallop to a rapid trot, then, after one frisky kick of jubilation, to an almost normal walk.

He raised his head to look at her. Her emerald eyes sparkled, and her flushed, peaceful face widened into the smile of an angel. His heart pumped another frisky kick.

"That was truly lovely, Adam."

"Indeed." He kissed the tip of her nose and started to move away, but she pulled him back.

"Stay awhile, please, I like the feel of you against me."

He was too weak to protest. Besides, she felt damn good against him. His depleted shaft lay between them, placid in the liquid warmth of its own spent fluid that coated her firm stomach. The sharp, fresh scent of his seed mingled with the dark, sweet perfume of her now-quieted excitement, enveloping them.

"Giving you my maidenhood was a special pleasure, Adam. Tis a pity I can give it but once to you."

He lifted his head, a frisson of alertness invading his peaceful lethargy. "I didn't take your maidenhood, Bethany," he said earnestly, gazing into her eyes.

"You didn't?"

He shook his head. Her smile was dazzling.

"Do you mean there's even more to look forward to? You *will* take it, won't you, for I want only you to have it, though I'm not sure I could bear something more wonderful than what just happened."

She'd come back to life, and his head cleared. He moved away quickly, tried to wipe her stomach dry, but dared not tarry there too long before pulling her skirts down.

"No, dear woman," he said, striving for firmness. He worked her dress back up to her shoulders to cover her luscious breasts and fumbled with the ribbon laces.

"Why not?"

He pulled away. "Damn it, Bethany, do you realize how close we came ... I came to truly taking you?" He avoided her eyes and shoved his rebellious shaft back into its unbuttoned prison. *She'd* liberated it, dear God. Still on his knees, he worked with the buttons, but his damnable fingers had lost their dexterity. "As it is, I've wronged you enough this day. You must wait for your true mate to show you the rest."

Lucky bastard, he thought with an unsounded moan.

"But you *are* my true mate, Adam."

The final button felt like a cold stone between his fingers. Troubled, he looked into her radiant eyes. She was sitting, completely poised, a portrait of composed assurance. His heart sank.

"What are you saying?"

"You're my mate. I listened to my heart, like you said, and it shouted your name. So you see, you've wronged me not at all, and you can have my maidenhood gift any time you want."

He stood and ran his hand through his hair. "Bloody hell, Bethany, I'm not your mate. I don't even *have* a heart, you know that."

"Of course you do, I've heard its strong beats many times."

"I've lost touch with it, then. And for sure it's without a voice. I've heard no names, shouted or otherwise."

"But you will, and it will speak 'Bethany' loud and clear. Just wait and see."

How in God's name could he reason with her? She was incapable of reason. She was scaring the hell out of him, too. He had to stop this nonsense.

"Let's eat, and then I think we should start back."

"Constant's eaten our food," she said with a giggle.

He saw she was right. The plates of food he'd laid out had been decimated. The dog was stretched beside them, sleeping contentedly. It figured, he thought with exasperation.

"We should leave, then. Now." He liked the no-more-foolishness gruffness he'd achieved.

She stood and fussed with her skirt. Thank God, she was obeying him. But her next words shattered his rising hopes. "Nonsense, Adam. The day is yet young, and my frock must be laundered." She shot a devilish, knowing look at his breeches. "And your clothing, too, is soiled, so I'll wash yours at the same time. There's sun aplenty left to dry them."

Horrified, he saw she was unlacing her bodice and intent on removing her clothes.

"We can't disrobe, woman! Have you gone completely berserk?"

Bloody hell, she was doing it. He turned his back to her and raised his eyes skyward, tensed. For a bloody innocent, she sure as hell knew how to bedevil the wits out of a man.

"Of course we can disrobe."

Behind him, her damnably confident voice was muffled by the cloth swishing over her head. He closed his eyes and counted to ten, then clamped his teeth into his lip—hard.

"I will *not* undress," he growled.

"Hand me your shirt and breeches, Adam."

Her hand reached out in front of him. She was so near that the heat from her body warmed his rigid back.

"We've both seen each other naked," she continued. "There can be no harm and you know we can't return to Ridgecrest mussed as we are. They may suspect we're not brother and sister after all."

That was reasonable but nothing else was. They couldn't spend the rest of the afternoon sitting around talking, as bare as Adam and Eve.

He was only human, damn it. How the hell much did she expect him to tolerate before he succumbed and truly invaded her innocence?

"Bethany, this is impossible."

"Why, for heaven's sake? Come on, hand me your clothing. Be reasonable."

That rankled. "Be reasonable?" he exploded. "If I remove my breeches, I can bloody well assure you that you might regret the inevitable consequences."

"What could I possibly regret, Adam?"

Her words were as smooth and calm as the peaceful river behind them, but they roiled him into an eddy of anger. After yanking off his shirt, he tore at his buttons, threw off his boots, and stripped his breeches over his feet.

Without turning around, he pushed his clothing over her waiting hand. "I've warned you, woman," he growled. "You're toying with danger. You'd better stay far away from me till our clothing is dry. *Damn* far away—or I promise you I'll bloody well give you a full demonstration of what it is a man and woman do!"

"I certainly hope so, Adam. I truly believe that's been too long delayed."

She walked away from him then and, by the sounds, was padding with merry confidence toward the river.

He held his breath and clenched his jaw. *You're bloody well asking for it, Bethany Rose Stewart,* his brain shouted.

Chapter Eighteen

The grass tickled his bare rump. Scowling darkly, Adam sat beneath a wind-curved sycamore back on a hill, as far from the river as he could manage. He remained near enough to protect her should she encounter danger, but, by God, he'd be damned if he would watch her, so he kept his back to the water. She'd have to scream like the devil if she required his help.

Good. Maybe a few seconds of fright would jolt some much-needed sense into her muddled head.

He conjured up a deadly copperhead asleep on a sunny rock pulled awake by her infernal splashes, slithering menacingly toward her or a catamount, perched in the branches above her, poised to pounce.

Hell, he could handle either of them. His loaded rifle was by his side. But then what? He envisioned himself, bare as the day he was born, rushing to comfort her wild hysteria. God, he knew where that would lead. Her naked body wrapped against his. . . .

He adjusted his position on the grass, cursing his damnable groin for betraying him. With a low growl, he banished his fancied snake and wildcat. He'd stay precisely where he was, knotted into a protective crouch, until his clothes were dry—and then they'd get the hell away from this abominable place.

"Don't you want to bathe, Adam? The water's truly warm." Her taunting voice lilted up from the shallow river.

"No," he yelled back over his shoulder. Hell, no.

"As you will," came the musical reply.

He grumbled. Placing his hand on his rifle's wooden handle, he alerted one piece of his mind to listen for cries of help, letting the rest wallow freely in the swamp of his misgivings about women in general—and one woman, in particular.

His mood grew as black as a moonless midnight, though the late June sun had imbued the world around him with the shimmering incandescence of an Albemarle summer's day. A thousand shades of green, from the pale slender leaves of the tender willows to the rich, moist darkness of weathered moss intermingled with the vermilion soil, the silvered rocks and multicolored wildflowers to create a palette of colors that would have made an artist's soul cry out with joy. The sky above was the blue of a sun-kissed sea. The air was astir with a symphony of birdsong.

Adam noticed none of it. He welcomed, instead, the layers of gray gloom piling around him. They provided covering—of a sort.

"Well, I killed the bloody thing, though it gave me quite a start at first, sneaking up on me that way."

He jumped at the sound of her soft voice as if she'd struck him across the back with a hefty club. With one swift motion, he was on his feet, his rifle ready, aimed toward the river.

No. It was aimed toward Bethany. He lowered the rifle, dazed, dazzled.

Bethany. Dripping wet. A silken image carved from ivory clay, gleaming with moisture as if newly molded by a master sculptor and just this moment brought to life. As that first magical time he'd seen her, she had ascended like Venus from the sea.

And the dreamlike aura was exactly the same. He blinked, trying to clear his vision, but she yet stood before him in gauzelike splendor . . . ethereal.

"You killed what?" he wheezed, the breath crushed from his lungs.

"A big snake." The vision had a voice like crystal bells. "I whacked it with a stick. It was as ugly as Satan."

She was as beautiful as an angel.

"Adam, are you all right? Why do you stare at me so?"

"Are you real?"

Her laughter—bells again. Silver bells.

"Of course I'm real, you ninny. It's me, in the flesh. Bethany. What's wrong with you? Did I awaken you from a deep dream?"

She glided toward him.

A dream. That was it. She was a dream. In the flesh. . . .

She reached up and touched his shoulders. Her fingers were tender petals of warmth, her large oval eyes, gemstones of vivid green.

"I am here," she said.

"I am here," he echoed, wispily aware he'd lost his battle—and won a treasure. He drew her close, breathed her name into her ear. "Bethany . . ."

The dream became reality; reality became the dream. She was petals and flames. He supped nectar from her lips, sipped honey from her skin, inhaled the fragrance of her silk-spun hair. His eyes absorbed the vision—nymph, airy sprite, angel; his flesh savored the essence—woman, lush, yielding, real . . . his.

Together they floated to their downy bed of feathery grass as a sensual medley flowed over them, from them, through them, surrounding them with the smoldering harmony of sight, touch, taste, sound, scent. She was warmed alabaster, springing alive beneath his fingertips, pink rosebuds swelling within his lips, a tender blossom opening its dewy petals to his tongue. Her moans were chimes he stroked into the resonance of rapture. The perfume of her desire wafted about him like a heated cloud of flowers.

Her caresses were fire; her kisses, volatile fuel. Her fluid, responsive movements beneath him were bellows. He was aflame, his veins engorged with onrushing streams of molten lava.

Pleasure her as she pleasures you, whispered his swelling heart. *Pleasure her . . . Pleasure Bethany*. There . . . there . . . she was burning with want, honied with desire, opening to him, pleading for him.

He moved over her, her hips rose, her throbbing sheath met his hardened shaft—her slender sheath, warm slick satin, pulsing with readiness. He entered her, a careful, slow, gradual entering. His heated, swollen tip gently opened her small gateway to paradise before slipping within. Her satiny sheath welcomed him with soft warmth, her responsive quiver drew him inward until he reached the tender veil that was hers alone to give him, and he paused, waited. He kissed her lips, gazed into her lovely eyes. They shimmered like stars, held him captive. She held him captive. He waited.

His shaft pulsed against the gossamer veil, against the pliant, accommodating walls partially surrounding him. With a low, loving moan, she lifted to him and the veil parted. She stiffened, her eyes widened, then filled with a shining acceptance telling him she was his. His eyes responded. He was hers.

She drew him deep within her, enveloped him. He trembled with the ecstasy of the feel of her around him, tight but yielding, compressing but embracing. For long breathless moments, he remained still, savoring her receptive tremors that drew him deeper, unfolding her before him as she enwrapped him, enraptured him. When he began the slow, easy cadence as old as time itself, she joined him. Her rhythm became his, his became hers.

His mouth captured hers, his hands played through her hair, gripped her head. She grasped his shoulders, moaning her pleasure deep into his throat. Her fingers pressed into his back, her legs clasped him, guiding him deeper, harder, faster.

Their rhythms built, coalesced into a unity of passion driving them far beyond the stars . . . higher . . . yet higher. Her beginning spasms triggered his, his bolstered hers, until the convulsive waves soaring through them were inseparable, merging, lifting them to their soul-fusing starburst. As his seed spurted forth, her welcoming vessel received his offering with strong pulses of gratitude matching his own.

Adam lay atop her, wrapped within their dream, suffused with a peace that surpassed contentment. His racing heart throbbed its one-word song over and over into his ears—Bethany, Bethany, Bethany.

"Bethany," he breathed with a ragged moan.

"Adam," came her shred of a whisper.

Neither spoke again for a long while, or moved. Her contentment radiated from her softened body through his, his through hers. A rose-tinged vapor embraced them, holding them within its glow, withholding the world.

A cardinal's ringing "cue-cue-cue" nudged through the vapor; Adam mumbled, wiggled one toe.

Bethany sighed, nuzzling closer. "Far better," she muffled into his beard.

"Hmmm?" He kissed her chin.

"That was far better than a dream," she said, nibbling his bottom lip.

"I think it *was* a dream," he heard himself say as he fingered a wispy copper curl and gently settled it behind her ear.

"But wondrously real."

He nodded. "That too." His hand brushed across her cheek. It was warm, wet. With a start, he raised his head. Her bliss-filled face was soaked with tears. They glistened still on her long, dark lashes.

"My God, did I hurt you, Bethany?"

She shook her head, smiled. "But a moment only. Tis the other that brought the tears. The joy you gave me. I've never experienced such sweet, pure joy."

Nor had he, he realized as he patted her cheek with light kisses. He tasted salt—and sugar. "I'm sorry about that moment, little sparrow, but I'm happy about the joy."

Her brow squiggled. "Was that moment the gift you spoke of?"

Reality hit with a hefty wallop. "Aye," he moaned, burying his face into her neck. Dear God, he'd done it. He had taken her innocence. His throat congested and he swallowed hard.

She threaded her fingers through his hair with the lightest of touches. "You, too, found joy, I vow."

He nodded, but his groan against her neck was mournful.

"I love you, Adam."

Her words stabbed into his heart. Rather the cold steel of an enemy's sword than that . . . that soft, sweet pledge of a woman who so richly deserved to be truly loved. She was love itself—spiritual and physical love—made manifest in the most beautiful, responsive body he had ever known, would ever know.

And yet, he could never love her, for his hardened heart had long ago shut out love. That was reality.

A chill ran up his back. He pulled away and rolled off her. Rubbing his eyes with the heels of his hands, he sat up with a heavy sigh.

A touch of a grimace crossed her still-radiant face. "You've donned it again, haven't you?"

"Donned what?" he asked, puzzled. Instinctively, he pulled his knees up and returned to his protective crouch.

"Your shield of armor, that's what," she responded with only a trace of a frown. "It's your defense, what you use to keep people distant."

Damn right, he thought, simultaneously remarking to himself that her on-the-target insight made him even gloomier. He tightened his arms around his knees and made no comment.

"Well, that matters not," she said blithely, rising to her feet. After bending to give the top of his head a brief, tender kiss, she added, "Your shield has opened to me, Adam Barwick, that's what's important. You need never be lonely again, and together we can make that silly armor crumble away completely."

He looked up, intending a scornful scowl. But her bright, open smile stopped him, and he ended up with an expression he figured displayed only his growing discomfort. "Love brings hurt, Bethany," he blurted out.

"Love brings joy," she contradicted him, the trill in her voice further unsettling him. "For heaven's sake, Adam, didn't we demonstrate that quite beautifully this afternoon?"

Not waiting for his response, she headed for the river, her steps as light and happy as her maddening words. He pressed his lips together and muttered an oath.

"We should bathe," she tossed over her shoulder. "And our clothes are dry, I believe."

Her pert bottom wiggled saucily as she walked with damnable assurance toward the water.

With a moan, he rose at last and followed her. He picked a spot for his own bath a good five yards away from her.

The sun was low when they reached Ridgecrest. Robert Castle came out to greet them, a slight edginess ruffling his customary calm demeanor.

"I'm glad you're here, you two. Mrs. Castle is in a fit of temper, Bethany. She wants her bath and is complaining you're hours later than usual."

Adam glowered at the man. "Our Sundays are free, so you told us. Your wife has no right to Bethany's assistance this day."

"It's quite all right, my dear brother," she chirped, dismounting from the spotted horse with fluid ease. "Mister Castle allows me many free hours during the week, and the lady dearly loves her Sunday bath."

Adam threw her a hard look, but at the sight of her, his guilty conscience dealt him a mighty blow. Dear God, she was aglow! As neat and tidy as she'd been when they'd started out, but all starry-eyed and radiant, emitting that telltale aura of a woman who has been truly fulfilled. Bloody hell, even a blind man could see what had transpired between them this day.

He cast a quick sidelong glance at Robert Castle. He seemed oblivious, but Adam wished like hell the man wasn't so proprietary with Bethany and didn't dote on her with such unabashed zeal.

"I'll hurry right in, Mister Castle. Forgive us our tardiness," she said, lifting her wide, shimmering eyes toward Adam.

He might have melted, but his misgivings had laced a scattering of frost over his vulnerability to her weakening gazes. Far too bloody late for frost, he knew with black despair.

Watch it! he wanted to shout to her when she wiggled her lips, preparing to add a parting word.

"The day was indeed glorious," she said, sounding not at all like a sister. "I look forward to all our future Sundays together. I'm sure you're wrong about its happening but once. I've figured out what you meant."

And, with that breezy comment, she ran up the steps, leaving Adam disconcerted as the devil and Robert Castle with a look of concerned curiosity on his face.

"What was she talking about?" the man asked, just as Adam feared he might.

"A—uh—surprise I sprang, I guess. A trick I'd taught Constant, a mere trifle, actually, involving retrieving a tossed stick and the stupid dog was too sluggish with food to accomplish it but once. But you know how Bethany's spirits soar with anything new." Bloody hell, he sounded like a blithering idiot.

"Aye, her soaring spirits ever brighten our days and, indeed, our very lives," Castle said with a blissful sigh.

Adam stared at him. The man was so damnably

265

captivated by her that he'd swallowed his flimsy fabrication? She'd *never* be safe at Ridgecrest. Damn him. Damn him straight to hell.

With an explosion of rage, his pent-up anger with himself burst upon a different target—Robert Castle.

"Declare your intentions with my sister!" he bellowed, grabbing for his knife.

Stunned, the man stepped back, paled, then looked up at Adam with a soul-searing intensity. Adam's hand around the blade's handle grew chilled, damp.

"I command you to declare your own intentions, George Stewart," came the firm reply.

Releasing the knife, Adam wiped his palm across his sleeve and dug his fingers into the contracted flesh of his arm. He slowly dismounted and stood erect before the silver-haired aristocrat.

"My intentions are to protect her, Castle."

"As are mine." A weighted silence fell between them.

He was taller than Adam remembered, standing sturdy, composed. His next words struck with the force of a cannon. "I know that you are not her brother."

Adam tensed, made no response.

"I believe we should have a serious talk. Would you join me in the library, please?" With the polite sweep of his hand toward the house, he had issued an invitation, not a command.

Thoroughly unnerved, Adam followed him up the steps.

"I've known you were an impostor from the beginning," Castle said, handing him a goblet of brandy and seating himself in a wingback chair across from Adam.

The setting sun bathed the richly appointed book-lined room with a golden warmth, but Adam's chill remained untouched. He waited for Castle to continue.

"I once knew Bull Stewart of Wildcat Hollow, met his son George, too. He was around twelve at the time, I believe. He was a squat, pig-eyed boy with black hair, doomed to grow up into the image of his father." He looked straight into Adam's eyes. "Do you want to tell me your true name?"

Adam placed his other hand around the goblet to steady it. "In time, perhaps. Keep talking."

Castle lowered his eyes, seemed to study his brandy. "Bethany, on the other hand, I recognized at once, though she was not yet born that summer I lay ill in the Stewarts' cabin." He raised the goblet to his lips but lowered it without taking a sip. "She is the image of her mother."

"You knew Bethany's mother?"

The man nodded, adjusted his position on the chair. "Mary McKeith Stewart." He spoke the name as though it were a musical composition. With a soft clearing of his throat, he crossed his booted legs. "She nursed me back to health."

Adam struggled to comprehend what he was hearing. Castle had known the Stewarts? This revelation was incredible and yet he sensed the undercurrent of suffering running beneath the man's sedate tones as he began telling his story. He was clearly relating truth—relating a truth that unsettled Adam, perplexed him, even as it transfixed him.

Twenty years earlier Robert Castle had joined a small group of gentlemen friends on an expedition to the lower Shenandoah Valley—a "mere lark for us," he called it. They'd heard tales from others who'd explored the fabled area beyond the mountains. Spurred by both "youthful verve for adventure and landed gentlemen's instinctive greed to seek vast new holdings," they'd begun their ill-fated trek. He was in his mid-twenties, a married man.

Foolhardy, they'd taken no guides. "It was to be a test of our courage, our keenness, our manly virtues. We looked forward to returning with boastful tales of our high adventures."

Disaster struck. They became lost in the rugged hills, and a series of tragedies ensued. One man drowned in a flooded stream; a second was torn asunder by a bear; the third plummeted from a craggy cliff and lay crushed on the rocks far below. Robert Castle was left to battle the wilderness alone.

He reached over to refill Adam's goblet, then refilled his own. Sitting back, but far from relaxed, he continued.

When Mary Stewart had found him, he was near death. He'd broken his leg in a fall and was wracked with fever. He'd been without food or water for days. "I beheld an angel above me, a flame-tressed angel with eyes like emerald stars and thought her a heavenly vision."

Adam's heart constricted.

"At that moment I welcomed death with the smile of one blessed with grace, as she told me later," Castle added with a soft chuckle.

He had remained under her tender care for more than two months, delirious and unconcious the first week, drifting with a minimum of awareness between the hell of pain and the heaven of that angel's nurturing all of the second week. During the third, he'd recovered enough to know Mary alone had saved him.

"She had a way with herbs and a will of iron that defied not only death itself but her husband's unrelenting harangues. I was an unwelcome guest who was 'fit fodder for the vultures and naught else,' he raged to her with ill-tempered frequency."

The gloom of twilight entered the library. Castle appeared strangely agitated and stood to light the room's candles. Sorely troubled, Adam realized in a mind-boggling flash that he knew the remainder of the man's story. He clamped down on the gasp that threatened to strangle him. Dear God, he knew.

"Bethany is your daughter, isn't she?"

Adam saw the small jerk of the sulphur-tipped stick in the man's hand as he held it over the candle, the leap of the wick's flame catching its fire.

Castle's tortured sigh filled the room. He returned to the wingback chair and crumpled into its cushions. "I never knew. God be my witness, I never knew I had left her with child. But the moment I saw Bethany, heard her name . . . It was the name I'd told Mary I favored above all others save her own, for it signified renewed life . . ." He stopped and covered his face with his hands.

Adam swallowed around the lump in his throat.

"I loved Mary with all my heart," Castle continued after a long pause. "I labored to convince her to come back with me to Albemarle. I abhorred the thought of leaving her behind with that abusive bastard Stewart. Her life was so hard there, but—"

"Did she know you also were married?"

"Aye, we had no secrets. I promised her I'd find a good home for her, a secure home, but she insisted she must remain in her own world, that our two worlds were separate, that our stolen pleasures of that August and September had brought us more joy and love than others could expect to experience in a lifetime." Castle pinched the bridge of his nose and issued a heartrending moan. "I left her! Dear God above, I left her."

Thomasina Ring

Deeply disturbed, Adam took a long sip of the brandy. He'd never developed a taste for the bitter-sweet wine, but tonight he sought its solace.

"I'm a weak man," Castle went on. "I was weak then, letting her convince me she was right, when all along I knew she was sacrificing herself because she sensed her presence would cause unfathomable problems for me and for my wife, Sara. I'm weak now, for I cannot tell Bethany. She would hate me for leaving her mother to her awful fate, and I couldn't bear that."

Adam's hand trembled. "Bethany has no hatred in her," he offered quietly. "She held love in her heart even for that despicable Stewart and his son."

Castle groaned. "My weakness runs far deeper, I fear. Knowledge of this would kill Sara. She's sickly, as you know."

Adam wanted to feel disgust for the man, but something more like heart-wrenching pity took hold. "What do you plan to do, Castle?"

The silvered head shook sadly. "I know not. I only know that God has given me an opportunity to make amends to Mary through our blessed daughter of love, Bethany. I will adore and protect her and never rest till I know she has a life of fulfillment ahead for her. Wedded, I trust, to a fine man who loves her true, and one far more courageous than I."

With stunning suddenness, Adam felt the pierce of the man's eyes. He flinched, and his hands grew moist around the goblet. He looked away from Castle.

"I am a man without love," he said at last.

"She loves you."

Adam put down the brandy and stood, moved restlessly about the room, running his fingers through his hair. "Bethany loves the world," he said, expelling a mournful sigh. "She deserves a man who can return

270

her love. I want that for her." He stopped, looked down into the anguished, guilt-torn face of Robert Castle. "I want that for her as much as you do, sir."

For a long moment, their eyes locked, held steady, searched unplumbed depths. An unspoken union was formed.

"Tell me who you are and what it is that tortures you so," Castle said.

Adam returned to his chair and sat back heavily. He bowed his head, pressing his fingers hard against his pounding temples. Castle had relieved him of his burden of responsibility for Bethany. No barriers held him now. He could go on with his life, fulfill his mission of hatred and retrieve his birthright. Nothing remained to stop him. Absolutely nothing, except . . . *No! I must let her go. For her own happiness, I must let her go.*

He raised his head. Sadly aware of a vast void spreading deep within him, he began to speak.

Adam Barwick told Robert Castle the truth about himself.

It took a long while—many questions to answer, many words to speak. When he had finished, Adam was drained, empty.

"We'll go to Brierwood early on the morrow, Adam. I can assure you that Hallston Lawrence will welcome you with open arms, as do I. Your father was a dear friend of mine." Castle leaned over with a warm smile and poured a splash of brandy into Adam's goblet and another into his own. "This news deserves a toast, my friend."

Adam shook his head. "Toasts must wait till James Wallace is defeated and Wendover is mine." He stood. "It's late, sir, and I'm weary."

"Aye, I too." Castle pushed himself up from the wingback chair like an old man, then straightened, reclaiming his stalwart, dignified demeanor.

Adam felt a rush of warmth for him. He was a good man. He would protect Bethany and provide for her well. He held out his hand, and Castle gripped it with firmness.

"Your secret is safe with me, sir, and you have my eternal gratitude for . . ." Adam couldn't continue, but the man's eyes told him he understood.

"Bethany has a strong spirit, Adam. She'll find happiness ahead, I promise you." He reached up and patted Adam's shoulder.

"Angus . . . Angus requested permission to visit her." The words lodged like bile in his throat, but he kept speaking. "I failed to mention it to her today. He's a worthy man, far better than—"

"I'll make note of it," Castle interrupted with a kind nod.

Adam started for the door, but before departing, he paused. "Please see that Bethany has some supper, sir. She might be hungry. The dog ate our food."

Without waiting for a response, he left the room and hurried from the house.

Chapter Nineteen

Never had a morning dawned with such dazzling splendor. As Bethany peered through the small leaded panes of her room's windows, her joyful eyes drank in the world's beauty. Sparkles of dew spangled the rose garden below, and each perfect ivory, pink, orange, and scarlet blossom in the profusion of rich blossoms proudly wore a tiara of sun-tipped diamonds.

She lifted the window to breathe in the fragrant perfume of the glorious new day, to revel in the sweet, contrasting melodies of a multitude of different birds.

"Humming already this morn, are ye now?" Ida asked, sounding as though her mouth were stuffed with muslin. Her sleep-mumbled greeting was followed by a resigned sough and a hefty puff of exertion. When Bethany turned, the woman had gotten as far as a sitting position on the edge of her rumpled bed.

Bethany hadn't realized she'd been humming, but she figured it was as inevitable as the rising sun. After all, she'd found her prince and knew him at last. Oh my, she *truly* knew him. Her heart skipped a lively patter.

"You're a slugabed, Ida," she teased with a giggle. "I've been up for *hours*. Tis a shame to waste a second of this beautiful day." She hadn't been up hours, probably but fifteen minutes or so, but she'd dressed and was eager to go to the kitchen. She couldn't wait till she served the men their breakfast. She couldn't wait to see Adam.

"Too much brightness, too much brightness," the plump woman admonished with a shake of her wiry gray head and what might have been a grumble. Only good-natured Ida Pumphrey was incapable of true grumbling, and Bethany laughed.

"You'll feel brighter yourself once you've washed your face. I've poured the water in the bowl for you and laid out fresh linens." She loved easing the woman's life whenever she could, for the aches of aging bones plagued the dear soul. Should she be blessed with a million years, Bethany knew she could never repay Ida for her many kindnesses to her.

As the woman shuffled across the room, Bethany turned again to the window. She hugged her arms and scrunched her shoulders with sheer happiness. Her face, she suspected, was plastered with a permanent smile.

When she saw the stable doors opening, she paid little attention. Someone was astir mighty early, but the field hands often were up and about before her. That it was Mister Castle atop his handsome gray stallion coming out, however, raised her curiosity. He seldom rode so early in the day. The rider following him had a far different effect. The sight of him set her heart on a merry pace. It was Adam . . . wonderful, perfect Adam on his beautiful chestnut horse.

She wanted to stick her head through the window and shout down to them to wish them a cheery good morning and inquire where they were headed so very early.

But something stopped her. Was it the easy manner they rode side by side, chatting congenially like old friends? Was it because Adam was clean-shaven, his sun-gold hair tied back with a black ribbon, looking for all the world like a fellow gentleman despite his buckskins?

A chill gripped her as she chewed at her lip. *Adam, where are you going?* She squeezed her dream catcher. It responded with a muted thump, comforting her not at all.

Knitting her brows, she slid partially away from the opening, holding to the wooden sill with tensed fingers. She watched the men break into a trot and pass beneath her. As Adam nudged the chestnut to a gallop, he raised his eyes toward her window. Then he looked ahead, and the two men sped away.

Bethany didn't think he had seen her, she was way over to the side. But she had seen him, had seen his dark, shaded eyes.

Dear angels in heaven, she'd seen his eyes.

They had told her farewell.

Hallston Lawrence did not greet Adam with open arms. His arms, like the rest of him, appeared stunned into temporary immobility when Castle presented his nephew to him. A wrinkle of hope lifted his gray brows, but Adam wasn't surprised to see doubt and suspicion pull them together into a tight knot.

He'd expected his uncle to require proof of his identity. He had none, but he prayed truth alone would prevail.

The three men sat distantly separated around the large burnished mahogany table in Brierwood's dining room. The rest of the family was yet abed, Lawrence told them, and he wanted none of them to have word of this until he himself was convinced the burly stranger before him was truly Adam Barwick.

After a Negro woman brought in cups and saucers of fine English china and a silver urn of coffee, Lawrence ordered her to retreat at once to the outside kitchen and to leave the heavy oak dining-room door closed tight behind her.

"Tell me of your father," he said to Adam when the trio were alone, searching the younger man's face with his sharp and penetrating brown-black eyes.

"My father was William Howard Barwick, born on the tenth of September, 1705, in Charles City County on the Chickahominy." He lowered his head. "I know not, sir, when and where he died. I was told it was within a year after my departure from Wendover. That was in 1754."

Lawrence stirred the spoon slowly in his cup, gazing into the concentric circles his motion aroused in the steaming coffee. "Do you know the names of his parents?" he asked.

"His father, my grandfather, was John Henry Barwick, born in Dorchester, England, in 1682. John Henry's parents, John William and Mary Henry Barwick, brought him to Virginia in 1685. He died in 1737 at Wendover on the James, the year of my birth." Adam was surprised with the ease his family's history leapt into his mind. He had recounted it to no one, not even to himself, for such a long span of years.

"William Barwick's mother was born Eleanor Howard to the Howards of Gloucester on the York," he continued. "She was called Nellie by all and kept her birthdate close to her bosom, determined, I believe, to remain forever young." The sweet memory of his grandmother brought a soft smile to his lips. "She succeeded, dying with the bloom of youth still fresh in her heart in January 1754. She was, I assume, at least seventy."

Lawrence, without his customary periwig, twiddled with a strand of silver hair that laid in lonely splendor across his pink scalp. "Name your brothers and sisters."

"I have none. I was the only son of an only son of an only son. The Barwick line was straight and strong, but woefully thin." It was something he'd heard his father say numerous times.

Hallston Lawrence's mouth quirked, but he didn't look up.

Methodically, he required Adam to recount the history of his mother's side of the family—the Lawrence side.

"My mother, Elizabeth Hall Lawrence, named for her mother and yours, was born July twelve, 1709; married my father in 1729; brought two stillborns into the world before bearing me and died in childbirth, 1740, when I was three," he began, continuing through the generations until Lawrence interrupted him with a weary sigh.

"Any impostor could set to memory such details. They're on record in the courts and parishes, the burial grounds . . . any number of places. My God, man, how can I know you speak the truth?" Frustration threaded a quivery fiber through Lawrence's words.

Robert Castle looked thoughtful. "Perhaps there is a way, Hallston. William Barwick was particularly fond of one prized object that he possessed. Do you know of what I speak?"

With a vigorous nod of appreciation to Castle, Lawrence eyed Adam intently. "Tell us of that possession he prized."

Adam searched through the dusty corridors of his memory. A possession other than Wendover that his father especially prized? An object? And then, his mind's eye saw it, glittering upon his father's proud, strong chest.

"It was a golden horseshoe," he said in a hushed, near reverent voice. "A small, jeweled horseshoe ornament handed down to him from his father who had received it from Governor Alexander Spotswood in 1716."

The air around them grew heavy and still, as though the room itself was holding its breath.

"Do you recall the ornament's inscription?" Lawrence inquired.

Adam closed his eyes, saw the small treasure clearly. "In Latin, *'Sic juvat transcendere monte'*. 'Thus joyous it is to cross the mountains.' On the reverse side, *The Transmontane Order*." He opened his eyes, but a haunting whisper echoed deep within him. *Joyous it is to cross the mountains*.

He paused for a moment, distracted by a soft flutter in his chest, then, after a quick clearing of his throat, he continued, "My grandfather had crossed the Blue Ridges with the governor, was one of the small group of gentlemen who Spotswood dubbed the 'Knights of the Golden Horseshoe.' My father indeed prized both the clasped ornament and the honor bestowed his father."

Two deep sighs of satisfaction skirred across the table. Hallston Lawrence pushed back his chair and stood, his deep brown eyes shining with tears.

"Welcome to Brierwood, Adam Lawrence Barwick. I rejoice that you are back within the bosom of your family."

He received Adam then, with open arms.

The three men talked for hours. They were served a hearty breakfast, and Adam briefly met the Lawrence household.

His Aunt Sally beamed at the news, but admonished her husband with a cluck of her tongue. "Faugh, Hallston, your requiring this young man to run through a gauntlet of questions was highly unneeded. One glimpse of his eyes should have told you he was your kin and his mother's son. Only the Lawrences look at this world through such orbs. Rich brown velvet I've ever called them. My own are blue, as you see, and I've often wondered if the brown provides a darker cast. Hallston, at least, views all with far too much suspicion, I vow. Welcome, Adam!" The woman, as warm and plump as a fresh-cooked dumpling, gave him a vigorous hug.

He wondered if Aunt Sally's silly remark about eye colors held any validity. *Bethany sees all through a cast of green—the color of spring, of life.*

Cousin Polly flitted about the room like an excited canary. "So *thrilled* to meet a true cousin at last, and one who's had such high adventures, too. You *will* regale us with stories of your exploits with the savage Indians and the French libertines, won't you?" A pretty girl, blessed with blond curls and dancing blue eyes like her mother's, she was as sunny as her yellow frock. Bethany had thought her "like a princess."

Bethany. Once again, a soft flutter skipped across Adam's heart. *Let her go!* his sterner judgment reprimanded. *She has a strong spirit, she'll find happiness ahead. She has far more sunshine than even this pampered darling of the Lawrences'. Far more gumption, too. She'll thrive under Castle's care. Please, God, let her thrive. . . .*

Despite the overheated reception bestowed him—perhaps because of it, came the discomfiting thought—Adam remained somber.

Marshall Lawrence's brows lifted with surprised recognition, then he chuckled. "I trust you'll not accept my hotheaded challenge now that we're cousins," he said, offering his hand.

Adam stiffened, but accepted the limp handshake. After absentmindedly wiping his hand across his buckskin breeches, he glowered down into Marshall's watery blue eyes. "My admonition still holds. Be damn sure you remember that," he warned.

Marshall shrugged good-naturedly and went over to the sideboard for coffee.

Evelyn Mason, the houseguest, was the last to arrive from upstairs. She was an in-law of Aunt Sally's, though Adam took little note of the convoluted family connections his aunt tried to explain. Dressed in a froth of blue, the young woman indeed was like a princess. She was truly beautiful, with smoothed-back hair as black and shining as a raven's wing and large, ebony-lashed eyes that were light gray with touches of silver.

Poised far beyond her years—she could be no more than nineteen, Adam concluded—she extended her hand. He noted its chill as his lips brushed across it, but her flirtatious wink when he raised his eyes belied the temperature of the marble-like hand he held a moment longer than manners required.

Though it had been a long time since he'd been subjected to the coquettish charms of a Virginia belle, he was quickly reminded of the shallow pleasures they offered. Politely, he dropped her hand and backed away. His "shield of armor," despite Bethany Rose Stewart's stubborn view to the contrary, was decidedly an intelligent defense.

Excusing himself, he followed Robert Castle and Hallston Lawrence into the parlor for a continuation of their morning's discussion.

The large portrait on the wall drew his attention at once. It was of his own mother and himself, painted by Charles Bridges when Adam was little more than two years old. The portrait ever had hung on prominent display in Wendover's vast dining room.

Adam walked to it, a flood of memories washing over him. Elizabeth Lawrence Barwick had been a ravishing woman. She wore a pale green satin dress in the portrait, its rounded neckline scooped low to reveal a creamy expanse of bosom. A deep green velvet cape draped around one shapely arm and swept behind her, emerging from the other side to lay like a protective swath across her lap, where her right arm reposed in a gentle curve, the stem of a single apricot-colored rose held in her hand. Her captivating eyes were wide-set and like dark almonds. Her hair was the color of chestnuts and, though pulled back severely, drifted in wispy waves about her oval face.

Standing ramrod stiff in the crook of her left arm, against the backdrop of the velvet cape was a small chubby boy with a head full of golden curls. He was dressed like a miniature man in black frock coat and breeches, an apricot waistcoat and a snowy-white ruffled shirt. His eyes, too large for the unformed face of youth, were the same color and shape as his mother's.

The young Adam Barwick was far from a cherub; he was definitely scowling.

"Why is this here instead of at Wendover?" he asked, scowling back at the early image of himself.

"James Wallace sold it to me."

"Sold it?" He turned to his uncle.

"He didn't want it, he said. Threatened to burn it if I didn't take his offer." His dark eyes looked up at the portrait. "She was my beloved sister and you were her beloved son. The picture was all we had left of either of you. I'd have paid him double his amount to save it."

Adam's face grew hot with anger. "Has the blackguard ravaged Wendover?"

Lawrence shook his head and sighed. "I know not, for I haven't seen it in more than five years. I've heard that it stands as proudly on the banks of the James as it ever did, but Wallace is often in debt. Has a great penchant for gambling, he does, and many of your father's furnishings and books have been sold to pay for his profligate ways."

With a pang, he remembered Bethany's determination to retain "penchant" and "profligate" in her memory.

"Damn him," he exploded, running his fingers through his hair. "He must be stopped. I should follow my instincts and ride east tomorrow and kill the bloody bastard."

"That would be foolhardy," his uncle said, sounding much like Dan Morgan on that black day in Battletown. "Wendover is yours, Adam, it's but a minor matter of reopening your father's will. Your instincts lead you only to the gallows."

Adam paced back and forth across the parlor's dark red turkeywork carpet. "I was told there had been a new will after my reported death."

"Aye, that's true. But your father was never reconciled to that report. He had faith that you were alive.

He said his heart told him you'd return, that you had come to him in a dream . . ."

Adam stopped, impaled by the man's words. God in heaven, *a dream?* He looked hard at his uncle who had paused at Adam's startled reaction and had a perplexed twist on his face.

"Please continue," Adam said, sitting on the edge of a cushioned settle.

"His new will left his wordly possessions to your stepmother, Mary Wallace Barwick, 'but only if my true son Adam's death precedes mine,' the testament clearly states. Mary died intestate two years later, and James petitioned the court. There being no other heirs, he prevailed. But, Adam, don't you see? Your death did not precede your father's. You're quite alive. Wendover is yours. We need only file a few papers and appear at court."

Adam studied his hands. They were tensed into hard fists. "How long will the process take?"

"A month or two, no longer."

"Two months?" he blurted out, jumping to his feet. "Am I to remain idle for months while that bloody scoundrel continues to dismantel Wendover?"

Hallston Lawrence smiled. "Two months might not be long enough to smooth you back into a proper gentleman, my son. I fear there's more frontier than aristocracy in your manner." He went over to the darkened hearth and lifted his clay pipe from the oak mantle. Slowly, he filled the bowl with tobacco from a filigreed brass box and tamped it with care.

"You will remain here at Brierwood, Adam. While Sally and the others work on polishing you back into a Tidewater Barwick, I will handle the legal matters myself, working with but a handful of honorable friends," he said. A frown tautened his face. "Above all, knowledge of your miraculous resurrection must be kept secret from all but a few. James Wallace must get no wind of this before we're ready to strike."

Adam liked that word "strike". It gave him a surge of satisfaction. In but a month or two, James Wallace would begin to suffer. The devil take him, he deserved to suffer.

Robert Castle nodded from across the room and rose to his feet. "I'll tell no one at Ridgecrest. He's known as George Stewart by all, anyway. I'll just tell them he's decided to move on to other work."

Adam's heart constricted as another peculiar flutter skittered over it. "Bethany knows my true name."

"We can trust Bethany, Adam, I'll have a long talk with her," Castle said, catching his eyes.

The flutter in Adam's heart kicked into an erratic thump. He knew the man was right. Bethany would never betray him. Had he, by God, betrayed her?

"Tell her . . ." He splayed his fingers across his cheeks and firmly ran his hands up against the rigid bones as though wiping away tears. But his eyes were as dry as his suddenly withered heart. He continued, his voice like a moan. "Tell her, please, that I'm truly sorry I never told her all this myself, and . . . and that I left without saying farewell."

Castle walked over and squeezed the tight muscles in Adam's arm. "She'll understand, Adam. She wishes happiness for you. That's her nature, you know that better than I."

"Aye, perhaps I do," Adam replied.

He had never felt so desolate.

Chapter Twenty

Bethany's dream catcher pressed like lead upon her chest, and it sang to her no longer. Its magic had sped away on a chestnut horse.

Adam was an aristocrat—an *aristocrat*, dear heaven. For two weeks, since that terrible day that Mister Castle had returned alone from Brierwood and confided to her the torturing truth, she had struggled to comprehend.

"It's precisely because he *is* an aristocrat that he would never entertain the thought of wedding you," Adam had told her, referring to Marshall Lawrence. Nor would Adam, she knew now. He was gone from her, forever gone.

Had her heart deceived her? No, it had spoken true. She loved Adam more than life itself and would ever do so. Had Adam deceived her? Again, no. He had mightily resisted her gift of love. She alone had been responsible, but she'd found herself unable to harbor even a skiff of remorse. That bright afternoon of miracles remained nestled like a small, curved rainbow in her heart. She would carry it with her to her grave, and well beyond.

She was far from her grave, however. Life continued, she'd discovered, though she was resigned to journey through it hand-in-hand with a new partner—the drab-cloaked, ever-hovering sadness of deep loss.

So be it. Mister Castle's carefully nurtured English roses still bloomed with glory, and the birds filled the summer air with their lilting harmonies. Colors and sounds were muted for her now, but they were there, and she found succor in their existence, found succor, too, in the tenderness and gentleness that Ida Pumphrey and Mister Castle enveloped around her.

Life continued. She'd passively accepted that fact, but today she was driven to become an active participant. She'd requested a private audience with Mister Castle, for he must know that Adam might be in danger.

"There are rumors among the servants, sir, low murmurings that disturb me. Some have seen Adam riding beyond the fields. They have recognized him and are saying 'George Stewart has been transformed into a gentleman.' The name Barwick, even, is being bandied about in low whispers." She wrung her hands. "We must stop them before the word spreads to Wendover."

With a look of concern, Robert Castle circled her hands with his own. "I've been remiss, Bethany. They must be gathered together at once. I shall talk with them, swear them to secrecy. I should have realized . . ." He paused, a soft light emanating from his eyes as he gazed into hers. "Thank you, my dear girl."

Bethany was encouraged by his words. Ridgecrest's servants held deep respect for Mister Castle. They would all take and abide by their oaths. Adam's plans to retrieve his Wendover would not be disrupted.

"I'll help call them in," she offered with enthusiasm. "I can ride to the western fields while you collect those on the eastern side. Don't overlook Mike. He sleeps beneath an oak at times when Angus isn't with him, though he's a worthy worker when he puts his mind to it."

Castle chuckled. "You've the temperament of a general, albeit a benevolent one, Bethany Rose. Aye, make haste westward and alert them to come immediately. Tell them we'll meet in the parlor within the hour."

Bethany frowned. "The parlor, sir? Do you think that wise? Mrs. Castle will not want the dusty men within her home."

"The parlor," he said firmly. "My wife's fastidious fussiness be damned. The walls of Ridgecrest must hear the oaths, and she, too, by God, will take her vow in unison with the servants."

His determination pleased her, though she found it difficult to picture the ill-tempered woman allowing herself to do anything in concert with her lowly servants.

But there was no time for quibbling. She lifted the full skirt of her brown calico work dress and began running toward the stable. "Whoever of us returns first should gather those in the kitchen and outbuildings," she shouted back over her shoulder.

"Aye, sir general," Castle rejoined under his breath. Bethany didn't see the twinkle of pride in his eyes.

He offered a silent prayer of gratitude as he hurried to follow her. The pink flush on her cheeks had been the first spot of color he'd seen on her porcelain-pale face since Adam's departure. A touch of her lively spirit had returned, praise God. True, it was her eagerness to help Adam that alone had triggered her renewal, but Robert Castle's faith in his daughter's inner strength had received heartening confirmation.

Ida Pumphrey warned her, thank heaven.

"Adam Barwick has come with them," she whispered as she walked into the pantry where Bethany was garnishing the roasted pigeons with sprigs of rosemary, preparing the dish for its presentation to the assembled guests.

"He's here?" The clump of herbs dropped from her hands.

Ida stooped to pick the rosemary from the brick floor. "In the flesh, I fear. It was inevitable once we all were informed and sworn to keep mum about his identity. Here, I'll carry in the pigeon platters. You run on out now to the kitchen and tell Martha to make haste with the asparagus and buttered potatoes."

"They're here already in the warming pan," Bethany said, a paralysis gripping all but her unthinking tongue. Sweet Ida was attempting to give her an excuse not to enter the dining room. She had only her motherly intuition to bolster her belief that Bethany's melancholy these past weeks was from a broken heart for Bethany had not confided in her; indeed, she'd worked hard to convince the woman that the gentleman who had brought her from Wildcat Hollow had been a trusted protector and nothing more.

"Stay in the pantry," Ida hissed with insistence. Her hooded blue eyes brimmed with compassion.

The compassion fired Bethany's courage. She raised her chin defiantly and pulled back her shoulders. "I will assist you in serving as is our custom," she said, lifting a platter. She was profoundly grateful it was heavy as iron. A lighter dish would have rattled about in an unseemly fashion in her trembling hands. "Please lead the way."

Worry creased deeper wrinkles in the kind woman's round face. "Bethany Rose . . ."

"Mrs. Castle is impatient, Ida," she reminded her with a firm steadiness that surprised even herself. She endeavored to insert a gleam of confidence in her eyes, but she wasn't sure she succeeded.

With a sniffle of resignation, the woman lifted the second platter of pigeons. "God love ye, my brave one, and protect us all from those with hearts of stone," she muttered as she pushed open the swinging door with her ample bottom and held it so that Bethany could enter the dining room.

She kept her eyes on the pigeons, depending on her well-tutored serving experience to guide her. Desperately hoping she wasn't revealing her distraught state, she placed the platter at Mister Castle's end of the table, stepped back with a prim curtsy, and waited till Ida had positioned the other in front of Mrs. Castle. Watching only Ida, she followed her into the pantry.

Lively chatter bombarded her ears as she moved trancelike behind the chairs. She heard only snatches of conversation: "Randolph himself guarantees the procedure will be swift. He's enlisted a bright young lawyer by the name of Patrick Henry to assist." "Truly, Evelyn, that peach frock enhances your complexion so." "The pigeons look divine, Sara, how on earth do you manage to . . ."

Adam's voice wasn't among the din, but he was there. Oh my, he was there, all right. Even the air reverberated with him. *Concentrate on the vegetables,* she ordered herself as she returned, sedately transporting them to the table. She walked with calmness and poise, while the rest of her stampeded like a herd of wild buffalo toward one seated, silent guest.

His eyes burned into her flesh, his magical woodsy scent wafted above the heavier fragrances of French perfumes, steaming food, and aromatic roses. She knew exactly where he sat, was acutely aware of every moment his dark eyes had touched her, but she never dared to make even the tiniest glance in his direction.

She didn't dare.

"He's a Barwick for sure," Ida babbled in the pantry as they arranged the tarts, cakes, and sweetmeats into the high pyramid Mrs. Castle insisted upon. "Larger even than his father, he is, and I thought *him* to be a giant among men, though Adam got his eyes direct from the Lawrence side, I vow. He's truly handsome in his gentleman's clothing and without that rat's nest of a beard, did ye notice?"

A delicate round ratafia biscuit rolled from Bethany's fingers. She fumbled a bit before retrieving it, then plopped it atop the towering mound they were building.

"I didn't notice," she said truthfully. His beard was never a rat's nest. It had caressed her skin like gold-spun silk. Trembling, she crumbled the edge off the tender crust of a plum tart.

"Faugh, there, Bethany. Let me finish this. You're all thumbs today, and little wonder, I'd say, his being here like this. Go on out to the kitchen, girl. Better I handle the rest of the serving alone than have ye topple this silly tower of confections on somebody's lap."

Bethany felt as if she had toppled. Whatever glue she'd held herself together with had come unstuck.

She gripped the corners of the worktable for support, and though she fought them, tears streamed in rivulets down her cheeks.

Ida stopped stacking sweetmeats. Reaching for Bethany, she wrapped her plump arms around her and hugged her close to her warm, soft bosom. "Find peace, little one," she crooned. "Adam Barwick is not for thee. He's stone, you're flower; he's darkness, you're dazzling sunlight. Forgive him if ye must, but forget him, too." With a large linen cloth that smelled of cinnamon and flour, she wiped Bethany's face. "Heed me, little one. Ye must forget him."

Bethany shook her head with heavy sadness. "No, Ida, I shall never forget him. Never, as long as I have breath will I forget him." Her shattered heart's anguish wrenched her throat with a choking sob and flooded her eyes with a rush of tears.

She fled from the house.

Returning to Ridgecrest had been a true mistake. God knew, Adam had been reluctant to consent to his uncle's proposal to accompany the Lawrence household on their weekly visit to the Castle home. But he'd allowed himself to be persuaded.

His own damnable restlessness had been the culprit. He'd been like a caged animal at Brierwood, pacing within its elegant rooms until Aunt Sally scolded him for "wearing thin the carpets with your massive boots," then stretching his restricted boundaries outside by riding Nutmeg with speed spurred by fury until Uncle Hallston tightened his reins. "Ridgecrest is safe now, Adam, but for the love of God venture no farther. Some planters might not be as trustworthy as Castle, and few have the loyalty of their servants as he does," his uncle had remonstrated.

"It's the bloody slave system that binds us, Uncle Hallston, that cuts so deeply into the fabric of this badly wrought tapestry Virginia is weaving," he'd retorted angrily. "Slavery binds us all, diminishing us all. It diminishes the owners as well as those owned."

"Wendover has near a hundred slaves," the man had reminded him in subdued tones.

"It will have not one after I retrieve it," he'd exploded. "I'll free them all, God be my witness."

Lawrence had shaken his head. "That won't be without complications, young man. No one wants a horde of freed slaves wandering about fomenting insurrections and God knows what else."

Adam had glowered down at his uncle. "And their freedom would wreak havoc on your blasted economy, wouldn't it? Too bad, kind sir. Bloody too bad that a few idle planters lose a portion of their ill-gotten wealth. The system must be aborted before it ruins us all." He'd lowered his voice, run his fingers through his hair. "I was enslaved by despicable French traders, I know what slavery does to a man. It lights raging fires of hatred in his soul and deadens his heart."

"But you escaped, Adam, after but a month you—"

"Not unscathed," he'd replied, and walked away.

Aye, his restlessness had driven him to Ridgecrest to dine. He'd known he would still be constricted by frivolous proprieties and richly garbed walls but there would, at least, be expanded company and different walls.

He hadn't counted on the lacerating effect of seeing Bethany Stewart.

Dear God, she was as pale as a specter, as stiff as a tethered sapling. More poised than he'd ever seen her, perfectly composed, even more beautiful, perhaps; she'd become truly polished. But it was as though her spring had snapped. She'd lost her spritely bounce.

The sight of her had ripped through him like a jagged spear.

Even now, several days later, he couldn't clear his mind of her. Had he brought her this great distance and accomplished naught but that for her? She was but a ghostly shadow of Bethany. Had he crushed her lively spirit with his own hands?

He hated himself. He tried to kill the memory of that afternoon when he'd fallen into her dream world, the way his heart had sung her name over and over and over. Dead hearts never sang. They laid inert within hardened chests, he knew that well. It was her dream he'd heard, or thought he'd heard. He'd been ensnared by naught but a fantasy.

Dreams destroy. Dear God, hadn't he warned her time and again?

No, it was heartless men who destroy. *He* had destroyed her.

Wisps of memory continued to torture him: the way her flaming hair had captured the sunlight as she knelt over a pair of shallow graves; her unbridled enthusiasm at a cobwebby window, a shaggy broom; a grain of sugar in the corner of her mouth; her gemstone eyes with the sparkle of emeralds when she was happy, the deep luster of jade when she was filled with passion. . . .

Damn. He must quiet his torment. He'd mount Nutmeg and ride like the devil till the fury of the wind swept her from his brain. He'd found a secret hidden spot less than four miles distant where he'd found solace in the past weeks. It was beyond his proscribed boundaries, but no one knew of his retreats there, and he crossed no land that was tilled or worked.

Today his tortured spirit cried for the freedom of the ride and the peace of solitude offered by the shaded falls he'd discovered on the low side of the nearest mountain.

He saddled his horse and jumped astride. "Let's fly with the wind," he muttered, bringing the chestnut to a speedy gallop. "It's freedom we need, Nutmeg. Freedom from stuffy parlors, freedom from bloody boundaries . . . freedom, by God, from bedeviling memories and one haunting dream."

"You must dismiss her, Robert. I find her work far from satisfactory and deteriorating daily, I may add," Sara Castle grumbled over her needlework. She was making yet another repulsive cushion cover. The house was pocked with the things as though an epidemic of unrelieved ugliness had struck the place.

"Bethany stays," Robert Castle said, keeping his eyes firmly on the book spread on his lap. The lines were a blur. He'd left his spectacles on his desk upstairs, but he had no interest in reading. The book was a prop to prevent his having to look at his wife's unpleasant face and her hideous embroidery while they shared their Sunday morning's "conjugal hour" together.

Sara's huffy snort crossed the room. "I don't understand you, Robert. The girl displeases me, and yet you insist on keeping her."

"Everyone displeases you, Sara. Your displeasure no longer qualifies for dismissal from Ridgecrest. If it did, we'd have no help, and then, milady, what would you ever do?" He hoped that would quiet her, and it did, though the stabs of her needle conveyed she was far from finished with the subject.

While he waited, he pinched the bridge of his nose to steel himself. Sara had better watch her tongue;

little did she realize he'd smother her with one of her hideous cushions before he'd shut his door on his daughter.

His wife had become increasingly fixated on being rid of Bethany and now, of all times, when the dear child truly needed a touch of kindness from everyone in her small world at Ridgecrest. And all, save Sara, willingly showered loving care on the withering blossom in their midst.

Sara, on the other hand, treated her with more harshness and impatience than ever. His anger rising, he found himself abstractly studying one of the horrid cushions propped in the corner of the pine settle. Quickly, he returned his eyes to the book on his lap.

She began talking again. "Before, you fought my wishes because dismissing the girl would cause you to lose an able hand—her so-called brother. Ha! Some brother he turned out to be—a Barwick, no less, in the disreputable disguise of a mountain man. Well, you've lost him now, that's certain, so what possible reason have you to keep this annoying girl in our home?"

"I believe she performs her work admirably, Sara. Besides, I promised Adam I'd give her a protected haven."

"*Adam*, you promised?" she exclaimed haughtily. "First you dishonor me by requiring I take an oath with unwashed servants to protect that man, and now you tell me you've promised him to shelter his doxy? You can rest assured, Robert, that stallion pleasured himself well enough with the redheaded filly during those months he was with her. She's well used, I vow."

"Cease, Sara."

She wasn't deterred. "Adam has far fairer merchandise to pleasure him now. I saw Evelyn Mason fondling his knee beneath the table the other day. At least this one is a lady and a marriage possibility. I'm sure Adam doesn't care a whit whether Bethany Stewart has a protected haven or ends up as a tavern wench, which is where her kind belongs."

Robert Castle stood with force and glowered down at his wife. The book slammed to the floor with a resounding clatter.

"Hold your venomous tongue, Sara Castle. I will hear nothing more on this subject, do you understand? Bethany stays at Ridgecrest." His voice was thick with anger.

Sara looked up from her embroidery and narrowed her eyes at her husband. "Is the slattern pleasuring you, Robert? Is that her hold on you? I do wonder how she finds the time for you. She's worked regularly by the field hands, that's fairly obvious, for she's often too spent to perform her tasks—"

"You are truly a vile bitch," he growled, his fists clenched hard by his sides. "You disgust me."

Never had he talked to his wife in such a manner. Sara's milky-gray eyes widened with shock. "You dare to—"

"Damn right I dare. Now go up to your pristine, frigid bed and stay out of my sight the rest of this day—the rest of my life, if I could have my way."

"Robert," she wailed, her fingers fluttering to her chest. "My salts, Robert. Fetch my salts. You've brought on one of my spells . . ."

He stormed across the room, picked up a small phial, and flung it toward the woman. It rolled up against her foot.

"Don't step on your medicine, Sara. You have a way of grinding your nasty heels into everything else in this world. Spare your medicine. You may need it."

He stormed from the parlor, leaving Sara gasping for breath, her face stricken.

He didn't give a damn.

Bethany was outside, saddling the spotted horse he'd given her. Castle pulled up short, his heated anger with his wife dissolving into deep concern for his daughter.

She had faded under his care like a rose without sun or water. He must find a way to help her. He'd move heaven and earth if it were in his power, but neither would suffice. He knew deep in his heart that moving Adam Barwick would be the only sure way to stop her decline. And that task might well be more impossible than moving either heaven or earth.

"Where are you going, my dear girl?" he inquired.

"Riding, sir." She mounted the horse and looked down at him.

The dark circles beneath her large oval eyes caused his heart to tighten.

"It's Sunday. I do still have the day free, don't I?"

"Of course," he said with a nod, anxiety wrinkling his forehead. "But alone, Bethany? Do you think it wise to ride out alone?"

Her smile was warm, though its light didn't reach to her eyes. "I have my bow, Mister Castle, and Constant—and myself. That's a braw team, as Angus would say. We managed quite well before back in the Hollow when it often was just me, the dog, and the bow." She stuck out her foot. "See? I'm shod for the wilderness, even."

She had on the sturdy but badly soiled Indian moccasins she'd been wearing when she'd arrived at Ridgecrest. Castle hadn't seen them since, had assumed they'd been discarded long ago. In fact, he noted with alarm she looked far more dressed for the wilderness than for a Sunday's ride in Albemarle County. She wore a pair of buckskin breeches, given to her by one of the younger servant lads, he supposed, and a loose white work shirt, possibly from the same source.

Except for the moccasins and that odd leather pouch she wore about her neck, she was dressed much like Adam Barwick had been when they'd first arrived.

He didn't like what he was seeing. Dear God in heaven, was she planning to leave Ridgecrest? Was she striking out to cross back over the mountains on her own?

"Don't go, Bethany," he blurted out.

Puzzlement lifted her brows. "I can't go for a ride, sir?"

She had no packs, no coat. Surely she wasn't leaving for good. He put his hand on the horse's bridle and gazed up into the green eyes so like his Mary's. "Only a short ride, perhaps. I was afraid for a moment that you . . ." He couldn't continue, but it didn't matter. He saw that she'd understood.

"I have no other home than Ridgecrest, Mister Castle," she said softly. "And it's a good home. I've found kindness here. I would never cross the mountains again, unless . . ." She hesitated. "I mean, no one should ever venture across the mountains alone, I know that well."

"I'm sorry Mrs. Castle is not kinder with you. It's her way, I fear."

"She's a truly unhappy woman, sir. I ache for her."

He ached, too, but not for Sara. She deserved no happiness. He ached for Bethany. He longed to see her regain her lively spirit, as much a part of her as her still-intact fortitude.

Like a bolt of lightning, it struck him. He would tell her. To hell with Sara! He was going to tell Bethany the truth. As her father, he could do so much more for her, could turn her into a propertied lady who would be the envy of every belle in Virginia. And she needed to know the truth about her heritage, about the deep love he and Mary had shared, even, God forbid, if she should hate him for his own lack of courage.

But Adam Barwick had spoken with wisdom. Bethany could hold no hatred in her heart.

"I must talk with you, Bethany," he said.

"Now, sir?"

Sensing her dismay, he dampened his eagerness to make his long overdue revelation at once. He smiled. "You want to ride now, don't you?"

She nodded. "I love riding. The speeding wind clears my head of foolish thoughts, and I've discovered a beautiful waterfall where I find a special solace."

"Crabtree Falls?" he asked, feeling a stab of concern. It was back in the hills, at least three miles away.

"I didn't know its name. Thank you for giving it to me."

He had something far more important to give her. Something that he believed with all his heart would give her more solace than a waterfall. But she should have both this day.

"Go on to your falls, then, Bethany. We'll have our little talk after you return. Mind you, however, you should be back well before dark."

She agreed, her appreciation for both his permission and concern lighting a near glimmer in her otherwise lackluster eyes. As she sped away, he watched her gallop westward till only a rising cloud of red dust remained.

Chapter Twenty-One

The brisk ride had helped. Being at last within the cool shadows of the dense trees helped, too. Already Bethany felt a small touch of comfort. Here, all alone, she could be as miserable as she wished without raising to even higher levels the concerns of her dear, compassionate friends at Ridgecrest.

Often of late she preferred shade to the bright sun, chilled dampness to warmth. When she'd first come upon this sheltered spot by the waterfall, she'd known she'd found a place where she could hide from the world for brief spells—a place, despite its beauty, that was gloomy.

She welcomed its dark canopy of green that allowed only a few thin shafts of pale sunlight to filter through, shielding her from the sky. Clouds no longer interested her. Their shapes offered no portents she could decipher, so she'd stopped looking for them long ago.

Even the waterfall echoed her mood. Holding no sparkle or colors, it plummeted from a rocky ledge high above and rushed its torturous course down through gigantic, craggy boulders of unrelenting grays. Bared tree roots clutched like gnarled fingers to black crevices in the wet, drab stones.

Bethany had heard stories of waterfalls that were like bridal veils. Crabtree Falls could be likened to a winding sheet, unfurled by a frenzied mourner and driven relentlessly downward by the cruel forces of nature.

Dismounting, she waited for Constant to catch up with her. He had grown heavier from his softer life at Ridgecrest and wasn't near as spry as he'd once been.

"Come on, boy," she chucked, patting her knee. "I vow you're becoming as slow as Ida."

He was panting when he arrived beside her, his pink tongue flapping rapidly, his tail wagging. She bent to give him a hug and couldn't help but smile at his simple happiness. Constant's life held no complexities and she envied him.

They sat together on a mossy boulder beside the rocky stream, shallow and narrow despite the force of the falls above that fed it, but its current was swift.

"The waters murmur here rather than making a merry babble, have you noticed?" she asked the dog. He stretched out on the spray-dampened moss, closed his eyes, and went directly to sleep.

Bethany sighed and idly rubbed his head. "Little company you are, Constant," she mumbled. Concentrating on the swirling water beyond her moccasins, she tried with all her might not to think.

When she heard the startling sound of hoofbeats approaching at a furious gallop up the hill, she leapt to her feet and grabbed her bow. Constant opened one eye, then resumed his nap.

She armed her bow and glowered at the dog. "You're no bloody help," she muttered under her breath. Despite the wild beating of her heart, she buttressed herself, aimed the arrow down the rugged path, and waited.

The horseman broke through the trees and Bethany pulled the string taut, then froze.

Adam. Adam?

Too stunned to move, she stared at him.

He stopped so suddenly the chestnut reared and whinnied.

"Dear God," she heard. He'd expelled it, as though a heavy fist had struck his ribs. His astonished gaze met hers. Neither moved.

"Why are you here?" she asked. She, too, sounded as if she'd suffered a hard blow to the chest.

Complete silence followed, save for the muffled rush of the falls. Then, the piercing shriek of a hawk rendered the air. Bethany's tense body jerked.

"For God's sake, Bethany, lower your bow."

It dropped from her chilled hands, its arrow still nocked on the slackened bowstring. She looked down in horror. She'd aimed it at Adam's heart.

He dismounted and walked toward her. She stepped back. Keeping her eyes down, she saw his black boots stop.

"I'm sorry I frightened you. You gave me a true start," he said at last. The boots were shiny, of very fine leather—gentlemen's boots.

"Why are you here?" she asked the boots.

They turned, walked away. She stared at the hard, gray stone where they'd stood.

"I come here often," he said. "I find a special solace by these falls."

Special solace. Odd—she'd used those exact words. She frowned down at her tightly clasped hands. *The falls hold solace no longer*, she realized, feeling empty.

His voice indicated he'd turned his back, and she dared to look up. Immediately, she was sorry. He was facing the stream, so at least she was spared from his eyes, but what she did see was wrenching torture for her. He was handsomely garbed in black riding breeches and a creamy balloon-sleeved shirt of costly linen; his gold-burnished hair was tied back with a black ribbon. A riding crop was tucked under his arm. He stood tall, stiffly erect.

Her heart twisted. Adam Barwick was indeed an aristocrat. Every hauntingly familiar muscled inch of him screamed that message to her.

With acute unease, she became aware of her own garb—the deerskin moccasins, the borrowed breeches and shirt of a servant lad's. From the untamed hair on her head to the tips of her moccasined toes, she was layered with a thin dusting of red soil. Adam had somehow ridden all the way from Brierwood without getting a grain of dust on him.

It was as though a thick block of clear, hard glass separated them now. She could see him, hear him, but she could never penetrate through that glass.

Her heart constricted and grew heavy as though additional clear, hard glass had suddenly encased it like a coffin.

"Why are *you* here, by the way?" he asked, turning to face her.

A flush of irritation heated her spine. She lifted her chin. "Not, I assure you, because I expected *you* to be here."

The weighted pause was torn by another shriek of the hovering hawk. "You're very angry with me, aren't you?" he asked, low.

She nodded. "Aye, I am, Adam. I am indeed angry." A surprising surge of relief accompanied her terse words. Anger felt far better than gloom and despair. Anger had sparks; anger had fire. Anger had *life*.

"Do you hate me, Bethany?" The fire died.

She shook her head. "I could never hate you," she said in a whisper, and then she made a terrible mistake. She looked up into his eyes. She lowered her own quickly, but she would never forget what she'd seen in that one impaling moment. His velvety dark, beloved eyes were beseiged with raw, naked suffering.

Had something gone badly amiss for Adam in his new world? She ached to know, ached even more to help him find relief. But no way was open for her to help him.

The world had separated them.

Bethany felt a weak flutter in her chest, followed by a deep chill. She shuddered, knowing with unbearable sorrow that the glass lid of her heart's coffin had lifted just long enough for a dying butterfly to escape and to allow inside an icy corpse who would forever lie there inside her.

Bethany's wounded dreams had flown; henceforth, harsh reality alone would be her partner and guide.

Issuing a long sigh of farewell and resigned acceptance, she sat back on a boulder and folded her arms across her chest. With her head bowed, she spoke to Adam.

"All along you have spoken wisdom to me, but I was too much the foolish simpleton to understand. Even now, your truth saddens me, but you've ever been right, Adam. The world is indeed a cruel, hard master."

A sound very like a groan was his only response.

She kept her head down and continued, "One should never expect it to be otherwise. I see that now with starkly clear eyes. Hope provides no strength; indeed, it leaves one without defenses. Harboring fantasies and dreams is even more futile. They can only weaken those who believe in them." She straightened her shoulders and raised her eyes. "You've taught me how to be strong, Adam, and I thank you. It was, I believe, your most valuable lesson."

"What in God's name are you telling me, Bethany?"

She steeled herself, gazed at him openly, forcing herself to withstand the powerful effect of his incredibly handsome face, clean-shaven, now, the dimple in his chin taunting her.

"Isn't it obvious? I'm sensible at last."

A whisper of movement shadowed across his tensed, square jaws. "You've ever been sensible and far stronger than I think you realize," he said.

She unfolded her arms and leaned back, splaying her hands out beside her across the cold stone. "I mean *truly* sensible, as you ever urged me to be—and as for strength . . . Well henceforth, I intend to achieve a more invincible variety. Like you, Adam."

"Like me?"

She nodded. "Shielded well."

His thick brows lifted, then lowered and pulled together. He expelled a ragged sigh. "Never allow yourself to become like me, little sparrow."

Hearing that term of endearment—the one he'd uttered but once before—unsettled her for a moment. She pushed herself upright and returned her hands to her lap, threaded her fingers together and held them tight.

"Why not?" she asked, keeping her voice steady.

"You know well that I'm not a happy man."

She threw him a sour look. "Who on earth said anything about happiness, Adam? We're talking about defense, about strength, about perseverance, I vow, and, with certainty, about survival."

What was wrong with him, for heaven's sake? He should be pleased she'd learned his lesson so well. While waiting for his response, she watched him push a wayward lock of tawny hair from his broad forehead and run his fingers back through the loose waves.

It pained her to see she exasperated him even when she was being so sensible.

And then she noted for the first time that Adam, too, was powdered with a thin layer of red dust from head to toe. The tip of his beautiful nose, even, held a smudge of soil. Dust, it seemed, landed with equal zeal on both sides of the glass.

She took no comfort in that discovery, for the glass was still firmly positioned between them.

When he spoke at last, she found herself totally unprepared for his words.

"Bethany, I've wronged you. Even if God should ever forgive me, which I truly doubt He shall, I will never forgive myself. You must heed nothing—do you hear me?—heed absolutely *nothing* that my thoughtless, embittered soul might have directed me to say to you."

He paused, lifting his grief-stricken face to the canopied trees above as if he hoped to find the remainder of his message to her written there. Tighter than a pulled bowstring, she held her breath and chewed at her lip.

He fastened his tormented gaze upon her own. "You must hold on to that special part of you that makes you Bethany. For you, hope is nurture. It's life itself.

Your spirit is entwined with dreams; your beautiful soul *is* a lively, colorful dream. Dear God, Bethany, please don't ever give up hope and always treasure your dreams and keep them alive within you."

The leaves above rustled, the falls roared, and the stream murmured its mournful dirge. Bethany sat, unmoving but not unmoved. He had spoken from the deepest recesses of his heart. Poor Adam. He'd broken through his stone and dug within only to discover something that no longer existed. Couldn't he see? She was different, no longer the silly girl who wove useless dreams but a woman who could face the world and endure with strength.

But, dear heaven, he was wracked with suffering—from guilt, she thought with a pang, and that was truly unnecessary. It was the old Bethany who was giving him cause to suffer and the old Bethany was suffering with him.

Suddenly, she knew what she had to do to release both Adam and herself.

She stood and spoke as though she were reciting an oath. "You're wrong, Adam. I have no dreams to treasure, nor do I intend ever again to fall prey to such superstitious folly."

Slowly, she pulled the leather strap holding her amulet over her head. Her fingers were steady as steel as she opened the pouch and removed the small piece of metal. It was cold and prickly in her closed hand.

"This, Adam, is what I believe should be done with dreams." Averting his hands that reached out to stop her, she flung her dream catcher into the water.

It swirled about in the rapid current and, in but a moment, it was gone.

After one soft tug of regret, Bethany knew she'd just taken the most sensible action in her entire life.

By releasing her dream catcher, she'd freed Adam from all need for guilt, and she'd freed herself from an imagined bondage that she alone had created.

Now, they both could continue on their separate paths.

She picked up the bow and arrow, nudged Constant awake, and mounted the spotted horse.

Feeling stronger than she'd felt in weeks, she urged the horse forward. "Farewell, Adam," she said to him softly. "And thank you, my dear man, for your many kindnesses to me. With all my heart, I wish you well."

She brought the horse to a full gallop and left Adam Barwick standing behind—a solitary figure, ramrod straight and rigid.

Farewell, Adam, her heart whispered plaintively, as she maneuvered the speeding horse down the twisted, narrow path through the thicket of trees. Wrapping the reins about her wrists, she gripped them tightly and headed home, to Ridgecrest.

Adam stood for a long while, trying to comprehend what had happened. She'd thrown away her dream catcher. Dear God, she'd thrown it away, seemingly without a twinge of regret. In fact, she'd grown stronger before his very eyes the moment it had disappeared beneath the water.

He didn't understand. She had acted as though she believed she'd freed them both from something. Perhaps she'd freed herself, but she'd increased his misery mightily.

Reaching down, he picked up the leather pouch she'd dropped. It yet held her warmth and was imbued with her flower-fresh fragrance. With a low moan, he fingered the frayed strap that had circled about her neck and pressed the small, empty pouch to his lips. He closed his eyes, engulfed by a wave of desolation.

The forlorn little bag, so redolent with memories of Bethany, was now but a symbol of loss and emptiness—of hers and of his.

His eyes swelled with the unfamiliar sting of tears. He blinked them away quickly and folded the leather-strapped pouch into his pocket.

An ache of anguish wrenched his heart. She'd done precisely what he had told her time and again to do, and yet he knew he'd been wrong from the beginning.

He'd taken far more than her innocence from her; he'd ripped away her very spirit. And, in the process, he'd lost the last remaining shred of his own tattered soul.

Feeling completely drained, he sat on the boulder where she had sat and stared with listlessness at the churning stream. When in the name of God had he grown so hardened and cruel that he could crush a tender, lively spirit? Where and why had he formed within himself the conviction that light, trust, and love led to weakness and defeat, while darkness, suspicion, and driving hatred demonstrated rational strength?

What had happened to him? What kind of ill-formed monster had he become?

Having long ago given up on achieving his own happiness, had he launched upon a mission to ensure that all who dared near him must suffer unhappiness?

With growing despair, Adam found his challenge-filled life had not prepared him for what he now saw was his most difficult challenge—facing his greatest enemy. Himself.

Dear God, he didn't even know what he should do with his life, let alone know what he might do or wanted to do.

Thomasina Ring

Restlessness had driven him to this waterfall today. Restlessness caused by what? Impatience with his shallow days of idleness at Brierwood, true, but he knew his future days at Wendover might well be but a long extension of such days.

Was that the birthright he had esteemed so highly?

No, he told himself. Wendover would be different. He would be involved in his land, work it with diligence alongside his men, his freed men.

Freedom. Odd how the concept of freedom had been gnawing at him of late. Today, his craving for freedom had driven him to this place. But freedom from what? Stuffy parlors and restricting boundaries? *From bedeviling memories and one haunting dream*, he remembered with a penetrating stab.

He had been seeking freedom from Bethany and yet, by an ironic twist of fate, he had found her here.

No. He had lost her here.

The plaintive call of a mourning dove repeated the slow, five-beat dirge: *He had lost her here.*

And yet another plaintive call: *She had let him go.*

He stood and walked to the bank of the stream. He had considered it his duty to let her go, but she'd had the greater strength. She had freed him.

With desolation, he realized she had only freed herself. He would never be free of her. A silken copper binding would ever hold his deadened heart captive.

Expelling a sigh of torment, he lashed his riding crop across an outcropping of rock, wishing it were his own shoulders.

At least, thank God, she had freed herself from him. He prayed that someday she would regain her own birthright—her God-given radiance of joyful light.

With a warming nudge of comfort, his faith in Bethany's sturdy spirit stirred to life within his darkened thoughts. Of course she would. With her native strength alone she would do just that, and the rewards for her would be far greater because she would know she'd found her way to happiness unaided by magic amulets or the dubious strength of lesser souls.

To hell with himself and his own deadened spirit. He had been moribund long before he'd met her, and even she had been unable to revive him.

As he turned away from the water, a tiny glint caught his eye. He stopped. Caught upon a rock in the stream was a small piece of gleaming metal.

Was it her dream catcher? With his heart quickening, he jumped down into the shallow, turbulent water and ran toward the twinkling object. Swiftly, he swept it up into his hand, just as the current threatened to carry it away.

It pulsed with warmth against his palm as he held it tight. When he slowly unclasped his fingers to look for the first time upon her treasured amulet, he gasped.

Dear God in heaven. Bethany's dream catcher was a tiny golden horseshoe—a clasped pin, studded with garnet nail heads, filigreed with miniature oak leaves, and acorns, and bearing a Latin inscription, "*Sic juvat transcendere monte.*"

His heart thumped as he gazed upon her amulet with stunned disbelief. How had this jeweled memento of Virginia's history found its way to Wildcat Hollow and become woven into the dreams of Bethany Stewart?

Her mother had given it to her, she'd told him. But how had her mother come upon the treasure?

A deep red garnet caught a ray of filtered sunlight, and Adam knew at once the heart-rending answer. Robert Castle had given it to Mary McKeith Stewart.

Castle's father had been one of the Knights of the Golden Horseshoe, and Castle, like his own father, had inherited one of the treasured tokens. Along with his heart, Robert Castle had left his golden horseshoe behind with Mary Stewart.

Adam closed his hand around the pin and walked with weighted steps from the stream.

No longer did Bethany require his protection, but, by God, he'd protect and shelter her dream catcher until he could return it to her.

Though he could never tell her why, he would have to convince her that she must always keep it close to her heart.

Carefully, he placed the golden horseshoe inside the small leather pouch and tightened the drawstring to keep it secure. After hanging the strap about his neck, he held the soft little bag in his hand. A warm, subtle vibration tingled his palm.

When he loosed his grip, the pouch swung free and swayed like a pendulum across his shirt before, at last, growing still. It nestled against his chest, directly over his heart.

As Adam moved toward the chestnut, his steps were lighter than they'd been for weeks. He didn't question why, for his mind was elsewhere. Bethany's dream catcher settled over his heart, and the soft stirrings within his chest had captured his full attention.

He didn't even try to comprehend what was happening to him.

Adam Barwick's heart was awakening beneath its shell of stone and slowly breaking through with strong beats of renewed life.

Chapter Twenty-Two

As Bethany approached Ridgecrest, she saw Mister Castle standing beside the stable waiting for her. She wondered if his wife was impatient again for her Sunday bath. The afternoon's sun was still high above the horizon. Mrs. Castle's nagging had started early today.

"I'll hurry right in," she said to him as she dismounted. "I'm certain the lady is eager to have—"

"The lady be damned," he interrupted.

Bethany stared at him, dumbfounded.

"Sara Castle isn't expecting your assistance today. She's taken to her bed with a fit of vapors," he added, sounding not at all concerned.

"I'm sorry, sir." She unsaddled the horse and began to unbridle it.

Thomasina Ring

"Your sympathy's misplaced, my dear. Sara's vapors are of her own making."

Puzzled, she slipped the reins from the animal's head and hung them over a peg. Mister Castle's mood was passing strange today. She'd never heard him speak of his wife with such bitterness, and he was extremely nervous.

"Have you forgotten I wish to talk with you?" he asked.

Oh my, she had. "I'm truly sorry, sir. My mind has been a muddle this entire day, I vow." She hoped her disappointment over his desiring a chat hadn't overshadowed her apology. All she really wanted to do was sit by herself somewhere and mull over the afternoon's events.

But then a chilling thought struck her. Dear heaven, did Mister Castle want to discuss the poor quality of her work these past weeks? The lady had been sorely displeased with her; she'd threatened her with dismissal many times. Had she, indeed, convinced her husband to release her?

She swallowed hard, feeling large chunks of her newfound strength slip away. Perhaps she deserved no better, but merciful heavens, where would she go?

Turning to face Mister Castle, she saw a flash of alarm very like her own reflect from his deep blue eyes.

"Why have you grown so pale, Bethany Rose? Are you ill?"

The concern in his voice smoothed away the sharpest edges of her apprehension, but slivers of worry yet lingered. He was mighty high-strung today.

She shook her head and lowered her eyes. "I fear I've been an unsatisfactory worker of late, sir, and I thought perhaps you were planning to dismiss me."

His hand touched her shoulder and embraced it lightly. "You've become essential to Ridgecrest, and you contribute greatly to our daily operations. You're not to heed Mrs. Castle's ill-tempered rages. She's ever been thus and we've learned to ignore her as much as possible. You should do likewise."

Heartened by his kind words, she relaxed considerably, though she pledged she'd go about her tasks with more vigor henceforth. After this afternoon at Crabtree Falls, she truly believed she'd find new sources of strength and energy within herself.

"Is that what you wished to discuss with me, sir?" she asked.

The intense probes of his warm eyes reached into her soul, soundly unsettling her. "No, Bethany, tis a far more vital matter, and I pray my words will bring you special happiness."

His gravity convinced her his matter was indeed serious. But she felt no fear; this man would never cause her harm.

How she knew that, she couldn't explain. Dear, sweet Adam would call it "foolish blind trust," bless him. It was neither foolish nor blind but it was indeed trust. She trusted her own instincts, and she trusted Robert Castle.

"I believe I want very much to hear what you wish to tell me, sir." She was suffused with a comforting sort of suspense. A feeling, she noted with interest, quite kin to hope.

Mister Castle smiled. "The stable is not a fitting site for our talk, and you must be hungry, my dear. Would you like some supper first?"

She shook her head and returned his smile. "I have not a whit of appetite. Would the rose garden be fitting?"

"Perfectly." He took her arm, and they walked side by side to the garden.

Robert Castle's startling revelations took Bethany's breath away. She sat awestruck, rapt, weeping openly, not daring to believe, but compelled to believe.

His wondrous story of the deep soul-binding love between her mother and him filled her heart with unbounded happiness.

She had sprung from a union of true love! Her beloved mother had been blessed with golden hours of a shared love that transcended time and space. And her father, sitting here before her, was gentle and kind—a prince among men.

For a long time after he'd stopped talking, she couldn't say a word. The lowering western sun bathed them in a glow of pink and lavender as they sat on opposite benches, their emotion-filled eyes speaking more to one another than their tongues could ever utter. She absorbed his love as she offered her own.

"You have given me the gift of life itself," she said at last, wiping the tears from her cheeks. The front of her shirt was soaked, but that bothered her not at all.

Unconsciously, she reached for her dream catcher, but her hand circled only air, a swift reminder of her impulsive gesture back at the falls. What had she done? Her mother had given it to her. It held magic, she'd told her, held wondrous dreams of a prince who. . . .

Bethany sat up with a gasp. Robert Castle's eyes . . . Her *father's* eyes were the blue of a summer's sky.

"What color was your hair?" she asked him, her voice a mere whisper.

"Brown, I suppose. Dark brown." He raised his hand to his still-thick silver hair and chuckled softly. "Your mother likened it to a beaver's fur."

Her heart quickened. "And your horse . . . Was it white?"

He nodded. "How did you know, Bethany?"

Fresh tears welled in her eyes. "It was *her* dream she gave me . . . Her love for you was its magic, its promise . . ." Wracked with emotion, she searched her father's attentive but puzzled face. He knew nothing of the dream catcher, so he couldn't possibly understand what she was talking about.

But she deeply wished she had it still. Not for herself, for she'd been right that she needed it no longer. She wished she had it for him. Robert Castle should have the dream catcher. Its magic had brought her to Ridgecrest, but the dream . . . the dream was her mother's—and his.

She bowed her head. "Mama gave me an amulet on my seventh birthday, the very summer she was taken from me. I believe she had a premonition she'd be leaving me soon, and she wanted me to have her dream catcher, as she called it. It held magic and would bring dreams of a prince who would carry me beyond the blue mountains."

"Was your dream catcher a small golden horseshoe, Bethany?"

She lifted her eyes in astonishment and nodded.

His low groan tore into her heart. "I gave it to your mother," he said.

"It was imbued with her dreams of you, sir. I saw the prince many times, but he was her prince, not mine." She remembered with a pang how her dream prince kept altering after Adam had come into her life—how he'd grown taller, his hair had lightened, his eyes were darker.

Dear angels in heaven, the amulet had been truly magical, even for her. And she had. . . .

"I threw it away," she said with a sob, burying her

face into her hands. "Dear God in heaven, I flung it into a stream this very day—and you should have it," she cried.

In an instant, her father had crossed the short distance between their benches and had her wrapped in his arms, cradling her head on his shoulders.

"The dream catcher brought you here," he crooned. "Its work was done, my love, its magic accomplished." He brushed away the tears on her cheeks, and she felt his gentling kiss on her temple.

His words and touches soothed her. He spoke with true wisdom; its magic indeed had been done. Neither her father nor she had further need for it. The dream catcher had known and its final guidance to her had led her to discard it forever—to free Adam.

Dear Adam. He nudged into her memory, and she bit her lip.

"Bethany, I want the world to know you're my daughter," Robert Castle said, still holding her in his comforting embrace. She could hear the deep resonance of his voice in his chest, the steady beat of his heart against her ear.

He continued, "With pride I shall tell them all, and you'll be the pearl of Ridgecrest—the true mistress of my home."

A jab of reality hit Bethany, and she lifted her head and looked with concern into his eyes. "But you can never do that," she said with a catch of her breath. "There would be shame heaped upon you because of me, and Mrs. Castle would die from the humiliation."

He frowned. "As I said earlier, Mrs. Castle be damned."

She shook her head and pulled away from him. Reaching for his hand, she clasped it tightly within hers. "'Tis blessing enough that I know the truth, sir, but I never want the world to know."

Worry shadowed his eyes a deeper blue. "That is my fondest dream, Bethany," he said.

His plea wrenched her heart. But she knew at once why Robert Castle's dream should never be fulfilled.

"No, sir," she responded with firm conviction. "Your dream would shatter any chance for happiness for us. I could never bear to see the beautiful love shared between you and my mother become an instrument of distress to anyone. Nor do I believe you could bear have it become something destructive."

He uttered an agonizing moan. "You received more of your mother than of me, my daughter. You're the embodiment of her selfless soul, and, like her, you're far stronger than I." Tears streamed down his finely sculptured face. He gripped his bowed forehead with his hand and kneaded his temples. His next words were a cry of despair. "Once again I'm facing a stronger will that would have me turn my back on one I love with all my heart."

Bethany leaned forward and kissed the top of his lowered head. "But don't you see, dear man? By turning your back, you're ensuring that your love for both my mother and me remains pure and whole—in your heart, in hers, and in mine. As long as we keep our special love to ourselves, it is ours alone."

His shoulders slumped. "Mary said those very words to me."

She squeezed his hand. "Mama was a far wiser woman than I, I vow. You mustn't keep torturing yourself, my father. You didn't leave her behind. She wouldn't come, I suspect. She had a wondrous, perfect love to retain in her heart, and she knew that perfection would have become something other, possibly something far less, had she entered your separate world where she might never have truly fit."

319

He lifted his face to her then. The hues of the setting sun tinged his sorrowful eyes with the delicate color of lilacs. Concern for her flickered from their depths. "Your wisdom appears to stem from troubled roots, my dear one. Are you beseiged by doubts about your own ability to fit into a separate world?"

She sighed and shook her head. "No more. I'm here because I was destined to be, I believe. The knowledge you've given me this day has indeed given me a special happiness I shall carry with me always. It bolsters my courage and strength." She smiled broadly. "It tells me I have your blood in my veins as well as that of my beloved mother's and assures me I can fit into either world. Maybe, even in all worlds." She placed her finger lovingly across his lips. "And if you promise never to tell another soul of our secret, perhaps someday I too shall find a love as perfect as the one you two shared."

"Adam knows I'm your father."

She gasped. "Adam?"

He pinched the bridge of his nose and expelled a sigh. "God be my witness, he's the only soul I ever revealed the truth to. He'll hold it close within himself, he vowed . . ."

"But why did you tell Adam? When for heaven's sake?" She was thunderstruck.

Robert Castle studied her eyes carefully as he spoke. "I felt compelled to confide in him, my dear. He was highly protective of you. I knew, of course, he wasn't your brother, since I'd seen the young George Stewart. I was protective of you, too, and was concerned about the times when he was alone with you."

He paused, searching, it seemed, for some reaction other than frozen astonishment from her. She was unable to comply and waited for him to continue, forgetting to breathe.

"After that last Sunday you two were together, he encountered me with fierce accusations about my intentions toward you. I countered with my own questions about his intentions. They were, he told me, but to protect you and he had a forceful earnestness that made me know his desire to see you safe and secure was as strong as mine."

He sighed deeply. "You love Adam very much, don't you, Bethany?"

His soft question jolted her and she jumped slightly. "Aye, very much, but—"

He stopped her with another deep sigh. "My revelation that I am your father released him from his responsibilities toward you, but I truly sensed he loved you. I didn't know at the time who he was and his true mission here in Albemarle but, even after he'd told me, I sensed his deep love for you. I still believe that with all my heart. It's just that he's so driven to regain his birthright and right the wrong done to him that he—"

"No," she interrupted. "Adam doesn't love me." Her heart wept, but her eyes remained as dry as a desert. "He's closed himself off from love for so long he may never be able to love anyone. I pray I'm wrong, for I hope someday he will open his heart to someone. He has a beautiful spirit, but he fears love."

In the long silence that followed, her own words echoed in her mind. She hadn't realized until she'd spoken them what her true discovery had been today at the falls—the one reason she'd freed him; the one reason she'd thrown away her dream catcher. She hadn't freed herself from anything. She loved him deeper than ever, she would always believe in dreams, and she'd harbor hope in her breast until the day she died.

But Adam was incapable of love, and so she'd freed

him. She had freed him from his burdensome obligations to her that had caused his gentle, tender spirit to suffer.

"It matters not that Adam knows of our secret, for he'll tell no one," she said to her father. With a loving squeeze, she released his hand, stood and walked to a bush of creamy white roses. Their delicate beauty and fragrance were soft affirmations that the earth abounded with glorious promises.

Glorious promises. Her heart kicked into a faster pace. Merciful heavens, what had been wrong with her? Why had she blinded herself to that one simple truth?

The evidence stood with proud splendor right before her. Roses might wither and seem to die during the cold grip of winter, but they awaited merely the touch of warm sunlight to bloom once again.

It was the same with hearts, she knew with sudden clarity. A heart, too, might wither and seem to die, but as long as there was a breath of life within a person, that heart could always revive and blossom fully. Hers was already sprouting with swelling buds of renewal. She could feel it happening.

And Adam? Why, Adam was *vibrant* with life. His warming spring's touch would come to him. His heart wasn't dead, it was only in a restless slumber. She pressed her face into one of the roses and inhaled the sweet perfume, remembering his lovely words to her back at the falls. "Little sparrow," he had said, and what else? "Please don't ever give up hope and always treasure your dreams and keep them alive within you."

Glory be, her burgeoning spirits sang to her loud and clear in a far stronger voice than even her dream catcher.

She wanted to shout with joy.

Adam Barwick was her prince, after all. It was as inevitable as the unfolding of the silken petals of this rose. Adam was the most glorious promise of all. Someday, in some way, her own sunlight would reach him and he would return her love as only he could do.

After fondling the blossom in her hand, she hurried back to Robert Castle and gave him an exuberant hug.

"I love you," she whispered excitedly in his ear. "Just wait and see, my dear father, all will be well with your daughter."

Her suddenly revived spirits had taken him by surprise, she could tell. But they pleased him, she could see that, too.

He patted her cheek. "I pray you're right, my dearest love."

"You can depend on it," she said brightly, and left him then, her steps springing with life as she ran toward the house.

A golden beam of morning sunshine stroked Adam awake. He lay naked on his tousled bed, reluctant to open his eyes. Remnants of his vivid dream lingered, and he struggled to piece it together, to recall its substance. It had been powerful, filled with color and motion, and passion. He groaned and rolled over, uncomfortably aware his aroused groin was holding on to the dream with more tenacity than his sleep-muffled memory.

There had been greens, he remembered, sparkling greens, a profusion of brilliant copper . . . a misty blue. He had flown like a bird. Flown? No, something swifter than a bird's flight, more impelling, more substantial. And someone had been with him. Someone as soft and yielding as. . . .

He opened his eyes. Dear God. He'd dreamed of Bethany. Moaning into the pillow, he scrunched it around his ears. Her dream catcher was beneath it. He'd placed it there to keep it safe.

Thrusting his hand beneath the pillow, he grasped for the leather pouch. It held incredible heat and buzzed against his palm.

His heart pounded as he pulled it out and raised up on his elbows to look at it. It was the same as yesterday—limp, worn leather with the little golden horseshoe laying quietly inside.

But the heat he'd felt? The buzzing? They'd been there. And what of that strong, rapture-filled dream? Was her amulet truly magical as she believed?

Adam shook his head. Was he going mad? He sure as hell had better return this thing to Bethany today. He rose quickly and splashed cold water on his face. After dressing, he stood for a while and stared at the leather-strapped pouch lying in the middle of his rumpled pillow. Magic?

Nonsense. He picked it up, slipped the strap over his head, and stuffed the dream catcher under his shirt.

Evelyn Mason and Marshall Lawrence greeted him with cheery "good mornings" when he entered the dining room. He grunted in reply.

"Our mood is bleak for such a lovely morning," Evelyn trilled with a pout.

"No, milady. *My* mood is bleak. Yours is as light and airy as your profoundest thoughts," he retorted, pouring himself a cup of coffee and taking a seat at the far end of the table well away from both of his breakfast companions.

"Your barbs sting me not, Adam Barwick," she said, fluttering her eyelashes. "Marshall's doting compliments this morn have cushioned my pride so well

I don't believe you could make even the tiniest of pricks in my fair flesh."

He ignored her baiting chatter and turned his attention to his coffee. The woman, despite her beauty, was truly the most uninteresting female he'd ever met. She oozed false sensuality and had flirted with him shamelessly since the day he'd arrived at Brierwood.

Resisting her dubious charms had been extremely easy, and she had, at last, diverted her attentions to Marshall. Good. They were cut from the same cloth.

But Evelyn's high-pitched shriek of horror caught him unprepared. He jumped to his feet, overturning his cup.

She was standing, her hand clasped across her mouth, her terror-filled eyes focused on the wall and one trembling finger pointing in the same direction. Marshall, too, was standing, his eyes wide with fright.

Expecting to see a catamount tearing through the wall, Adam stiffened. Unarmed, he quickly reached for a sharp table knife.

When he saw what had caused the uproar, he rolled his eyes upward in disgust.

With a disdainful snort, he walked over, plucked the tiny spider off the wall, and pinched it between his fingers. Scowling with scorn at the ruffled couple, he wiped his hands across his buff breeches, hoping mightily he'd left a speck of smashed insect and blood across his thigh to further unsettle them.

Evelyn fanned her pale face and flopped back on her chair in a poof of filmy blue muslin. Marshall circled his fist over his mouth and coughed nervously before sitting beside her. Both of them stared at Adam as though he might have been a stranger from a different world.

"Spiders terrify me," Evelyn whimpered.

Adam shrugged and went back to clean up the coffee he'd spilled. Bethany bounced unbidden into his thoughts. Bethany with an arrow aimed at a murderous stallion's neck; Bethany clubbing a deadly copperhead without a second thought. With wry amusement at the contrast between Bethany Rose Stewart and the sniveling Virginia belle before him, he sopped up the liquid with a cloth and righted his cup and saucer.

Suddenly, his already tenuous patience with both his present company and the pampered society they represented collapsed. He desperately needed a breath of fresh air. With dispatch, he placed the cup and saucer on the sideboard, tossed the cloth beside it, and headed for the door.

"On your way to Ridgecrest?" Marshall inquired, daintily dipping a toasted sippet into his coffee.

"Perhaps," Adam answered. "I have business to attend to there." He did. He wanted Bethany to have her dream catcher.

Marshall snickered wickedly, and Adam stopped, throwing him a dark look.

"The kind of business that will improve your humor, I vow," Marshall said, keeping his own eyes on the soggy sippet.

Adam leaned over and spread his hands across the burnished wood of the table. "State your implications," he ordered.

Marshall lifted one eyebrow and smirked. "The red-haired servant girl serves you well, I wager. Tis little wonder you aborted my own dalliances. You wanted to keep the wench untired for your own—"

He didn't finish his sentence. In three swift strides, Adam had circled the table, got a handful of Marshall's shirt collar in his fierce grasp, and lifted him from his chair. With his free hand, he delivered a punch to his dandified cousin's jaw that sent him reeling across the room.

Other than two overturned chairs, a soft tinkle of disarranged silverware, and the strangled gasp of an aghast young lady in a blue muslin dress, the grandly furnished dining room was relatively undisturbed.

Not so, Marshall Lawrence, who lay sprawled across the turkeywork carpet, rubbing his jaw and sputtering with pain. And not so Adam Barwick, who stood over him, his face hot with anger, muttering a string of oaths never before heard by the staid, portrait-hung walls.

Thus was the scene greeting Hallston Lawrence when he entered his own dining room.

"Holy God, what has happened?" Lawrence exclaimed, standing in the doorway as though he'd been pinned to the spot. His wig was slightly askew.

"Your son is much in need of proper table manners," Adam said gruffly, and stepped over the groaning Marshall to stand in front of his uncle.

Hallston Lawrence's dark eyes focused hard on his nephew's face. "My home is not a crossroads tavern, Adam. We settle our differences here with more refined means."

Adam narrowed his eyes. "With obscenities, sir?" he roared. "With venomous tongues and scurrilous accusations? Are you telling me those are the stuff of refinement? If so, I want no portion of your bloody refined ways."

Lawrence was taken aback, but he remained poised. He looked down at his son, who was sitting up with a dazed expression on his slightly swollen face. Evelyn Mason was bending over him, clucking her sympathy and patting his head, but positioning herself to avoid any undue mussing of her pristine frock.

"What did you say to your cousin, Marshall?"

Lawrence asked, an undercurrent of accusation in his tone.

Marshall only shrugged. Evelyn's gray eyes shot pointed darts at Adam, but she addressed the older man. "Marshall spoke only the truth, sir. Adam's uncivilized reaction was truly excessive considering such scant provocation."

Adam's growl rumbled deep in his throat. Lawrence looked up at him, and, surprisingly, despite his stern expression, his eyes twinkled.

With a harumph, he turned to his son. "Apply a cold poultice to your face," he suggested. "And, henceforth, I advise you to restrain your tongue with whatever judicious wisdom you can muster."

Marshall and Evelyn stared at the man, their mouths agape.

Taking Adam by the elbow, Lawrence nodded his head toward the parlor. "I have some news of import," he said under his breath.

"Marshall no doubt deserved the hefty blow to his jaw," he said to Adam with a low chuckle as he closed the parlor door and the two were alone. "Sally and I have coddled him far too much, I fear."

"Brierwood isn't Battletown, sir. I apologize for my unbridled temper; it's just that he provoked me beyond reason and I—"

"No matter, no matter," Lawrence interrupted, dismissing the subject with a flip of his hand. "Something of far greater importance requires our immediate attention."

Adam's brow furrowed.

"I've received a disturbing message this morning," his uncle continued. "James Wallace is on his way to Brierwood and may arrive by this afternoon."

Adam clenched his teeth. "What is the bastard's purpose for coming?"

Worry creased Uncle Hallston's face. "The message didn't say, though I suspect he's coming to solicit a loan. It's unlikely he knows of your presence here. My contacts in the Tidewater assure me he's totally unaware of our legal maneuvers."

"Then he's in for a bit of a surprise, isn't he?" Adam said with a dark smile, relishing the opportunity to confront James. Today, at last, he would meet the bastard head on and. . . .

"No, Adam," his uncle admonished. "He's not to know you're here. I've arranged with Robert for you to stay at Ridgecrest during James's visit. The message spoke of but a day or two. John Randolph tells me the hearing on your father's will is scheduled this coming court day. That's next week, mind you. It's paramount you remain out of sight and hold to your patience. James must have no forewarning."

Damn, once again he was being buffeted about like a bloody pawn. But he knew his uncle spoke with wisdom.

Clamping down on his long-festering instincts for quick vengeance, he nodded his assent after a long pause.

A strange flutter within his chest, beneath the very spot where Bethany's hidden dream catcher rested, caught his attention. Ridgecrest? He was truly pleased to be returning to Ridgecrest.

Chapter Twenty-Three

Making soap wasn't one of Bethany's favorite chores. The stirring was tedious, the lifting cumbersome, and the awful stench bit at her nose. But the process was far less a burden at Ridgecrest than it had been in Wildcat Hollow, for she had the able assistance of three strong-armed women servants. Nevertheless, the task took most of the day.

By the time they'd finished, she, like the rest of them, was thoroughly smeared with ashes from top to bottom, and her gray work dress and white apron were woefully splashed with grease.

At last, the reward stood before her—two fine barrels of beautiful soap, and the stink hovered no longer. Quite the contrary. One barrel was scented with bayberry, the other, with fragrant lavender.

"Tis fine work we've done this day," she said with

satisfaction to the women, wiping her perspiring forehead with her soiled sleeve. "But I vow it might take the whole of both barrels to clean up us soap makers."

Millie, Christine, and Bette giggled behind their ash-stained fingers. They were a giddy trio, but they'd been willing, competent help all day, and their merry chatter and playful attitude had lightened the heavy chore and made the hours flee.

Her spirits high, Bethany acted on an impish impulse. "We deserve a bath, ladies," she exclaimed, reaching in for a great handful of the still-warm soap. "Let's be off to the river yon and wash away our toil!"

The three women took to the idea with enthusiasm and followed her lead, gathering up globs of soap and running after her toward the river.

Bethany noted with amusement that the others had scooped from the lavender barrel. She, of course, had chosen the bayberry.

From a window, Adam watched them disappear behind the trees, compelled to smile despite his frustration. He'd been waiting all day to have a moment alone with Bethany so he could return her dream catcher. Now, he'd have to wait a while longer.

Off and on during the past hours he'd been drawn to the window to watch her at work. She was the animated, lively Bethany he remembered so well, ordering the others around like a little general, but doing double their work with a spritely exuberance that amazed him.

Her spirits and gumption truly had returned, and he was genuinely happy for her. Robert Castle had told him about his conversation with Bethany last evening, and he figured the knowledge Castle was her father had liberated her from the self doubts he'd sensed in her.

But her stubborn refusal to let Castle acclaim to the world that she was his daughter pained him, though it hadn't surprised him. How like her it was to think of others before herself.

Bethany Rose Stewart indeed was an unusual woman, unlike any he'd ever known. She was blessed with far more courage than a dozen men; more beauty, even with an ash-smudged face and grease-stained frock, than every fair, fashionably gowned plantation damsel in all of Virginia. Bethany, in a word, was wonderful.

Feeling a notable tug at his heart, he jerked erect, stunned. Dear God, he was beginning to sound like an addled man who'd been captured by the snares of love! But that was insane. Adam Barwick had no room in his heart for a frivolous commodity like love and certainly no time to waste on pursuing such a fancy.

Time. Hell, he was plagued with a blasted over-supply of idle time at the moment. That was his biggest problem. Having nothing to do but peer from windows was driving him crazy. And he would have to stay hidden and idle here at Ridgecrest for at least another full day.

A spell of good honest back-breaking labor was what his soul craved. Lord, he'd missed heavy, useful work. Pushing himself away from the sill, he made a quick decision. Angus would have plenty of chores he could do.

With a surge of energy, he ran from the house to find the Scot. Adam wanted to get his hands, brawn, and body occupied with mindless tasks, for his thoughts and heart, he realized with a pang, were leading him down a mighty dangerous path.

Angus not only welcomed him, he set him to repairing a near mile of fences. Though it took till well past nightfall, Adam accomplished the task with frenzied zeal.

"My God, that exertion felt good," he said to the Scot as the two sat alone in the servants' quarters. Adam had been assigned a spare bedchamber in the main house, and he'd be heading there soon. But, for the moment, he was content to put his feet up and enjoy a cup of rum in the company of Angus McInnes.

Bethany, he'd found, had already retired for the night, so his return of the dream catcher would have to wait for the morrow.

"Are ye finding the life of a gentleman a wee boring now?" Angus asked with a light chuckle.

"Far worse than boring," he responded, running his fingers through his hair. "Fresh air to most of them means a half-opened window to stir up a perfume-laden room, and labor is carving a leg of venison or lifting a tea cup with the little finger extended just so." He demonstrated comically with the full stoneware cup, managing to splash a drop of rum on the table.

Angus laughed. "Sounds like a braw life to me, laddie. If ye're looking for sympathy from McInnes, ye're barking up the wrong pine tree." He sipped his rum, sticking out his little finger, and waggling it in a taunting fashion.

"I'm serious, you bloody Scot. To labor till you sweat is a gift. Wide open spaces are to be treasured. Freedom . . ." He paused, took a deep breath, and looked longingly into Angus's pale blue eyes. "Freedom, by God, makes life worth living."

"What's holding ye from freedom, Adam? There's not a thing in this world I can think of that could stop ye from jumping atop that braw chestnut and riding west where ye could find all the damn wide open spaces ye profess to treasure and labor enough to busy ye for a lifetime."

Adam stared at the man, dumbfounded. What the hell was he talking about? What, as a matter of fact, had he been talking about himself? He frowned into his cup.

"I'm befuddled, I guess," he said in a hushed voice. "For six years I've had this obsession about returning home to Wendover, ruling like a grand pasha, I suppose, over that vast estate. But the years have changed me, I'm finding." He slouched down farther in the chair and let out a weary sigh. "Hell, Angus, I don't even know what I want anymore."

Angus sat back and crossed his arms. "Most men want happiness, lad, did ye ever think of that?"

"Happiness? What kind of a fool goal is that?"

The Scot snorted a soft laugh. "Happiness isn't a goal, lad. It just is. Ye either have it or ye don't. It's way inside, and when it's there, nothing or no one or no place can take it away from ye. That don't mean ye can't improve your lot or try to do better or any of those worthy things but a man's got to be happy with himself first. Ye, Adam, strike me as a man who's unhappy with himself."

Adam narrowed his eyes in deep thought. Angus was right. He *was* miserably unhappy with himself. And why the hell not? There was precious little inside him to make him happy.

A tiny warming buzz vibrated against his chest and he straightened up quickly, placed his hand over the small pouch beneath his shirt. The damn thing was acting up again. Only he discovered with astonishment that he was more comforted than annoyed. His eyes must have widened, because Angus looked at him with concern and started to rise.

"Having a pain in your chest, lad?"

Adam shook his head and removed his hand from

the pulsing dream catcher. "No, I was just thinking about something."

The Scot sat back in his chair. "Something or somebody?" he asked with a grin.

"Both, I guess." Bloody hell, what had gone wrong with his tongue? He was saying things his mind hadn't formed.

"Would the somebody by chance be a bonnie lass with flame-red hair and eyes the color of a bright laurel leaf?"

"Emeralds. They're emeralds, Angus, not laurel. Laurel leaves are a dull green, relatively speaking." He was doing it again, babbling like a blithering idiot.

Angus reached over and topped Adam's cup, then replenished his own. "Laurel or emerald, tis one and the same, lad, to the rest of us, that is. She sees only ye through those green orbs, ye know that, don't ye?"

The buzzing had stopped at last, but his chest was alive with a hammering racket. He couldn't hear himself think; he covered his ears and moaned.

Angus jumped up and came over to him. "What's wrong, lad? Are ye ill? You're as pale as a ghost."

Adam rubbed his eyes and kneaded his forehead. "I'm all right, just a bit tired, I guess." He put his hands on the table and pushed himself up, straightened his shoulders, and expelled a heavy breath. "Not used to working so hard. My life at Brierwood has been a mite on the soft side, I reckon." He attempted a smile, but it felt more like a sneer.

The burly Scot gave him a friendly punch on his arm. "Tis good to have ye back, Adam, even if tis for just a couple of days. We've missed ye. Want to work a bit on the morrow? We've got horses to shod. Ye were always good at that, and ye might find it less grueling than repairing fences."

"Aye, I'd love to shoe the horses." He clasped Angus

on the shoulder and his smile was easier, broader. "Have a good night, my friend. Tis good to be back."

As Adam was opening the door, the Scot stopped him with a parting remark. "She let none of us come for a visit, by the way. You're a lucky man, Adam. She's bonnie and true, and a lass who could help any man find happiness within himself. She's chosen ye. You're a bigger fool than I think ye be if ye don't accept her choice and do some choosing of your own."

Adam left without a response and closed the door with a quiet thud. The buzzing and hammering accompanied him into the house, up the stairs. He couldn't escape either, and they climbed with him into his narrow bed.

He had a thoroughly restless night.

Adam was at Ridgecrest! Bethany was beside herself with excitement. She hadn't seen him yet, but she would. She knew she would. In preparation, she'd donned her prettiest work dress, a green airy muslin with wisps of creamy lace circling the prim neckline and elbow-length sleeves. Her apron and cap were of the same ivory lace.

With her heart singing, she carried Mrs. Castle's breakfast tray into the woman's bedchamber.

"Good morning, Bethany," she heard. She came close to dropping the tray.

"Why, good morning to you, Mrs. Castle." The woman was *smiling*, for heaven's sake, and she'd spoken her name correctly. Indeed it *was* a good morning but at the same time, a highly peculiar one.

"You may place the tray on the table yon. I'm dressed, as you see, and I'm weary of eating my breakfast in bed propped up by plump pillows."

"Aye, ma'am." *Highly* peculiar, but wondrous, too. Perhaps, just perhaps, the woman was emerging from her dark night of misery. Why the change, she couldn't imagine, but whatever the cause, she was happy for Mrs. Castle.

"Will that be all, ma'am?" she inquired with a polite curtsy.

Sara Castle tilted her head, studying her with her pale gray eyes. They held a glimmer of life, further puzzling Bethany.

"You look lovely today, Bethany Rose. Are we expecting company?"

Her cheeks grew warm. "None that I know of, Mrs. Castle."

A thin silver eyebrow lifted. "Adam Barwick is here, I understand."

Bethany lowered her eyes. "Aye, though I haven't seen him, ma'am. He's in the stables shoeing horses for Angus."

"Unfitting work for a gentleman, don't you think?"

She didn't know what she thought, but the woman expected a reply. She raised her eyes, looked openly at Mrs. Castle and found herself speaking with heart-felt earnestness. "Mister Barwick is a true gentleman, ma'am, but I believe he enjoys heavy work."

"Interesting" was the reply.

Bethany felt a need to change the subject. "It's a pleasure to see you looking so well, ma'am. Mister Castle told me of your unfortunate vapors of late, and your frail health has concerned us all."

The woman's long thin fingers tightened on the padded arms of her chair. "Was Mister Castle concerned?"

"Truly, ma'am," she lied. No, not a lie. Robert Castle was ever concerned about his wife. Only she'd kept him so distant, had kept him away from her. Oh, how she hoped that the woman was truly changing. . . .

The knock on the door startled them both. Bethany ran to open it.

"Good morning, Robert," Mrs. Castle trilled.

He stared at his smiling wife, astonished. "Good morning, Sara," he said with a stiff bow of his head.

"Bethany and I were just having a lovely chat. But you're all abother about something, I fear. How may we assist you?"

"Uh, I have need of Bethany for a minute or two if you don't mind, Sara. Something has come up that requires immediate attention, I believe." Obviously baffled by his wife's changed demeanor, he fixed his awed eyes on her briefly before turning to Bethany. "Could I talk with you outside?" he asked her.

Bethany looked at the woman for permission.

"Certainly, Bethany. Go on, the two of you, and tend to the urgent matter. And . . . Robert?" She managed a surprisingly warm smile. "You will come up for a visit later, won't you? I would dearly love to spend a bit of time with you, my dear."

Robert Castle nodded and motioned to Bethany to follow him.

"What in heaven's name has happened to her?" he whispered after he'd closed the door and they were walking down the hall.

Bethany shrugged, but her face lit with a brilliant glow. "'Tis a miracle, I vow. Do you suppose an army of angels paid her a visit during the night?"

His brow crinkled then his eyes widened, as if a surprising thought had occurred to him. "More likely a devil or two," he said with a low chuckle. "By God, something might well have given Sara a fright. Something long overdue . . ."

Bethany puzzled over his strange words, but remembered suddenly he'd come for her with a purpose of some urgency.

"You needed me for an important matter, sir?"

He stopped and grabbed her arm. "God, Bethany, she befuddled me so I came near to forgetting. You must run to the stables at once and warn Adam. James Wallace is on his way to Ridgecrest, and Adam must stay hidden."

"James Wallace? Coming here? Why?" Alarm triggered her heart into a fury of leaps.

"I've no idea. The message only said he'd be arriving within the hour. Now run, dear girl. Alert Adam!"

She ran like the wind. Not until she was opening the doors of the stable did an odd thought strike her. Why had Robert Castle sent her rather than warn Adam himself? No matter, she decided with a surge of excitement. She was delighted he had.

"Adam?" she called softly. She squinted, adjusting to the dusky light. When she saw him, behind the stallion, her mind went blank, but the rest of her tingled. Oh my, he was gorgeous. He'd heard her, seen her, and now he was coming toward her, pulling on his shirt. Twas a shame to cover those massive bronzed shoulders, that muscled silky-haired chest, she thought fuzzily.

When he stood before her, so close she breathed his heady scent of wood smoke blended with bayberry, her knees turned liquid.

"Bethany?"

His dark, velvet eyes burned into hers, and then—glory be!—with a low gasp, he enfolded her in his arms.

With dizzying ecstasy, she greeted the hungry pressure of his lips on hers, the thrusts of his heated tongue. Her weeks of unsated hunger for him gathered into a massive force, driving her to devour his frenzied kisses as he devoured hers, again and again, till she was so weak she would have fallen to the straw-covered dirt had he not held her so tight, kept his wonderful mouth clasped to her own.

Time stood still. Her heart raced, her swirling brain cheered. Adam's kisses avowed the wondrous truth. He loved her. *Adam loved her!*

"Dear God, I've missed you," he moaned into her neck, cradling her head, embracing her, kissing her ears, her eyes, her cheeks, her nose. His lashes touched hers, and then, his lips returned to cover hers with an encompassing tenderness that sealed his love.

A chorus of jubilant songs rang within her. What at last had awakened his love she knew not, but his fervent affirmation of that love pervaded her. She accepted it with pure joy, and her heart and soul bounded to join his in a blessed, eternal fusion.

When his mouth left hers, his sweet gasp of acceptance and relief caressed her ear, filled her with his promise. His love for her pulsed from his strong, loving hand as he held her head to his chest. She heard his hammering heart, and she smiled into his shirt, nuzzled her face into the sweat-dampened linen.

"I've missed you, too, Adam. Lord, I've missed you," she sighed.

He was quiet for a long while, stroking her hair. She listened to his vigorous heartbeats, completely content.

"Why did you come here?" he asked. His husky assuring voice soothed her with its underlying message of love.

"To see you." The truth. Why else would she have run to the stable like a light-footed deer?

And then she remembered. Good heavens. . . .

She stiffened in his arms, looked up, aghast. "Mister Castle sent me. James Wallace is on his way to Ridgecrest, and you're to stay hid—"

"James?" he blurted out.

She nodded, far too happy to work up any regret that she'd delayed her ominous announcement. He'd delayed it, actually, and the imminent arrival of James Wallace paled in comparison to what had just happened.

Even Adam didn't look as disturbed by the news as she would have expected.

Glory be, he wasn't at *all* disturbed. He smiled at her, in fact, tapped the tip of her nose with his finger, and followed the tap with a soft peck of his delectable lips.

"I'll finish the shoeing, little sparrow. The forge is at the back of the stable, so I promise to stay hidden. You'd better run on to the house, for if you're near me a second longer, I might well send you in a bit too disheveled to serve tea to my charming stepbrother."

Devilishly, she ran her finger over the beautiful dimple on his strong chin. "Disheveled strikes me as far more appealing," she teased, moving toward him.

"On with you, my love," he chuckled.

With a gentle twirl of her waist, he had her facing the door. He gave her bottom a soft pat, and she complied, secure in the knowledge that dishevelment by Adam would occur with decided frequency in their glorious future together.

But before she opened the door, a twinge of worry made her pause.

"What if he knows you're here, Adam?"

"Then by all means shout out the news to me loud and clear, little sparrow. I'm eager to confront the bastard."

Oh dear. She'd hoped that day could be postponed forever.

As she returned slowly to the house, she pushed down her concern. Adam would be victorious whatever happened.

Little sparrow. She smiled and hummed a merry tune. Oh my, she did so love the way he spoke that name.

Chapter Twenty-Four

Adam bent over the blazing forge, pounding the red-hot metal on the anvil with renewed vigor. Lord, but being in love was bloody wonderful! Why he'd fought it so long was a true puzzle. His heart had been trying to convince his stubborn gloom-ridden brain since the moment he'd met Bethany.

Well, perhaps not since the *first* moment, he corrected with a wry smile, remembering the wild hellion who'd had an arrow aimed at his chest but, by God, swift and soon thereafter.

What had finally shaken him awake might forever be a mystery. He didn't care what the hell it was, be it magical powers of an amulet, the wise, prodding words of an amiable Scot, or his own crying need for Bethany.

All that mattered was that the moment he'd seen her

standing before him in the musty stable, wide-eyed and expectant, he'd known with jarring certainty he loved Bethany Rose Stewart with every fiber of his body, mind, soul, and heart.

He hammered the glowing metal at the end of the tongs into the glorious shape of a horseshoe, then plunged it into a barrel of water, relishing the satisfying sizzle and burst of steam that enveloped his sweat-greased face and shoulders.

Bethany was indeed sizzle and steam but she was far more. She was the warmth of a glowing hearth, the fresh breath of a May morn, the vibrancy of a meadowlark's song, the beauty of a fragrant blossoming rose.

He chuckled, his jubilant heart crowing with delight. Hell, she'd turned him into a bloody poet.

And why not? Bethany was a perfectly wrought poem of love. She'd be a wonder of a mate. He'd be blissfully content with her anywhere. She'd breathe life into any place they might find themselves—any place in this wide, beautiful world. At Wendover, for sure, should that be their destiny. But in a rugged cabin in the middle of the mountains it would be the same.

He accepted that truth with satisfying ease. Bethany had swiftly become his life's most essential component.

Though he'd tried to work up some of his old hatred for James as he'd watched through the stable window when he arrived with Uncle Hallston, only a tinge of blackness had brushed across his euphoria. That tinge had dispersed without a noticeable trace.

James was stooped, weary, as pale and limp as the underbelly of a dead rat. The man oozed defeat. He had, apparently, done it to himself with the help, perhaps, of a just God.

Adam raised his eyes skyward. *Thank you, God*. "And thank you, Bethany, for teaching me the greater power of love," he added quietly, his heart suffused with gratitude and a mighty, unending love for Bethany Rose Stewart.

As she prepared to carry the tea tray into the parlor where the three gentlemen were holding their conversation, Bethany noted a strand of hay clinging to the hem of her skirt. She brushed it away briskly and smiled, wishing with devilish glee she had hay and stable dirt all over her.

She could barely believe the wonders that had occurred since she'd flung away her dream catcher. Good heavens! She'd found her true father; she'd seen a miserably unhappy woman begin to crack through a self-created shell of loneliness; and—the most wondrous happening of all—Adam had opened his heart to her!

In two brief days her world had truly filled with a magical bounty of sparkling, life-bestowing sunshine.

Double-checking the tray's contents, she lifted it and pushed open the swinging door with a frisky shove of her bottom. She dreaded seeing James Wallace again. Lord, he was a mean-looking rascal and devious. She could see it in his shifty eyes the instant she'd opened the front door to admit him and Mister Lawrence.

The man had hurt Adam so deeply. An unfamiliar surge of something far darker and more bitter than mere distaste pushed into her breast. With a jolt, she knew exactly what she was feeling. She shrugged. James Wallace deserved her hatred. He had come dangerously close to destroying Adam.

If she'd had a drop of poison, she might have placed it in the dastardly scoundrel's cup.

When she walked into the parlor, the men ceased talking. Robert Castle and Mister Lawrence had deep frowns on their faces. The despicable James was slumped in a chair, a nervous twitch pulling at his pale, weak face.

He was suffering. Good.

"Where shall I lay this, sir?" she asked her father, giving him a secret wink to ensure him all was well with Adam.

"The table there will be fine, Bethany. Thank you."

His "thank you" was for more than the tea, she knew, but his concerned expression bothered her. Did she need to warn Adam? Was something truly amiss? Her eyes questioned him; he shook his head lightly, and his kind blue eyes, though deep with worry, told her James knew nothing of Adam's presence.

Encouraged, she approached the table that sat next to James Wallace. A taunting glint on the man's magenta frock coat caught her eye. As she neared, she saw the object clearly.

My God! The silver tray dropped from her suddenly frozen hand, its contents crashed to the carpet in a heavy rush of flooding tea and splintering china.

Bethany heard only the strangled gasp of her paralyzed brain, saw only the haunting glitter on the abominable man's chest.

James Wallace was wearing her dream catcher.

She clasped her hands over her horrified face. Choking on sobs and a rising swell of bile, she fled from the room, ran from the house.

"Adam!" she screamed, rounding the stable, frenzied, wild.

In a whirling second he had her in his arms, holding her close, trying to calm her but she couldn't be calmed. She clung to his strength, sobbed into his chest, grasped him tighter.

"He has the dream catcher . . . He has the dream catcher," she sputtered over and over into the sweaty nest of silky hair on his hard, heated chest.

"Who, Bethany? What? Calm yourself, sparrow. Tell me what's happened, for God's sake."

She heard his softening tones, felt his encompassing comfort. But her shocked mind couldn't comprehend what she'd seen.

"That awful man . . ." she sobbed, gasping for breath. Adam's arms tensed, pressing her to him, enveloping her with his protection. "He's wearing it, Adam. He's wearing it!"

"What is he wearing?" he asked, his face buried in her hair, his concerned voice a smoothing whisper in her ear.

She lifted her tear-streaked face to his. "My dream catcher," she groaned.

Brief puzzlement clouded his eyes, then they cleared with a soft light. "No, my love," he said with a soothing smile. "I have your dream catcher. It's here with me. Here, sweet sparrow, here's your dream catcher." Removing one of his arms from around her, but still holding her with gentle firmness, he squirmed his hand between them.

She heard his comforting words, felt the heat of his hand, the reassuring thump of soft leather against her breast.

But comprehension was slow. Keeping within the security of his embrace, she pulled back only far enough to see what he was talking about. Her dream catcher was there, against his heart. Her trembling fingers circled the pouch, vibrated with the warm pulse of the amulet nestled inside.

"But how? I just saw it on . . ." Stunned and thoroughly confused, she stared up into his gleaming face.

Thomasina Ring

"I found it in the stream, or maybe it found me," he added with a light chuckle. His deep brown eyes glowed his love. "I would have returned it to you before now, only—"

"You've had my dream catcher since Sunday?" she interrupted, her heart leaping with joy.

He nodded, kissed the tip of her nose.

Her eyebrows squiggled with aroused curiosity. "But the other I saw . . . it was the same. I don't understand."

He hugged her close. "It's a long story, Bethany." His lips nibbled their way across her cheek, reached her ear. "Come to my room tonight, little sparrow, and I'll explain it fully, though it might take the entire night," he promised, his heated whisper causing waves of tingly shivers to billow through her insides.

His warm, salty kiss made her forget everything but Adam. She let her responding lips convince him that she fully expected more than a convoluted tale about two golden horseshoes.

Neither was aware they were being watched. Adam noted the onlookers first. She felt his body jolt, but he kept her closely within his embrace. Though she knew some invasion into their special, private world had captured his attention, he didn't loose his hold. On the contrary, he squeezed her into a securer grasp and serenaded her with his soft avowal that his concern for her held priority over whatever or whoever had appeared.

"Stay here, don't move," he crooned. "Are you all right?"

She nodded beneath his cradling hand. Even after her nod, she felt his face in her hair, the caress of his lips as they told her he loved her and that all would be well.

Only then did she hear his resonant voice speak out to someone else. "Have you something on your minds, gentlemen?"

Staying pressed to Adam, Bethany wiggled her head, twisting enough so she could peer behind her. Startled, she dug her fingers into Adam's back. Robert Castle, Hallston Lawrence, and James Wallace stood like three wooden soldiers with three differing painted expressions. Lawrence's face was dumbfounded; James Wallace's, staggered, fearful; and Robert Castle's showed worried concern with a heavy overlay of radiant delight.

Though she appreciated her father's delight and knew precisely what caused it, his worried concern alerted her. She might be safe as a cocooned butterfly in Adam's arms, but Adam was in danger. And, God in heaven, her own wild outburst had placed him in that danger. She'd led James Wallace back here, had led him to discover Adam was alive and a decided threat to him.

She held tighter to Adam, but kept her head twisted so she could watch the men.

James was the first to speak. His voice quavered, his words as thin as the milk of a sick cow. "Is it truly you, Adam?"

"Aye, James." His rich, strong tones told her he was in full control.

"We thought you long dead."

"As you can well see, you thought wrong."

A nervous cough. James Wallace looked to Castle and Lawrence for support. Neither offered him anything but stiff frowns.

"Well, then . . ."—he coughed—"we have occasion for celebration, I believe. My little stepbrother has returned from the dead and he's grown into quite a—uh—strapping man, I vow." Though he'd tried for a light cheerfulness, his stumbling speech had the lightness of a funeral dirge.

Nobody said a word. Adam's hand was steady and relaxed as he stroked her hair, but the air in the stable yard was snapping with tension.

Bethany saw with alarm that James Wallace had a large pistol strapped beneath his frock coat. He was armed, and Adam was without a weapon! Cautiously, she began to unwind herself from his sheltering hold.

Robert Castle spoke up. "Adam, James has come to Hallston and me for a hefty loan. He may lose Wendover within days unless we help him."

"Don't help him," Adam said.

"But there will be nothing left," Castle protested.

While Adam was distracted, she wiggled looser. Only the tiniest bit. She didn't want him to notice, but she had to find a way to protect him.

"When is the court in session, Uncle Hallston?" Adam asked.

He tightened his hold on her arm, but the rest of her had worked free. She stood quietly beside him, facing the men.

"A week from Thursday," Lawrence replied. "We can't wait till then if we're to save Wendover."

Adam released her arm long enough to comb his fingers through his hair, and she jumped up to give him a quick kiss on his cheek and a restraining squeeze of his hand before scurrying away from him. She'd disconcerted him, and he started toward her, but she threw him a look with a threefold message: She loved him, she knew what she was doing, and he must trust her.

She wasn't sure he'd gotten all of it, but at least he stayed where he was. She detected the whisper of a smile curl his handsome mouth, and his eyes definitely twinkled.

"Excuse me, gentlemen," she said, bobbing a brief curtsy. She darted around the corner of the stable, leaving the three of them in varying degrees of astonishment. But only James Wallace looked truly unnerved.

She slipped unnoticed through the stable's door. Her bow and arrows hung inside. She figured she might be needing them.

Adam walked up closer to the men. He'd noted James's pistol and wanted to be where he could observe the bastard's eyes and movements. He suspected what Bethany was up to, God love her, but he doubted he'd be requiring her talents with the bow this day. James Wallace, even with a pistol, was hardly the danger of a bucking stallion.

He glared at his stepbrother. "Why do you need this hefty loan?"

James squirmed. "Debts, Adam. The tobacco's not done well this year, what with the blight and all, and the taxes have risen mightily."

"Balderdash!" he growled. "Wendover could survive years of bad crops and ten times the taxes. What's the true reason, James?" He wanted the satisfaction of hearing the man's confession.

"I lost some livestock. The animal barn burned, ten of the slaves were—"

"The *truth*, James."

He seemed to shrink. "I had a long spell of bad luck at the gaming tables, but—"

"How long a spell?"

"Very long." His tattered sigh deflated him further.

"What is the amount of the loan he's requesting?" he asked his uncle.

"Twenty thousand pounds."

Adam's heart sank. An impossible sum!

"We'd willingly give him the loan, but it would be for you, Adam, not for him," his uncle said. "Without it, there will be no Wendover for you to regain."

James jerked to attention. Adam took a quick check of his arm. He hadn't neared his pistol. "Regain? What do you mean?" the stunned man asked Hallston Lawrence.

His uncle threw Adam a questioning glance. Adam nodded.

Lawrence turned to James. "The will is to be reopened, Wallace. Adam is the true heir to Wendover, and his father's wishes will prevail."

Whey-faced, James cringed. "But . . . but that's not possible. The court gave me the rights—"

"The court knew nothing of your heinous deceptions, Wallace," Castle interrupted, his icy eyes fixed on him. "They will not, this time, look with favor upon you."

Adam stared down at the panic-stricken shadow of a man. He was as wan as death, as shriveled as a faded leaf. Fully deserving of contempt, and Adam could do naught but view him with contempt. But he bore, too, an overriding sorrow that any man could wreak such misery upon himself. Dear God, he might never forgive James Wallace, but he harbored pity for him.

Knowing at once what he had to do to release himself from the bondage he'd allowed James to chain around him, he turned to Castle and Lawrence. "You shouldn't consider lending this man even a shilling. He'd throw it the same direction he's thrown the rest of his ill-gotten fortune."

"But Wendover, Adam, we must secure it for you," Lawrence protested.

Adam focused his eyes on James, but spoke to his uncle. "Wendover is James's to secure or lose. I no longer desire to regain it, for I would regain only a debt-ridden shambles that would take me a lifetime to restore."

A flicker of relief crossed James's ashen face, but despair followed in quick pursuit. "You must persuade these gentlemen to lend me the resources. I've exhausted all other—"

"No," Adam said with firmness. "I've given you Wendover. With God's help, perhaps you shall find the means to hold it, and I pray you'll change your despicable ways and maintain it properly henceforth."

James flinched as if Adam had slapped him. But then, acting with the irrational impulse of a desperate man, he yanked the pistol from his coat, aiming it directly at Adam's chest.

His steellike nerves on full alert, Adam instantly analyzed the man's stance, their distance, planned his attack. But before he could move, a swift arrow zinged between them, impaling the sleeve of James's magenta frock coat with the force of a cannon shot. The pistol dropped harmlessly from the man's hand.

"Give me the order, Adam, and this next one goes straight through his bloody, black heart!" Bethany screamed.

Holding up his hand in restraint, Adam bent to scoop up the heavy, cold pistol. Only then did he look at her. He let his love for her pour forth in his approving smile. "That won't be necessary, little sparrow. Drop your weapon and come here by my side where you belong."

Smiling brightly, she threw down her bow and ran to him. He put his arm around her waist and patted her hip, pulling her close beside him.

James was whimpering, staring with horror at the still-quivering arrow pinned through his sleeve. He held his arm away from him, his widespread fingers jiggling with tremors.

Castle and Lawrence stood in dazed disbelief.

"Maybe your luck is turning, James," Adam said. "This lady's aim is true. Had she wished, you can be damned sure that arrow would be through your wrist or any other part of your spineless body she might have chosen to strike."

Holding Bethany by his side, he went up to his shaken stepbrother. After flinging the pistol away, hard against the stable's side, he reached forward and ripped the arrow from the man's sleeve. Bits of magenta thread clung to the arrow's tip, but not a drop of blood. He handed the arrow to Bethany.

"Now, James, she's given you your life this day, and I've given you a second chance to right your wrongs. I believe you owe us both a debt of gratitude," Adam said.

James only moaned and looked as though he might crumble.

"Say thank you," Adam persisted.

"I . . . I . . . thank you," came the choked whisper. James staggered, kept his head bowed.

"And I have yet one more request, James Wallace. You're wearing the golden horseshoe that belonged to my grandfather and my father after him. I want you to unclasp it and hand it over to me. That, James, is my birthright."

Though the broken man nodded, his shaking hands were unable to comply. He fumbled, sobbing.

"Here, I'll do it for you," Bethany offered, a tiny tear of sympathy sparkling in the corner of her eye and tugging at Adam's heart as she moved up to James and unfastened the clasp.

With an endearing smile directed only to Adam, she placed the treasured pin into his palm and held her hand tenderly over it. Her emerald eyes glowed up into his. "Your birthright is yours, dear love," she whispered.

He bent to kiss the back of her petal-soft hand. "It's ours," he corrected her.

With his heart chanting her name and clamoring with joy, he gingerly placed the golden horseshoe alongside its partner in the leather pouch that hung about his neck. Taking her hand, he started for the house.

"Send James on his way, please," he called back to Castle and Lawrence. "Keep his pistol, though, he should have no further use for it. Mister Wallace has skills enough to find a way to keep Wendover. Henceforth, I trust he'll use those skills with forthrightness and honest wisdom."

"But, Adam," the semi-recovered Hallston Lawrence croaked. "Do you mean you're truly relinquishing Wendover?"

"I have other plans, Uncle Hallston," Adam replied with a broad smile. "And, believe me, sir, I have all I will ever require to see my dreams come true." He heard Bethany's wee gasp, and he squeezed her hand.

As they walked toward the house, both Adam and Bethany looked back at Robert Castle.

The gentle man's smile stretched from ear to ear.

"You relinquished Wendover?" Bethany asked, truly awed.

Adam closed the door of his bedchamber behind them. He beamed. "Aye, my love, and I've regained far greater wealth—my soul, I vow, and you." With hearty enthusiasm, he wrapped her in his arms, gazing down into her eyes with such fiery love that she melted like candle wax thrust into blazing flames.

She lost her breath along with any sense of time,

place, and, for sure, propriety. Duties? She should be cleaning up the mess she'd made in the parlor . . . Nonsense, Adam was kissing her with beautiful, persuasive pressure. Duties be damned.

Everyone at Ridgecrest would know what they were doing. Excellent. His hands were cupping her bottom, drawing her hard against his wondrously aroused staff, so alive with his life-giving power and pleasures.

How he managed to unloose her frock, she never knew. His magical touches had burned through cloth, then were searing into her bare flesh, lifting her to him. Glory be, he too was bare!

Adam worked miracles. She loved him, God, she loved him. Her back sank into a cool puff of feathers, his heated body never left hers, pressed, promised. His lips, his hands, his sure, stroking fingers caressed her to a frenzy of throbbing desire . . . there and there and, "Oh, please, Adam, *aye, there*. . . . "

She moaned her plea, arched to him, clasped him, opened, received him deep, full, hot, sleek, pervasive, pulsing, thrusting . . . *more*, yet more, splendidly, magnificently more, till he carried her with him to an encompassing burst of ecstasy—*their* ecstasy, shared, complete, wholly one.

"I love you, I love you, I love you," he groaned again and again, his fingers threading through her hair, his soft lips breathing into her ear, his body blended with hers.

"I know" was all she could say, too limp, too content to express her full heart's ringing song of joy.

That mattered not. No further words were needed. Her transcending love for him, as his for hers, emanated throughout the sunlit room, enveloped their joined bodies, and spread beyond the walls of Ridgecrest.

Indeed, their love was strong enough, powerful enough to suffuse its radiant hues throughout the entire glorious world.

Forever.

Epilogue

The mid-September wedding of Bethany and Adam Barwick was a lively occasion at Ridgecrest. The festivities continued over a span of three days and, save for massive cooking, little other work was done around the place. Servants drank and danced with the Tidewater gentry who'd come— some of them, alas, from curiosity—to celebrate the marriage of "one of their own" and to see for themselves that Adam had "returned from the dead."

The bride, everyone agreed, was radiantly beautiful, though the Tidewater folk lamented her lack of heritage. But, after all, Adam Barwick had relinquished Wendover, or so they'd heard. It was probable the man's terrible ordeals in the frontier had made him a wee daft.

For the ceremony, Bethany wore a stunning gown of white lace, sewn by the loving, if no longer nimble, hands of Ida Pumphrey. Both the gown and ceremony were quite traditional. Little else, so it was rumored, was in any way traditional.

She didn't wear a veil, for example. Adam wouldn't allow one. "Her hair shall not be covered," he'd insisted. And who could blame him? Her flaming tresses were indeed lovelier than any veil, and the tiny white flowers woven through the long flow of copper curls provided a proper bride-like touch.

Rather than holding an arm full of Robert Castle's glorious English roses, as one might expect, she carried a single pink flower—a wildflower, at that. She'd found it blooming robustly in the crevice of a large stone. Actually, she'd found two, thriving side by side. Adam wore the other pinned to his handsome gray frock coat.

The guest list was a hodgepodge. Beaming servants stood shoulder to shoulder with primly smiling aristocrats. By the day after the ceremony, no one appeared in the least disturbed by the odd mingling. But by then, of course, barrels of wine had been drained and many more waited to be opened. Dancing continued throughout the nights.

The bride and groom, strangely enough, were never seen after sunset—not even once. That, too, defied convention, but most agreed they possibly tired easily.

Sara Castle, on the other hand, was extremely energetic. Everyone commented on the vast improvement in her health. Herbs had done it, some suspected; others, those with a religious bent in particular, attributed her recovery to a heavenly miracle.

Only her husband, Robert, apparently knew the true cause. For once in his life, he'd given Sara a well-deserved tongue-lashing. Lord, he wished now he'd done it years ago. His wife was yet far from anybody's definition of a docile, loving woman. Oh, he knew she might never be that. But the little nudges of warmth he'd seen glimmering were increasing daily.

Hearteningly so.

Warmth bred warmth. No longer was there need to speak harshly to Sara. She'd even stopped embroidering cushion covers, thank God. Robert Castle found himself believing in miracles.

Angus McInnes became distracted quite early in the festivities. Mister Castle had hired a new girl to replace Bethany. She had golden hair and eyes of blue that twinkled like stars. Aye, a bonnie lass, she was, with a name that rolled off the tongue—Rachel Morris.

By day two he'd kissed her rosy lips; on day three . . . Well, he knew by then. Soon enough Mister Castle would be requiring another servant girl *and* a new foreman. Angus had saved shillings aplenty, and his dream was beckoning on the western horizon. At the moment, Rachel was beckoning from the stable loft.

A peculiar thing happened to James Wallace. Some called it good fortune, others—Adam, for one—considered it rather amusing. He received his loan from, of all people, Benjamin Mason, Evelyn's father. The belle had taken a fancy to Wallace, so the gossip ran; Mister Mason had ever doted on his daughter and was delighted she was to become the mistress of Wendover.

That big wedding was yet weeks away, and the Tidewater gentry was truly looking forward to it. By then, they figured, they'd be recovered from the Ridgecrest gala.

Neither Evelyn nor James were present at the Barwick wedding. Poor dears, they were *sorely* beset with making preparations for their own. It occurred to but a few that perhaps they hadn't been invited.

The Lawrences all enjoyed themselves mightily. Even Marshall, who'd matured more than a tad, according to those who hadn't seen him in a spell. Love had done it, many suspected. The third Williams daughter of *the* Godwin Williams of Afton Hall had caught his eye. From the looks of it, Afton Hall would be issuing invitations in the near future, and events there were *truly* magnificent.

Perhaps the strangest guests at the Ridgecrest wedding was a couple by the name of Owens. *She* was an Indian! One of their sons looked full-blooded; the other was, well, an obvious half-breed. They seemed a happy family, though, and the lads were polite and proper. Mina Owens stood with Bethany during the ceremony. The pair seemed to be special friends. And the way both bride and groom embraced that Indian boy! Most everyone found that a bit out of the ordinary.

Early on the third day, the bride and groom made their departure. Off to the Shenandoah Valley they were headed. Settling there, so the guests were told. Though no one could figure why, Robert Castle had gifted them with a tract of land he'd held for years, fifty acres of prime land near the river with a small cabin.

Adam had big dreams. He'd build a home grander than Wendover there someday, he told one and all. Somehow, he made it sound possible. He and Bethany would begin a new dynasty, he said, start new traditions.

They were, many said, an untraditional couple at that.

The assembled guests gave them a rousing leave-taking. (Angus and Rachel, alas, were otherwise occupied and missed it.)

The bride and groom both wore buckskins. At least the bride had the decency to wear a buckskin skirt and sturdy boots; they rode a pair of heavily packed horses. Bethany's steed was near white, *another* fine gift from Robert Castle.

Indeed, the man richly deserved the warm hug of farewell from Bethany Barwick. Who could blame her for being so grateful?

She hugged Sara Castle, too, and the older woman actually reciprocated.

Possibly that was because of the dog. The bride left her black dog behind for Mrs. Castle, who'd grown uncommonly fond of the animal. He was far too plump and complacent now to journey across the mountains, anyway.

Angus's wedding gift to the couple was a younger dog—a frisky red-haired pup of no known breed. They named him Scot.

Another gift Bethany Barwick especially admired was the feather pallet from Ida Pumphrey. Wrapped in a tidy roll of deerskin hide, the pallet rested behind the bride's saddle. Ida knew Bethany had become partial to feathers.

As they headed west toward the mountains, Adam reached over for his wife's hand and gave her a scandalous wink. One could only assume the man planned to stop early this day. He was, after all, intending to begin a dynasty.

Odds were high among the assembled guests that this Barwick line would be long, strong, and plentiful indeed.

Many expressed curiosity about a small but noticeable item worn by both bride and groom. Pinned to each of their buckskin coats was a tiny gold jeweled horseshoe—a matched pair, it appeared.

When asked about the pins, Bethany simply stated, with a sly wink to Robert Castle, that they were their "dream catchers" which would carry them safely beyond the blue mountains.

Sic juvat transcendere monte! Thus joyous it is to cross the mountains!

Author's Notes

Battletown, Virginia, is now called Berryville. This lovely, peaceful village in the lower Shenandoah Valley is named for Benjamin Berry, the tavern keeper, who platted the town. Though chartered as Berryville in 1798, the once-rowdy crossroads generally kept its old name until the 1830s. By then, "Battletown" hardly fit the calm community.

Dan Morgan, later General Daniel Morgan of Revolutionary War fame and hero of Cowpens, was, indeed, the legendary "hands-down champion" of Battletown's tavern brawls in the era of the novel.

The Shenandoah River that flows through the beautiful Shenandoah Valley runs from south to north. Thus, the "upper Valley" is south; the "lower Valley" is north.

A Wildcat Hollow does exist. It's approximately twelve miles southeast of Berryville, and I've not yet ventured there. I used only the name and moved it closer to Battletown. Otherwise, Adam and the dastardly Stewart men never could have made their journeys in the time span required by the story.

The "old Indian trace" traveled by Adam, Bethany, and Sammy ran approximately the same path as the current well-traveled, scenic Skyline Drive.

I located the fictional Brierwood and Ridgecrest in what is today Nelson County, Virginia. In 1760, Nelson County was part of Albemarle County. Virginia began with only a few very large counties, but as settlement increased, the populace demanded smaller counties. Their courthouse, they believed, should be close enough for a day's journey. Nelson County began as part of Henrico County (1634), was part of Goochland County (1728), of Albemarle (1744), of Amherst (1761) and, finally, became Nelson County in 1807.

Nelson County is 468 square miles of unspoiled beauty in central Virginia, bounded by the James River on the southeast and the Blue Ridge peaks on the northwest. Its rolling, red soil lies about thirty-five miles south of Charlottesville. The upper James River, which runs by Wingina, is a tree-lined mirror.

Crabtree Falls, off Virginia Route 56, is a delightful sight, well worth a visit. Unfortunately, Bethany was in a gloomy mood when we joined her there. Her description doesn't do the place justice.

The "golden horseshoes" were mementoes bestowed by Governor Alexander Spotswood to a dozen or so gentlemen who accompanied him on an early expedition (1716) over the Blue Ridge Mountains to the Shenandoah Valley. At that time, horses were seldom shod in the Tidewater. The rough terrain taken by the expedition, of course, required horseshoes. Governor Spotswood chose that symbol for his commemorative gifts to his "Knights."

Though it's believed the treasured pins have been handed down through the generations and zealously guarded by the lucky families who own them, none are available for public viewing.

Mr. James C. Kelly of The Virginia Historical Society was kind enough to provide me with the copy of a photograph of a golden horseshoe pin believed to have been given to Robert Brooke, who died in 1744.

I'm also indebted to Rosann Meagher of the Virginia State Library who provided additional information such as the Latin inscriptions on the pins and the garnet "nailheads."

For their personal "hands-on" tour of Berryville and their helpful guidance with flora and fauna of the area, I express special gratitude to my longtime friends, Berryville residents Marilyn Lister and Patricia McKelvy.

My favorite ex-Eagle Scout, Larry Criswell, made it possible for Adam and Bethany—and me—to survive in the wilderness; and two wonderful, knowledgeable Maryland ladies, Joanie Taylor Gillen of Brandywine and Betty M. Taylor of Belvidere, saw to it that Bethany learned to ride horses properly.

Adam, Bethany, and I thank them all!

DISCOVER THE REAL WORLD OF ROMANCE WITH LEISURE'S LEADING LADY OF LOVE!

Shirl Henke

Winner of 5 *Romantic Times* Awards

RETURN TO PARADISE. Separated at birth and raised in vastly different worlds, the sons of the House of Torres could never know that fate would cast them into a hell of their own making. Yet in the end, the power of love would redeem their sins and destine them for a glorious return to Paradise.

_3263-5 $4.99 US/$5.99 CAN

PARADISE & MORE. Fleeing the persecution of the Inquisition, and the evil of Ferdinand and Isabella's court, Aaron and Magdalena crossed storm-tossed oceans to discover a lush paradise fraught with danger and desire.

_3170-1 $4.99 US/$5.99 CAN

NIGHT WIND'S WOMAN. Proud and untamable as a lioness, Orlena vowed she would never submit to the renegade Apache who had kidnapped her. For a long-ago betrayal had made this man her enemy. But a bond even stronger than love would unite them forever.

_3096-9 $4.50 US/$5.50 CAN

LEISURE BOOKS
ATTN: Order Department
276 5th Avenue, New York, NY 10001

Please add $1.50 for shipping and handling for the first book and $.35 for each book thereafter. N.Y.S. and N.Y.C. residents, please add appropriate sales tax. No cash, stamps, or C.O.D.s. All orders shipped within 6 weeks via postal service book rate. Canadian orders require $2.00 extra postage. It must also be paid in U.S. dollars through a U.S. banking facility.

Name _____

Address _____

City _____ State _____ Zip _____

I have enclosed $_____ in payment for the checked book(s).
Payment <u>must</u> accompany all orders. ☐ Please send a free catalog.

SPEND YOUR LEISURE MOMENTS WITH US.

Hundreds of exciting titles to choose from—something for everyone's taste in fine books: breathtaking historical romance, chilling horror, spine-tingling suspense, taut medical thrillers, involving mysteries, action-packed men's adventure and wild Westerns.

SEND FOR A FREE CATALOGUE TODAY!

Leisure Books
Attn: Customer Service Department
276 5th Avenue. New York. NY 10001